HELL AND GONE

A Wakeland Novel

SAM WIEBE

HARBOUR

Harbour Publishing Co. Ltd.
P.O. Box 219, Madeira Park, BC, VON 2H0
www.harbourpublishing.com

Edited by Derek Fairbridge
Cover design by Anna Boyar
Text design by Carleton Wilson
Cover photograph by Carly Reemeyer
Printed and bound in Canada
Printed on FSC-certified paper with 100% recycled content

Harbour Publishing acknowledges the support of the Canada Council for the Arts,
the Government of Canada, and the Province of British Columbia through the BC
Arts Council.

LIBRARY AND ARCHIVES CANADA CATALOGUING IN PUBLICATION

Title: Hell and gone / Sam Wiebe.
Names: Wiebe, Sam, author.
Description: Series statement: A Wakeland novel
Identifiers: Canadiana (print) 20210291842 | Canadiana (ebook) 20210291850 |
    ISBN 9781550179637 (softcover) | ISBN 9781550179644 (EPUB)
Classification: LCC PS8645.I3236 H45 2021 | DDC C813/.6—dc23

Whatever I do with all the black
is my business alone.
—Don Paterson, "Filter"

You just live there and you keep your head down.
—Stephen King, describing his hometown

PART ONE: HEAD DOWN

ONE

BLACK MASKS

Fireworks let off indoors.

At first I thought I might have drifted off, and the sound belonged to the tail end of some already-dispersing dream. Five-fifteen in the goddamn morning, and I'd been up all goddamn night.

I'd driven back from Hope in the early hours, chasing down a scaffolder who'd moved north owing five months' child support. He'd been drunk and quarrelsome, and it had taken some bare-knuckle convincing, but he'd paid. Instead of going home and waking up Sonia, I'd driven to the office. The plan had been to write up my report, make tea and fall asleep, in whichever order those things happened to come.

The half-finished document lay in front of me, and if I'd dozed off it was only for a second. The small office was still, the only sound the burble from the Zojirushi, heating water for tea. Quiet, too, outside, with dawn just breaking behind the new office towers of Chinatown. I could hear the diesel drone of a vehicle idling in the street, and the groggy gabble of commuters waiting for the first bus of the morning.

The office was on the third floor of a brick tenement on Keefer Street, surrounded by larger, newer pre-fab structures. The office window was wedged open with a copy of Kim Rossmo's *Criminal Investigative Failures*. Over the frame, with its trench of pigeon spikes, I had a view of the six-storey office building across the street. Locals had christened it Gentrification Central.

A panel van idled to the left of the building's entrance. Late nineties vintage, painted a lustreless black, exhaust dribbling from its tail. The engine made guttural sounds like the phlegm-clearing horks of a smoker.

The windows were tinted, so I couldn't see inside.

I looked for the Calendar Man, the only other person I'd seen this morning. I'd passed him walking up from the Korean market on Hastings, coffee in hand, dragging his cart of merchandise behind him. He hawked *Light in Darkness* calendars at the corner bus stop, catching early morning traffic from Chinatown to the Financial District.

Only this morning he wasn't by the bus stop. Looking down I saw a pair of Asian women in heavy green coats zipped over dark skirts, a white man in a charcoal suit, and another with his back to me, wearing a tan fedora and a suede jacket, his head crooked to talk on his cell.

Movement on the corner up from the front entrance of the building, around the side. A figure in a battered peacoat knelt with one foot in the gutter, gathering up something in his hands. It was the Calendar Man. His cart was tipped over and dozens of shrink-wrapped calendars were spilled across the road.

He righted the cart with a sharp kick and hurled calendars into its basket. He was out of place. There was no foot traffic on the side street, no potential customers that far from the bus stop beneath my window. I wondered if the sound had come from him.

I heard it again, the muffled boom of fireworks, coming from inside the building across from me. Ripples of sharp bass echoes, erratic, that could be felt through the morning air. Then heavier sounds that grew louder till they shook the panes of the glass-fronted lobby. A shattering sound. Then nothing but the rev of the van and a chirp of confusion from the bus stop.

During the lull I noticed the fissures in the glass doors. Not fireworks. Maybe I'd known from the jump.

I have some experience with violence. I fetched my shoes from the front door and shut off the Zojirushi, abandoning my mug with the string of Twinings wound around the handle. As I laced one shoe, I glanced out the window and saw a figure emerge from the building, soon trailed by others.

Each of them was dressed in the same deep-blue janitor's coveralls, their faces masked, thick gloves on their hands. The first figure out held a pump-action shotgun and walked calmly to the van, as if he were guarding it. He changed direction as he noticed the two commuters who'd ventured into the street.

Black neoprene covered the bottom of his face, the bleached jaws and fangs of a skeletal dog stencilled over his mouth. His exposed skin was dark and his hair dark brown and cut short. When he spotted the commuters, he swung the barrel of the shotgun toward them.

I felt the breath steal from my lungs.

The next out of the building was a woman, who opened the rear of the van and slung a black and orange hockey bag into the hold. She held an automatic pistol and tapped the shoulder of the man with the shotgun. All clear. The man nodded. The woman climbed in, joined quickly by a third figure, limping and cradling one arm.

The commuters, the man in the hat and one of the women, had walked into the street to see what was going on. Now they froze. The man slowly raised his hands.

A gunshot from inside, close, maybe from the lobby. A startled cry from the commuters below.

The last man came walking out sideways, shouldering the door of the building to throw it open. He swung around and crossed behind the man with the shotgun. Pale skin and blond hair atop the same dog mouth. He held a rifle of some sort. When he saw the commuters, the blond man didn't hesitate. He swept the barrel up to aim at the closest of them.

Wait—

The barrel jumped and flashed fire. The man in the fedora made a horse-like whinny as he dropped backward. His hat miraculously remained on his head during the fall, but tipped back under his neck as he struggled, limbs flapping desperately. The other woman ran and the blond man fired at her back. A ghastly black smoke bloomed from the gun.

The man with the shotgun discharged his weapon, an explosive noise louder than the rifle. My eyes closed reflexively. When they opened, the man was sprinting to the van's side door.

The blond man fired into the small crowd by the bus stop, emptying the rifle, the black mist rising around him. Maybe thirty rounds. Then he walked to the door and the door slid closed and the van drove off.

The commuters had first made a communal sound, almost a swoon, that in the aftermath broke into separate sounds of panic and agony and fear. A male voice stuttered and sobbed as a keening rose up from the street. A sharp slurp of breath from someone in pain.

During all of this I hadn't moved from the window. One shoe still dangled stupidly from my fingers. I became aware of it, blinked, let it fall to the office floor. I muttered to myself, words that felt empty and inadequate even as I mouthed them.

Oh,

shit,

what am I going to do?

I have some experience with violence. Nothing like this. I forced myself to breathe.

Then I went out the window.

TWO

CATCH YOUR BREATH

This is so fucked up.

With trauma your mind spins. Collects arbitrary data and makes decisions a sane person would question. I could hear whimpers of pain from the sidewalk below. There were key-operated doors at the top and bottom of the office staircase. I'd save maybe a minute using the fire escape. It seemed like a precious minute.

I struggled out the window, slicing my thighs on the bed of pigeon spikes. The fire escape took my weight with a moan. I clambered down the stairs to the edge and swung down, dropping to the concrete.

This.

   Is.

      So.

         Fucked.

         Up.

I landed badly, pain jolting up my legs. I hobbled over to the bus stop.

The man with the fedora lay in the middle of the street, unmoving. The pair of women had crumpled by the gutter, one face-down and the other on her back. The moans came from them.

The smoke from the rifle still loomed over the street, a corrosive smell, rust and piss. The man in the suit sat on the curb near the women, his blazer placed beneath the seat of his slacks to shield them from the grime of the concrete. The left arm of his white shirt was bloody.

"I was on my way to the Financial District," he said to me. His fingers prodded the wound.

"Keep your hand tight on that," I said.

His cellphone lay on the curb beside him. "Should I call someone?"

"Nine-one-one, maybe."

"Right. Hey, yeah, right." Financial District looked at the phone blankly, then picked it up with the fingers of his injured arm.

The woman nearest me had fallen forward, almost toward the other woman. A protective gesture. She was maybe in her fifties, hair cut short and a patterned dress beneath the coat. A leather file tote nearby. I touched her shoulder, moved her purse, noticed the stain below her shoulder blade.

"Miss," I said, "I know a little first aid. I'm going to help you. That all right, Miss?"

"My daughter first," she said.

The younger woman next to her stared at the sky, blinking slowly. Her left hand was draped over her stomach, rising with each slow breath.

"Your daughter's okay," I said. "You need it more than she does. Let's get you onto your back."

I turned her, supporting the head. *How's this go? Airway, then breathing, then cardiac.* The first aid course all but useless, coming back in pieces and broken mnemonics.

The entry wound was just above the woman's left flank. The exit wound was a frothing hole a palm's width from her navel. She'd been shot from behind.

I bunched her dress as I turned her, setting the excess fabric over the hole in her back.

"My name is David Wakeland," I said as I worked on her. "What's your name?"

"Diane. Diane Cui." Pronounced "*Tschway*." "My daughter…"

"Yep," I said, tearing her dress, "your daughter's gonna be fine. Where do you work, Diane?"

"Sinclair Centre. I'm CPA."

"An accountant? That's really interesting work. Hold still."

"Jingjing—my daughter—she work—works with me."

"Oh, that must be nice." I had her dress open at the belly, exposing a grey sweat-stained bra and below that, the wound. Blood burbled out of it with her breathing. I closed my eyes tight to fight off a fizzy wave of nausea. Pressing my hand over her wound, I shrugged one arm out of my flannel shirt.

"It's nice to work with family, isn't it?" I said. "Though it can be—" I switched hands—"it can be stressful too."

"Yes." Diane Cui's mouth clamped shut as a groan escaped her throat. Beside her, her daughter coughed.

"My sister Kay works with me. Half-sister, I guess, if we're being technical. Most of the time it's great to have her there. Will you do me a favour, Diane, and put your hands over mine?"

She did, crossing them over her belly like a corpse posed in an open casket. There wasn't much force in her hands. I slid mine out and clamped them on top to add to the pressure.

I looked over at Financial District. "They on their way?" I asked.

"Who? Oh, the ambulance. Yeah, on their way." He was staring at Diane and her daughter. "Are they gonna die?"

"Nope," I said. "They're gonna be fine. Would you grab me some napkins, please, or paper towels? Maybe check that purse?"

Diane groaned. The blotch near her shoulder had darkened and spread. Another bullet, maybe, or a fragment of this one. I hoped it hadn't turned to shrapnel inside her.

"Diane," I said, "how long have you lived in Vancouver?"

"Nine—teen years," she said, the syllables tumbling out. "Jingjing was born here. Vancou—ver General."

"Wow, that's where I was born too." With my free hand I tore at the fabric over the shoulder. It looked like a graze. There was blood on it. Blood everywhere, the smell like freshly turned earth and old coins.

Financial District passed me a wad of yellow Wendy's napkins and I balled them and wiped off the wound. Diane seized up and bent forward, her head turning to look at her daughter. I shushed and lowered her.

"No worries. What city were you born in?"

"Suzhou," she said.

"Near Shanghai, right?"

"Not so near."

"My partner was born in Guangzhou. His family's still there, most of them, other than his cousin. That's my work partner, not my partner-partner."

I moved her hands and kept pressure on the stomach myself.

"My partner-partner doesn't have much family. Me neither. Maybe that's why Sonia and I get along. How're you feeling?"

"It hurts," Diane said.

"That's good, right? It means the body's still sending signals."

"Are you a doctor?"

"I'm a private investigator."

"A police?" She tensed.

"No, I work for people that hire me, like you do. Do you like your job, Diane?"

"I like to work," she said. "My hus—band, he died with no money. I went to school af—ter."

"That's good." Sure it was. *Hi, how are you, where are you from?* The absurdity struck me along with another bout of nausea. My mouth had gone cottony but I managed to say, "Education, right? Without education—"

We heard the sirens.

"Sirens," Financial District said.

About fucking time. To Diane I said, "You hear that? Just a little longer, Diane. You're being really brave."

"Jingjing," she said.

"Yep. You just hold this in place"—my shirt over the stomach wound—"tight as you can, all right? And I'll check on Jingjing."

When I looked up Financial District was pointing at an ambulance, approaching from the intersection. "They're waiting," he said. "Just sitting over there."

Behind them was the number three bus, parked, its destination sign reading NOT IN SERVICE. The driver stood out front leaning on the bicycle rack, his phone out, watching us.

"Waiting for the cops," I said. "Protocol to a shooting is to make sure there's no threat to the EMTs. Did you tell the operator the shooters had left?"

"I honestly don't remember. Sorry, man."

"Okay," I said. "Flag them over here."

The ambulance crawled forward, parking diagonally in the middle of the street. The paramedics came out with the gurney. I was kneeling and I shuffled back as they approached Diane, making the same judgment about the body in the street that I had.

"Gunshot to the abdomen," I explained. "Blood loss but no respiratory problems. Another nick to the shoulder which could be a fragment."

"Thanks, we got it," the EMT said brusquely. She removed my shirt from the wound. Diane moaned.

"They'll get you to the hospital," I told Diane. "You did really great."

"My arm." Financial District thrust his bloody cuff under the face of the EMTs, who ignored him while they finished transferring Diane to the gurney.

"Jingjing," Diane said, her head moving as she was lifted up. The EMTs moved to either side of her.

I looked at her daughter's crumpled form, at the ruined pulp that had been the back of her head. At the blood in the gutter, running past cigarette butts and trash.

"She'll be fine," I told Diane. "We're all going to be just fine."

THREE

INSIDES

Keefer Street was a mess. Traffic had bottlenecked between the stalled bus, the ambulance and the arriving patrol cars. A Lexus crossed into the opposing lane and tried to weave around. The driver saw the bodies in the street, backed up and turned down the side street, the cars that had followed him forming a perfect jam.

Speaking of the side street, I looked for the Calendar Man. At some point he'd disappeared, along with his cart and merchandise. Good for him, I thought.

I bummed a cigarette from the bus driver, let her light it for me, no sense bloodying her Zippo. My hands felt gummy, like they'd been spattered with paint.

Eventually a patrol car got through, swinging to park across both lanes. The officers conferred. No doubt the situation was already spinning out of hand. Traffic, evidence, first aid, witnesses. To make matters worse it had begun to rain. Finally one officer moved to hold back the crowd of cars and passersby, the other watching over the bodies.

I threw the cigarette butt away and crossed behind the bus to the opposite sidewalk. Whatever this was, it had started within Gentrification Central.

In front of the entrance I saw cartridge cases, a dull steel colour, and the red plastic tube of a shotgun shell. I opened the door gently, avoiding the handle, and slipped inside.

The lobby was unadorned except for a large black and white photograph over the reception desk. A horse at full gallop, ridden by a helmeted and bent-backed jockey. Passing the desk, I looked down, saw an elbow, a bent arm, orange fingernails. The body of the receptionist lay awkwardly behind the desk, as if in the midst of turning over in her sleep.

The polished metal staircase swung up from the rear of the lobby. On the landing I looked down. A few smeared footprints in the centre of the white tile. Others close to the reception desk.

I thought of Shuzhen. My partner's cousin had been Wakeland & Chen's first receptionist. Shuzhen was now a law student, but she was only a few years younger than the dead woman below.

The thought sobered me enough to question what I was doing in here. Satisfying a perverse curiosity? Collecting more mental images I wouldn't be able to forget? Or worse—did I think I could "do something"?

In truth it had been reflexes and nothing else. I'd started toward the building and no one had stopped me, so in I'd gone.

Upstairs. The hallway walls were bare and coated in primer, masking tape framing the outlets. The doors were metallic green with small inset windows. A few fresh stains matted the dark carpeting.

Halfway down the hall, a man lay on the floor in a jackknife pose, forming an L that barred my way. He looked to be Chinese, in his twenties, dressed in tailored jeans and a silk shirt, a thick, gold, segmented chain circling his neck. His face was frozen into something like disappointment. Not how things should have turned out.

As I stepped over him, I noted the black automatic pistol by his knees.

The door behind the body was wedged open a fraction by what I realized was a foot. I touched the door with a knuckle and it swung open. A stench of cigarettes and fast food, copper and excrement and flesh.

This had been the start of it.

The room was small and unfinished. Bare wires hung down from missing tiles in the ceiling grid. The stray foot belonged to a body that lay near the outstretched legs of another. Both had been shot multiple times, leaving blood on the walls, dark pools on the carpet. More cartridge cases, a mix of brass and the dull steel from the blond man's rifle. Amidst those were trash bags, rubber bands, McMuffin wrappers, flattened cans of 7up and Wong Lo Kat. A broken currency counter, the machine's cord still plugged into the wall, its tray crushed into clear plastic shards. And money—US and Canadian bills around the legs of a collapsible table, now overturned.

In the corner behind the table was a dark, bloody something. A fourth man or woman, face-down, wearing a shredded garment that looked put on backward. White athletic strings hung off the collar, and I realized it was a man, and he was face-up. Or rather, faceless. The drywall behind the form had been nearly destroyed. Peach-coloured powder and crumbs coated the clothes and the body's dark red no-longer-insides.

You wanted to see this, didn't you?

You wanted to know.

Well. What do you know?

How much more sense does it make? How much better will you sleep with THIS rather than questions?

Face it. You are so fucking far out of your depth, Wakeland. You don't belong here.

I took the fire exit down, nearly colliding with two uniformed officers. My hands went up without being asked.

"The hell are you doing here?" one said. "You were outside."

"Thought maybe someone was alive in here and I could help."

"And?"

I shook my head.

Both officers looked young, and the one who spoke was sweating. Not a time for provocation. I didn't resist when they near-dragged me outside.

The scene had become further cluttered since I'd gone in. Both ends of the street were blocked off by patrol cars, traffic rerouted down Gore. A crowd had formed near the front end of the stalled bus, white lights from cellphone cameras strafing the scene.

A support van was nearby. One of the VPD's forensic technicians carefully placed white letter markers on the concrete. Another tech documented the scene with a camera. Uniformed cops at either end of the street. The illusion of order, of everything under control.

The cops escorted me up the street toward a Dodge Charger parked halfway up on the curb. The word SUPERVISOR was decaled in blue on the white side panel, above a swooping Coast Salish design. The back door was open and a woman sat with her legs in the street, drinking a coffee and chewing on some sort of protein bar.

"We found him," the perspiring cop said. "Inside. The guy the shirt belongs to."

"Does it?" the woman asked me.

For a moment I was confused. A flinch of self-consciousness hit me. I was in jeans and a Soundgarden T-shirt, one shoe on. My flannel shirt had been used to stanch a wound in Diane Cui's chest.

"If it's faded blue-green it's mine," I said. "The blood's not."

The woman stood up. She was thickset, a shade below my height, her hair silver and trimmed short. If she was perturbed by the bodies or the hectic action around her, it didn't show. Her gestures were friendly, her handshake warm and firm.

"Superintendent Ellen Borden," she said. "This is quite an ordeal. From what I've heard, there's a woman going to the hospital that has you to thank. Very heroic."

"Basic first aid," I said.

"And modest too." Her expression was somewhere between mocking and sincere, but I was too tired, too something, to parse it. "Can I get you anything?" she asked.

I told her a cigarette would be heavenly.

"Four years quit myself," Borden said. "What we're going to do is get a medic to look at you. Then we'll need to talk to you at the station. We can scrounge up a smoke for you there. Sound all right to you?"

"Not much to say," I said. "I got here after."

Borden's head canted to the side in a shrug, *we'll see.*

A Black officer approached us and informed Borden in a Québécois accent that there were four more inside the building, on the second floor. Borden drank the last of her coffee and told the officer, Sergeant Dudgeon, to hold on a second. "This fellow was inside." She pointed at me.

"You disturb anything?" Dudgeon asked me.

"No."

"Why you go in, then?"

"See if I could help anyone."

"You know what's inside? You maybe see it happen?"

Images of the shooters coming out the door cycled through my mind. Their masks. How the man with the shotgun had tilted his head in the moment before the shooting. Giving an order to the blond man? Warning him off? Or just a meaningless tic?

I said to Borden, "My office is across the street, third floor. That one there with the open window. I keep a pack of Gauloises in the desk drawer. You mind? Otherwise I might throw up."

"We'll get you sorted in a sec," Borden said.

Across the street, a pair of forensic technicians were sweeping the gutters. Jingjing Cui's body had a white marker placed beside it, number two.

Dudgeon headed into the building. Borden looked through my wallet. Licenses, business cards. Her brow knit and her smile disappeared. She looked at me critically.

"Your name is David? Dave all right?"

I told her Dave was all right.

She handed back the wallet and the smile returned, warm and welcoming, no trace now of irony.

"Dave. Listen. You're a private investigator. You know how dicey eyewitnesses can be. Even good ones. How important it is to get what you saw down."

"I got here after," I repeated.

"But with your office right above, you heard something. Might even have seen something too and not realize it, something critical. I'm sure you're aware how often that happens in our line of work."

I nodded, seeing again the face of the man in the hall, his expression, the awareness that this was it.

"Dave. You did a great thing helping Ms. Cui. And now we need your help. You might be in shock now, and we'll get you seen to right away. But to do our jobs—to catch these people—we're going to need your help. Your cooperation."

"Honestly," I said,

and I saw the blond man shoot down the commuters. The man with the fedora falling, hands raised to ward off the violence. The woman, Diane Cui, pivoting at impact from the shot. Seeing her daughter struck down. Mother and daughter dying next to each other.

and I said, "nothing. I honestly didn't see a fucking thing."

FOUR
MEMORY BOX

In a fluorescent-bathed room in the Cambie Street station, I went over my statement with Sergeant Dudgeon. Heard gunfire, heard a scream, dropped out the window to help. Really that's all I can tell you.

Dudgeon regarded me with a disappointed scowl. He'd scrounged up a pack of Parliament Super Slims, but before handing them over, asked me to run through it one more time, the morning's events, from the top.

I understood. When you interview a witness, you want to hear everything they have to say, and multiple times. Speech and memory trigger each other. On the third run-through a person might describe someone in more detail, or remember something peculiar.

You want those inconsistencies, self-justifications, revisions. "I was just standing there" becomes "I was waiting for my friend" becomes "I was buying drugs from him for another friend" until you end up with, "I was planning on jacking his stash but I swear I wasn't planning to shoot him."

Dudgeon flipped a page in his notes. "When'd you get to the office, what time?"

"Four, maybe."

"Hour, hour and a half before the shooting. And you were doing what?"

"Writing. Making tea."

"And you don't see no one suspicious. You don't hear nothing before the shots."

"Three to five it's usually pretty quiet," I said.

"Usually. So you do this regular. Work this kind of schedule."

"I don't really keep to a schedule," I said.

Dudgeon scraped his pen's cap across his teeth. "Okay. So you go down, you help this woman. Ambulance show up. What do you do after?"

"I went into the building to see if there was anyone in need. There wasn't, so I left—was on my way out when I ran into the officers."

"You're a private investigator," Dudgeon said. "Just like Magnum, right?"

"That's right, exactly like Magnum."

"You think, hey, I can do better than the police."

"In what sense?"

Dudgeon didn't answer right away. I sighed.

"No, officer, I don't think I can solve murders on my own. I'm a PI, my job is mostly to find people."

"Maybe you think you can find them first. These shooters."

As he spoke the last word, Dudgeon cocked his fingers into a gun, aimed it at me, *pow*.

"Maybe you think Phil Collins was better after Genesis," I said. When he blinked: "I don't want to answer any more maybes. I told you what I saw."

Dudgeon wrote in his notes. I leaned out of my chair and saw him write *uncommunicative* at the bottom of the page, pausing to double-check his spelling. He caught me looking, snapped the book shut.

"How 'bout we have that smoke," he said.

We walked out through the parkade, into the alley between Cambie and Yukon. Dudgeon took a cigarette for himself, then handed me the pack. It was no longer raining, the sky a cold blue.

"Why do you think this happen?" he said.

"Why do you?"

He blew smoke out of his nostrils. "Ever hear of the Rock Machine?"

"Bikers, right?"

"Where I'm from, when I'm a kid, Rock Machine had it out with the Angels. Montreal fucking gang war. Still get talked about. Territory, drugs, weapons." He drew on his cigarette and coughed. "This today, to me it got that same feel."

"Could be," I said.

"Something illegal get done in that building, somebody shoot off his mouth. Other guy hear about it, get an idea."

"Why the civilians, then?" I said.

"Make a big noise," Dudgeon said. "Show everybody they're real."

I finished my cigarette. "Could be."

"My point," he said, "even tough guys want no part of a gang war. They might see something and think, smarter to keep shut."

"Wouldn't speak well about public confidence in the police," I said.

Dudgeon spread out his hands and shrugged. "What can we do, if nobody take the risk? If nobody—what's the phrase—step up."

A patrol car dropped me at home. I had keys but my wallet and phone were still locked up in the cubbyhole office. They could wait.

I had a healthy shot of Buffalo Trace, then mixed another with water and took it over to the couch. Bourbon and music had always worked wonders. I flipped through my records, put *Dig, Lazarus, Dig!!!* on the platter. Nick Cave and the Bad Seeds had seen me through a lot over the years.

My needle drop technique is solid, my hand usually steady. This time, though, the stylus skidded off the record with a loud *frrrruuuuppp.*

For a moment I regarded the silent spinning record, the arm bouncing beside it. Accidents will happen. But maybe I wasn't ready to relax just yet.

Peeling off my clothes, I examined myself in the mirror. Deep scratches from my trip out the window, punctures in the thighs of my jeans. A soak in the shower, a few bandages and I was ready to return to that drink. This time I used the automatic lever to start the music.

Dudgeon had said he thought this was a gang shooting. As solid a hypothesis as any. The dead men in the building had been Chinese, the shooters mostly white. Bikers, maybe? That would mean The Exiles, which would mean Terry Rhodes.

I'd had run-ins with Rhodes before, none pleasant. Ruthless and unpredictable, he wasn't above murder if it suited his business—or if it pleased him. Still. The receptionist. The onlookers. What purpose could that serve?

Send a message, Dudgeon had said. *Fear us.* Terry Rhodes had no need to send messages like that. Not to me, at least. But if not Rhodes, then who? One of the suburban gangs, like the League of Nationz?

I saw the shooting unfold again.

The way they walked and moved, the formation, seemed practised. Professional. And yet what professional would shoot like that? Into a crowd—

Enough. I wasn't going to think about it any longer.

Easy to say that—

No.

You're done with all this. No more speculation, no more dwelling on those images. Today goes in that airtight box of bad memories you don't allow yourself access to. No matter what you saw. You're done with this. Trust me, it's for the best.

Good. Now have a drink, wipe the tears out of your eyes, toss these clothes in a garbage bag and count yourself among the very fortunate. This morning the shadow passed low over your head. And you're still here. Live with that.

When Sonia came home she found me sprawled over the couch, well into my fourth drink. She dropped her gear by the door and nearly bent my spine with her embrace.

Her first words to me: "When did you start smoking again?"

"I'm not," I said. "It's just the stress."

"I came home soon as I heard," she said. "You should've called me. I was fucking worried."

"My phone's still in the office," I said.

"Dave, are you okay?"

"I don't know," I said.

We lay down together on the couch, stretching out to share the length. As a patrol officer, Sonia Drego had her own gallery of bad memories to draw on. It wasn't unprecedented for one of us to come home morose, be distracted for a couple of days. Eventually we'd knit ourselves back together, good as new, usually without discussion.

Sonia took a sip of my drink and replaced her arms around my neck. "You remember what we said when we got back together, what we agreed to. No secrets."

"Never," I said. "None."

She kissed my forehead. "If you need help, you ask. We'll figure things out together. But you don't get to close up about this, Wakeland. You don't have my permission."

FIVE

THE HERO OF KEEFER STREET

Whenever I fought with Jefferson Chen, I tried to keep certain things in mind.

Private investigation and corporate security wasn't the career path Jeff's family envisioned for him. As a satellite kid, studying abroad, Jeff had made the decision to defy parental expectations. He'd spurned business school in favour of an apprenticeship at Aries Security, before he and I struck out on our own. That defiance had cost him. Even now, with Wakeland & Chen turning a generous profit and our offices thrust into renovation chaos due to expansion, he felt the need to defend the business from everyone, his family included.

Working under Bob Aries had taught Jeff the value of reputation, if only by negative example. He'd seen firsthand how cutting corners gave Aries the reputation of being a glorified confidence man—not so glorified to those of us who'd worked with Bob, seen the way he treated his clients. Jeff had tempered his own ambition with a strong work ethic, which I admired and mostly agreed with, and usually adhered to. Wakeland & Chen stood for something, and that was mostly Jeff's doing.

For years he'd sublimated his ego, shirked his personal life, in order to grow the company. We both had. But whereas I'd poured work hours into cases, Jeff had mastered the business skills he'd once scorned. He'd somehow found us the capital to start up, despite neither of us having much of a track record. He'd learned about advertising, public relations, choke points and credit lines and other terminology that made my eyes glass over. Jeff spoke Mandarin and a little Cantonese, and worked his connections to build an international client list. Nowadays Jeff was a family man, with a second child on the way. If he thought nothing of asking employees to sacrifice for the good of the company, it was only because he'd done so himself.

So when I showed up at the head office at eight, the morning after the shooting, Jeff wasn't fazed. Neither of us took many sick days. His only complaint was that I didn't want to capitalize on the event in the name of corporate goodwill.

"Forget for a second that it's free advertising," Jeff said, as if the effort to do so would be great. "It's something you actually did, Dave. Something you should be proud of."

Jeff's personal office was the first renovated, fitting since he was president and manager. The walls of oak panelling gleamed with fresh stain, and the room still reeked of chemicals and cleanser. Photos of Marie and their son peeked out from boxes around the desk.

He turned to the paperwork hillock atop his file cabinet, pulled something from its summit. A copy of today's *Vancouver Sun*, the headline reading,

SEVEN DEAD IN "GRISLY"
CHINATOWN SLAYING

A large photo of the scene below the fold: the edifice of Gentrification Central. White markers and yellow cordon tape. A uniformed cop pointing at something. Near the edge, a silver-haired figure in a trench coat that looked like Superintendent Borden.

No bodies in the photo, but I saw them.

I folded over the paper and looked at Jeff. "So what?"

"Your name's not even in there," Jeff said. "I'm not talking about being exploitative, if you're worried about that. Like I said, it's what you did. It's heroic. You should be proud."

"I don't want to be proud," I said. "I want to be busy."

"Christ. If this was Aries, he'd have six cameras on Diane Cui's hospital bed, you next to her, smiling, every time she wakes up."

"You're making my point, Jeff. We're not him."

"A couple interviews."

"No."

"A statement, then. I'll write it, you don't want to."

I looked at Jeff, tilted back in the ergonomic embrace of his leather office chair. I understood. His partner wanders onto the scene of a crime, helps save someone, and the son of a bitch won't speak of it for who knows why. A missed opportunity caused by nothing more than false modesty and a general aversion toward the press.

"Do what you want," I said.

I read through the article in the boardroom, which the renovators were using for storage at this stage. The offices were in shambles. That was part of the reason I'd asked Jeff to find me a cubbyhole somewhere else, in some other building.

Part of the reason. Beyond that was my own not-so-secret feeling that the Wakeland & Chen offices were a great place to visit if you didn't have to work. 675 West Hastings was an elegant building, from the brass and marble in its modest lobby to the wood-panelled offices, to the view of Burrard Inlet and the North Shore Mountains. The East Van kid in me felt anything beyond a flat surface and a cup of tea was ostentatious, and that I didn't belong there. The small office on Keefer Street had felt more appropriate.

I hadn't gone back there, though.

Jeff sent someone for my things. Cellphone and cigarettes, a jacket, one shoe and the half-finished report on the child support case.

The news story in the *Sun* by Natalie Holinshed segued from facts to speculation to vows by the authorities to find those responsible. I hoped they would.

The article estimated there were three to six shooters, Caucasian males with automatic rifles. Holinshed threw out the same possible suspects I'd thought of, Exiles, League of Nationz, along with tongs and triads and fraternal organizations the dead men in the building were allegedly connected with.

The article was most concerned with the dead. They were enumerated, summarized by name, age and occupation, followed by some fact or accomplishment that elicited sympathy:

Qiu Xin Yi, Theresa Qiu, 27, a receptionist. Four years in Vancouver, taking part-time hotel-management courses at BCIT.

Jingjing Cui, 22. Recently completed her CPA certification. Honours student. Oboe player in the Vancouver Youth Symphony.

Owen Kazarian, 41, a retail manager. Survived by a wife and stepson.

(There he was, falling, crushing the peak of his hat as he struggled.)

The others were written about in slightly less eulogistic terms:

Chang Chia-Yang, 36, former card dealer at Waterfront Casino.

Vincent Ma, 28, occupation unknown.

Huang Shao Wei, 33, occupation unknown.

Zhou Li, 21, student.

Financial District's name was Bryan Mulgrew, 30, a junior partner at an investment firm. I found a video clip of him telling his story to a nodding newscaster, comfortable speaking for the camera.

"So being punctual is important to me, right, which is why I'm there at four-fifty, and how I know what time it started, which was five-ten exactly. We all hear the shooting, and kind of look at each other—what's going on? Maybe they're making a movie. I mean, it *is* Vancouver.

"So these four guys come out and just start shooting. *At us.* I'm in shock. This guy I've seen at the bus stop for months, I don't know his name but he just—goes down, y'know? And these two nice Asian women, who I've seen before also, they go down."

Mulgrew rubbed his neck and turned his face away from the lens self-consciously. "Guess I was just lucky."

The news anchor mentioned the lifesaving efforts of Mr. Mulgrew and another man. A blurry photo flashed on the laptop screen. Me at the scene, smoking. Then B-roll from a busy hospital trauma unit.

Mulgrew continued:

"So this guy jumps down out of his window—crazy, like a twenty-foot drop. We start giving first aid to these ladies. He starts removing the bullets, or—no, more like stanching the wounds?—and I call nine-one-one. The one lady died but the other I heard is doing all right. Guess we saved her."

A photo of Diane Cui in business attire, smiling.

"What is for sure," the anchor said, "is that for Bryan Mulgrew and the rest of those involved, nothing will ever be the same."

Jeff showed me the statement just before noon. Three brief, declarative sentences that said I'd been the one to offer life-saving assistance at the scene, that I was co-founder and senior investigator at Wakeland & Chen, and that the company extended its sympathies to the victims.

"What do you think?" Jeff said.

"Poetry, buddy. Philip fucking Larkin."

"Harder than it looks to write simple," he said. "Are you up to doing some casework?"

"About all I *am* up to."

"I figured that." Jeff hesitated, studying my face. "There's not a part of you that wants to get involved in this, is there? Try and solve it?"

"Not in the least," I said.

"Good. Gang stuff, it's always better to keep far away. You know better than anyone."

"What's the job?" I asked.

"More of a favour. My cousin didn't say much, just that someone she works with has a missing relative. I was going to go myself, but if you'd rather do it."

"Love to."

He nodded. "Shuzhen said to meet her out at UBC at one. Museum of Anthropology, there's a café around the back. And Dave"—Jeff stressed this with a hand gesture—"it's a university. You know what parking's like out there. Whatever happens, save your receipts."

I nodded, then got ready, left, thinking,

David Wakeland, 34. Private investigator. Saver of lives and receipts.

There were worse epitaphs.

SIX
THE CITY BEFORE THE CITY

The UBC Museum of Anthropology lay on the outskirts of the campus, near the edge of the endowment lands. Arthur Erickson had designed the building in the seventies, melding his brutalist architecture with the post-and-beam style of the coastal First Nations. The building was a hefty slab of aged concrete grafted onto the slope of Burrard Inlet.

I parked along the side and climbed the hill of yellowed overgrown grass that brought me to the entrance of the museum café. Standing in the courtyard were Shuzhen Chen and a stout older woman who leaned on a long, elegantly carved umbrella.

Shuzhen—Suzie now, since starting third year—had worked for us for a couple of summers until the pressures of law school picked up and her time was better spent studying in the library. Thursdays she volunteered at the law school's free legal aid program. I gathered the woman next to her was one of her clients.

Suzie hugged me—eleven years younger, my partner's cousin, and beautiful, no impure thoughts clouding my mind—and asked how I was doing.

"Good enough," I said. "And you? You look like you're thriving."

She did. I'd taken her for a fellow introvert, but that had been homesickness, unfamiliarity with the city and the language. Now she spoke with confidence, with a slight accent, and a more-than-slight valley girl lilt. She presented her acquaintance to me with the assurance that the two of us would be natural friends.

The other woman had a solidness to her that went beyond the

34

physical, an authority unasked for but shouldered all the same. Black hair with a silver blaze hung down the back of her raincoat in a long plait. When we shook hands I noticed the bands on her wrist, rawhide and silver, ornamented with jade.

Shuzhen introduced us. "This is Martha Youngash. She's with the museum."

"Not quite," Martha said. "I'm guiding a tour for a special exhibit. c'əsnaʔəm. You've seen it?"

Sonia and I had gone on one of her rare days off. c'əsnaʔəm had been the trading and community hub of the lower Mainland, going back almost five thousand years. Colonized and paved over into Richmond and Vancouver, the original site had been excavated after a long legal battle.

Like most Canadians I'd had little idea of what my city looked like before European settlement. The c'əsnaʔəm exhibit was less about artifacts than connections—oral history to digital media, trading posts to strip malls. It was preservation of a different sort—maybe resuscitation. And it was troubling; it had kept me up a couple nights.

"A few times a month they bring in someone from the Musqueam band to lead the exhibit," Martha said. "Today is my turn."

"You don't sound enthused," I said.

"No, I love it." She gave Shuzhen a five-dollar bill. We followed Jeff's cousin into the café and sat at one of the tables.

"It's exhausting, though, trying to explain things. People have such different expectations. Sometimes they're shocked, which is good. But it's been such a long process, and there's so much left to do. That's really the issue—I have other things on my mind these days."

Martha accepted the coffee from Shuzhen, along with her change. She opened her purse and pulled out a folded pile of printouts.

"First," she said, "I should make sure you're up to this. Suzie told me you witnessed that shooting yesterday."

"Not witnessed. I showed up after."

"Dave saved someone's life," Shuzhen said, rubbing my arm and batting her eyelashes like Daisy Duck. "My hero."

I aw-shucks-ed and told Martha I was fine.

"Good to hear." She unfolded the papers. "When I talked to Suzie at the Law Society, she said you knew how to find people. I need my nephew found. My white nephew, Jaycen."

She smoothed out the top page, a graduation photo of an acne-scarred teenager. A blow-up from a yearbook. The pages beneath were printouts of online photos, Jaycen at a ceremony of some sort, another with three other teens posed in someone's rec room. Dragons and cannabis leaves and Johnny Cash flipping the bird adorned his T-shirts in the photos.

Martha sighed. "It comes back to status," she said. "Always. And the onus is always on us, even after Bill C-31. You have no idea how fucking tiresome it gets, telling people what parts of you come from where."

I told her no, I didn't.

"Jaycen is my nephew, despite everything—*because* of everything. I have money for him, and no idea where he's at."

She explained how her older sister had married an American and moved to Oregon, returning years later, divorced, with Jaycen in tow. Her husband had run out on them, even though Jaycen was his son from his first marriage. There'd been nobody else, so Jaycen had been raised in Martha's house, with her own children.

"My uncle died last year," Martha said. "He left some money to be divided among the kids. Most are all grown now. Jaycen would be, let me think—thirty." The number sank in.

"When did he leave?" I asked.

"He moved out in his twenties but he used to keep in touch. After his mom passed, I didn't hear from him too often. Maybe a Christmas card."

"Was he in trouble?"

"Well, he was *troubled*," she said. "It was hard for him. I think he was used to having more stuff and more privacy. There wasn't much of those in my house back then. Plus, he was maybe ashamed, his dad running off like that. They never patched things up."

She showed me a sheet with his date of birth and vitals, a decade-old tax form from a part-time employer. "Jaycen worked a lot of odd jobs. He did some fishing, drove a delivery van. My kids used my house as a mail drop rather than change addresses every few months."

"Are you worried for him?" I asked.

"I hope he's okay. I think if he's in the right mind, this money could help him. That's an education. A down payment."

Shuzhen said she had to get back soon. The Society was understaffed this week.

Martha deposited her paper cup in the recycling bin. "Jim—the current chief—says we can't expend the resources. It'd be different if he was my kid, he says. That's where Jaycen fits—he doesn't fit."

I told her I'd find him, and outlined the Wakeland & Chen fee structure, applying the friends and family discount. She told me she'd send a cheque to the office, along with Jaycen's inheritance.

"When you see him," Martha said. "I should say if."

"When."

"You could ask him to call me. His cousins would like to hear from him. If he says no, tell him I understand."

She tapped the tile with her umbrella.

"Not everyone's proud of where they come from. Some I guess might like to forget." She added, "Him being white, he's lucky society lets him."

SEVEN
WHITE SHEEP AND SHEPHERDS

Jaycen Waid's father had been dead two years, leaving behind the third-largest realty and brokerage firm in Northwest Oregon. His third wife had been sole inheritor. Waid's lawyer and executor had no idea Jaycen existed.

It's usually not difficult to find someone to accept twenty grand. I talked with people who knew Jaycen from high school, his co-workers, friends of his mother. Nice guy, they all said, but we didn't keep in touch. I let them know that Jaycen could accept his money with one meeting, no questions asked.

I worked until seven, phoning and emailing from the couch in my East Van flat while Sonia got ready for the party. She was a nervous wreck. I'd once seen her repel a knife attack, earning scars in the process, yet fretting over the ratio of carrots to cauliflower on the appetizer plate had defeated her. Lucky her attacker hadn't wielded an invitation to dinner with colleagues.

When she barricaded herself in the washroom to get dressed and made up, I lugged the television into the bedroom and changed the bed-sheets. I set the parental controls and made sure there were kid-friendly movies.

The whole thing felt to me like something you did because you were a certain age and people expected it. I'd've happily had any of those people over by themselves. Hosting a cop party was different.

Sonia felt it, too, I sensed. We weren't a couple that entertained. That level of normalcy felt foreign, maybe undeserved. She'd grown up without knowing her parents or any sort of family life, and while we'd been living together for almost three years, she hadn't yet sold her apartment. We both still thought of this as *my place*; now we were presenting it as *our home*.

Sonia emerged in a white print dress with her hair teased up. I felt my heart flutter. I had wine decanting—she'd actually bought a decanter— and was pulling out records. She poured herself half a glass and stood looking over my shoulder.

"This is your idea of appropriate party music?" she asked.

"I know my audience," I said. "We start soft, a little Rage Against the Machine, then segue into Ice-T and Body Count—"

"We don't have enough space," she said. Looking at her, I saw she was serious.

I snaked my arm around her and took her wine glass with the other. "There's the patio too. It'll all be fine."

And it was. Frank Keogh and his wife Lorraine arrived early, with a case of Bud Light, and KFC for the kids because the kids didn't like Indian food. Lorraine explained this apologetically. Despite the overwhelming pull of her Desi ancestry, Sonia had in fact cooked salmon filets, roasted potatoes and spinach salad. She shrugged off the Keoghs' assumption, smiled and found space for the bucket on the already-cramped counter.

Keogh was a sergeant in Robbery, close to retirement. Sonia had been told she would be transferred to that unit within the next few months. She liked Keogh. After years of patrol, the chance to work Robbery had renewed her enthusiasm and given her hope for her career.

Ryan Martz showed up with his fiancée, Nikki Frazer. Ryan took a can of beer, but didn't refuse when Nikki handed him a wine glass. I saw him slip the can into the pocket of his cargo pants.

"The mark of a broken man," I said. "Giving up your choice in beverages."

"Which is why I see you downing bourbon left and right."

He grinned and we shook hands. Ryan, Sonia and I had gone through the Justice Institute, had served as rookies together. Ryan had been chosen for Missing Persons, while Sonia had toiled in a patrol car. As for me, I'd found out quickly I wasn't cop material, and I'd made my way into another line of work.

"Got something to ask you about," I said to Ryan.

We moved to the patio while Nikki and Sonia admired Nikki's engagement ring. As we spoke Ryan frequently glanced back inside at his fiancée, as if worried the distance might be too great. They'd been dating for less than a year, but the change in him was profound. Ryan Martz was the son of negligent parents, hippies, and had been angry since I'd met him. On his best days, he was abrasive and volatile, with a shock jock's sense of humour. Nikki had mellowed him, and he'd been smart enough to know the changes were all to the good.

"This about the shooting?" Ryan asked. "I heard what you did."

The wound in Diane Cui's chest geysered, frothing red. I willed it out of mind.

"I didn't do much," I said.

From inside I could hear Keogh's big-chested laughter over the strains of Jimmy Ruffin, "What Becomes of the Brokenhearted."

Moving away from the door, Ryan said, "From what I hear, there's a fuck-ton of pressure to solve this."

"I can imagine." Vancouver didn't have many homicides per year, and this added seven. The city was on track to set a new record.

"More than just stats, Dave. White shooters, mostly Asian vics. Everyone's worried this is the start of a gang war."

I took a long drink of red wine and fought against asking for details. Fought hard and won. Ryan supplied them anyway.

"Word is, the place was being used as a count room. Two of the vics had records, gang connects. One was fired last year from the Waterfront Casino."

"And these shooters ripped them off," I said.

"How it looks, yeah." Ryan set his wine glass on the concrete steps leading out to the street. He popped the beer can. "They go in, surprise everyone. Must've figured it was easier to leave no witnesses."

No witnesses, not one.

"They seemed professional," I said. "From what everyone's been saying."

"Ruthless, definitely." Ryan sipped his beer. "There's another theory," he started to say.

The sliding screen shuddered and Frank Keogh stepped out. He had two cans of beer in each hand.

"Two for you," he said, handing one to each of us, "and two for me. Cheers, boys. Dave, hell of a nice place you got."

Keogh had a thick frame, with a friendly, dimpled, ruddy face. Sonia thought he dyed his hair. It was a dark brown that seemed slightly off its natural colour. His eyes looked compassionate, though I got the sense that was an attribute he cultivated and deployed as part of his job.

"Really glad you came," I said. "Sonia's grateful learning from you."

"She'll be teaching me soon," Keogh said. "Smart girl. Was I interrupting?"

"Just talking about the shooting," Ryan said.

"Sad shit," Keogh said. "Sad, sad, sad. My heart just bleeds for Uncle Roy Long and his crew."

I'd heard the name before, but couldn't place it.

"As I was telling Dave," Ryan said, "it might be a straight robbery that got out of hand. Or it might be retaliation, bikers or whoever sending a message."

Keogh wrapped an arm around Ryan's shoulder, still two-fisting the beers. He rubbed Ryan's cheek with the side of his own head, grinned at me with drunken affection.

"Sherlock Martz here," he said to me, "is one of the great armchair detectives. You got an armchair in there, Dave?" He craned his head, exaggerating as he looked through the mesh.

"It's all anyone's been talking about," Ryan said.

"Sadly. No one wants to see the city turn into the Wild West. Right, Dave?"

Keogh looked up at me, all smiles. Hard to gauge how drunk he was, how much of an edge might lie behind his words.

I told him he was right. Right one hundred percent.

After dinner, when Keogh had taken his family home, and Nikki and Sonia and her friend Kiranjit were finishing off wine bottle number three, Ryan motioned back to the patio.

"What'd you want to ask me about before?"

I had Jaycen Waid's details written out on a slip of paper. Ryan glanced at it and put it in his pocket.

"No problem. Glad to see it's a male this time. Anything I should know about this Waid?"

"His aunt's a former chief of the Musqueam band."

Ryan's head fell to his chest. "It's never simple with you, Dave."

"Just a peek at his record and anything outstanding on him."

"I'm too fucking nice to my friends."

"That's what everyone says about you, Ryan."

For a moment his jaw clenched and he looked like his old self. He looked through the patio door, where the screen had been until Keogh's daughter had crashed into it and knocked it out of its frame. Ryan looked at the blonde woman talking to Sonia and Kiranjit. Constable Nicole Frazer, currently assigned to support services.

"Ever catch yourself thinking, Dave, just how fucking lucky you are?"

"Never," I said. "Not once."

Before we crossed back inside, Ryan said, "I don't need to tell you there's a lot of interest in this case. Some people figure you know more than you let on. If you saw something—"

"I didn't."

"—I'm saying *if*, Dave. I can smooth it with them. We're not talking about open-court testimony. Shit, you could call Crime Stoppers, all I fucking care."

"The second I hear anything," I said.

Something struck the side of my head. I looked inside at the women, staring at us, on the verge of giggling. A wine cork bounced off the carpet and rolled to the edge of the door frame.

"That's it," I said, "all of you are cut off." I pointed at Sonia. "And you, young lady, can look forward to a severe reprimand."

"What about a ring?" Kiranjit said. "When can she look forward to one of those?"

Nikki added, "When are you proposing to her?"

Sonia looked at me, fingers covering her mouth. "I didn't put them up to this," she said.

I bit my bottom lip and blushed. I didn't have an answer.

EIGHT
A NICE LITTLE CHAT AMONG FRIENDS

Fatherhood suited Jeff Chen. His hairline had receded an inch, and he'd started to form a pot belly. He now kept his bespoke suits for special occasions, and he'd taken to dressing business casual around the office. Yet the result made him look younger, more distinguished, and both less and more comfortable. I doubted even he could answer if he was happy or not, at least without dictating a novel.

"Sorry about last night," he said, in a tone that said he was anything but. "The kid is just coming off that cold going around, and Marie might have a touch of it."

"We missed you," I said. "All we did was sit around, 'Where's Jeff? Why isn't Jeff here?' More of a wake than a party, actually."

"It won't happen a fourth time," he said, with slightly more sincerity. "Tell Sonia I'm sorry. Now what's going on with this case?"

"Jaycen Waid," I said. "Thirty years old. Recently minted twenty thousand-aire. If I can find him."

"Is he in trouble?"

"Doesn't look like."

"So you're working a paying case? That isn't outrageously dangerous? And you're not obsessing and putting in an insane amount of time?" Jeff let his jaw fall open in mock surprise. "Who the hell are you? Where'd Dave go?"

"New and improved," I said. "Steadfast and boring."

"I fucking love it," he said.

Our Monday morning strategy session, as he called it, involved coffee and char siu bao. Jeff headed the company—we were nominal partners, but it was clear who should have final say on business matters. I floated, oversaw hiring and worked the cases I wanted. It was ideal.

Almost before I had, Jeff sensed that there was value in the way I did things. Early on I had some high-profile successes, longshot missing persons cases. Even the failures—Jasmine Ghosh, Chelsea Loam—had their value. People saw the dedication. It was tangible, it gave them hope for their own happy resolution and it worked better than any guarantee.

You couldn't run a business with employees all doing what they wanted, but one added that something. Name recognition when we started, reputation later on. Most importantly it gave Jeff something to gripe about.

"This other thing," Jeff said after he'd thrown some budgetary stuff at me that I'd nodded and uh-huh'd through. "The shooting. How are you feeling about it?"

"Nobody believes me when I say I'm not interested."

"It's your kind of thing," he said.

"No it's not. I don't like violence."

"You boxed."

"As a teen, till I realized getting hit hurts." I wiped crumbs off my shirt. "This is different. It's too big for us."

Jeff leaned back in his ergonomic swivel chair, a gift from Marie. She'd also given me one. It was in the boardroom, swapped out for the straight-backed wooden chair I sat in now. My back felt ergonomical as hell.

"Just want to make sure you won't look into this behind my back," Jeff said. "In these circumstances, staying away is only smart."

"Sure," I said. "Fair warning, though."

"What?"

"You don't eat that last pork bun in the next thirty seconds, I'm taking it."

He smiled and slid the box toward me.

After our meeting, I talked to a friend of Jaycen Waid's who worked with him on a fishing boat for three summers. She told me Jaycen was hard-working and hard-partying. He'd been sleeping on someone's couch. The friend couldn't remember whose.

Another fisherman said Jaycen had an accident and nearly lost his thumb. He explained the hospital trip, the stitches. Jaycen had been proud of his new scars. He'd drifted out of the fishing business, gotten work driving a forklift. The friend didn't know where.

I talked to someone at WorkSafeBC about whether a Jaycen Waid had ever received a forklift ticket. She said she'd check.

When I phoned back she told me yes, two years ago a Jaycen Waid had been granted a licence through instructor Leonard Tunney, who also happened to own a warehouse, Tunney Bros. Logistics.

"It's a cost-saving measure with him," the clerk confided. "He hires unskilled workers, teaches them himself and gives them their ticket. Better than offering higher wages or paying for training. I can't tell you the number of accidents at that warehouse."

Tunney was out but his office manager said he'd be back tomorrow morning. The manager sort of remembered Jaycen. Nice kid. Hadn't seen him in a long while.

I wrote it up, looking at the pattern. Jaycen had drifted from job to job in his twenties, aimless. Who hadn't? He could be selling dope, doing manual labour under the table. It all depended. He could be dead.

Maybe he'd expected to be given more in life. When it didn't show up, he soured on hard work. Maybe he took up crime. A remembrance of yesterday's violence hit me out of nowhere. The coppery smell of the count room, the dead men inside it. I closed my eyes till the images disappeared.

I made a note to tell Jeff to cancel the small office on Keefer. He'd hated the expense of a satellite office anyway, and had only arranged it as ammunition to get me to do something else later.

Tunney Bros. was in Richmond, a good thirty-minute drive. If I hurried I'd make it back before rush hour. I passed Jeff's door on my way out of the office, saw that it was open.

Superintendent Ellen Borden was sitting in my wooden chair. Sergeant Dudgeon leaned against the wall behind her. Jeff was pouring them each a cup of tea.

"Speak of the devil," Borden said. "We thought we'd speak here, away from everyone else. Unless you'd rather talk at the station."

NINE

IF THEY'RE AFTER YOU

I settled into Jeff's chair, avoiding his look. Sitting behind the desk lent me some authority. "What can I help you with?"

"Still our multiple homicides, I'm afraid."

Borden moved papers from the edge of the desk and set her mug down. Jeff hurried to slide a coaster under it. Antique rosewood and condensation circles: I'd heard the lecture before.

"First of all, how are you coping?" Borden asked. "Seeing someone die is traumatic. It's very hard to wrap your head around." Her look implied she had personal experience to draw from.

"I didn't see anyone die," I said. "Or anything else."

"Young Ms. Cui."

"Her, yeah." I leaned into the chair and the chair tipped back. I caught the edge of the desk. The slip wasn't lost on Borden. Dudgeon caught it, too, looking up from his phone.

Jeff returned with two rolling chairs, gliding one toward Dudgeon and seating himself to my right. Borden had taken a digital recorder from her pocket and set it next to her mug. "Do you mind if I take this down?"

"Are we working on new material, or just doing our greatest hits?"

"See, that's interesting," she said. "That frivolous tone. Either you're still in shock, and the weight of this hasn't yet hit home—"

"It's hit home," I said.

"—or you simply don't care about the deaths of these people."

I crossed my arms and stared at her.

"Let's approach this a different way," Borden said. "Have you had any dealings with Roy Long?"

I saw Jeff swing his face away from Borden, toward me.

"Don't know him," I said.

"Anyone who works for him? Anyone connected to the criminal underworld?"

"We run a pretty square, pretty above-board business," I said.

"I'm sure you do." Borden and the sergeant made eye contact. Dudgeon had seated himself next to her, his mug on the floor between them.

"What about the Heaven's Exiles Motorcycle Club?" Borden said. "What have your dealings been like with them?"

"Exceedingly positive," I said. "They're a bunch of good-natured lugs. Sweethearts, really, who just love choppers. The wind in your hair and all that. And also the occasional murder and gang rape."

"You've met the West Coast chapter president, Terry Rhodes." Not a question.

I nodded. Not only met but I'd traded fists with him, coming out poorer on the exchange. Nothing Borden needed to know, if she didn't already.

"Are you afraid of him?"

When I didn't answer immediately, Borden added, "I certainly wouldn't blame you. If half of what he's rumoured to have done is true, it's a wonder he's not in prison for life."

"Yeah, funny about that." Rhodes had overseen the murder of at least three people I knew of, one I'd considered a friend. "It's almost like he's free to act above the law."

"Rhodes is clever but he's not immune," Borden said. "Outlaw motorcycle gangs are a priority for us. For the RCMP too. There's a task force—"

Understaffed and underfunded, I thought. Chasing half-patch affiliate gangs and cut-down kilos, while Rhodes and his Montreal connections bought car dealerships and department stores. Strip clubs into strip malls, loansharking into online poker. An empire held together by violence, bribery, collusion.

Ask me again if I'm scared.

I said, "If you're implying I held back out of fear, I wish you'd just say that."

"All right."

"Also, if I had to ask that of a witness, I might wonder why someone would feel that way, if they might not be justified. And that might lead me to wonder why there are two big-time criminal groups operating in my backyard, and why rectifying that doesn't seem to be a priority."

"Duly noted," Borden said sympathetically. "Who was it said, it's not paranoia if they're really after you."

"And if Terry Rhodes can shoot people with impunity, don't ask why there aren't more witnesses."

Borden collected her recorder, switched it off and pocketed it. She thanked Jeff for the tea.

At the door, she said, "You might consider it's a two-way street. If no one speaks up, there's little we can do. Maybe you saw nothing and I'm pushing you too hard.

"But I think," she added, "you did see something and won't speak up, for reasons I simply can't fathom. I don't believe for a second you're afraid. I believe you're hiding something."

"Believe away," I said.

"I will. And I'll have your help on this. Eventually you'll want to."

"And why's that?"

"Because either you're a good person who wants to see justice done."

"Or?"

"You'll realize I'm not a good choice for an adversary." Borden smiled and moved to let Dudgeon pass through the door. "Self-interest usually wins out in matters like these."

TEN
NEW FACE

After Borden left I decided to put off my trip to the Tunney Bros. warehouse until tomorrow. I had other leads on Jaycen Waid I could follow. Electronic leads.

I opened my laptop. The first headline in my news feed:

GANG WAR LOOMS

Natalie Holinshed's article in the *Sun* suggested the shooting tied into rising tensions between Lower Mainland organized criminal groups. You had bikers, you had triads, you had the loose affiliation of multiethnic gangs. There was only so much dope, so much real estate. Treaties eventually broke down.

Holinshed didn't mention Roy Long by name, or the Exiles. Her anonymous source was quoted as saying, "This is a power struggle, pure and simple. It's about who's going to be the new face of Vancouver crime."

Holinshed's take: The money from the count room was less important than the message the shooting sent. This kind of breech could destabilize a leader who'd let something like this happen, cause that person to lose face. It would have to be answered in kind.

It doesn't matter. I don't care.

I repeated that to myself and focused on finding Jaycen Waid.

I had left a message with Ryan Martz but he hadn't gotten back to me. I reminded myself he did have other things going on.

The last job Jaycen held before the warehouse was with a painting crew, college kids who paid their part-time help in cash and didn't keep the best employment records. They played the hapless newbies, out of their depth with things like paperwork, but I knew their corporate tax forms would be in order, their retirement plans maxed out. Cut us a break, we're just starting out here. I felt nostalgia; Jeff and I had done the same thing.

The painting crew turned over staff quickly, semester to semester, but one of the crew chiefs had worked a few jobs with Jaycen. A so-so worker, the chief recalled, reliable but not above copping an attitude. Sometimes Jaycen could act like he was too good to roll paint.

Sixteen months ago he'd stopped showing up. No one had bothered to ask what had happened, since no-showing was common among their work force. The crew chief thought he remembered Jaycen mentioning a girlfriend. Jessica? Jennifer? The chief was pretty sure their names alliterated.

That evening I asked Sonia, if she saw him at the station, to ask Ryan to call me. She headed out to work her shift, leaving a desolate void in the apartment that faintly smelled of her body scrub. I lay on the bed and tried to sleep.

With my eyes closed, the shooting would come back to me. Details broke into my thoughts. Sometimes I'd feel like it was happening now, just out of sight. Like a flickering television screen casting its erratic glow on the surfaces nearby.

Not good, I thought. *Not good but normal. Give it a few days.*

I made tea and concentrated on work.

Martha Youngash's children seemed shocked when I phoned about Jaycen. He'd borrowed money from the oldest, four hundred bucks, which, no big deal between family, but it could definitely be put to use if Jaycen paid it back.

The youngest was miffed that their uncle had cut Jaycen in. He wasn't blood, was he? He could get his own inheritance from some white uncle.

Before I called Martha and informed her of my progress, I tried Ryan's desk at the Cambie Street station. It went to voicemail.

A minute later he phoned me back on his cell.

"You think I didn't get your fucking messages?" Ryan said. "You maybe think my not answering *is* your answer?"

"Tough night at work?" I asked.

"You don't know the shit you stirred up," Ryan said. "MacLeish called me. We had fucking drinks on the sixth fucking floor."

"And what did the deputy chief constable want?" The VPD's head of the General Investigations Unit usually kept his distance from the rank and file.

I heard Ryan's hand cover the receiver, a low muffled conversation. He sounded like he was outside when he came back on the line.

"MacLeish made it clear," Ryan said. "Not in so many words, but I got the fucking message. Said he knew you and me were friends, and it was sometimes hard to keep work and friends separate."

"Was Borden with him?"

"Just MacLeish," Ryan said. "The two of us talked about my future, all the places I could go, if I didn't get hamstrung trying to stay friendly with people who were bad influences."

"I'm a bad influence?" I said. "Ryan, I'm hurt."

"Fuck your hurt. I can't help you any more."

"Ryan—"

"Good luck with that kid Jaycen or whatever. Hope you find him. Good luck, Dave, but Dave, fuck right off."

ELEVEN
FUCKING THE DOG

The first thing Len Tunney said as he ushered me into his private office: "Not every day I get to meet a hero. That was some firefight, huh?"

"It was a bad day," I said.

"That's an understatement. Understatement and a half. Guess you're tired of talking about it." Phony sympathy, almost gainsaying a negative response. No, it's fine, of course let's talk about it.

I said, "I'm looking for Jaycen Waid," but added, thinking I might as well use it, "It's not the kind of thing I can talk about, really. Nothing prepares you for it."

Tunney nodded, impressed. He wore a polo shirt with the company logo printed on the breast pocket, dark slacks marked with warehouse dust. A florid-faced man with an easy smile, a sweat-dappled forehead and a slightly clammy handshake.

After a respectful pause, Tunney said he'd be happy to talk about Jaycen. He showed me his employment records. Pay stubs ending in March, the barebones resumé Jaycen had submitted.

WORK EXP: Commercial fisherman. 2 yrs.
SKILLS LEARNED: Fishing, boating, hard work, puntcuality.
WORK EXP: Painting. 3 summers.
SKILLS LEARNED: Communicat with people, dealing with customers.
WORK EXP: Landscapeing. 3 years [off + on].
SKILLS: Driving, yardwork, working long hours.
REFS AVAILABLE UP ON REQUEST

"Someone must have vouched for him who already worked here," I said, putting down the resumé.

Tunney spun the paper on the desk, looked it over, then laughed. "That would be Paul," he said. "Paul Lagana. If I remember, he brought Jaycen in to handle the Christmas rush." He hit his intercom. "Ask Paul to come up here, please."

A moment later we heard a woman's voice over the warehouse PA, "Paul to the office, please, Paul to the office."

"Jaycen seemed like a good kid," Tunney said. "But a few weeks in he started to slip. Looked tired all the time. I can't have that, Mr. Wakeland. A good day, we can get a few hundred orders sorted and sent out on the Purolator. It can be hard to keep up. I know 'cause when it's busy I'm not sitting on my tush, I'm out picking with the rest of them."

"You also trained him on the forklift," I said.

"I train all my employees. It's cost-effective, plus then I'm sure they know how to do it right. What passes for education these days, it's best to do it yourself."

"Sure," I said. "So what happened to Jaycen?"

"Things reached the point, I had to tell Paul to send him home. We can't have anyone here who's not giving a hundred-and-ten."

"Does that happen often?" I asked.

"With college kids, sometimes, yeah. Not with people used to putting in an honest day's work."

"Do you think something happened to Jaycen? Or was it just ennui?"

"En-what?"

"World-weariness," I said. "General dissatisfaction with where he was in life?"

Tunney's face reddened even further, stopping just short of supermarket beef. "I didn't go to college," he said. "I just know there's people who put in the work, and then there's the other kind. Jaycen showed me who he was."

A booming knock on the door. Paul Lagana entered without waiting for a go-ahead. Slender and tanned, head thrust slightly forward, his weathered face shadowed by the brim of a grimy Jays cap. He nodded at me as Tunney made the introductions.

Lagana said he had to check on the dog treats orders, but I could tag along. I followed him onto the warehouse floor. We passed signs ordering hard hats and steel toe boots to be worn at all times. Lagana hopped onto one of the motorized pallet jacks and told me to climb onto the forks.

"Hold on or it's your ass," he said.

He spun the machine in a tight donut and we blasted up the aisle. The shelving was three stories of blue steel, the corner posts silver where accidents had scraped the paint. Shrink-wrapped pallets hung on the top shelves.

All it takes is one, I thought.

"Jaycen do this?" I asked.

"Sure. Picked orders mostly, did shelving."

"How'd he like it?"

"How would you?" Lagana said.

At the end of the aisle near the back door, three Korean women crouched beside a pallet. They had lined up a row of shipping boxes near their feet, and dropped order components into the boxes as one of them read from a stack of orders.

"Newman," she said in tired, accented English. "Three chicken, four organic chicken, two doggie delight, one weight-control."

"No more weight-control," another called.

They looked to Lagana, pointed at the second shelf, maybe eight feet off the ground. He mimed climbing up. They stared at him. He said to give him a minute, he'd come back with the lift truck, but for now, do the orders without the fucking weight-control.

I waited near the women as Lagana fetched the lift. None of them wore safety gear. The shelves loomed above us. One of the women smiled at me. When she turned her head back to her clipboard, I saw something dark seep out from the back of her scalp.

Diane Cui's daughter—of course it wasn't her—

"Here you go," Lagana said, at the wheel of the lift truck, dropping the skid near us. The tines clanged on the concrete.

"You gotta count on people to be fuckups," Lagana said, as we cruised back down the aisle on the pallet jack. "Or lazy."

"Which kind was Jaycen?" I asked.

"He was a difficult cat to read," Lagana said, steering out of the shelving, across to the loading docks. "I wouldn't say lazy, exactly. Unmotivated might be better."

Lagana brought the jack to a sharp halt, my knee catching on the battery housing. He loosed a long grey cable from the charging station on the wall.

As he coupled the charge cable to the battery, he said, "If Jaycen did all right with the orders, we planned to move him up to the loading dock. I didn't exactly promise him that, understand. But then Len caught him fucking the dog a couple times. Once Len thinks you're not pulling your weight, it's pretty hard to change his mind."

We started back to the office on foot, Lagana's pace almost as breakneck as his driving.

"Jaycen have any friends here?" I asked. "He ever mention his girlfriend?"

"After the shit about the promotion, we didn't talk much. Jaycen might've felt I should've stuck up for him more. Here he was, my old landscaping buddy, pulling ten-hour shifts, making a bit over minimum wage. Him doing another four months of order picking wasn't my decision, y'know? But he wasn't exactly hitting home runs at the jobs we gave him."

"Did he want more?" I asked.

"In his place, I would," Lagana said. "But I got kids. That means I have to be here, I don't got a choice. Jaycen had all the choice in the world. The fact he ended up here at all tells you something about that kid. Like my dad used to say, some people take the easy road all the way uphill."

TWELVE
FLINCH

When Sonia came home I was stretched across the carpet in my under-wear, an almost empty tumbler of Buffalo Trace next to me, the stereo blaring Soundgarden's *Down on the Upside*.

She looked at me and shook her head. "So when I texted you an hour ago and asked if you were ready, I take it you were lying? Or are you plan-ning on going out in your undies?"

I propped myself up on my elbows and tried to look apologetic.

In truth I'd been ready long before that. I'd come home from the warehouse, showered, made tea, put on fresh clothes. I'd killed time writing up notes on Jaycen Waid, started rereading Leonard Gard-ner's *Fat City* for the fifth or sixth time. And then something had broke.

It had suddenly all seemed so fucking futile. The unprotected women in the warehouse, no different from the dead people in the street. A tape that's played out one time only, to the end of its spool, and then torn off and tossed away. And we all had to shoulder this knowledge, and smile, and pretend it wasn't so.

It took time to pull myself together. I'd taken a second shower, applied the home remedies of bourbon and vinyl. Now I told Sonia I'd be dressed and ready in five, before she could change into her gym strip. And I was.

We walked up Broadway, the sun just beginning its descent. Tuesdays and Thursdays she trained no-gi jiu-jitsu at the Gracie Barra on Main. I'd wait for her, browse the shelves of Pulp Fiction or the Mount Pleasant library, or walk. After, we'd get takeout from Budgie's and either stroll home or, if the weather held, head to Jonathan Rogers Park and sit over-looking the field.

It was an ideal routine, something I'd never had before. Tonight, as we walked, Sonia told me she had good news.

"I'm having a talk with the deputy chief tomorrow," she said, smiling. "Just out of the blue, MacLeish's secretary asked could I meet with him before my shift starts. How cool is that?"

We'd been walking arm in arm. She gripped my elbow tighter, squeez-ing with both hands, giddy. I ripped my arm from her grasp.

Both of us paused in the middle of the sidewalk. I apologized and told her it was just a reflex. I offered her my arm again.

"What's going on with you?" Sonia said.

"I'm just a bit jumpy, ever since that thing. Sorry again."

"Jumpy is right. I tell you good news and you flinch like I'm going to hit you."

I stepped into the doorway of a pho restaurant to allow passersby to thread between us. "I don't know that it *is* good news," I said. "Ryan had the same type of meeting yesterday. Informal drinks with the deputy chief. He was warned not to help me."

"Why would MacLeish…" Sonia massaged her brow. "The shoot-ing," she said. "This is about you helping them."

"I think so, yeah."

"They're exerting pressure on you, through us."

"And I don't think they've even started," I said.

After a moment we resumed walking, no longer arm in arm.

At the entrance to the dojo I told her, "Have fun. Beat the shit out of someone for me." I couldn't quite pull off the tone, but she nodded and kissed me goodbye.

Alone, I bought Chinese cigarettes and found a vacant patch beneath an awning. I listened to the drumroll crack of rain on concrete, slowly changing into the loud susurrus of a steady downpour.

Sonia's career meant everything to her. She not only aspired to make rank, she had a path mapped for herself to get there. Patrol, then detec-tive work and only then command. That way, later, no one could accuse her of lacking street credentials. It saddened me that even in her dream scenario, she anticipated being challenged, criticized. But then she was aware of the realities of being brown-skinned and female in a system where those could be used against you.

If her career was damaged on account of this mess, I'd regret it, and I'd feel ashamed. But it wouldn't change my decision to stay out of it.

In my own brief career on the job, I'd messed up, bad enough to be summoned to the sixth floor. I was told, in so many words, that all could be forgiven. But I would owe. I hadn't quit out of superior virtue, only a sense that the marker would be too steep.

Primal forces threaded through this shooting, any of which would annihilate a person without warning or reason. To hell and gone. No career was worth that.

I watched a woman collect bottles and cans from the garbage containers along Main, tossing them into the cargo pouch of a rain-soaked baby stroller. She made me think of the Calendar Man. His positioning that morning had been wrong. Opposite side of the street, far from the bus stop. Either he'd taken a strange route to his usual place, and his cart had overturned, or someone had accosted him. Or he'd known something. In any case, I hoped he made it away from the scene unscathed.

I couldn't think of him in isolation from the rest, so I concentrated on the last drags of my Double Happiness, then headed to Kafka's. Armed with a London fog, I started back toward the dojo.

Behind me a young woman speed-walked across Broadway, barely making the curb before traffic resumed. I turned my head to look at her. She spun to face the doorway of Fable Diner.

I look, you look away. Two probably unconnected events. Something said *wrong* to me. Before the shooting I might have called it a born detective's unerring sense of human guilt as revealed through body movement. The post-shooting me would chalk it up to paranoia.

But the fact remained, the woman looked into the restaurant but didn't enter. When the light changed and I crossed Main, she followed me.

From what I could see she was Chinese, in her early twenties, give or take. Large, dark shades and a formless green raincoat hid most of her. Her mouth was coloured bright purple, which stood out in my periphery as we crossed. Not a surreptitious shade. An amateur, or else someone drawing attention there to mask some other feature.

The woman kept two storefronts' distance between us. When I sped up, so did she. I walked past the dojo. The woman did too.

At the corner I about-faced and headed toward her.

She did what I hoped she'd do, what a professional would strive to avoid. She entered the bookshop. Trapped. One entrance, and nowhere to hide.

I stepped inside, passing the new releases section and the counter piled high with trade-ins. A small group of wet-haired customers were lined up near the till, operated by a rangy, bespectacled proprietor. I looked down the aisles, saw people browsing. No woman in green.

She could be crouching near the back. I took two steps down the centre aisle, peered over the shelf into poetry, stepped around a stack of crime books waiting to be shelved.

On top of the stack was a hardcover with a black and white image. The door of a police car, porous with bullet holes. I saw and smelled the inside of the count room, the walls punctured to dust, the one man's face hardly recognizable *as* a face. Fine powder over ruined red-black.

Dizzy.

I heard rapid footsteps, caught myself, turned, saw the door close and a green blur run up toward Broadway.

"The fuck was that?" said the proprietor.

Outside, I couldn't see her, and when I reached the corner, she was gone.

So much for the pro's advantage. She'd outmaneuvered me in a bookstore—in my local bookstore, even worse. Something athletic in her movements, skittish. I couldn't tell if she meant me harm. I hoped I hadn't pissed her off.

THIRTEEN
TERMINALS

Sleep-deprived and neck-cramped, and peevish to begin with, my half-sister Kay explained why she and Tim Blatchford had given up their surveillance on Mrs. Bostick's house.

"It was only one night," Kay said, "and only for a couple hours. We were dead tired, Dave. And anyway, it's not like the old girl's in danger."

"That," I said, "has four-fifths of fuck-all to do with whether or not she feels she is."

Kay took this in, nodding. We'd had vastly different childhoods, she and I. The troubled woman who'd left me on the steps of her sister's East Van house had since moved to the Prairies, cleaned up, found Christ and raised her second child in suffocating suburban bliss. I didn't think of that woman as my mother, and for the longest time her daughter River had been only a distant relation. We'd become closer when she moved to Vancouver for college. She'd changed her name to Kay for reasons known only to her, declared her classes dull and a waste of time, and decided private investigation might be fun. I'd paired her up with Tim Blatchford hoping they'd learn from each other.

Kay and Blatchford looked almost comical standing side by side. My half-sister was short, compact, dark-haired, dressed in light denim and light-brown suede. Blatchford's pro-wrestler physique had shrunk after kicking his various unhealthy habits, but he was still well over six feet, his hair sheared to a dirty blond fuzz that darkened and greyed as it wrapped around his chin. He was wearing the dark blue pants of his Wakeland & Chen security uniform, one knee torn and the rest pocked with stains. His grey warm-up jacket was zipped to his throat.

I heated the brackish water I'd left in the Zojirushi the morning of the shooting. I hadn't been back to the Keefer Street office before now. The window was still partway open from when I'd gone through it.

I could see traffic pass across the street. No sense that the drivers knew or cared what had happened here days ago. Plywood had been affixed to the door of Gentrification Central in lieu of glass.

"The Bosticks are one of Wakeland & Chen's better clients," I said. "Mrs. Bostick feels alone in the house while her son's in Toronto. You patrol the grounds before bed and stay out there. Makes her feel better, which makes him feel better—"

"Which makes Jeff feel better," Kay finished.

"That's really what this is about," said Blatchford. "The way that compound is set up, nothing's getting through all those motion detectors. Jeff doesn't trust his own handiwork."

"He doesn't have to. He has you." I poured hot water into the mug, the week-old tea bag still inside.

"What were you doing up that late anyway?" Blatchford said.

"Not important."

"Of course it is, Dave," he said, ever so sweetly. "We care about you."

"Then don't make me fight Jeff to keep him from firing you."

"You don't mean that," Blatchford said.

Kay interrupted him to say I was right, it wouldn't happen again. Not that she bought my bluff any more than Blatchford did. She knew I wouldn't fire him. He'd helped me when I was starting out, and while he was a Costco-sized pain in the ass, Tim Blatchford was still an able PI.

I offered them tea. No takers. I looked out the window, briefly, then turned my gaze back inside.

"Why are we meeting here," Kay said, "and not at the head office?"

"I didn't want to have this conversation in front of the others. Better you realize it can't happen again and save yourself another penalty."

Jeff's system of reprimands was charmingly, needlessly complex. In a year's time you were allowed a hundred points' worth of reprimands: thirty for lateness, sixty for dereliction, eight for leaving a mess in the break area. There were also fireable offenses. Kay hadn't posted a single point this year. Blatchford was hovering around eighty.

He stared at me, his fingers tapping the arms of his chair. "You haven't been back here since it happened, have you? You just wanted someone else here when you opened up."

"I don't want you getting yourself fired," I said, working myself up to where I almost believed it. "Jeff's strict and has his quirks, but he's right, you need to shape up."

Blatchford smirked. "Sure, Mom."

I said to Kay, "Some time in the future, when you're running your own business, and some washed-up, broken-down bum asks you for a job, playing the for-old-times'-sake card, think long and hard before answering yes."

"What if it's you?" she asked.

Later, after Kay and Blatchford had gone, my cellphone rang with an unlisted number. Ryan Martz, asking if I'd tried the brewery on Lonsdale Quay.

"If you haven't, you should," he said. "They have one of those hop-heavy IPAS you love so much. They're open for lunch. There's a SeaBus at twelve-ten you could probably catch."

"Thanks for the tip," I said.

From the office, I walked to Waterfront. There was mild cloud cover and a breeze coming off the water. I kept my eye out for the Calendar Man, but didn't see him on my route.

Would anyone notice if he was suddenly gone? The Calendar Man was part of the class of near-invisible city dwellers whose presence you'd feel—but their absence? Would anyone notice that he, specifically, had vanished?

The receptionist at Gentrification Central would have, I thought. Theresa Qiu. I'd seen her talk to the Calendar Man a few times. Once during a rainy morning she'd brought him a cup of coffee. Maybe she would have missed him—but then she was dead, and his subsequent disappearance might be connected in some way—

No.

Stop.

Not your business.

You already have something you're supposed to be doing. So do it, okay?

I reached the terminal at noon and watched the squat, antennaed SeaBus slowly cross Burrard Inlet and let off its passengers before boarding. There was a crowd of thirty or so, plus a half dozen stragglers who ran down as the glass doors and gangplanks swung to close.

I sat with my back to North Vancouver, on a string of white benches all to myself. Across from me I saw a floating copy of the *National Post*, open to the real estate section, with a pair of yellow-striped pants splayed out beneath it, legs cutting over onto the adjacent seats.

"I'm not that crazy about hop-heavy IPAs," I said to the newspaper.

Ryan folded the *Post* and tossed it onto the seat next to him. "Hops, malts, who gives a fuck?"

"Thought that might be some sort of code," I said. "I order one and there's a self-destructing message under the coaster."

"You joke," he said, "but MacLeish is serious."

"I know. Sonia is meeting with him tonight."

Ryan turned his head toward the window. The industrial cranes along the port were receding as we neared Lonsdale. "I don't get it," he said. "Why they want it solved, of course, but why they have it out for you. You specifically."

"Maybe they think I'm in league with the shooters," I said.

"Doubt it," he said, taking me literally. "I get the sense you're making it hard for them. Fuck if I can figure out why."

"I'd just as soon not find myself in the midst of a gang war," I told him.

"Sure, but still. There's a lot of dead people. Can't expect them to be happy to eat seven unsolveds, 'specially with the chief's every-person-counts mandate."

He spoke the last part with added sarcasm. Of course every life should count. Of course an administrator would make that a talking point.

Unspoken between us, though, was the fact that if the seven had all been gang members, if there weren't civilians involved, there would be less public pressure on the department to solve it.

"Fuck it," Ryan said. "Most likely next week or so we'll find these shooters, chopped up and dumped behind the night market."

Ryan had a hoodie on, his gear bag tucked under his seat. He pulled a piece of paper out of the pouch pocket and handed it to me.

"Your boy Jaycen Waid," he said. "He was picked up during a raid last year on a grow op in Surrey. Charged with illegal manufacturing with intent and pled it down."

"This a pro operation?" I asked.

"Doesn't seem like it. They found plenty of dope and psilocybin, some hydro gear, but it seemed pretty thrown-together from the reports. If it was an Exiles grow op, there'd've been guards, and more care taken to disguise the power overrun."

The ferry docked, doors on the opposite side sliding open. The other passengers lined up to exit.

"Anyway," Ryan said, "address is on there. The rest you can find out easy enough."

A transit officer passed by. Ryan nodded to him, made a circle with his finger to indicate he was staying aboard. I thanked him.

"No worries," he said. "Tell Sonia, hi. Tell her I hope MacLeish doesn't chew her ass out too bad." He grinned at me, a flash of his old self. "That should be your job, anyway."

I got off and walked to the market and had a beer I didn't want. I looked up the news stories from the grow op raid. The homeowner's name was Alyssa Canejo, owner of Canejo Developments Ltd., former insurance saleswoman for Waid & Associates. Jaycen's father's firm.

Canejo was quoted as saying she had no idea what her tenants had been up to. She knew she was supposed to go through her rental properties every year, but she was busy and her tenants had supplied really good references. They'd seemed like such nice people.

I'd heard that from others about Jaycen Waid. No one seemed all that worried by his disappearance, or surprised, or sad. His effect on the people that knew him best, that were most disposed to like him, was something close to learning your favourite chain restaurant had moved into a strip mall five minutes farther away. They all assured me he'd turn up soon.

I finished my beer and took the SeaBus back, thinking, wouldn't that be nice.

FOURTEEN

TRADITIONAL VALUES

At the main office, I set up a video call with Alyssa Canejo. She was on vacation in Florida. Her laptop camera displayed a fiftyish woman in a cranberry-coloured bathrobe, sunglasses on, in front of a patio shaded by palmetto trees. She sipped orange juice as we talked.

"Jaycen's father gave me my break, helped me scrape together my first down payment." Her mouth spread into a smile tinged with nostalgia and maybe regret. "He always said put everything you make into land, 'cause they're not making more of it. He wanted the best for Jaycen, he really did."

"Of course," I said, thinking that was easy to say.

"When Jaycen got in touch about the house, I maybe didn't check out his friends with the proper due diligence. That was my mistake. I tried to do something nice for him."

"Jaycen asked you to rent to his friends?"

"What he said was, they needed some place with privacy. He had health issues, this friend. Crohn's disease. If I could rent the house to them a little below market, they'd be grateful. Plus with disability, they'd have no trouble making the rent."

She paused, drank some juice, and checked something in another window on her laptop. She nodded at the screen, but not looking at me.

"The first eight months, there weren't any problems," she continued. "They paid in cash, dropped it off at my office. They didn't complain or ask for improvements—of course, now I know why."

Alyssa Canejo let out a long sigh, probably remembering what she'd paid out in renovations after the house had been stripped, first by the tenants and then by the authorities.

"Maybe deep down I knew," she said finally. "I'm not an idiot. If they were dealing a little dope, so what? I didn't think it'd be that bad—didn't think they were growing the stuff in my house."

"How many were there?" I asked.

"I only met the two, Jim and Jenna Balfour. They really did seem like nice kids. It felt good to help them out a bit."

"Ever see them again?" I asked.

"In court, the once."

"Was Jaycen there?"

"Now this is the really dumb part," Canejo said. "This I have no excuse for. Other than, again, trying to do a good turn for my friend's boy. I heard Jaycen was picked up. He told me it was all a misunderstanding. He'd just been there to drop off some tools. Babe in the woods, right?"

"And he asked you to vouch for him," I surmised.

"Which I did. Until I get to court and he's out front having a ciggie with Jim and Jenna, the three of them looking like it's all a big joke. He didn't see me but I turned right around. Last I saw of him."

"And the Balfours?"

"Charged, copped, no jail time. And me on the hook for the damages. From what I heard, Jim put on quite a show for the judge—brought his crutches and a Safeway bag full of bloody snot rags he kept adding to. Sixty thousand in damages—I didn't make half that my first year at work."

"Any idea where Jaycen went?"

"Who knows?" Canejo said. "Hard to believe he's his father's son. His mom was part Native or something, wasn't she?"

Asking me, as if that explained it.

At home, I browsed around and found an online dating profile for a Jim Balfour. His cover photo showed a man of sixty bench-pressing a thick stack of plates on a machine. *Looking for a thin nonsmoker who shares my love of lifting. Traditional values important. No dogs. No vaccines.* Probably not Jaycen's friend.

A local small-business website had a page for Jim Balfour Customized 420 Glass Enhancements. The only images on the site showed Bob

Marley smoking a joint, and a circle of religious icons wreathing a giant dollar sign.

UNITED UNDER ONE GOD,

the banner read.

I messaged this Jim Balfour and said I was looking for something epic for a bachelor party. Could he maybe show me some of his work?

I made dinner while I waited for an answer. Impossible burgers and a salad with homemade vinaigrette. Far from gourmet, but it would be ready when Sonia got home. Her moods swung on her blood sugar, like mine did, and she needed no encouragement to opt for takeout.

When she did come home it was eighty minutes after shifts' end. Not unexpected: as a cop, things come up. Sonia lugged her gear bag over the threshold and dropped it next to the shoes. Her face seemed blanched and she was gnawing her bottom lip.

She accepted a hug and poured herself a drink, then sat on the couch while I fired up the stove. "That bad?" I asked her.

I'd been a cop for less than two years and had plenty of horror stories: abused animals, children dead from neglect, bodies discovered weeks after expiry. Sonia had those and more.

Sometimes over drinks we'd share them, to gross the other person out, to make them laugh. It seemed callous; it *was* callous. It was also a distorted and mangled way to share, to request solidarity, to let someone know the burdens you had to carry.

I handed her a salad bowl and leaned on the table, one eye on the skillet.

"How was the meeting?"

"Short," she said between bites, looking at the television though it wasn't on.

"No threats?"

"No."

I checked the burgers and flipped them. Pea protein doesn't sear like fresh ground beef, but these looked brown enough. I turned off the stove.

"So what happened?" I said. "Why are you late?"

"I'm late," she said, "because I was busy cleaning out my locker."

Sonia was most beautiful when angry, which was something I'd never tell her. But this wasn't an anger that flushed the cheeks and set the mouth in a predatory sulk. This was a dull, beaten-down resentment, not aimed at me but not excluding me. Her look hurt.

"For what?" I asked. When she didn't respond: "You can fight this, right?"

"I wasn't fired," she said, beginning to tear up. "I was promoted."

Relief hit me. I tried not to smile at her reaction. "To what?" I asked.

"Public fucking relations. I'm going to be a fucking spokesman."

I turned off the stove, sat down beside her and rubbed her shoulder blades. "I'm sorry."

"MacLeish said Robbery was full and PR is where he needed me. He said he knew I deserved promotion, that there wasn't anyone else he'd rather see in that position."

Her face scrunched up, her head falling onto my chest.

"It'll work out," I told her. "It won't be forever."

My foster father, technically my uncle, had remained a constable his entire life. He'd had an engrained hatred for "the bosses," the desk-riders and bureaucrats who he saw as working against "real" cops. In his mind the cops who fled the streets to hide in the upper ranks were those least qualified, the police department a kakistocracy save for a few of the good ones.

All of this might have been due to a lack of ambition, or a preference for cracking skulls rather than taking complaints from people with head wounds.

Sonia was more ambitious. Part of that was a "twice as good" mentality, partly a way to neutralize anticipated complaints from white male street cops about taking orders from someone who got above them without ever being one of them.

Above all she abhorred anything to do with public relations. Not only would it take her off the streets, it made her the designated apologist. When an officer stepped over the line, she'd be the one vouching for him—not only him, but the institution's ability to punish him fairly.

Her skin colour and gender would be used to validate an institution she was hoping to improve. And it would ruin her credibility with the rank and file.

She wept a little. I thought of how there'd be no danger in her job now, no worries that today she'd take the wrong door with the wrong person behind it. And I pushed that thought away and comforted her as best I could.

FIFTEEN
SMOKE

Dragonflies, alien larvae, a winged dolphin in Rastafarian colours. The storefront window at Broadway and Fraser was packed with elaborate bongs, hash pipes, hookahs and vaporizers. The man behind the counter called to the back for Jim Balfour. A pain-filled voice said he was just finishing up.

I'd brought Kay with me to view Balfour's glassware. Despite being tired, she was thrilled to do something other than security detail. We wore slacks and our shirts buttoned up, and tried to look out of place.

The clerk told us we could go back and wait for Jim, as long as we didn't touch anything. We passed the display cases and walked through a bead curtain into the back.

Balfour was seated at a workbench, a quad cane next to his chair. He was starvation-thin and wore shorts and sandals and an oversized T-shirt that hung off one shoulder, the collar cut out. He waved us over, apologizing for not standing up.

On the workbench sat a clear glass pig, the mouthpiece above its haunches, and next to it, a long rainbow-coloured wizard's staff. The glass lay on rags, amidst mounds of bloody paper towels.

"Nosebleed," he said, swiping the tissue to the floor. "I got a condition. What are you looking for—you said it's for a party, right?"

"Our brother's bachelor party," I said. "We're thinking of something crazy. Can I?" When he nodded, I touched the staff. "Beautiful. Think he'll like that?"

"He's not really a fantasy guy," Kay said.

"Still, look at the craftsmanship."

"These are samples," Balfour said, "not for sale. What does he like—sports, video games? I've done a race car."

"He's into sci-fi stuff," Kay said. "Could you maybe do a lightsaber?"

He nodded disdainfully, disappointed at the lack of imagination and skill required. "I could do a whole Death Star, you want. Give it tripod legs. Smoke the glass so it's slightly grey. You name it."

"The guy we talked to who recommended you," I said, "told us you were the best. And the prices were reasonable. What would something like that run?"

"Size and materials and detail all depend," Balfour said. "Between two to eight grand, though, for the high-end custom. If you're looking for budget, there's some imported stuff in the window that'll do. I'm an artisan, I do artisan work, that pulls an artisan price."

"Artisan is exactly how Jaycen described you," I said.

Balfour's face soured like someone had offered him a cat turd to chew on. "Jaycen Waid? He said that?"

"That you were the best, yeah. A real craftsman."

"Like he'd know," Balfour said.

"You guys aren't close?" I asked. "Not that I want to get between you."

He rubbed the flesh around his nose and reached beneath the desk for the roll of paper towel.

"If you know Jaycen, you know what he's like," he said. "Did he say anything about a commission for himself?"

"I can't remember—we were at a party, a mutual friend. He just told me about your skills and that I should check out your website." I added, almost as an afterthought, "He's not in shit or anything, is he? I mean he looked kind of, I dunno, troubled."

"He always looks like that," Balfour said. "Like everyone's against him and he deserves better."

"That's the look, that's it exactly."

"And the thing is," he said, "Jaycen still talks like he's better than you. Like someday his daddy will raise him up. My sis calls him 'the Deposed Prince.' Except it's all bullshit. His dad's dead and left him sweet FA."

"He told me…" I looked at Kay, projected shock. Then to Balfour I said, "You're kidding, right? About his inheritance?"

Balfour's laugh was cynical. "You lent him money?"

"Five hundred—aw, hell. I thought it was a mistake when the phone number he gave me was wrong. You don't"—I paused to collect myself, breathe, look like someone trying to regain control—"You wouldn't know where I could reach him?"

"Trust me," Balfour said, "I'm the last person he wants to see. You think he owes you?"

"Is there any way I could get in touch? Anyone who might know where he is?" I looked downcast. "I was planning to pay you with what he owes me."

Balfour thought about it, saw his sale evaporating. "I could ask my sister," he said. "Leave me your number. Did we decide on the Death Star?"

I left him a down payment of a hundred bucks, apologized it wasn't more, but told him once I'd seen Jaycen, I'd bring him the balance. He said when he had the first thousand in hand, he'd start work.

Outside, I paused to light a cigarette.

"You didn't really need me here," Kay said.

"You never know."

She nodded and lit her own cigarette.

"You shouldn't smoke," I said. "Blatchford is a bad influence."

"Tim doesn't smoke," Kay said. "Why do you keep him around if you don't trust him?"

"He's a clutch hitter. He comes through when I need him."

Kay exhaled, coughed. "Jeff really doesn't like him."

"It takes all kinds," I started to say. Then noticed up the block, approaching us, a heavyset man. Grey T-shirt, leather pants, leather vest. Moving swiftly for his size.

"Go that way," I told Kay, indicating the other direction. "See you back at the office."

But around the corner came the Leather Man's twin, pinning us between them. They closed the distance fast.

"What do we do?" Kay asked.

I couldn't think of anything.

Before I had to, a cream-coloured Chevy Avalanche roared up, jolted to a stop in front of us. In the passenger's seat, leaning his arm out the window, was a thin man with a braided red beard. He hoisted a tattooed arm, an automatic pistol in his hand.

"You're Wakeland?" Redbeard said.

I didn't answer, but I didn't have to.

To the two in leather, he said, "Just him." And to me, "Get in. Friend of yours wants a talk with you."

SIXTEEN
HUMAN CHESS WITH LAND MINES

On a stretch of Commercial Drive, there are a pair of by-the-slice pizza shops next to each other. The one on the right uses fresher ingredients, and relies a lot less on the heat lamp for longevity. The shop on the left will sell you cocaine cut with fentanyl if you know to ask for it.

Both places were owned by the Exiles Motorcycle Club. Both were fronts to launder money.

The story was that the shop on the right was used by Terry Rhodes as a meeting place. A long time ago he'd fed a slice to one of his dogs. The animal had developed severe gastroenteritis, nearly requiring surgery. Rhodes had seen to the dog's health. Then he'd come back to the store, and talked with the manager. Him, his dog, the manager and the manager's son. Soon after, the right-hand shop instituted its present quality control.

It was a short ride over to Commercial, but felt as cold and long as a naked trek through the taiga. The inside of the Avalanche smelled of sweat and stale beer. I was wedged into the middle seat, the two leather giants on either side. Redbeard watched me from the front seat, smirking, his gun hand waving in my direction like the drunken gesticulations of a barfly. The driver wore sunglasses and looked bored as he flouted the rules of traffic.

The Avalanche stopped in the middle of the Drive. The three men climbed out, ignoring the honks of the cars behind. I was dragged out onto the pavement, marched into the pizza shop on the right.

The boy at the counter looked up and gaped. Redbeard shoved him aside as the others muscled me through the narrow kitchen. One of the leather giants caught a tub of grated cheese with his shoulder, knocking it off the shelf.

The backroom was barely big enough for two people to play cards. One wall was stacked with milk crates of liquor. Bowmore, Bladnoch, Macallan Twelve. A collapsible table and two wooden chairs. Terry Rhodes sat in one of them.

Redbeard nudged me into the room and shut the door, leaving me alone with Rhodes.

He wasn't as large as the men that worked for him. Older, with a face like a rail-splitting wedge. Yet given the choice, I would have preferred my chances taking on the other three together. Part of that was due to the aura Rhodes projected: ruthless, explosive, always one breath from scorched-earth savagery. I'd seen it firsthand.

But I'd also seen what lay behind it. A predatory business sense that sized a person up, decided value and acted without hesitation. All threats neutralized, all desires gratified, all opportunities seized by the throat. I'd once likened meeting with Rhodes to human chess, played on a minefield.

If I'd lasted this long in my dealings with him, it was for one of two reasons. Either Terry Rhodes hadn't quite found a use for me, or he didn't view me as a credible threat.

Rhodes had his cellphone out, held sideways, watching the screen. His blunt hatchet-face chuckled. When the video ended he grunted one loud laugh, then threw the phone onto the table.

"Beheading video?" I asked. "Or the one with the kitten that looks like Gene Hackman?"

The smile lingered on his face, though his eyes looked me over with an auctioneer's disdain for shoddy merchandise.

"Business thing," he finally said. "Sit."

Rhodes kicked the other chair at me. It stung my shin. I sat.

"You get around," he said. "It's been, what, three, four years since we seen each other?" He poured Blue Label into the glass in front of him. "How the fuck did you manage to get mixed up in this?"

No use insulting him, pretending I didn't know what "this" was.

"I'm not mixed up," I said. "I didn't see—"

"Yeah," he barked over me. "Yeah yeah yeah yeah yeah. Right. So how'd you end up there?"

"Just happened to be in my office—"

"Just happened to be there."

"Yes."

"In the neighbourhood. Just happened. A fucking coincidence."

"Heard shots and tried to—"

"—and jumped out a fucking window," he said. "You're a hero, Davey Boy. My little fucking hero. And guess what my little hero's going to do now?"

He scratched at his gumline with a yellowed fingernail.

"You know Uncle Roy Long?"

"I know how to read a newspaper."

"That's a good skill to have," Rhodes said.

"I didn't see anything. So whatever happened between you—"

"Between me?"

Rhodes shot his chair backward into the wall of crates, making the bottles clink and shudder. He leaned over me, pressing his forehead into mine until I backed up, my shoulders hitting the opposite wall.

"Between whoever," I said slowly. "It's not my business."

"No, it fucking isn't," he said. "It fucking isn't, but it sure fucking will be."

I waited for him to explain.

Rhodes picked up his drink. I moved my hands up, ready to ward it off if he threw it at me. Instead he drank it and put the glass upside down on the table.

"Dead Chinks," Rhodes said. "You think it was me? My guys?'

"No."

"You just saying that 'cause you're afraid?"

His hand reached past me, snagged a bottle from the top crate. He pushed the glass toward me. "Have a drink."

I righted the glass and he filled it. Rhodes drank from the bottle. Arran Ten, Robbie Burns special. In different company it would have been pleasant.

"Fact is it wasn't me," Rhodes said. "But everyone thinks it is. So what do I do about that?"

I didn't have an answer.

"Fucking headaches I got from this. Everybody's ready for the shit to fly. And nobody wants to look weak, and I can't 'zactly tell Uncle Roy, hey, sorry for your loss, but some other cocksucker has it out for you."

Again, I said nothing. Rhodes put the bottle down and looked at me. Appraising something.

"I don't explain shit to anyone," he said. "Rather have 'em think I'm crazy. But I want to know who done this."

"I didn't see."

"So make some inquiries. Ask your partner."

"Why would—"

"Do your fucking job," Rhodes growled. "You find people, don't you? So find these motherfuckers."

"So you can kill them—"

"So I can buy them a shot and a fucking blowjob."

"I'd rather not," I said.

"You'd rather not."

"I'm busy."

Terry Rhodes's laugh scrunched his features into a mask of pain. He coughed out absurdly high-pitched giggles. When he finished, he slammed his hand on the table, as if angry at his own sense of humour.

"You're not afraid of me at all, are you?" he said.

"I'm very afraid of you."

"But you're busy. You got plans. You run your mouth."

"Compensating," I said.

"For what?"

"Being scared shitless."

Rhodes nodded seriously, as if I'd made a cogent point in a dead-even debate. He handed me the bottle and watched me refill my glass.

"For a guy scared shitless you're not shaking. Haven't pissed yourself yet. No tears. Guys scared shitless tend to do that."

"Caught me on a good day," I said.

"Catch you any fucking day I want."

His hand went up and I flinched and pushed back to the wall. Rhodes smiled. The hand opened the door a crack.

"I want to know who," he said, "and where they are. Figure it out."

I walked past Redbeard and the others, back through the kitchen. The manager paused mid-slice on an onion to scurry out of the way.

Terry Rhodes called to me before I could exit.

"You do what I say, Dave. Couple humps and a van shouldn't be too hard to find, not for a tough guy like you."

SEVENTEEN
DEAD END FRIENDS

I held it in till I'd walked the few short blocks to my apartment. Held it in like one long breath. Once inside, with my door closed, it all spilled out. I kneeled and beat the floor with my forearms, and dry-heaved, and reminded myself to breathe.

Breathe

while you can.

Eventually I calmed down. I phoned Kay and told her I was all right. Phoned Jeff to say the same. Before I could speak, though, Jeff said he had a favour to ask of me.

"A reporter called," he said. "Natalie Holinshed, she said you know her. She liked your statement, the one I wrote for you, about the shooting. She wants to know, can you come down to St. Paul's for a photo shoot?"

"Why would I?" I said.

"Diane Cui's condition has been upgraded. She can receive visitors. A photo of you two together would be news."

I saw Diane Cui. Smelled her blood.

"It's not a good idea," I told Jeff.

"Right. Free publicity. Terrible idea."

"To be honest," I said, "I'm a little fucked up right now." Knowing he wouldn't believe me otherwise, I added, "I just ran into Terry Rhodes. Or he ran into me."

"Shit, Dave," Jeff said. "You're okay?"

"Define 'okay.'"

"He didn't hurt you?"

"Threatened to, I don't find the shooters for him."

"That's insane," Jeff said. "Listen, you can stay around the office for a few weeks. We can protect you. There's plenty to do here."

"Not a chance," I said. "Just let me do what I'm good at, Jeff. I'm close to finding Jaycen Waid. I can do that. That makes sense to me."

He agreed, provided I checked in regularly and didn't take any risks.

I sat on my patio and smoked a cigarette, one of the Super Slims Dudgeon had left with me. The clouds above the mountains signalled a storm coming in the next few hours. It was nice for the present, though, chill but clear.

Jim Balfour had gone home for the day. The clerk at the vaporizer store described his hours as "usually in around one and here till whenever." I told him I'd been in earlier, and owed Jim some money. Could I get his cell number? Him being disabled, I might save him the trip.

Balfour answered on the first ring. I reminded him who I was.

"Right," he said, "Mr. Death Star. You come up with that thousand yet?"

"Hoping to get some of it from Jaycen Waid. You mentioned your sister might know where he is."

"She's got no clue," Balfour said quickly. "Guy comes and goes, depending on who's paying. He runs through friends." Balfour pulled away from the phone and coughed and blew his nose. "You might want to start thinking of that money as gone."

"I'd hate to," I said. "Your sister say anything about who Jaycen hangs with?"

"Prob'ly someone with a few bucks. That's what he does."

I pried a bit more, to no avail, and then thanked him.

"No problem," Balfour said. "Let me know when you get the cash together. I got lots of ideas about that Death Star."

Jenna Balfour's address was a trailer park in Surrey. I drove through New West and took the Pattullo Bridge across the Fraser River, the water green-grey in the afternoon light. Turning off the highway, I followed Old Yale Road until I found the address.

Built in the midst of the industrial waterfront, the park bordered an auto-wrecking yard. A steeple-roofed pub sat in the centre, the trailers arranged in semi-circles around it. Strands of clothesline festooned the small lawns, shirts and halters flapping lethargically.

I parked and went searching for Jenna Balfour's trailer on foot. Unit 24. I found it. A white trailer stained at the edges with dark green moss. Yellow polka dot curtains drawn across the window.

It was entirely possible Jim Balfour had been forthright with me and had no idea of the whereabouts of Jaycen Waid. I got the sense, though, that Balfour was scornful partly because Jaycen was still in his life. Jaycen's boss had mentioned a girlfriend with a name like Jenna. Balfour might disparage his sister's partner, without wanting to sic a creditor on him.

I expected to talk to Jenna, to work Jaycen's location out of her, or maybe to leave him a message through her. I didn't expect to knock on Jenna's screen door and see, through the mesh, Jaycen himself sitting on her couch, shirtless, playing Mario Kart.

He squinted at me, blinked, and his eyes opened wide.

"Hi Jaycen," I said.

He pushed himself to the edge of the couch and drew up his feet. The controller slipped to the floor.

I held open the screen. "Your Aunt Martha sent me to find you," I said, stepping inside. "I have some money for you. An inheritance."

"Show it to me, then."

"It's at my office."

"Sure. And I'm 'sposed to go with you and get it, right?"

"You can pick it up any time."

He looked at me skeptically. Jaycen Waid was skim milk pale, slight, with tattooed arms and neck. Thinning blond tendrils hung down to his shoulders. He had moccasins on, and cargo pants.

"Inheritance," he said. "You're a lawyer?"

"Private investigator."

"How 'bout showing me some ID?"

He waited till I had my wallet out, then he bolted out the back of the trailer.

"Jaycen," I called to his back.

Jogging around the side of the trailer, I saw Jaycen sprint across the grass to a rusted hedge of chain-link fencing. Beyond that was a waste-land of machine parts and derelict cars.

I thought quickly but very hard about letting him go.

The fence was bowed and curled over. Jaycen vaulted to the top, threw his leg over and tumbled into the long grass. He ran left, threading between the metallic hazards with familiarity.

I followed from my side of the fence, hoping I'd find a door or a gap. No such luck. I clambered up, my feet slipping on the rusty links.

As I grabbed a handhold near the top, I felt a stabbing pain. I removed my hand, exposing a wayward spur of wire. Blood filled the cut. Nothing to do about it now.

Poised at the top, I bent my legs and scanned the grass, and then let myself drop.

Impact. I opened my eyes onto Keefer Street, saw the body of the man in the fedora, thought how clownish he looked with his hat crushed beneath the corner of his head—

No. Not now.

Jaycen glanced back and saw me. I started after him. He approached the edge of the auto yard, a high fence topped with barbs. Fortunately for me, he veered right.

The mouth of the auto yard led out onto Old Yale Road. Jaycen raced onto the pavement. A tow truck lumbered past him, swerving, the driver letting out staccato blasts from his horn.

We were approaching the small stretch of grassy beach along the riverfront. The road swung to the right. Jaycen was faltering. I wasn't much better.

He crossed the railway tracks just ahead of me, cutting across the grass to a beachfront path. I'd need to get parallel with him, close enough to tackle. I ran to his right, one foot on the paved walkway, the other on grass.

Jaycen slipped. By the time he was up I'd just about closed the gap. He looked back as my arm clasped his shoulder, slipped off, grabbed hold again.

Blood on his shoulder. My hand shrank from it.

Jaycen ran, sensing freedom, swinging his arms frantically. The red smear across his trapezius, blood from my hand. By the time I could orient myself, he'd put distance between us, and I was in no shape to pursue.

Panting, I sat down on the cold grass and watched Jaycen Waid disappear. When he was gone, I watched the river.

"Who fucking needs you anyway," I said.

EIGHTEEN
CINDERELLAS

Jenna Balfour stood in the doorway smoking as I approached her trailer for the second time. Wearing a white bathrobe, feet shoved into oversized gum boots, hair turbaned in a faded blue towel. She looked at me like you'd look at a water stain on someone else's ceiling, a rainbow puddle of transmission fluid beneath the car next to yours.

"If you're here to collect from Jaycen, knock yourself out." She waved me inside, and gestured with her free hand around the trailer's narrow interior. "TV's mine but you can take his Nintendo."

Dishes filled the sink, cereal bowls covered the counter. There was a stack of red plastic beer cups still in their plastic wrap. I gestured toward them, *may I?*, then filled one from the faucet and drank.

As I rinsed my hand, I explained to Jenna that I was here to persuade Jaycen to collect his inheritance. I showed her my security worker's licence unbidden, then leaned on the arm of her couch while she made up her mind.

It took her till the end of her smoke to decide. Jenna Balfour was close to forty, pretty and seemed neither ashamed nor thrilled about her surroundings. Not going out of her way, because her way wasn't going anywhere.

Eventually she said, "He usually phones once he's sure he's got away. Then, lucky me, I get to go pick him up."

"How often has he done this?"

"Often enough. Jaycen owes money to a few of his friends. When he's not washing dishes at the pub, he's thinking up schemes to get clear.

Course, usually those schemes cost something. 'Startup capital' is how he phrases it."

"Like the grow op," I said.

Jenna winced. "Don't remind me. Jim wanted to put in generators—raised most of the money for them himself. But Jaycen was all like, my buddy can help us siphon power for free."

She lit another cigarette. I looked at it longingly until she offered one and lit it for me.

"How'd it go wrong?" I asked.

"Jaycen's friend ratted us out. He wanted to be a full partner, but Jim was like, fuck that, not for doing a bit of wiring and then sitting on your ass. Jaycen kind of forgot to relay that message. Then the guy felt cheated, called the cops, and we got shut down. Jim'll never forgive Jaycen. We all put everything we had into it."

My toe nudged a plastic bag with two pairs of chopsticks and a wad of paper napkins. I took a few napkins and held them over the wound in my hand, which felt less like stigmata now and more like an irritating scrape.

"How much does Jaycen owe?" I asked Jenna. "All told, to everyone, you had to guess."

"Six grand at least. Two to me, plus he's been living here rent-free since Christmas. Fifteen hundred to Jim, and there are a few others. How much did his rich daddy leave him?"

Instead of correcting her, I said, "Enough to get him square if that's what he wants."

"Un-fucking-believable. I always thought that Deposed Prince stuff was bullshit. I guess his family actually was worth something." Her laugh had a bitter inflection to it. "Jaycen Waid, the trailer trash Cinderella. Can't think of anyone deserves it more."

A phone rang from somewhere beneath the mess on the floor. Jenna picked up a plastic hamburger from beside the couch. She held the top of the bun to her ear.

"Yeah… Yep, still here. Says he's got money for you. Inheritance… He already showed it. You don't believe me, dumbass? Fine."

She covered the bun's mouthpiece. "He'd like you to show me some ID. Yeah, I know, again."

Before I could open my wallet, she said, "Yep, he's totally holding it up in front of me. It looks legit." Rolling her eyes, she said to me, "Jaycen thinks it's still bullshit."

I handed her a business card. "Tell him to look up Wakeland & Chen. He'll see my face on our website. His cheque will be at our head office, 675 West Hastings, any time he wants to pick it up."

Jenna relayed that and nodded.

"Also tell him, if we could wrap this up by morning, I'd greatly appreciate it."

She talked to him a while longer, in a lower voice. He seemed to be pitching woo. She okayed him, each one slower and deeper-pitched. Her irritation finally peaked. "Okay... Yep... I will... See ya."

Lighting a fresh cigarette, Jenna let the burger fall back to the floor. She sighed. "What a fucking flake," she said. "Least he gives good head."

NINETEEN
WHAT FRIENDS DO

When I arrived back at the office, the lights were off in the reception area. Jeff's door was open. He was inside, using a level and a drafting pencil to mark the walls where his photos and credentials would go. I could hear the renovators at work in the adjacent office—my office.

I sat at Jeff's desk and opened the bottom drawer, removed the first aid kit. I set about disinfecting and bandaging my hand.

"Help yourself," Jeff said.

"You got a minute to talk?"

"Actually," he said, "I was hoping we could. We need to double up the patrols on the construction sites. There's been some supply theft. When Kay is done watching over the Bostick residence, we'll need to add her to the rotation."

"Blatchford could do it," I said.

"You mean because he's ditching surveillance anyway?" Jeff paused to look at me, to verify that I already knew. "That puts him over a hundred demerits, Dave, and it's not even summer."

"So we'll put him on process serving," I said. "Or maybe let's rethink the repossessions department. That might suit him better."

"Promote him, you mean."

"Put him to proper use. He works better alone, and he doesn't mind conflict."

"About that I have no doubts."

Jeff raised up a panoramic photo, the Coast Mountains wrapped around the city on a rare cloudless day, gold glinting buildings against layers of blue and grey. He lowered it slightly, nodded to himself and put it down.

"He's using again," Jeff said. "Ralph mentioned he saw Blatchford in the washroom."

"I'll talk to him."

"Talk. He's forty-two and you treat him like a kid brother. And you already have Kay."

"Kay isn't a liability."

"So you admit Blatchford is."

I held my hands out across the desktop, *what do you want from me?* My bandage itched.

"Not that long ago Tim Blatchford took a knife for me," I said. "And he'd do it again. I can't fire him."

"Part of what separates us from the Bob Arieses of the world is our reputation," Jeff said. "It has to be impeccable. And he might be your friend, but Blatchford—"

"—is pretty fucking peccable," I finished. "I know. I'll deal with him, okay? Let's talk about our sterling reputation for a minute."

Jeff nodded. I watched him select another photo, the two of us in suits at some business function, standing on either side of the Governor General. We were smiling, holding up an oversized charity cheque.

I said, "While I was driving back from Surrey, I had a disturbing thought. I wrapped up the Waid case, by the way. He should be in tomorrow to collect his money."

"Nothing disturbing about solving cases," Jeff said.

"The disturbing part comes when I started thinking about how I found him. Jaycen helped his friends rent a house to start a grow op. He told an old friend of his dad's they were looking for a cheap place. It's pretty common, isn't it? Friends helping friends find real estate. Especially here, where everything's so goddamn overpriced."

Jeff stopped what he was doing and looked at me.

"The shooting's been on my mind," I said, "much as I wish it wasn't. After what happened I can't work at that office on Keefer. I forget if I asked you to cancel the lease."

"You did," Jeff said.

"Right. Because you used your contacts to get it for me cheap in the first place. And I got to thinking about whether the property owner might be the same as whoever owns the building across from it, where the shooting happened. Gentrification Central."

Jeff said nothing.

"It wouldn't be too hard to check—to see if the companies are the same, find out who the owners or the chief shareholders are. Then check whether any them are fronts for Roy Long."

I gave Jeff a mean-spirited smile. "But then of course I remembered that the Wakeland & Chen brand is built on impeccable reputation, and there's no way in hell you'd ever do business with a known gangster and not tell me."

For a second Jeff looked like he wanted to walk out. His tongue explored the corners of his mouth. Finally he collapsed onto a client's chair and rubbed grit from his eyes.

"It's not like that," he said.

"So what's it like?"

"Roy—Mr. Long—is a member of the Benevolent Association. That's how I know him. It has nothing to do with whatever else he does."

He pointed at the picture of the Vancouver skyline. "Not like he's worse than half the *gwai lo* owners of other buildings. More than half."

"So you don't owe him," I said. "We don't owe him."

"I wouldn't do that to you," Jeff said.

"But you'd keep it from me."

"I mean—" he looked at me, putting on his confession face. "You got to understand. I came here with nothing."

"'Cept money, an apartment, a Mercedes—"

"Culturally nothing," Jeff said. "Going against family means something different when you're Chinese. I know you don't have much family, so maybe you can't understand. For me, my whole life was about them, what they wanted, until I decided it wasn't. I make more than most accountants, a lot of engineers, and my father's still pissed at me."

"Which has what to do with Roy Long?"

"The Association helped me make connections," Jeff said. "And Roy was a part of that. A small part, okay? It's nothing illegal, I promise. I swear."

"So long as we don't owe him," I said.

"I should've told you. We shouldn't have secrets. I'm sorry."

He returned to hanging pictures. I watched him put up the skyline, then I went home. The rain outside was beginning to pick up.

TWENTY

NIGHT THOUGHTS

At ten that night, as I tried to sleep, a stray sensation hit me. I felt my hands push down on a chest, applying pressure. And then they simply sank in, all the way up to the elbows. My hands moved through viscera, warm and wet and vital. A feeling of panic forced me from my bed.

Sonia still slept. I'd woken from my not-quite-dream to her soft snores and thankfully hadn't disturbed her as I'd left the bedroom. We hadn't spoken much since she told me about her promotion. I tried to think of the last time we'd made love.

If I was to confide in someone, by rights it should be her. I held back. *Confide what?* I might've asked, if pressed. I was making do. Hadn't I tracked down Jaycen Waid—by myself, the way I had time and again?

Of course I was shaken, off my game these days. I'd witnessed horror. Processing that took time.

Terry Rhodes wanted answers, but let him find his own. It wasn't my fight.

In the morning I met Jaycen Waid out front of the office. The last remnant of the storm was a pulsing rain that beat against the pavement. Jaycen ran to the door with his jacket worked up over his head. I escorted him up in the elevator.

"Good to see you fully clothed," I said.

We used Jeff's office. I had the cheque ready, but I told Jaycen there were a few outstanding questions, some blanks in his history I needed to fill in. He was happy to oblige.

Following the grow op fiasco, Jaycen had been at a loss. He'd spent months researching crop yields, hydroponics, soil pH. Without the capital to start again, he was forced to rethink his life's direction. He spoke of his time playing video games and occupying Jenna's pull-out couch as a holy endeavour, a cleansing period necessary to discover his purpose.

"No offense," Jaycen said, "but I'm not 'sposed to be a guy working in an office forty hours a week. That's not me, man."

"You're built for something better," I said.

"We all are." Jaycen looked earnestly at me, as if I knew that as well as he did. "I'm not saying I'm too good for work, just that I've done that already. I've seen where that goes."

"And where does it go?"

He didn't answer. I made a few notes and asked him what happened with his warehouse job.

"Bullshit happened. My supervisor Paul was a good dude. But the owner, Len, promised a bunch of stuff and screwed me over. So I walked."

"Maybe he thought you hadn't earned it," I said.

"But I did earn it."

"Maybe not in his eyes."

"Here's the thing," Jaycen said. "Can I smoke?"

"In the office, absolutely not."

"Okay. Well, this whole thing is built on earning it. Paying your dues."

He spread his arms out, taking in all of modern society.

"You put your time in, you climb the ladder. Work your way up. And it's all bullshit, dude. It's a fucking pyramid scheme."

Jaycen stood up and walked to the window, pointing out at something. Performing for me, and enjoying himself.

"See, people think it's about hard work and keeping out of trouble. But think about it. If you're a good worker, who's gonna promote you? They'll just say they will, in order to keep you working. It's all a con. You have to see through it."

"And then do what?" I asked.

"Then find a way in. See—sure I can't smoke?—it's like what my dad told me this one time. Risks only seem like risks to people who don't take them."

"Meaning a risk is safer than putting in the effort?"

"Maybe that seems fucked to you," Jaycen said.

"It seems a little fucked to me," I admitted.

"Sure, and no offense, but between you and me, who's delivering the money and who's getting it? See what I mean?"

He wasn't being rude or pulling rank. He was trying to open my eyes to a better way. I handed over his cheque.

"It's something to think about," I said. "Your aunt wants you to call her. It's not a condition of the money, but as a courtesy. Can I tell her you will?"

Jaycen held the cheque on his lap and stared down at it. In spite of his speech he looked surprised. "Aunt Martha, right? How is she?"

"Good. Spent her own money to hire me to find you."

He folded the cheque and slid it into his wallet. "It's weird. When you said 'aunt,' I thought you meant someone on my dad's side I didn't know about. His family has money and I kind of always suspected something like this—I pictured his family remembering about me, helping me out. Stupid, right?"

Whether or not he deserved pity, I felt for him. I understood the need to fill the absence of parents with all sorts of fanciful thoughts. My parents had been young when they left, taken in by a guru who promised them enlightenment and mastery of the realms beyond. Their decisions had done as much harm to themselves as to me. Those had been tough truths to face. But I'd faced them, there being no other option.

"Trust me," I said. "Phone your aunt. You have someone who cares about you. That's about as miraculous as it gets."

He left, still a bit stunned his good fortune had come from the less privileged side. Jaycen Waid, who'd figured out the machinery of the world, arriving at the right answer despite all the wrong operations.

I wondered what exactly the lesson was, and whether Jaycen would learn it. A car, an education, a better set-up to grow dope. He'd have his chance. That was more than a lot of people got.

Best to him. I had other things to worry about.

TWENTY-ONE
A SLIGHT BETRAYAL

Roy Long did in fact own both office buildings, along with another in Strathcona and two in the suburbs. He was partners in a chain of produce marts, held an interest in a carpet wholesaler on Terminal Avenue and sponsored two art galleries in Gastown. He paid taxes, supported left-leaning politicians, and was every bit the community pillar Jeff made him out to be.

His latest and most high-profile project was the Waterfront Casino in False Creek, built next door to the stadium. News articles hinted that some of the money that flowed through the casino might have illegal origins. That was about as close as any public accusations came to connecting Roy Long with organized crime.

So why, then, did Terry Rhodes name Long as his rival? Why did Sonia's colleagues joke about the shooting's effect on Long's organization? Even Jeff had hinted that Long had another side to him, hidden from the respectable world.

The pictures of Long online showed a man of sixty, smiling behind gold-rimmed glasses. His thick black hair showed wisps of white along the part and was beginning to recede. The photos showed Long in cap and gown receiving an honorary doctorate, with a Tartan scarf around his neck for a Gung Haggis Fat Choy celebration, him with his wife and son. None of the pictures screamed "gangster." If they screamed anything at all it was "executive"—pensive, shy and affable.

I'd researched Long after Jaycen left, and again when I got home. Part of me felt guilty for delving further into the matter, after Jeff had come clean with me. Another, smaller, angrier part thought it served Jeff right for keeping his connection from me in the first place. Everyone I dealt with seemed to know Roy Long, at least by reputation. If the man had nothing to hide, there was no harm in verifying that. I told myself part of being a private investigator is having a porous and ambivalent relationship to concepts like privacy and trust in the first place.

Sonia came home after her second day in public relations looking, if not happier, less burdened. She kissed my cheek and hurried through her shower, then dressed in her lay-around-home clothes—pajama bottoms and a paint-stained halter. We ordered Thai food and ate on the couch, watching *Manhunter* for the thousandth time. As a couple we didn't have "our song." Instead we had films we could talk through, drink through or watch quietly while cuddling. *Mona Lisa, Zodiac, The Long Kiss Goodnight.* Things we could reach for that we'd both be in the mood for, always.

We waited until after the Brian Cox scenes to pause for refills. Cox was the best Hannibal by far, had the killer's gaze down pat. Normal at first, but lingering a little too long. Terry Rhodes had that same look.

Before we started the film again, Sonia said, "Have you ever heard of Sheryl Lynn Axton? Shelly Axton?"

I said I hadn't.

"I heard her name mentioned today, in connection with the shooting."

"Connected in what way?" I said.

"One of the perps, I think."

I put my bowl down on the coffee table. The woman in the jumpsuit and mask who'd carried the bag out of the building, who'd tapped the shoulder of the man with the shotgun. That was right before—

I blinked. Sonia had her hand on my shoulder.

"So you do know the name," she said.

"No. Just thinking of the—about what happened."

Her hand dropped and took up her plastic fork. Between mouthfuls of bean sprouts, she said, "They're holding off from announcing it, but it sounds like they have something connecting Axton to the shooting. Fingerprint or photo ID. From what I heard, Shelly Axton and her husband Percy are their first real lead."

"That's great," I said.

"They're both Americans." Sonia paused to see if I'd say anything, but I was busy chewing pad see ew. "If they cross the border under their own names, it's easy enough to track them. And it gives us a starting point with the others, if there were others." Again, a pause. "Do you not want to talk about it? I thought you'd be happy."

"Thrilled," I said.

"Sorry I brought it up."

We finished our meal and the movie. As Sonia brushed her teeth I slipped on my shoes, took my jacket from the hook on the door.

"Where are you going?" she said from the washroom doorway, alerted by the tinkle of keys.

"Forgot that Jeff asked me to check on one of the construction sites." I spoke quickly, already half out the door. "Supply theft thing. Be twenty minutes. Love you, see you soon."

In my Cadillac, I drove toward Cambie Street. I used the car's audio set-up to dial the police station and ask if Superintendent Borden was still in her office.

"She is," the voice said. "Working late. One moment and I'll transfer you."

I told the voice no need, I'd meet her there in person.

TWENTY-TWO
SCARS

Never enter a police station angry.

The drive helped to calm me, and I spent another minute in the car after parking, thinking about how to handle this. Straight-on but level-headed seemed the best approach.

When I entered the lobby I saw Sergeant Dudgeon, listening to the receptionist tell him something funny. His face held the premature grin of someone hoping to break off conversation once the punchline was delivered.

"…and you can imagine the look on Dale's face when he saw all our muddy gear, thrown across his brand new, however many thousand-dollar floor. Cindy and I just looked at him. I mean, what else could we do?"

"Hilarious," Dudgeon said, and turned to me.

"Is the superintendent around?" I asked him.

"Why don't we go see, uh?"

We rode the elevator up to the third floor. Dudgeon's expression remained neutral. Down the hall, into the same small interview room. He said Borden would be in when she could. Would I like something to drink while I waited? One Coke Zero, coming right up.

There were all sorts of advantages a cop could exploit to put a suspect on edge. A wobbly chair, for instance, creates discomfort, prevents the suspect from settling in. I tested my chair and found it pretty much level. Slightly lower, though, than the ones across from me.

When Dudgeon came back, I'd been in the room for twenty minutes. It felt like the temperature had crept up. The sergeant handed me my drink and sat down, opening his notebook in front of him.

"Ellen will be a bit longer," he said. "Meantime how about we go through the events once more. Warm you up a bit."

"I'm not here to go over this a million times," I said. "If it's something I'll have to repeat for Borden, I'd just as soon wait for her."

"Suit yourself."

Dudgeon read and jotted notes. I stared at the ceiling and tried to talk myself out of the growing sense that I'd made a mistake coming here, that I'd done exactly what they wanted.

Borden entered, no knock, a thick binder held in both hands. The Crown report for the robbery-homicide. She looked composed and good-humoured, but the flesh around her eyes was puffy and dark. I got the sense I was the last obstacle between her and a well-earned night's sleep.

"Terribly sorry for the wait," she said. "And how are you doing tonight, Dave?"

I told her I was just fine.

She sat down next to Dudgeon, across from me, and opened the binder.

"To reiterate," she said, "you've told us you saw nothing. Not the suspects or their vehicle."

"I didn't," I said.

"And as to what you heard: gunshots followed by a vehicle driving off."

"That's right."

"You didn't attempt to get a licence number?"

"From a car I didn't see?"

Borden put a picture in front of me, a black Aerostar, side windows tinted black. She asked if I'd seen it before.

It was the van from that morning, or at least the same make and vintage. The paint had the same matte black, touched-up look. The windows were darkened like the shooters' van.

"Is this what they were driving?" I asked.

"We think so." Borden put another photo, a profile shot, next to the van. "How about her?"

It was an arrest photo of a fortyish woman, a hard face framed by a wild buoyant mane of black hair. Pale eyes and a slightly odd angle to the right cheek.

I thought of the black-haired woman who'd eluded me in the bookstore. I'd only seen her briefly, beneath shades and distracting make-up, and I'd assumed she was Asian. The woman in the photo was white and looked much older. Was it possible they were the same person?

"Who is she?" I asked.

Instead of replying, Borden slid the photo to the side and added another mug shot. This one showed a sandy-haired man, stocky and slump-shouldered, with the same hard scowl as the woman.

"Nothing on him either?"

"Never seen either of them," I said.

"Is it true you were visited by Terry Rhodes?"

"I visited him."

"Of your own volition?"

I tried some of my lukewarm cola. "He says it wasn't his guys, for what that's worth."

"And you believe him."

"Nice thing about not being involved," I said. "I don't have to make those calls."

"You don't strike me as someone who's content to watch people die from the sidelines," Borden said.

"You think I've got elaborate theories charted on the wall of my garage?"

"Do you?"

"Don't have a garage."

Borden showed me her palms. "My mistake, then. You are uninvolved and uncurious."

I studied the faces. They could've been terrorists or college professors—community college, maybe. The woman's right cheek looked as if she'd puffed it out with her tongue. Yet her mouth was partway open, and it seemed to be the natural shape of her face. Reconstruction, maybe.

"Scar tissue?" I asked. "She have a military record?"

"She does," Borden said. "Sheryl Lynn Axton." She tapped the other photo. "Her husband, Percy Axton. From Oklahoma and Michigan, respectively."

"They've done this sort of thing before?"

"Something similar," Borden said. "The Axtons are methodical and proficient with firearms."

"Do you have them in custody?"

"You and I wish," Borden said.

Dudgeon excused himself from the room. Borden looked at me for a while, a tired version of her sarcastic smile returning briefly to her face.

"How is Sonia Drego?" she said.

"She passed along what you wanted her to."

"I don't understand."

"Right," I said, tapping the photos. "Her overhearing something about these two, telling me so I'd come here. None of that was your doing."

"Constable Drego is a fellow officer," Borden said. "I'd never ask her to do something she wasn't entirely comfortable with."

"Meaning what, exactly?"

Borden didn't answer. I ran through the possibilities, none of which I liked.

"If these are the people you saw," Borden said, indicating the photos. She held up her hand to stop my objection. "I'm only saying 'if.' You should know that the Axtons are very dangerous people, that they're likely to be dangerous until they're in custody. Anyone asking you to leave this to us is probably thinking of your safety."

We left the interview room. Borden escorted me out the side entrance, to the alley. Dudgeon caught up to us as Borden was about to open the door.

They talked, Borden's arm blocking the exit. I wondered if this was a performance they'd worked out.

Borden sighed and said, "It'll wait, then, till Monday." She turned to me. "Monday morning works for you?"

"I'm done talking to you," I said.

"That's all right. This is a request from Deputy Chief Constable Mac-Leish. Monday morning, his office. I'll tell him you'll be there for nine—he appreciates punctuality."

TWENTY-THREE

GRAVEYARD WATCH

Driving:

Cambie. Kingsway. Grandview. Anywhere but here.

It wasn't that Sonia had lied to me. It wasn't even that she'd chosen sides, agreed to be part of Borden's manipulations. I knew what her career meant to her, and I could imagine the conversation she'd have with herself. *In his own interest. Best for everyone. Think of the victims, of the dangerous people still out there. He'll come around eventually. If he knows something, we need to know too.*

What I couldn't get past was the paranoid thought that it had always been like this. That trusting her, anyone, was inherently foolish. That I'd brought this on myself by letting her in.

First Jeff and now Sonia, and maybe it was in my head, but I felt that in the moment when I'd needed unquestioning support, I'd reached for them and found nothing.

The last thing I wanted was a neighbour-rousing shouting match with the woman I loved. I drove till I could think calmly, could see my hurt as one part of some larger, slightly damaged mechanism that still functioned and was worth the maintenance.

To be fair/to be honest/to put my feelings aside: I *had* lied to them. As much as anything else, it was the strain of keeping up that fiction that had created this sense of betrayal. I was justified, sure, in saying I wanted no part in the investigation. Sonia hadn't been there. To her the shooting was abstract. To me it was still unfolding, every time I closed my eyes.

I drove home, parked, unlocked the door. Sonia was gone. Her gear bag and toiletries and a few of her clothes had left with her. Back to her place, most likely. I reminded myself she was about as good at confrontation as I was.

I flipped through my records and put on *Wilderness Heart* by Black Mountain. I filled the kettle and set it on the stove as the drums kicked in on the first track.

You thought you were alone before.

The masked woman I'd seen the morning of the shooting lined up well enough with Sheryl Lynn Axton. Neither the dark-skinned man with the shotgun or the pale blond shooter could be mistaken for her husband Percy. The other man, who'd limped out of the building, holding his arm? I hadn't gotten a good look at him. The van had been idling, and judging from the speed at which they took off after the shooting, there'd been a driver waiting for them. Five of them overall.

But that wasn't my concern. I didn't care. I repeated that mantra as I drove into Shaughnessy. *I don't care I don't care I don't care—*

The city's wealthiest neighbourhood was asleep this time of night, the Victorian street lamps casting haloes across the winding lanes. Motion-sensored porch lights blinked on as I drove past. I parked on West Forty-ninth, and walked among the dark and silent estates until I reached the high brick fence that surrounded the Bostick home.

With its spot-lit parapets, gabled roof and turrets, the manor house looked like the chalet of an ss high command. I half-expected to see Lee Marvin and John Cassavetes sneaking across the lawn. In the driveway I saw a Wakeland & Chen security van, cleverly disguised as Big Nate's Fireplace and Chimney Repair. I let myself through the gate and knocked lightly on the passenger door.

Tim Blatchford jolted awake. Of course he'd fallen asleep. As he squinted and realized who it was, he turned the map light off, then back on. I saw him try to hide whatever had been open on his lap. He shoved it down into the driver's door pocket.

"Busy night?" I'd brought a Thermos with me. I refilled his takeout cup, verifying first that it was empty, and still used for coffee.

"Yeah. Sorry, fell asleep."

"Let's see what you're reading."

When he didn't relinquish it, I reached past him and grabbed the booklet. He caught my hand with the outside edge of his knee, then relented.

The cover was familiar. *Advanced Techniques for the Contemporary Interviewer* by Jun Fei Jefferson Chen.

"Jesus," I said. "Haven't seen this in a while."

Jeff had written a book on interrogation, laying out "the Chen System" for inducing confessions, taking down descriptions from witnesses, establishing a rapport. The flow of text was interrupted with sidebars, or "Chen Tips." As a wedding present I'd taken it to a small publisher in North Van, who'd done a modest print run. The book had been my favourite running joke, to the point where Jeff refused to talk about it with me.

I flipped through. Chen Tip Number Seven: "Always, if possible, approach a subject from the left. Studies show people are more trusting of persons introduced from that side. Orientation is important. Use it to your advantage."

"It was on the shelf in the boardroom," Blatchford said. In the low light I couldn't tell if he was blushing, but he wasn't making eye contact. "I was gonna read it to take the piss, y'know? But some of the stuff in there is pretty smart."

"You're kidding." But flipping through I could see he'd underlined passages, drawn asterisks or question marks next to others.

That made it all the funnier. Maybe it was the lack of sleep.

"There's useful stuff in there," Blatchford said. "Why doesn't everyone at the office have to read it?"

"Have you ever seen Jeff interview someone?" I said. "He's great at pitching people and talking to clients. The second he has to lie, or deal with someone who does, he folds like origami."

"So where's *your* book, then?" Blatchford asked. Indignant, sticking up for his author.

We had our coffee. It was touching, in a way, his desire to improve, the grudging respect Jeff had earned from him. He'd probably never admit it to Jeff's face. Maybe the Chen System would help turn Tim Blatchford into an employee Jeff would want to keep around.

Which brought me to my purpose for being there.

I should have told Blatchford that Jeff wanted him to shape up. No, that was shifting the blame. He *needed* to shape up. Jeff spoke for the company, which meant he spoke for me.

But I didn't say anything. I was tired, and for all his faults, Blatchford at least could be trusted, if only to remain himself.

We watched the house until dawn.

TWENTY-FOUR
NO RETURN

It was a Sunday, and the office was empty save for the renovation crew. I kept to the front desk and out of their way. Inquiries needed to be made on outstanding missing persons cases. Paperwork needed to be checked. A day where nothing happened would be welcome.

Martha Youngash had left a message the day before. I called her back and told her I'd send the invoice Monday afternoon, and that there was no rush on payment. She said Jaycen had phoned her. They'd talked for almost an hour—well, Jaycen had talked. She still sounded exhausted from the conversation. But it was a start, she said. It was something.

Jeff usually dropped in Sundays around noon, if only to check that the renovators hadn't smashed anything essential. Today, though, he didn't show.

I kept busy into the afternoon. Behind everything was tomorrow's meeting with MacLeish. I tried to think of how he'd come at me, what he'd be prepared to do.

At one, I came back from lunch to find Sonia standing in the hall outside the office.

I let her inside and took her coat. As I did she leaned close to my collar and smelled me. "You're smoking again," she said.

"I figured you knew but wouldn't care, long as you didn't have to deal with it. Sorry."

"Well I do care," Sonia said. "But that's not even the point. You told me you'd stop. You promised."

"I'm sorry."

"Stop fucking apologizing. Tell me what's wrong."

I sat behind the reception desk and beckoned Sonia to a client's chair. I leaned back, crossed my arms.

"You took Borden's side," I said.

"You know that's not what this is about."

"It is to me."

"You're not dealing with what you saw."

"That your official diagnosis, Anna Freud?"

"I spoke to a counsellor," she said.

"About me. Without telling me."

"You're defensive, withdrawn. Smoking again. You barely look at me. I needed to talk to someone about this, so I asked Dr. Shibata to meet me for coffee."

"And what did she say?"

"That you're in pain, and don't feel you can trust me, for whatever reason. She said a lot of cops go through that after trauma. They shut down."

"PTSD," I said.

"If you can't admit to me you're not okay, Dave, if you don't trust me enough to see you when you're weak, then what am I to you?"

Sonia wiped below her eyes. I could hear something clatter from the boardroom, followed by a string of *shits* and *motherfuckers*.

"I'm supposed to be honest with you," I said, "even though you and Borden—I don't even know what deal you made with her."

"Just to tell her when you were willing to talk. That's all." She added, "She thinks you're afraid."

"For good goddamn reason."

"She's also worried you're trying to solve this on your own."

I uncrossed my arms and leaned forward, over the desk. Sonia reached for my hands. I placed them on hers, feeling the coolness of her palms.

"Between us," I said.

She nodded.

"I saw them. They came out of the building and shot at the crowd watching them from the bus stop. No hesitation, they just shot them and left. There was nothing I could do."

"Of course not," Sonia said.

"The way they moved, they knew what they were doing. They weren't panicked. It was almost like cover fire. And..."

I paused, unsure how to go on. In the other room the renovators were hammering the walls. Someone switched on a radio. Loverboy, "Working for the Weekend."

"And," I said, "I keep thinking of that time last year you took me to emergency. Remember?"

Jeff had been off for two weeks to take his family to visit Marie's parents. I was covering for him while working my own cases. A fresh lead had appeared in the Jasmine Ghosh disappearance. A couple in northern California were suspected of abducting teenagers, jailing them in their basement and assaulting them.

Three young women had been recovered from the couple, one matching Jasmine Ghosh's age and ethnicity. Mr. Ghosh and I had flown down to San Francisco. I'd comforted him during the whole trip, hoping it was true—what a fucking thought—because then there was an answer, then at least it was over.

The victim wasn't her. Both of us had been relieved. I kept Mr. Ghosh's spirits buoyed, telling him it wasn't our last chance, that Jasmine might still turn up.

I'd come back and spent a day in the office dealing with what I'd missed. And then, that night, I was unable to sleep, then unable to breathe.

Sonia had taken me to the hospital, where I stayed overnight hooked to a saline drip, telling anyone who'd listen I felt fine.

It was walking pneumonia. Common with people who work long hours and are used to charging through illness. I was back at work Friday like it didn't happen.

But since then something had changed. I hadn't realized it at the time.

I said, "If you hadn't've been there, I'd be dead. And seeing what these shooters are capable of, I decided it wasn't worth dying. Nothing is."

We stood and took hold of each other, kissed.

"Everyone I talk to thinks they know me," I said, still embracing her. "They think I'm secretly looking into this, pretending not to care. Truth is, Sonia, it's taking everything I have *not* to get involved. I'm fighting against myself, desperately, because I feel like if I can't..."

"What?"

I held her even tighter, kissed her shoulder and her neck. The end of the sentence was painful to think, let alone say. But it forced itself out, the second we broke our embrace.

"Because if I can't, I don't think I'm coming back from this."

PART TWO:
ALL THE BLACK

TWENTY-FIVE
THE BLUE WALL

Deputy Chief Constable Ferguson MacLeish had been a patrol officer around the same time as my adopted father. Their careers hadn't intersected much that I could tell. My father had been a proud beat cop for life, working the rowdy East Van neighbourhoods of District Two. That might be one way MacLeish would come at me. I knew your old man. He and I were buddies. That makes us buddies too, doesn't it?

MacLeish had done his patrol stint in District Four, assigned to the more respectable areas of Point Grey and Marpole. He'd transferred to Missing Persons around the time that the disappearances of who-knows-how-many low-income women were being routinely written off, before it became a national concern. His career had survived the inquiry. That told me he knew how to negotiate choppy political waters, accept a portion of blame in a had-I-only-known manner, while deftly maneuvering others into the line of fire.

After six years overseeing Support Services, MacLeish had taken command of Investigations. I watched a PR video of the announcement. He had a warm, genteel, avuncular demeanor, coming across like a revered baseball coach being handed his new team's jersey. But he wasn't as camera-ready as he thought, and he stuttered and mumbled at times.

When asked his thoughts on taking his new position:

"Oh, it's a big honour, real big, definitely. Mike's a good guy, fine officer, sorry to see him go. A lot, lot, to live up to, that's for sure."

What kind of changes could we expect?

"I feel like one thing I bring is communication. Y'know, Support Services is all about connecting people, making sure various departments get what they need to do the best job they can. That's what I'd like to do here, increase intra-department, sorry, *inter*-department communications. Streamline."

He'd been in the position seven months. Not much streamlining had occurred. No new initiatives or major reforms. He oversaw Missing Persons, Major Crimes, the Gang Crime Unit and various special programs. He preached stronger community ties, officer safety and communications, always communications. Mostly he was business as usual.

I phoned Natalie Holinshed at the *Sun* and asked for her take. She told me MacLeish was more than his interviews let on.

"He plays the old school beat cop really well," Holinshed said. "He's got the Scots-Irish thing going for him, the white hair and kindly old-man smile. Guy's a shark, though. Lot of people are afraid of him."

"I've noticed that," I said.

"And for good reason—if I was a betting woman, I'd say that's our next chief. The last one used to joke about catching MacLeish in his office, measuring the curtains."

"So with the shooting," I said, "he's sees this as a career case?"

"Wouldn't you? I've heard he's working poor Ellen Borden to death."

"Are they close?"

"Publicly, sure," Holinshed said. "Privately, well, when they do start looking for the next chief, Ellen's name will be in the conversation. So if the count room slaying doesn't solve, she's likely to eat the blame. If it does, they'll fight over who gets credit."

All my research led me to no useful conclusions about MacLeish. Behind the professional veil he could be anyone, have any agenda. I arrived at the station at 8:40 a.m., waited in the lobby to be summoned.

On the walls around the elevators were photos of officers who'd died during active duty. My father's was there. No biological resemblance, though we shared the same pissed-off scowl at having our picture taken. I wondered what he'd think of the meeting I was about to enter.

The newest addition to the photo wall was Chris Chambers. Sonia had partnered with him for a time. His handsome face smiled winningly down on me. I turned my back to the wall and studied the trophies in the display case instead.

Nine o'clock came. I readied myself to be yelled at, sweet-talked, implored, cajoled, lied to, given looks of disbelief and disappointment and fatherly consternation. I was ready to be kept waiting.

The elevator chimed and my plans went to hell. MacLeish himself walked out, alone. A wiry man of sixty dressed in jeans and a polar fleece, his white hair combed straight back. He nodded to me and shook my hand.

"Beautiful day out there," MacLeish said, opening an umbrella. "How about let's take a walk."

TWENTY-SIX
CAPTIVE KILLERS

The Cambie Street Bridge leads into the downtown core, fording False Creek. As we crossed the bridge we saw sailboats pass beneath us, and the small rainbow-canopied ferries making their circuit to Granville Island.

Rain speckled the concrete and beaded the underside of the guard-rail. MacLeish didn't offer to share his umbrella.

"I know you Vancouver boys like the rain," was his opening comment.

"Not you?" I asked. All the research I'd done and I hadn't thought to delve into his origins.

"I'm a Prairie lad at heart," MacLeish said. "Brandon, Manitoba by way of Saskatoon. Ever been to the Prairies? Amazes me how many of you on the coast haven't. Even Alberta's another world."

"I was in Winnipeg once," I said.

"And how did you find it?"

"It's Winnipeg. Other circumstances it would've been fine."

MacLeish cut a quick pace, shouldering past cyclists and couples on the bridge's narrow walkway. We moved single file for most of our trip. Then at the apex of the bridge he paused and put his hand on the rail.

Below us a pair of sailboats came abreast of each other. People on the decks waved. Music reached us, a treble-heavy new-country whine.

"I've heard orcas can come all the way up here," MacLeish said. "Never seen one, except at the Aquarium. Used to love taking my kids. Shame they don't still keep them."

"They don't do well in captivity," I said.

"I'm aware. It's cruel to them, I know. And yet think how many animal rights activists got their start as wide-eyed kids, pressing their hands to the glass to watch the killer whales."

MacLeish leaned on the guardrail and stared down at the water. He reminded me of a dictator, addressing the masses from a balcony.

"It's discomfiting to have to calculate pain or sacrifice, things of that nature. Unfortunately that's sometimes our job. It's an awesome responsibility, in the true meaning of the word. And awful, in all its meanings."

I wasn't sure what this was a preamble to. I looked out at the condominiums, at the bright white towers of Yaletown.

"There's a story about Robert McNamara. You know who that is?" Without waiting for an answer MacLeish said, "Secretary of State under Kennedy and Johnson."

"So?"

"During World War II McNamara worked for the oss, strategic planning. His job was to calculate what altitude bomber pilots should fly at. The lower they flew, the more precise their runs would be."

"And the more casualties," I said.

"How many more can you kill, weighed against how many more can you lose. He's a misunderstood man, McNamara. His reputation's suffered on account of Vietnam. But I think he's heroic, in a sense, making those decisions. Committing to that, whether or not the war itself was the right course."

"Wasn't he also a weirdo who had his middle name classified?" I asked.

MacLeish smiled. "Strange. That was his middle name. Robert Strange."

"Step up from 'Danger,' I guess."

He didn't acknowledge the joke. I waited for him to continue. MacLeish wouldn't be rushed to his point. As still-seeming yet propulsive as the current below us.

"So this shooting," he said at last. "Let's start with congratulations. You helped save that Cui woman's life." Pronouncing it "Kwee."

"I know a little first aid," I said.

"Everyone should. You did right, Mr. Wakeland. Now we need the shooters caught. I hear from Ellen Borden you're not being too cooperative."

"I thought I was," I said. "This is about the fifth meeting I've had."

MacLeish raised himself onto his toes in order to stare straight down. He wasn't a tall man. His gaze was contemplative, peaceful. He'd probably never looked down at water from a bridge and wondered about the plunge.

"What you're telling me," he said without looking up, "is in all those meetings, nothing has enticed you to speak up. Is it a stipend you're looking for?"

"I'm not holding out on you for money."

"Then what will it take?"

I'd thought about it. If there was a time to bargain, here it was.

"It has to be on my terms," I said. "An official consultancy, either to you or the Crown Prosecutor's office. Assigned on paper to another case, something innocuous. Billable and taxable, at your top consultancy rate."

"So money is a factor," MacLeish said.

"No, that's not extortion, it's just what I'm worth."

"What else?"

"Full access to files on Terry Rhodes and the Exiles, on Roy Long and his organization. Everything on the suspects. Trust works two ways or it doesn't work."

He'd been nodding throughout my demands, small dips of the head that meant comprehension rather than acquiescence. He looked over at Coopers' Park, green against the grey of the water, sky and buildings.

"And here I was hoping we could accommodate each other," he said.

Turning and stepping toward me, pressing his finger to my chest.

"For a kid who seems to have a good head on his shoulders, you have massively overplayed your hand. Why would you think this is at all negotiable? Why would you think you have a choice, other than to save yourself some grief?"

"I'm used to having old people yell at me."

He shook his umbrella, pelting me with rain. Close, I could smell coffee on his breath. His look held that cold kind of anger that lives to dream up surprise revenges. The look said we were far from finished.

"There are things going on with this case you can't possibly understand," MacLeish said.

As he began to walk back, I lit a cigarette and thought, *no shit*. I wondered what he was hiding.

TWENTY-SEVEN
A DEATH IN STRATHCONA

Sometimes the world seems hell-bent on verifying your deepest terrors. Months ago I'd signed up for a neighbourhood watch service, which monitored police bands for East Van. I'd been meaning to unsubscribe. Either the messages came too often, in flurries of petty thefts and drug use, or weeks went by without hearing anything. Monitoring police bands was probably a hobby for the service provider, one they felt comfortable ignoring when not in the mood.

That morning I woke up to find a text alert on my phone. The remains of an unidentified man had been found in Strathcona Park. Homicide was a possibility.

I read the alert and thought selfishly, solipsistically, *Rhodes*. His way of saying to me, if you don't deal with this, I will.

If I walked down Commercial Drive and along Venables, I would pass the park on my way to the office. As I dressed, that seemed important. I wasn't going out of my way. Just passing by, and thought I'd take a look.

Not that I expected to see much. By now the scene would be cordoned off, any witnesses separated and hauled to the station. Like I had been, days ago. I'd pick up gossip, if I was lucky, and if I caught sight of Borden, I'd know the death was connected.

It wasn't six yet, but the sky was already a luminous grey. The shop windows along the Drive were still dark, except for the Italian bakery. The smell of bread warmed my mood, distracting me from my purpose.

Strathcona was full of older houses that had once belonged to dockworkers and immigrant families, and now sold for multiple millions. The park was a hangout for all sorts of folks, depending on time of day.

For a while it had been the site of a homeless encampment, a tent city. Gone now.

The northwest corner of the park showed activity as I approached from the east. I crossed the grass, as if out for a walk and attracted by the crowd and the silent flashing lights.

A low chain-link fence enclosed a baseball diamond. It would have provided a natural cordon, except that the police activity was focused on the home team dugout rather than the field. A patrol officer kept the half-dozen onlookers pushed to the sidewalk.

I skirted the field and came up behind the gathering. Pressing close I looked for a body, couldn't see one and felt relief. A bleary-eyed resident with a plastic coffee mug said, "Crazy way to start the morning, huh?"

"Sounds like," I said. "Overdose, you think?"

"Not with the guy's hands all messed up like that. My upstairs neighbour's the one who phoned it in—I mean he was asked to phone by the guy who found it. My neighbour said the dead guy's hands were all chopped up and bloody. You can still kinda see."

He pointed at the gravel inside the dugout. It was stained dark grey from the morning rain, but there were black patches, glimpses of red.

"Anybody know who it was?" I asked.

"Nah. Cops don't think he was local."

"Why's that?"

The resident shrugged and took a long slurp of coffee. "Just what I heard."

The police attending didn't include Borden or Dudgeon, though maybe they'd already left. A pair of techs collected gravel and documented the scuffs in the turf behind the dugout. I continued my walk to the office.

There was no reason to assume the corpse was connected to the shooting. It could be a rage murder. It could be drug-related. The suspect could already be cooling in a pre-trial cell.

But say it was connected, for the sake of argument.

Maybe I was right to think of Terry Rhodes. He favoured dogs, and the mutilated hands could be a sign of that. But Rhodes was known to disappear bodies, or use them to send a message. If this was meant as a show of force or retaliation, his work would be more thorough, and probably more creative.

That didn't mean I ruled him out. It could be Roy Long's people too. Or the shooters themselves. Without knowing who the victim was, how he fit, it was guesswork.

As I walked, I was struck by how easily I'd assumed my own involvement. In fact, I hadn't even questioned it. The alert had probably gone out to hundreds of people, but I'd interpreted it as a personal message, and put myself in the midst of things, as if it were only natural. Even if I was done pretending I didn't care, it felt uncomfortable to declare myself an active investigator. This was murder and I had no right to interfere.

But then I was involved, and not by choice. Borden and MacLeish and Rhodes and the others had put me in the centre of this. If I wanted out, this would have to be resolved. I had doubts about how the others would go about doing that—especially Rhodes.

I stopped at Matchstick on my way, sat and had a cup of tea and used the coffee shop's Wi-Fi to check for info on the body. "Unidentified Caucasian male, mid-twenties" was all the description I could find.

Ryan Martz wasn't in his office yet, and I didn't leave him a message. I thought of phoning Sonia but realized I didn't have her new work number. I texted her cell instead. We'd left things on a reasonably good note, though she'd spent the night at her False Creek apartment. She said it was only because her gear was there, and that was undoubtedly true. I tried not to dwell on what else it could mean.

I reached my office building at half past seven. The lobby was locked to the public till eight. A woman was waiting out front, peering through the glass door at the office listings on the far wall. Slim, tall and black-haired and wearing a formless green trench coat. I recognized her as the woman who'd followed me along Main Street, who'd run from me in the bookstore.

Her attention was still on the lobby. From across the street, I continued past her, taking the next three crosswalks in order to keep out of her sightline. Car traffic was steady but few pedestrians were out, most heading toward Waterfront Station.

If she'd been older, larger or male, I might have avoided confrontation. She didn't look furtive or hostile. She was too young to be Shelly Axton—the wrong ethnicity, no facial scars. She didn't seem violent.

I got closer to her, within tackling distance. I could have pinioned her arms and put her on the ground before she knew I was there. Instead I asked her, with my hands out and ready, "Are you looking for me?"

She turned. Her sunglasses slipped down and I saw red-rimmed eyes, noticed a wet spot on her upper lip below her nose. The same bright purple slash of lipstick. Her expression showed shock and desperation, and once she recognized me, anger. She lunged past me.

I had a hand up and was beginning to say how we could talk things through in my office, if she wanted. Her hand shot out on a rising diagonal, fingers jabbing into my left eye.

I turned away, shielding my face. The woman darted past me. By the time I could see, she'd turned the corner and disappeared.

Once the shock faded, the eye felt more irritated than damaged. I wiped away tears, then made my way into the building. There'd be footage of my assailant on the security cameras.

I wondered if her visit had something to do with the corpse in Strathcona. She probably didn't subscribe to the same neighbourhood alerts, which meant either this was a coincidence or she'd known about the body some other way. That opened all sorts of ugly possibilities.

With my good eye, I looked at myself in the reflection off the elevator brass. The left half of my face was scrunched up like an exaggerated wink. I got this covered. Sure.

TWENTY-EIGHT
A PART OF THINGS

Jeff ran the security video back, his lips pressed tightly together to suppress a smirk. For the third time we watched the woman turn from the doorway and strike me. As the video-Wakeland staggered back, Jeff snorted and rewound it again. By the fourth time through he was openly laughing.

"You're lucky she took pity on you, didn't finish you off. Teenage girls these days."

Instead of responding to the bait, I adjusted the ice pack so it rested flush against my cheek. Jeff printed a screenshot of the woman's face, indistinct behind the sunglasses.

"No idea who she could be?" he said.

"Thought you might know."

"Because all Asians know each other, right?"

"Since Roy Long is involved," I said, "and you two are so close."

Jeff's smile faded. "I explained already."

"And there's nothing you want to add to that?"

He shook his head.

I leaned back in the office chair. I could see out of the eye all right, but it felt good to keep it closed and the ice pack on top. One of her fingers had struck my cheekbone, to the left of the socket, leaving a dark brown crescent-shaped mark.

The woman could be connected to the shooters, or one of the dead. Or the police, for that matter. I couldn't guess what she wanted from me. She hadn't attacked. Hadn't even followed me, really—she'd been waiting outside the building. It was even possible she didn't know what she wanted from me. Blood, answers, an apology.

"You gonna tell Superintendent Borden?" Jeff said. "You should. She ought to know someone's after you."

"So she can offer her congratulations?"

But he had a point.

Jeff left to take Marie to lunch. Before I closed his laptop, I checked the news feeds to see if there was any new information about the body in Strathcona Park. Nothing I didn't know. A short video clip showed the bagged remains being carried out, cordon tape being strung around the baseball diamond, somber cops standing watch in rain gear.

The police receptionist told me the superintendent would get back to me at her convenience. I put the ice pack in the office fridge and texted Sonia, who still hadn't responded to me. *Love you*, I texted, *hope everything's okay*.

The face of Jingjing Cui flashed to mind. I remembered telling her mother something similar. *Everything's going to be okay.* At the time lying had seemed a necessary kindness. Now it felt like the beginning of a long period of denial. I hoped I was moving past that.

Borden phoned me back on my cell during her lunch break. I moved into Jeff's office and closed the door. As we talked, I heard Borden chewing, heard her fork stab lettuce. I imagined she'd gloat, but her tone was uninflected, businesslike.

She listened as I explained how the woman had been waiting for me, had struck me when I got close and how days before I'd seen her following me. As I finished, I heard her swallow and clear her throat.

"It's an interesting story," Borden said. "I'm not sure why you'd share it with me."

"It's possible she's somehow connected to the shooting, isn't it?"

"You'd know that better than I."

"I'm not asking you to care about my safety," I said. "But if she's involved somehow, don't you want to know?"

Eating sounds. A napkin being scraped across a mouth. A sigh.

"I'll send someone to pick up the footage," she finally said.

"That's some swell police work," I said. "Amazing you haven't caught the shooters, that kind of dedication."

"High fucking praise coming from you," Borden said. "You realize I have a family that's barely seen me the last week? That this is the first meal I've had sitting down since Sunday. You lie to me, waste my time, then all of a sudden when you're threatened, I should drop everything."

"This woman might be a part of things."

"*Everything's* a part of things," Borden said.

She hadn't meant it philosophically. It was hyperbole, a way to express how hopelessly all-consuming the shooting had become. I sympathized.

"The body in Strathcona Park," I said. "Can you at least tell me if it's connected to the shooting?"

"Not even if I wanted to," Borden said.

"Do you think your boss is hiding something?"

"My boss."

"MacLeish," I said. "I get the sense there's something more to his involvement. And if I get that sense from meeting him once, I bet you have it too."

Borden didn't answer immediately. Through the window of Jeff's office, I saw a small Iceland-shaped patch of blue sky stretch and expand as smoke-grey clouds travelled around it.

"Goodbye, Mr. Wakeland," Borden said. She hung up.

I'd missed a call from Sonia, but when I phoned back there was no answer. I thought about what else I could say to her, what deeper sentiment could be squeezed into text form. After a moment of indecision, I scrolled to my previous text and hit resend. *Love you, hope everything's okay* seemed to say it all.

TWENTY-NINE
THE MAN IN THE PARK

Ryan Martz preferred to drink alone, away from other cops. He favoured the kind of low-rent bars you'd find with hostels or backpacker's lodges above them. The Cambie was one such place.

Ryan was already inside, at a table against the wall. Three-quarters of a glass of beer sat in front of him. Normally after shift's end he'd be piss drunk, grousing about the addicts he dealt with, the pushy families who wanted their babies found right away, the bleeding hearts who'd hold · him accountable for every missing person everywhere.

But then he wasn't that person anymore. His engagement to Nikki Frazer had calmed him. He'd learned how to separate criticism of the system from criticism of himself. It was a profound change that had come incrementally, until it became clear that the new and improved Ryan Martz was more likely to nurse a beer and call it an early night.

A waitress swept steins off a nearby table. Ryan's eyes roved over her ass. He grinned at me. "Day you stop looking is the day you die."

"And I was just thinking how much you've changed."

"Not that much," he said. "Or I wouldn't be here with you. You're a bad influence, Wakeland."

"That's probably true."

I ordered a pitcher of whatever rusty draft beer they had on special.

"Czechowski," Ryan said without prompt, once the waitress had left. "Rudolf Petr. Spelled just like it sounds."

"The man in the park," I said.

"He wasn't in the park for long. They're thinking it's a dump job."

"Is he connected to the shooting?"

"Looks that way," Ryan said. "He's an ex-infantryman. Twenty-seven years old, five years since his discharge. Since then he's worked a couple security gigs and been a supermarket assistant manager. They found his CV online."

"But no criminal record," I said. "Was Czechowski blond?"

"Brown hair. Why?"

"Heard a rumour one of the shooters was blond," I said. "How does Czechowski fit with Shelly and Percy Axton?"

"No clue, other than they're all from back east, and from the States. Weird they'd come here. Has to be a count room to rip off back home, right?"

"Maybe that's the point," I said.

"They're imports? For who?"

"Terry Rhodes, maybe."

After ordering another beer, I asked him about Czechowski's hands.

"Crushed," Ryan said. "'Pulped' is how one tech described them. Odd body part to torture. Lopping hands off, I get, makes identification harder. Breaking an arm for intimidation, sure. But why just the hands?"

"Maybe he fought back."

"Not defensive wounds—'pulped,' remember."

Ryan put his glass down and focused on his own hands, threaded around his beer. He unclasped the gold band of his watch, and placed his fingers over the narrow, scarred armrests of his chair.

"Say you got me tied up," he said.

"And I want you to talk? You're asking which body part I start with?"

I pictured myself standing over him, tapping my palm with some sort of unpleasant tool. Hammer, maybe, or saw.

"The hands aren't a bad place to start," I said.

"I'd go with the eye," Ryan said. "'Specially if I was in a hurry."

I realized his long, hard look was him picturing that happening to me. My taste for beer waned. I held the glass to the bruised socket.

"You could also go kneecaps," Ryan said.

"Unless he had to walk somewhere."

"Stroll through the park?"

"Or pick up something—the money, maybe. You get an amount yet, what was taken?"

"Two to three hundred grand is what I heard."

"Focusing on hands isn't specific to bikers or triads," I said.

"Which is maybe the point," Ryan said. "Makes it hard to figure who's doing it."

By eleven we were finishing up, talking about his upcoming wedding, about Nikki and Sonia, about how ten years ago he'd never have expected to be here.

"I don't know what I expected," Ryan said. "Video games, football parties and shit. This is way more serious, y'know? But I guess that's good. This is the time of your life to get serious."

"Is it?" I asked. "Who says?"

"You and Sonia don't plan on getting married? Just gonna drift through your thirties, living in that first-floor dump?"

"What's wrong with that?"

"It's sad," Ryan said.

"To you. Sad to me is a mortgage in the suburbs you can't afford, an suv you don't need, a job you hate and kids you're not ready for."

"Nikki and I are ready," Ryan said.

"Then good on you."

"Maybe it's for the best," he said. "Bunch of little Wakelands running around, terrorizing everybody. That's a nightmare scenario."

His eyes fixed on whomever had come through the door. He tensed.

I turned. Sergeants Dudgeon and Frank Keogh were pushing past the tables toward us.

THIRTY
WILDERNESS

"Nothing like an afterwork nightcap," Keogh said. "Take the edge off. 'Cept you don't want to take too much of that edge off, right?"

"Stay hungry," Dudgeon said.

"Keep your wits about you."

"Maintain a professional what-you-call-it. Demeanor."

There were empty seats and tables around us. Dudgeon and Keogh waited for a formal invitation from the waitress before sliding a table over, pinning Ryan and me close to the wall.

"Too bad Sonia's not here," Keogh said. "It sucks she won't be working with me. I like her."

"She likes you," I said.

"I prob'ly bored the pants off her, all that Civil War talk."

She'd mentioned it to me, Frank Keogh's obsession with Pickett's Charge and Wilderness and Shiloh. Sonia had conceded to watch the Ken Burns documentary. Doris Kearns Goodwin's bio of Lincoln had adorned her nightstand for the past month, becoming as much a fixture of my nighttime periphery as the vintage auto calendar where she charted out her shifts.

"It's a way of staying sane," Keogh explained. "Though opinion's divided on how successful it's been. We all have our ways to unwind."

"Which brings us all here," Dudgeon said.

Their drinks arrived, bourbon and cola and a Bud Light. They leaned back in their seats and insisted on clinking glasses and a here's-to-us toast. The vibe they created was more than just affable menace. They genuinely liked us, I thought. And genuinely had a problem. With me, at least.

Dudgeon said, "You guys must'a heard about the dead man. What's his name again?"

Neither Ryan or I said anything.

"Not important, I guess. Somebody really want him to get the message—some kind of message, any case."

"Someone smashed my hands," Keogh said, "might make me think about certain choices I made. What about you fellas?"

"What about us?" Ryan asked.

"Someone did that to your hands, mushed them to pulp, would it make you wonder what you did to end up there."

"Guess that'd depend," Ryan said. "Maybe I deserved it."

"Fair point." Dudgeon said to me: "You gonna solve this for us, Dave?"

"We can surely use the help," Keogh said.

"Nothing we appreciate more, really, a private eye doing our work for us."

"Just don't make us look too bad," Keogh said.

Ryan's face was set in a scowl. He was nearing his volatile phase, where even innocuous statements would be taken by him as invitations to a fight.

I said, "Nobody appreciates the job you do more than me. If I'm looking for information it's only to make sure I stay out of your way."

"Sensible," Dudgeon said.

"I've always said Dave's sensible. Mr. Sensible is what Sonia calls him."

"I try," I said.

"Course, what would've been *really* sensible is you helping Ellen from the get-go, coming clean, not standing by to watch your woman get punished for you not speaking up."

"That would be way more sensible," Dudgeon concurred. "Maybe the most sensible."

"The sensiblest."

"But I guess you can't be sensible all the time."

"Lay off him." Ryan had the look of someone searching for an excuse to throw down.

"Martz." Keogh tut-tutted. "We're just talking."

"If a guy can't take a ribbing—"

"Fuck your ribs," Ryan said. "Fuck this passive-aggressive shit. Dave was attacked today."

"We heard." Dudgeon's face brightened. "Call come in, guy grabbing some girl, real aggressive. But I'm sure there's more to it. Right, Dave? You don't grope women, do you?"

"I grope for words with them," I said. "It's been fun, but time for us to go."

I hustled Ryan out onto Cambie Street, averting whatever violent response he was thinking of.

"You shouldn't have to do that," Ryan said. "Assholes."

We walked up to Hastings, the air noticeably chill. I made sure Ryan Martz got on a bus that would take him by the new condo in Burnaby he shared with Nikki. We didn't have more to say, other than goodbyes.

It was a sobering three-block walk to the office to retrieve my car. I thought how much had changed in twelve years. Ryan and I had bonded as recruits over a shared anger: Ryan toward his parents, me at a world that would take mine from me. We'd wanted the same things: action, pussy, power, responsibility. None of which we deserved or were ready for.

I'd found new ideals, learned that you weren't right just because you had the force to compel others to say you were. Ryan had been slow to follow. When he had, though, he'd done me one better. He'd found a way to function within the institution. Marriage loomed, kids soon to follow. Ryan was heading through the blindingly brilliant archway of full-fledged adulthood that seems a keyhole when you're a kid.

Goddamn if I didn't find myself looking up to Ryan Martz.

I phoned Sonia, wanting to hear her voice. After three rings it went to voicemail. I hung up and dialed again, mostly to hear her repeat her name on the rings.

"You're probably sleeping," I told the phone after a pause. "I'm walking to the office. No, I'm not drunk. What I am is hopelessly, tragically, lamentably—"

The phone chirped, out of time.

I took the elevator up to the office, thinking of other adverbs. *Forlornly. Disconsolately.*

Lights were on in Jeff's office. I called his name, thinking if it wasn't him it must be the renovators. The crew had left buckets and paint-speckled sheets strewn around the boardroom, furniture shifted into the hall. I maneuvered around it.

Jeff's desk lamp burned. I stepped into the room, making sure it was empty, and turned the light off. As I did, a view of the city seemed to rise out of the window, office towers lit with golden light, a golden reflection off the dark water of the inlet. My own image imposed over the view.

My reflection, and someone else behind me.

The silhouette moved away from the door. A thin-barrel target pistol in its hand. I recognized the face, and fought to hide that fact.

The shadow told me to turn around, slowly, and sit down.

THIRTY-ONE
A WAGER

My arms were pushed out from my torso as I was patted down. A one-handed frisk, shoulder to shoulder, waist, crotch, down each leg.

The voice, a weary-sounding baritone, told me to sit down.

The man stood to the side of the desk, just out of my reach. The pistol remained pointed at my chest. A broad-shouldered Black man of my height, hair buzzed in a military High and Tight, a week's stubble on his face. Before, I'd only seen the top of his face, above the dog-skeleton mask. I recognized him now as the man who'd held the shotgun.

His expression gave away nothing. I couldn't tell if he was making up his mind about me, or if he'd already decided.

Jeff's chair wobbled beneath me. The man's pistol arm extended slightly. I held my breath, held my palms up and planted my feet flat so the chair wouldn't shift.

I exhaled, slowly, slowly.

His foot gestured toward the bottom drawer of the desk. "Open it."

I did.

"Take out the computer."

I had to push the chair back slightly and angle my knees so I could extract the laptop and set it on the desk. He took me through booting it up, logging into the building's security system, calling up the cameras.

"Erase tonight," he told me.

The screen was tilted between us, so the man could see what I entered. I blanked the last twenty-four hours of recorded footage. The laptop made that crinkling-paper sound effect as I cleared the trash folder.

"Are the hallway cameras still on?"

"They all are," I said, "but not recording."

"That footage can be recovered, can't it?"

"Probably, yeah."

He nodded. His free hand folded the computer closed and set it on the desk's edge. He backed up to the wall and leaned against it, holding the gun lower, still trained on me.

"Why were you at the other office that morning?" he asked me.

"Writing a report."

"You were watching for us."

"No."

"But you saw us."

Admitting it would make me more of a threat. Lying would make me untrustworthy. I weighed up the options and their likelihood of survival, and decided it was better to go out with the truth.

"I saw," I said.

"Why were you there and not here?"

"Renovations. My partner rented the Keefer Street office so I'd have a quiet place to work."

"You're here now."

"The other office has a few bad memories now."

He nodded. "You don't usually work that early."

The realization that he knew my habits and had clocked my routines glaciated my blood. My jaw and throat seemed resistant to speaking, but I forced them into employment. "I wanted to be alone. I work better when others aren't around. Sometimes I need that."

"Did you tell the police what you saw?"

"No."

"Not even your girlfriend?"

Another shiver hit me. My legs trembled and I was thankful the chair was underneath me. I locked my knees and hunched forward, looked into the gun and tried to appear truthful.

"I told her I'd seen you. I didn't describe you."

"Why not?"

Often intuition takes you partway down the path, only to abscond. There's not just the terror of moving forward in faith, but the knowledge that every step so far has been a wager against unknown odds. I tried to shake the feeling that I was already dead, and that being honest with the man was only providing him with future targets. I felt begging would be useless, mercy unforthcoming.

"Because you're professionals," I said, "and either you'd disappear, or whoever you stole from would kill you."

He took that with a nod, go on.

"I've regretted getting involved since I went out that window."

For a moment we looked at each other, each waiting to see what he'd do. The man coughed. His breathing was slightly congested, air pulled in, let out in bursts. The gun rose up, its empty eye raised to my chest.

"What time is it?" he said. "Slowly."

I slid my phone from my pocket with two fingers. "Just after twelve."

"Unlock the phone permanently and give it to me."

I did, disabling the passcode feature. He tested to make sure the screen lit up on touch.

"It still hold a charge?"

"Well enough. It's last year's."

"You keep handcuffs here?"

"Zip ties and cuffs in the supply closet."

I walked there, the gun at my back. Unlocked the closet and took out two pairs of cuffs and a bundle of ties. The man herded me back to Jeff's office.

He told me to sit behind the desk. He zip-tied my arms around the chair's backrest. My feet were strapped together. I felt the cords cut into my ankles.

Once I was immobile, he took the phone and entered a number. He spoke into it, his telephone voice louder, more authoritative, a shock in the silence.

"It's Kent... Yes, dealing with him now... Don't know. I'll ask... About forty minutes... Black Cadillac sedan, ten years old at least. Understood."

He pocketed my phone, took my key ring and fanned it out on his palm. He pointed in turn at each key. I nodded to the one with the molded plastic grip.

"What stall?" he asked.

"Fourteen."

He swept up keys and wallet, put the laptop under his arm. "Any cash in the office?"

"About three hundred and change in the reception desk. Top drawer, box marked 'petty cash.' Key is on that ring."

"The cleaning staff arrives at seven, don't they?"

Opening the centre drawer of Jeff's desk, the man took a wad of tissues from a package. He put the gun on the desk while he inserted the tissues between my teeth. He had electrical tape with him and ran it around my head, making sure to leave my nostrils unobstructed.

At the door, when he looked back at me, I wondered if there was part of him still evaluating, *mightn't it be safer to shoot.*

But he left.

I watched the hall lights blink out in his wake.

The room was cold, drowned in shadow, like a burnt-out camp left by an invading army. I sat very still for a while, breathing through my nose, thinking thoughts of gratitude and revenge.

THIRTY-TWO
DECISIONS

One-thirty-three a.m., and I thought, *fuck. this.*

For over an hour I'd sat there in the dark, listening to the building's sighs and crepitations. Staring at the feeble orange line below the door, the residue from the lights above the elevator. I told myself Kay and Blatchford might be in early. If not, seven wasn't that far away.

A view would at least help pass the time. I'd turned the chair toward the window, nearly upsetting it and sending me to the floor.

What I saw in the window was the outline of someone restrained. Kleenex spilling from his mouth beneath the tape. The slumped, defeated pose of someone with their hands behind their back. Eyes carrying their share of fear, but also acceptance.

Keeping my head down had done nothing to improve my chances. It just meant waiting for something like this to happen again.

And so, *fuck that. Deal with Kent and Rhodes, Borden and MacLeish, Roy Long and the others in their time. But first things first. Let's see if you can escape on your own.*

You can cut zip ties, snap them, slip them or use a shim. Hard to do anything when you're tied to a chair. So step one, get rid of the chair.

It was sturdily built out of metal and leather, but I started the chair rocking on its castors. Picking up momentum, I hit the backrest against the edge of Jeff's table, then slammed it, and me, backward into the floor.

As I landed, I heard a snap. Testing the restraints, I felt no extra give. My shoulder hurt and I was no closer to being freed. *Smooth, Dave. Break a couple bones but don't injure your partner's stupid chair.*

On my side, I bent forward and back, and felt the metal support give.

When I wriggled, the backrest creaked and rattled. Screws and bolts held this ergonomic, mass-produced piece of shit together. No match for the wiles of one desperate East Van kid.

I swallowed some particles of tissue and gritted my teeth. Bent forward. Strained at the metal. The top half of the chair came with me.

The backrest slipped out from between my shoulder blades. There was now more play in my hand restraints, but I still couldn't slip them. I flexed, grunted, cursed Jeff for buying the metal-reinforced zip ties.

Okay, step one was a moderate success. Step two, find a shim.

I felt around for any bolts or small bits of chair on the ground, but nothing useful came to hand. It was hard to sit up with my feet still secured to the base of the chair. I got to my knees and crawled to the desk.

Rubbing the ties against the corner of the desktop didn't do much good. I was already imagining the bawling-out I'd get from Jeff later. I took that as a positive sign. Maybe I wouldn't live that long, but it was good to set goals.

Leaning against the desk, I pulled myself up onto its surface. I turned onto my side so my hands could work the top drawer open. Scissors? Exacto knife? Nope and nope. A flat metal something—not flat, tubular. I managed to palm it.

Turning it in my hand I thought I recognized the feel. An ornate gold fountain pen Jeff told me a client had left behind. I'd always suspected Jeff had actually bought it himself and been too embarrassed to admit the extravagance.

I uncapped the pen and used it to tap the plastic encircling my wrists, locating first the strand of excess tie, then the lock. A simple latch held the ties in place. I stabbed the pen into it. In and down. After a couple of tries I felt the latch release.

My wrists hurt but I could move them. I sat up on the desk and unwrapped my head, spat the tissue onto the floor. Untied my feet, then tossed the chair base aside. I stretched gloriously, luxuriating like a pardoned felon.

Looking around the office I saw the thrashed remnants of the chair, the scuffed edge of the desk. Ink stained my hands and leaked from the bent nub of the pen. Laughing, I thought, that would teach Jeff not to have nice things.

Free.

So what next?

Find Kent. Find the other shooters. Try to stay alive while doing so. Not easy, but it's not like you have a choice.

I smoked a cigarette, had some water and then found Ellen Borden's cell number. She didn't appreciate being roused at two in the morning from her first decent sleep in two days. I told her she'd forgive me once she heard what I had to say.

THIRTY-THREE
LESS THAN SIXTY

I could hear kitchen sounds on Borden's end as I recited the night's events. Faucet, coffee grinder, the whistle of a stovetop kettle. By the time I'd finished, those sounds were replaced by pouring liquid and the pestering clink of a spoon on the lip of a ceramic mug.

She sipped and *ahhh*'ed approval at her concoction. "I appreciate the call," Borden said, "but you should also make an official report. If and when we catch this man, it will hold up better to have it on record."

"Remember our last conversation?" I said. "You couldn't deny your boss was hiding something."

"I'm pretty sure he's not," Borden said.

"I have to be more than sure."

"You're actually afraid," she said.

"More than ever. Doesn't change the fact, I still want this solved."

I gave her details on my car and the laptop, told her what I could about Kent and the pistol he'd carried. Borden's pencil made fervent scratches as she wrote it all down. I hung up, wondering how much Borden would tell her superior and what MacLeish would do with the information.

Sleep wasn't coming soon. Instead of going home, I turned on the rest of the office lights, and sat down at the reception desk.

Using a cheap gel pen and a piece of paper from the printer tray, I made a list of every investigative avenue. Soon I had filled both sides of the page.

Shooters
    Kent
    Czechowski
    S + P Axton
    Blond man (?)

Witnesses
    D. Cui
    B. Mulgrew
    Calendar Man (?)

Victims
    T. Qiu
    J. Cui
    O. Kazarian
    Chang C-Y
    Z. Li
    Huang S-W
    V. Ma

Weapons
    shotgun
    rifle (modified?)
    target pistol (.22?)
    others

People of Interest
    Borden
    MacLeish
    Rhodes
    Long

Misc.
    Vehicle (Aerostar, matte black finish)
    Money (2–300K)
    Building (Gent. Central)

There was one name I couldn't bring myself to put on the list. I told myself I'd speak with him tomorrow. For now, I needed to go back to that morning.

Replaying in my mind the sequence of events, I felt my heart rate increase, my mouth go dry. Yet the feeling of stupefied shock had lessened. As if admitting I wanted to solve this had curbed some of its power.

The sound of gunfire. The van idling outside. More shots. The bystanders crossing the street to see what was happening. Kent with his shotgun, pointing it at them. Shelly Axton with the hockey bag. The wounded man, who might have been Czechowski. The blond man last. And then the shootings in the street.

Either they'd gone in to rob the count room, and the killings had resulted, or the goal all along had been to kill the men inside. The receptionist, Theresa Qiu, where did she fit in? She might have been first, to prevent her from warning the men upstairs, or the blond man might have shot her on his way out. Or at any point in between. This was conjecture, after all.

The police estimated two to three hundred thousand had been the take. Who knew how accurate that was. Say three. For five shooters, for seven deaths, that was sixty grand per participant. Less. It didn't factor in the money outlaid for the van and tools and weaponry. Or a share for whomever tipped them off.

It was horrible to put a number on it. Horrible every way.

Kent, Czechowski, Percy and Shelly Axton had carried out their work professionally. Had the blond man panicked? Or had he meant to shoot all witnesses? Had he simply reckoned, what were a few more deaths?

That old saying that life is cheap—one person's low appraisal and you blink out like a carelessly nudged light switch.

The blond man had shot the bystanders. Kent had fired too. In the air or to the side, not hitting them in any case. He hadn't expressed shock or displeasure. Instead he'd walked to the side door and climbed into the van as if the dead were immaterial.

There's a difference between a desperate man and a professional trapped in a desperate circumstance. When I'd been tied up, Kent hadn't killed me. Not because I was smart or I'd caught him on a good day. Because, to a professional, it was simply less hassle not to. That was rare. That wouldn't happen twice.

THIRTY-FOUR
RED LANTERN

Liu's Red Lantern occupied the top floor of a three-storey, turret-shaped building on Main. The restaurant was known for elaborate seafood dinners, but it was noon when I arrived. Dim sum time. Wait staff in starched white jackets and black aprons trolleyed baskets and shallow dishes from the kitchen, trailing steam and savory smells.

I was seated at a four-person table, given a stubby pencil and a bilingual order sheet. A pot of tea was dropped off. The Red Lantern did a brisk lunch-time trade. Families occupied the large circular tables, while business duos in smart suits filled the small square tables along the walls. The dining room was high-ceilinged and the acoustics travelled, merging every conversation and table noise into one collective clamour.

I poured a cup of tea and studied my options.

Jeff was seventeen minutes late, unheard of for him. He scanned the room from the entrance, then cautiously made his way between tables, turning his back to the other diners when he had to squeeze past.

"Trouble finding the place?" I asked.

"Of course not. Why'd you choose here?"

I shrugged, scratched below my lip with the nub of the pencil. "Gets us out of the office. You been here before?"

"You know I have," he said.

The waitress dropped off a second tea cup. Jeff declined when I asked if there was anything he wanted to add to the order. "Suit yourself, but let's be quick. Busy day today."

I ordered shumai, ha cheung, sticky rice, chicken feet, taro cakes, cold octopus in vinegar sauce, and a Coke with a slice of lemon.

"We can always take it back with us," I said. "So what's new?"

"You tell me." Jeff's hands were under the table. He shifted his chair so his back was to the kitchen door.

The first of our dishes arrived. The waitress cut the rice noodles with scissors, removed the basket lids with low-key panache. She checked the items off our bill.

As the food rolled out, Jeff loosened up. He outpaced me, even beating me to the last purse of sticky rice, prying apart the lotus leaf with alacrity. Business was forgotten for the moment.

"Delicious," I said.

Jeff nodded, said with his mouth full, "When my parents visit we always come here."

"We should tell the owner. Compliment him in person." As the waitress approached, I asked, "Is the owner here?"

"I'll check for you," she said.

She was already in motion when Jeff called to her back, "Don't."

I used my chopsticks to slice off a quarter of the taro cake. "Why not?" I asked innocently.

Jeff's gaze followed our waitress. She approached a table in the corner near the kitchen, interrupting two men eating bowls of noodles. The older man looked up and over at us, squinting. The younger man spun in his chair as if alarmed.

The waitress was very young, and a look of doubt had begun to darken her face. Both of the men looked at Jeff and smiled.

"Why, Dave?" he said to me as he nodded and grinned at them.

"Why what?" I said. "I'm just here for the food."

"I have to go over there now," Jeff said. He wiped his face with the napkin. "I have to say hello."

But before he was done grooming, the younger man was at our table, offering his hand to Jeff. He was in his mid-twenties, hair teased up to cascade diagonally over his forehead like a movie star. His suit looked expensive, unbuttoned at the throat to show thick braids of gold.

144 · SAM WIEBE

He spoke to Jeff in what sounded like Cantonese, his tone familiar, almost chastising. Then he turned to me and took my hand. I heard Jeff make introductions, "Dave Wakeland" the only words I understood.

"Dave," Jeff said, hiding his resentment pretty well. "This is Rui Fei Long. Felix. He's Roy Long's son."

THIRTY-FIVE
EMPTY FORTUNES

Felix Long spoke English with a suburban, hip-hop edge. He said, "Good to meet ya, Dave. Glad you guys enjoy the food. Anything else you need, you just holler."

"We're fine," Jeff said. "How are you doing?"

"Business is business." Felix added something in Chinese that sounded aphoristic. Jeff nodded. "You want to say hi to Pop?"

"We don't want to bother him," Jeff said.

"No bother. He's always glad to see you."

We left our food and followed Felix to the corner table. The older man had pushed his bowl to the side. He stood as we approached, took Jeff's hand and pointed at my partner's hairline, maybe remarking how tall he'd grown.

Jeff deferred to the men. He spoke low and graciously and didn't make introductions. I guessed he was putting the interruption down to my well-meaning rudeness, wanting to thank the owner. The old man waved it off, nothing.

In person Roy Long had the same unassuming charm that the photos hinted at. He was stockier, the white in his hair slightly more prominent, his jowls a bit less resistant to gravity. Dressed in a royal blue shirt with white trim and slate-coloured slacks. A Timex on a rubber strap and a wedding band decorated his hands, a few orange liver spots visible below the cuffs.

The overall effect was too deliberately humble, especially given how Felix and Jeff acted toward him. I tried to see if there was something dangerous lurking behind Roy Long's expression. Results were inconclusive; if I did see something, it was probably because I knew his reputation.

He shook my hand, his smile cautious, more reserved than it had been for Jeff. "I'm Roy Long," he said. "So glad you enjoy the food."

Long beckoned us to sit down. I thought Jeff would beg off. Instead he sat promptly, motioned for me to take the corner chair.

"You a drinker?" Felix asked me. "Get you a beer?" He had ice water and Tsingtao in front of him, green tea for his father.

I started to say we were fine but Jeff accepted a cup of tea. Roy Long took the lid off the pot and rotated it so it sat overturned. It was swept up and replaced by a waiter.

"Real Dragon Well," Felix boasted, "not that supermarket shit."

"It's very good," Jeff said.

"Terrific," I echoed. My palette for tea bent toward Twinings Earl Grey, but the green was subtle and comforting.

They talked around me, Roy Long asking Jeff questions, Jeff searching for the words in Cantonese. I heard Marie's name. Long pointed at his son, maybe sharing something about what Felix had been like as a kid.

"I still *do* think that," Long's son said, exploding in self-deprecating laughter. I gauged its sincerity as low-grade, covering embarrassment. He turned to me. "How 'bout you, Dave? You got kids? Why not?"

"My girlfriend has a demanding career."

"Modern woman, huh. Modern problems." He cracked a joke and looked to Jeff for approval. Jeff smiled and explained something to him.

Felix's response was a quick sentence, laced with repulsion. Jeff kept the smile on his face.

"That's cool," Felix said to me. "I love cops. Takes all kinds, right?"

Long spoke to his son without looking up. The words were soft, the intention pointed, adamantine. Felix's smile grew broader and less sincere, a tricky feat.

"Me and my dumbass mouth," he said. "Pop thinks sex talk doesn't belong at the table, and maybe he's right. So how's business, Jun? Making that money. Few more years you're gonna be making the big bucks." Turning his head to include me. "Both of you. Hope you'll still give us your business when you're eating caviar and smoking cigars."

"This is a good location," I said. "You must be happy it's not closer to downtown, what with all the violence there recently."

Roy Long stared into his tea cup. His son looked over at Jeff, who stepped around the issue, smiling and saying, "This is definitely a good location. Good parking, lots of foot traffic."

"Yeah," Felix said. To me: "Hey that's right, you're the guy that saved that lady. Big hero. We should break out the Cristal."

"Thanks but we've got work this afternoon."

"That's Pop's attitude too. No drinking on the job, and the job lasts all the time." He took a swig of the Tsingtao, smiling at his father.

"We should probably go," Jeff said.

"Okay. Good to meet you, Dave." One more handshake. Felix slapped my arm. "Glad you enjoyed the meal. Prob'ly not what you expected, huh? No chicken chow mein, no bright pink sweet and sour. Still pretty good, uh?"

"Terrific," I said.

"Want me pack it up?"

"We're good."

"Great. Just pay the cashier. Catch y'all later."

Jeff lingered to say goodbye to the old man. I paid up and met Jeff on the staircase. We silently walked down to the parkade. He'd parked his wife's hybrid next to my rental.

"What the fuck was that about?" he said. "Seriously, Dave. Why the fuck?"

I lightly slapped my forehead. "I forgot. I was going to thank Roy for renting us that office. But then why not thank him for co-signing our loan agreement eight years ago?"

Jeff didn't deny it. "You think springing this on me accomplishes something?"

"Spring it on you—imagine how I felt, finding out our business was bankrolled by a gangster."

"Not like that at all—"

"Then what's it like, Jeff?"

I'd found out that morning, after making my list. The file cabinet had been right there. I'd gone through our old incorporation documents, to assure myself my partner couldn't possibly be involved. Jeff's name couldn't belong on my list. He wouldn't do that to me, wouldn't be a party to that.

The papers had meant nothing to me when we'd first incorporated. The names were just part of a never-ending list of loan officers and other signatories. I found Long's signature, his name printed next to it. Co-signing, guaranteeing we'd pay back the bank. Even serving as witness for Jeff's own signature.

"You don't understand," Jeff said.

"Well that's true."

Jeff looked past me as the elevator doors opened. The white-jacketed waitress came forward, holding a small box. She handed it to me and nodded and quick-stepped back before the doors swung closed.

I opened the box. Inside were our leftovers, along with two fortune cookies.

In a calmer tone, Jeff said, "I'll explain everything to you. Promise."

"Damn right."

"But I have to see someone first. Give me a couple days."

He disabled the alarm and opened the car.

I held up the box. "Want this?"

"Never liked them," he said.

"Check your fortune. Maybe it'll be good. 'Long life and riches to someone close to you.'"

He accepted the cookie, cracked it. "Don't think that means someone standing close."

"Open to interpretation, right?"

He pulled out the ribbon of paper, letting the halves of the cookie fall to the pavement.

"Exciting opportunities are come your way," he read.

I broke mine. "Are come?"

"You gonna correct the grammar of a free fucking cookie?"

I ate some of the shards and pawed through the rest. "Odd," I said.

"Why, what's yours say?"

I held up the crumbs. "Doesn't have one."

Jeff stared at the pieces in my hand. He grinned, then laughed, more a release than a sign of amusement.

"That's not ominous, is it?" I said. "Some kind of symbol?"

"What do you think?"

Jeff's laughter carried him into his car, and up the ramp into the alley off Main Street. I let the crumbs fall and followed him.

THIRTY-SIX
BANG BANG BANG

My rental Saab had all the leg room of a Parisian handbag. I drove with both front windows open, clearing out the stench of amalgamated air fresheners. Six of the things clogged the glove box. Pine and lavender, ocean spray and summer breeze.

I made a circuit of suburban gun ranges, starting in Delta. Since the shooters' van had been stolen locally, I figured the weapons had probably been acquired in the same way. The target pistol Kent had pointed at me didn't seem ideal for his purposes. That suggested he was making do with what he had.

The Delta gun range was located in an industrial park, no sidewalks or trees to break up the dull grey vista of warehouses and manufacturing plants. The range rented guns—the front counter had a display case filled with glimmering automatics and large-calibre revolvers. Novelty targets hung behind the case, zombies and sports team logos in addition to the familiar human silhouette with concentric rings.

The proprietor dealt with a costume party ahead of me, college kids in fedoras and bootlegger pinstripes. They wanted to rent a Tommy gun. The steady crack of gunfire from inside the range stoked my headache.

When the party had moved into the waiting room, the proprietor smiled at me. She was the same age as the customers, hair tied back in a ponytail, wearing a black T-shirt with the company logo in crosshairs on her breast. I told her I was interested in any reports of missing or stolen firearms.

"Our customers mostly rent ours, and we're super careful," she said.

"Has anyone tried to buy them from you?"

"All the time. Then I tell them they need a licence, and that shuts them down. They only get to shoot here because they're under our supervision."

I gave her my card and told her to call if she heard of any stolen guns. She spun the card between her index fingers.

"Private investigator," she said. "Not quite law enforcement."

"More like 'law suggestive nudge,'" I said.

She smiled. "Know what? If you want to shoot today, I'll give you the twenty percent police discount anyway. I wasn't going to, but I'll make an exception, 'cause I like your face."

"It's a hell of a face," I said.

"Twenty percent, plus a box of .22s if you spend a hundred or more."

I told her thanks, that was sweet of her, but I had miles to go.

Driving to Langley, I fed Mad Season's *Live at the Moore* into the Saab's treble-heavy sound system. I thought of Jeff's promise to divulge the entirety of his connection to Roy Long. The conversation worried me. If he lied, that was the end of our partnership. Worse, if he told the truth…

It wasn't just the hypocrisy of being in debt to someone like Long, though that ate at me. It was that for almost a decade, Jeff had kept it to himself. I hadn't even known I was compromised. Even if we patched things up, that trust would be hard to regenerate.

I had no luck at the Langley range. Its clientele brought their own weapons and shot on a strict timetable. Green light on: inspect targets and reload magazines. Red light on: range is hot. Fire till you're empty. Green light on: firearms down. Repeat.

The range officer wouldn't divert his attention. Maybe that was for the best. He did provide me with earmuffs, an index card and a magic marker.

I wrote:

STOLEN FIREARMS

IF YOU KNOW ANYTHING

PLS CONTACT

And then my number, adding at the bottom:

ALL CALLS CONFIDENTIAL

I pinned the card on the range bulletin board, atop ads for

WINCHESTER .30-30 FAIR CONDITION
INTERESTING TRADES EXCEPTED

and

NEXT SAT & SUN MILITARY GEAR EXPO!!!
MAJOR COLLECTION OF WW2 KOREAN + CONFEDERATE GEAR!!!
DOOR PRIZES TO FIRST FIFTY ENTRANTS!!!

From Langley to Abbotsford, Soundgarden's *Live on I-5* replaced Mad Season. I drew much-needed comfort from those old Seattle records. Each gunshot, no matter how muffled or faint, made my stomach lurch, my shoulders lock together. I'd had guns pointed at me before. A few on purpose, many more by careless weekend shooters. Often when you'd step away from the barrel, they'd look at you with confusion or contempt. I know what I'm doing. It's not even loaded. Don't be so touchy, man.

The Abbotsford club featured four separate outdoor ranges, built against the foothills of a mountain. It was cold and wet, the sun going down, and only one range was in use. A Mazda pickup had the gravel parking lot to itself. I pulled the Saab in next to it.

There was a sheltered shooting area with tables and a locked door. Cement barricades ran along the edge of each range. The backstop was the steep mossy earth of the mountainside. High-powered pistol shots whip-cracked and reverberated from the range. I waited for the light inside to turn green before tapping on the door.

Nikki Frazer opened it.

She wore her uniform, along with earmuffs and a tinted shooting visor. A Velcro holster belt was cinched around her waist. She grinned at me and let me inside.

"Didn't know you shot, Dave."

"Following up on something," I said. "Ryan with you?"

"Nope. He's a pisspoor shot. I'd only embarrass him."

She turned the light to red and began checking her pistols, then reloading the magazines. Two automatics, each with a holster, a .22 and a 9mm. Ten clips for each.

"I shoot competitive," Nikki said. "Quickdraw and the obstacle course, mostly. It's expensive but it's fun. You and Sonia should come out some time. How is she, anyway?"

"Wish I knew," I said, more truthful than I wanted to be. "Since her promotion we haven't spent much time together."

"Rough break. Mind helping me with these?"

I picked up a clip and began thumbing cartridges into it, much slower than Nikki.

"I did PR for a while," she said. "I loved the classroom visits, all the community stuff. Sonia will do fine. It's really not that bad."

"It's safe," I said.

"That make you happy?"

Nine bullets. Ten. I picked up another clip.

"Honestly, yes. It's patronizing, but it's how I feel."

"Ryan got a call the other day," Nikki said, her hands flying, adept and at ease with her tools. "A tip this missing kid was staying in the Baltic, that run-down SRO on Pender. He goes into the room, the guy inside tries to stab him."

"Shit," I said.

"Shit is right. Nothing happened, and don't get me wrong, I know Ryan can handle himself. But I did have a guilty thought that if he wasn't on the street, well, I'd never have that need-to-shit-on-an-empty-stomach feeling again. You know the one?"

"Too well," I said.

Nikki smiled. "That's probably how you feel about Sonia. I know how much you two care about each other. It'll work out."

I was grateful to bask in her optimism. Before she resumed firing, I asked about gun thefts at the club.

"Not that I've heard," she said. "A friend of a friend might have mentioned losing his gun. Or guns. I never got the full story, but I can ask. This about a case? Not that shooting, is it?"

Before I could answer, she said, "Actually, I'd prefer you don't tell me. This'll just be us shooting the shit at the range."

"Works for me."

Her clips filled, Nikki loaded her guns and tucked them into their holsters. She practised her quick-draw motion at tai chi speed. Each hand in turn, then both together.

She said, "You should know, Dave, Ryan pisses and moans a lot about helping you. Like, *a lot*. But deep down he likes to. As much as he can be a dillweed sometimes, no one has a better heart than him. I knew that right off the bat. Same as with Sonia and you."

"I'm glad," I said. "It gets murky sometimes, doesn't it?"

"Not to me." She tapped her chest. "I know in here, Dave."

Mystified and somewhat envious, I nodded and left her to her target practice.

It was a dark drive home to my dark East Van apartment. I played albums I hadn't listened to in years. PJ Harvey, The Gutter Twins. I thought about where to go next.

From guns to witnesses. I'd have to talk to Diane Cui and maybe Bryan Mulgrew. Then I'd have to track down the Calendar Man. Maybe one of them had seen something I hadn't, and maybe I could convince or coerce them into telling me. Maybe one of them was involved.

I wished I believed, like Nikki Frazer, that a person's character was discernable from their face or behaviour. Their *heart*, as she'd said. I knew too many instances of the opposite. It seemed sometimes that everyone was hiding something. That made it hard to function among other people, always waiting for them to reveal their true and horrible selves.

Inside the apartment I turned on the light in the hallway-kitchenette. Shucked my coat and flannel shirt, tossed wallet and keys onto the dusty top of the fridge. I heard a sound from the patio, a steady *pop pop pop*, like smashing lightbulbs—

Something hit the patio glass. Cracked it.

I dove for the floor.

THIRTY-SEVEN
OPEN SEASON

I heard shots pepper the fence and ding the glass. Some ricocheted off the concrete, others making a dull thud into the stucco. Small calibre and semi-automatic from the sound.

They're here to execute you. One is waiting in the hall, hoping you'll try to escape. They've probably scouted the bedroom window too. Now that you're frightened, they'll close in, taking pleasure in how helpless you feel, and you are helpless, because this is it…

Silence. I looked up at the crystalline patterns cut into the glass door. Like snowflakes under a microscope. Without raising my belly, I reached for the top drawer next to the sink, cutlery, and took out the first knife my fingers ran across. Lunatic thoughts came, terror and bravado.

The front-facing patio was hemmed in by a high wooden fence, greyed by Vancouver weather, with a wooden divider between mine and the next unit. A raised grass walkway ran in front, leading to a side gate near the building's entrance. No footsteps on the grass. No squeal from the gate. Night traffic from Broadway and no other sound.

After another minute I stood up and put the knife away. I drew out a long-barreled aluminum Maglite that had belonged my father. Useful as a torch as well as a bludgeon, but mostly a comforting totem. I felt more competent with it in hand.

I walked to the patio door, stood to the left, behind the retracted blinds. Peering out, I saw no one. A light snapped on in the unit next door.

I unlocked the door and slowly slid it open, feeling the bite of surprisingly cold spring air. Casting the flashlight beam over the patio revealed new perforations in the wooden fence, chips taken off the latticework.

They'd fired from the street. Blindly, but knowing which unit was mine. Which made this a warning.

From who, though? Roy Long, Kent, Terry Rhodes. The woman who'd followed me. All of them working together. I pulled back from thoughts of conspiracies when I heard a fist beating on the hallway door.

The spyhole showed Marty, the stay-at-home half of the couple next door. He was shirtless, wearing orange and blue pajama bottoms. His daughter, Lea, was in his arms, the child naked, held snugly against her father's bare chest.

"Are you all right?" he asked me. I told him I was. "What was that, was, was it gunfire?"

"Small calibre," I said.

"That doesn't make me feel better."

Other than hallway greetings, we'd had three interactions over the years. He'd once asked me to turn my stereo down. Another time he'd needed baking soda, but had politely declined the year-old box in my fridge. We'd spent an hour in the laundry room one rainy Sunday, griping about rents and the black streaks forming at the corners of the building's peach-coloured exterior. Somebody should do something, we'd both decided. The landlord sure as shit wouldn't. Then of course we'd both done nothing.

"I phoned nine-one-one," Marty said. "One of those, those bullet-things, it hit my window. Why would, who would do that?"

I told him I didn't know.

The patrol officers took statements and searched the patio, plodding over the dead garden to examine the punctures in the wood. They talked to Marty, who told them he had no idea, he was just changing his kid and watching TV, when all of a sudden it started.

My statement wasn't much different. I added that the officers might want to talk to Superintendent Borden. They seemed skeptical, but after a brief phone call they drove me over to Cambie Street.

I was led into the familiar interview room. Sergeant Dudgeon was already waiting, writing in his notebook. I sat down and watched him. The night before, in the company of Keogh, he'd been sardonic and vola-tile. Now he'd resumed his pose of disinterest.

Without looking up, he said, "If it wasn't for bad luck, Wakeland, you'd have none at all."

"I'm still here, though."

Dudgeon's eyes travelled up, and his mouth pursed in the slightest of smiles. "Guess that counts as something," he said.

He wrote another paragraph in his clear, tight script. When he'd filled the page he put the pen down and closed the book with a flourish. He checked something on his phone. Stood up. Opened and held the door.

"Deputy chief wants a word," he said.

Up three floors, taking the stairs. MacLeish's office with its crossed flags and framed commendations awaited us. It was empty. Dudgeon turned on the light and told me to sit down.

A framed picture on the desk was the only personal touch in the office. It showed the deputy chief embracing a young redheaded woman in military uniform, their heads pressed together to fit in the frame. Daughter, it looked like.

MacLeish entered, dismissing Dudgeon as he settled into his seat. His perfect grooming hadn't changed, but there was a desperate cast to his eyes. He looked like a monument in the aftermath of an earthquake, outwardly preserved, inwardly cracked, precariously balanced and awaiting ruin.

"Some shots were thrown around," he said. ".22s, outside your building."

"My apartment," I said.

"Let's not jump ahead of ourselves. From what I hear, the fellow next door to you had his patio defaced too."

"Defaced."

"It's not uncommon," MacLeish said. "Sadly, kids like to do this kind of thing."

"Kids."

"Is there an echo in here?"

"I was fucking shot at," I said.

"Language, son." MacLeish folded his hands. "As someone who's scorned our protection before—"

"They shot at me," I said.

"*They*?" His eyes widened in mock innocence. "Did you see this *they*?" I shook my head reluctantly.

"So this time you also saw nothing. A pattern seems to be emerging. As I was saying before you interrupted me, since you've turned down our protection before—"

"What protection?" I said. "What have you done besides spin your wheels and talk about the hardships of command?"

"Let me fucking finish," MacLeish near-shouted.

"Why? It'll just be more bullshit."

"You're scared."

"Frightened for my fucking life," I said. "Out of my fucking wits."

He managed to get out the line he'd been wanting to say.

"The department has no protection left to give you."

Despite their theatricality, I felt the impact of MacLeish's words. He grinned, his torso thrust forward over his desk, imposing in his triumph. I wanted to say, you can't do that. His look replied, *just you fucking watch.*

But his posture gave away something.

"This is personal to you," I said.

"You're damn right it's personal. When law-abiding citizens are cut down in the streets—"

"Sure, but beneath this bluster this is about you. You personally. That's why the threats, isn't it?"

"I make promises, son, not threats."

"Bully for you," I said. "Here's one of each: I am not going to be owned by this. I'm going to find those shooters and figure out what's going on."

"You involve yourself in my investigation—"

"I'm already involved."

"—and I'll put the complaint in on your business licence myself."

I opened my wallet and threw it on his desk. "Take it. Driver's too, if you want. Bus pass, credit card. Then bring charges. This still ends with your secrets out."

"You stay out of this," MacLeish said. "Or I swear to Christ you'll pay."

"There is no out. 'Cept further in. Thanks for making that clear." I grinned at him as I collected my wallet. "See if you can keep up."

THIRTY-EIGHT
COME CLEAN

It was a short walk across the bridge to Sonia's apartment. Rain and wind licked at my face and pasted my hair to my forehead. I thought of how best to tell Sonia my plans. That meant thinking hard about exactly what my plans were.

I had three advantages over an official investigation, and one major drawback. First, I'd been there, and I knew what I'd seen. Second, I knew what *others* had seen. Third, I had no boss, no MacLeish to steer or hinder my investigation. I could do things the way they needed to be done.

True, I lacked official authority, but that wasn't the drawback. It might even work in my favour. The drawback was who I worked with, and my relationship to them.

Anybody I dragged into this would have a personal connection with me. I'd be asking them to put themselves in peril. Which meant I'd have to come clean with each of them in turn, lay out what we were dealing with. Trusting them, and asking them for help.

Starting with Sonia.

I tapped the intercom outside her building. My key to her place was at home. Behind me, False Creek glittered with the reflection of the towers, jewels spilled across black felt.

Sonia's voice came from the speaker. "Yes?"

"Me," I said. "We need to talk."

"We do. I'll come down."

I didn't know what that portended. After a few minutes she emerged from the elevator, buckling her cream-coloured Burberry jacket as she crossed the foyer. From her pocket, she slipped out the top of a mickey of Bulleit, to show me she'd come prepared.

The False Creek promenade was nearly deserted, save for the occasional late-night jogger. No matter how thoroughly gentrification pervaded the area, a few drops of water could clear it out quickly. We walked by Science World, headed in the direction of Olympic Village.

Sonia told me her work was going fine and there were aspects she enjoyed. She'd done her first classroom visit, and the kids were much more engaged than she'd anticipated. Police reform, systemic racism: these were issues she cared about. She'd spoken her mind, with no reprisals so far. It wasn't Robbery, but for a time it would do.

"And you?" she said. "How have you been?"

"Well, I was shot at this evening, which wasn't all that fun."

"Dave."

"I'm fine," I said, "though the patio door looks like Sonny Corleone. After that I was bawled out by MacLeish and told to stay away from his case."

"You're not going to stay away, are you?"

"Can't, even if I wanted to. Which I don't."

She produced the bottle and we each took a swig. We avoided the brightly lit plaza of Olympic Village and continued along the Seawall toward Granville Island. Lights in the waterfront apartments winked out. Driftwood bobbed in the water.

"Here's where the thing stands," I managed to work up the courage to say. "I need to see this through to the end. I'm terrified, probably out of my depth, definitely in danger. But this needs to be solved."

"So let's solve it," Sonia said.

"Just like that?"

She uncapped the whiskey and shared it.

"You could've let me finish," I said. "I prepared about twenty minutes of brilliant oratory."

"I told you when it happened," Sonia said. "You're not allowed to shut me out. You don't have my permission. And yet what did you do, almost right away?"

"I was hoping it would go away. Stupid thought."

"Very stupid," Sonia said. "The only way we work as a couple is by accepting that there are risks to what we do. Not pretending we're not scared, but understanding that. Right?"

"One hundred percent," I said.

"Good. So I'm in, you idiot. I've always been in. Catch me up on what's happened."

We started back and I told her everything. We worked on how to proceed. Holding hands, passing the bottle, pausing often to kiss her, feel her fingers stroke the soaked nape of my neck. We said our I love yous.

As we entered her building, she told me there was a catch. I agreed to it unquestioningly. Loosening her jacket in the elevator, feeling her hands grope me through the rain-soaked fabric of my jeans. We barely made it to her apartment, and before the door had closed, I'd stripped her. The fine hairs on her arm stood up, her skin taut from the cold, small dark nipples erect. The familiar black sweep of hair above her crotch. I joined her, lifting her onto the counter.

It had been weeks. It felt new. Her hands roughly kneaded my shoulders, legs threaded around my hips. It was rough and quick and it felt like it had been a million years and worth every moment.

Later, on her bed, we took our time.

Afterwards we lay together atop the blankets with my arms wrapped around her as she slept. I thought of how little you have to do to demonstrate love to someone, and how often even that was left undone.

I wanted to wake her up and ask her what condition I'd agreed to, but Sonia slept peacefully. I held tight and didn't move.

THIRTY-NINE
SOLIDARITY

Walking into the office the next morning, I felt a pang of anxiety. The new alarm system was still active, and I punched in the eight-digit code. I'd brought the Maglite with me, as well as a box of Cartems assorted for the meeting. After filling the kettle and flicking on the coffee machine, I set about clearing the renovators' junk from the boardroom.

Jeff arrived at eight, followed five minutes later by Kay and Blatchford. My sister spied the box of donuts on the table and said, "Something must be wrong if you're springing for pastries."

"If you don't want any…" I said.

She took a custard-filled and sat down.

Once we were all provisioned, I closed the door and stood by the whiteboard. I laid out what I'd seen the morning of the shooting, and what I planned to do about it.

"If anyone doesn't want to be involved, I absolutely understand. These are dangerous people. One broke into the office and held me at gunpoint. Someone else shot up my apartment. If they suspect we're looking for them, they might do worse."

I looked at them each in turn. Kay nodded eagerly and took another donut. Jeff I couldn't read. Blatchford crossed his arms and yawned.

"All right," I said. Part of me wanted to thank them for the gesture of solidarity. Instead I quickly moved to the details of the case, remembering what I'd thought last night, about how rarely we take the time to let others know how we feel.

I wrote out the names of the shooters, the victims and the witnesses.

"The shooting was motivated by one of three things," I said. "Money, status or straight-up execution. I think it's status, and here's why. The robbery yielded two to three hundred grand. Divided by five, that wouldn't be worth the risk. A low-rent stickup man could walk up to a bank teller and clear almost that much."

"Maybe they thought there'd be more," Blatchford said. "Most people in the life don't got a good grasp on money. Somebody could've shot their mouth off at a bar, what a big deal they are. It happens."

"Sure," I agreed. "But from how they acted, the shooters had some idea what they'd find in that room. None of the victims were high-ranking or important, which puts a dent in the execution theory. They could have believed a top guy would be in the room, but I doubt it. Someone like Roy Long probably never sees that money until it's cleaned up and laundered."

Jeff shifted in his new chair, the twin of the one I'd destroyed while freeing myself. He caught me looking at him and raised his eyebrows innocently. Then he lifted the lid of the donut box as if that had been his goal all along. He chose the chocolate glazed.

"Status is most likely," I said. "Unless Roy Long deals with the shooters, he looks weak. That would benefit someone trying to usurp control. Terry Rhodes and the Exiles, maybe."

"Doesn't have the feel of a biker hit," Blatchford said.

"Rhodes is canny enough to know that, and set it up for that reason. If he has an agreement with Long, this gives him deniability."

"But he talked to you about finding the shooters," Kay said. "He threatened you."

"I wouldn't put it past him to do that for appearance's sake," I said. "Hiring me shows how uninvolved the Exiles are. If I did uncover his involvement, he could always muscle me into silence."

"But to be clear," Blatchford said, "if it's him, you're not going to let him go."

"No."

"Good to hear."

He pulled the box close to himself, inspected the remaining donuts, then pushed it away in an act of willpower.

"So Rhodes hires these guys to hit Roy Long's count room, give himself deniability. That's Option One. Option Two is someone within Long's group, ripping him off. Option Three is they're independent operators, taking advantage of gang warfare to make a score."

"Option Four?" Kay asked.

I hesitated. "At least one of the suspects is ex-military," I said. "So armed forces or law enforcement could be involved."

"Jesus."

"It's unlikely," I said, thinking of last night's meeting with MacLeish. "But it is a possibility. Any others?"

Kay put up her hand. "Do you think they all knew each other? The shooters."

"Most robberies, it's a crew of people you know. Same gang or same group. You put a crew together of people you've served with, served time with, grew up with or know from the life. There are probably exceptions."

"So this Jigowski guy—"

"Czechowski."

"Whatever. If we find out about him, that'll lead us to the others."

"It could," I said.

"Good. Then I want to do that."

I hadn't got around to dividing the workload. Of all of us, Kay seemed the most eager to run into danger and the least able to deal with it. One for the nature side of nature/nurture, I thought. My adopted mother, her aunt, would filet me like a fresh-caught sockeye if anything happened to Kay. And Kay's mother back in the Prairies—*our* mother, who I'd met maybe six times in my life—how would she feel?

Kay was twenty-four and deserved more, deserved better. She also deserved to take the risks she felt necessary. I told her that was fine, she and Blatchford had Czechowski.

"Jeff and I will start with the victims. We'll talk to the witnesses too. Our next meeting is tomorrow, same time."

"Are we getting paid for this?" Blatchford asked.

"Of course."

"In actual, physical, spendable money?"

"Sure," I said. "Just deduct all the hours you spend napping or watching Japanese wrestling. I'll happily pay the balance."

He grumbled something about making rent, and he and Kay left. Jeff held back until we were alone.

"Problem with any of that?" I asked.

"No problem. Just that I'm surprised you let Kay handle that. Thought you'd keep her in the office till this is over."

"I want to," I said. "But I'm trying this new thing of trusting people. I'll let you know how it works out."

"About that." He coughed. Together we gathered the coffee cups and used napkins, swept up the table.

Jeff said, "Remember I told you I had to talk to someone? Well I did. He'll meet with us. Explain things."

"'Less I'm mistaken, I remember you saying *you*'d explain once you saw him."

"It's easier if he does it," Jeff said. "You'll believe him. He said he'll be at the Garden till noon, so we should head."

I slung my coat over my arm. "We meeting your lawyer?" I asked.

"My uncle," Jeff said.

FORTY

GUANXI

The route to the Sun Yat-Sen Garden took us up Carrall, into China-town. We made the trip on foot. Late-morning traffic along Pender was sluggish. Men and women in tailored suits hurried along the sidewalks, as if fearing too much exposure to poverty from the panhandlers and shopping-cart pushers they passed.

I told Jeff I wanted to see the building.

We detoured up Taylor through the shooting scene, passing Gen-trification Central. The glass doors had been replaced, the lobby floors polished, the reception island taken out entirely. Lights were off inside.

Like it never happened.

To our right, the window of the small third-storey office was shut and dark. A healthy crowd formed a line to the bus stop. Up the street from where the Cuis had fallen, crows nipped at a popcorn bag discarded in the gutter.

The clean white walls of the Garden came into view. They sur-rounded a pond and convoluted walkway, a museum and cultural cen-tre and a contemplative space. By the entrance was a marble bust of Sun Yat-Sen, a few filaments of spider web clinging to the good doc-tor's brow.

We paid our admission and threaded through a tour group that had paused by a half-submerged willow. Their guide was explaining the con-nection between the garden's shape and Chinese martial arts, and why there were few straight lines in either.

Covered rooms displayed Chinese antiquities. We passed through a moon gate and crossed a narrow, arching bridge. Below us, koi darted through murky, burbling water, streaks of red-gold that disappeared amongst reeds and lilies.

Eventually we came to a terrace shadowed by a hillock of volcanic rock. Roy Long sat on a bench beneath the grooved awning of the terrace, holding a notebook on his lap. One of the terrace gates had been drawn closed, which, with the styled leak windows atop the wall, gave us the suggestion of privacy without promising the real thing.

Long greeted us and beckoned toward the bench across from him. He wore slacks and a checked dress shirt, penny loafers, their leather grooved and shined. He unstrung thin wire reading glasses and set them on the bench.

"I'm glad you came, Mr. Wakeland. Jun Fei has great respect for you. He's a good young man."

Away from the restaurant and from Long's son, it was easier to see the depth of the connection between them. Jeff looked upon Long with filial respect. Pride showed in the older man's face.

I reminded myself he was dangerous.

"Jeff's a prince," I said.

Long nodded. "We met when he first came to Vancouver. He was a student at the same time as my sons—my older sons. He asked me to…" he looked to Jeff for the phrase. Jeff told him in Cantonese. "Yes. Straighten out things between you."

"Things aren't all that crooked," I said.

"But you have doubts about him. And me."

"Let me put it this way," I said. Beside me Jeff winced in anticipation. "I'm a very simple guy. I do one thing well—better than anyone. I don't compromise, and I don't let myself owe."

Long nodded. "Wise philosophy."

"When we started Wakeland & Chen, our goal was to be superior to everyone else. More ethical. Owing favours complicates that."

"Of course."

"There was a shooting a few days ago. Seven people are dead. Respectfully, sir, I'm going to find the people responsible."

"I very much hope you do," Long said.

"This connection Jeff has to you—*we* have to you. I need to know that it doesn't make us party to anything illegal. If it does…" I shrugged. "I have to trust the people I work with. I hope you understand."

"Perfectly," Long said. "In your place I'd feel the same. I *have*. It hurts to feel your trust is…"—he struggled for the word—"misused. Hard to decide to continue or to separate."

"That's about where it stands," I said.

The tourist throng passed us on the other side of the gate. Roy Long gazed at the pond in the opposite direction until they'd moved past.

"Jun Fei said you know something about Chinese culture."

"Less than he thinks," Jeff muttered.

"It's very important to have connections to people. From all walks of life, business and friendship. It's so important."

"*Guanxi*," I said.

"Right. When you're away from your home and family, when so much happens you don't understand, good *guanxi* is very important. Sometimes people need a favour."

"But favours have to be paid back," I said.

Long paused and pressed his hands together. He had the look of a schoolmaster coming up with a third example to give a pressing student. He seemed to light on one, and focused back on me.

"David," he said, "I've been thinking about a story I know." He glanced down at the notebook. "My English isn't so good, but I'd like you to hear it and give me your advice, if you have the time."

I told him I did.

FORTY-ONE
ROY LONG'S STORY

Perhaps the best way to explain the importance of connections is to mention someone who had none. My father came to Vancouver in the 1960s, fleeing the Cultural Revolution. In China the Red Guards stripped him of nearly everything. He'd been tortured, forced to denounce his so-called bourgeois lifestyle. He was sent away from his home, into the countryside, for re-education. He never discussed how he got here, or how he arranged to bring over my mother and older brother.

He came to Canada speaking no English and knowing nothing of the culture. He worked jobs that paid nearly nothing. He was stolen from and beaten. But what got him through was that he wasn't alone.

The people he worked with introduced him to others. He met people from his hometown, people with the same name as his. Each group would meet and look after its members—clubs and societies and organizations.

A few years passed. My father worked many different jobs. He had several children to support. He and his friends started a business, but of course they could barely feed everyone—and no bank would lend them much.

Fortunately they knew a member of a club that was known to lend money to people starting promising business ventures. When this group met, each member would put up a certain amount, so that the total sum was available. My father and his friend borrowed this money and paid them back with interest. In time they both became members of this group, lending out money to others.

Now across all these groups, were there some members who came by their money through dishonest means? Has any group of people ever been assembled who could say otherwise? Some people might claim that good *guanxi* involves knowing people across all fields.

The government we fled used hard labour and relocation to punish us. And only a generation before, Canada's government didn't allow Chinese immigration. My father did what made sense for his family.

In any case, his business did well, and I took it over when my brothers died. My older sons will run it at some point, I hope.

A lot of what I know about my father I learned from his friends. When he died I felt I barely knew him. But I knew the struggle he went through to bring us the good things, so we wouldn't have to want the way he did.

A few months after my father died, my sons introduced me to a friend of theirs, a promising young man whose family had sent him here to study. His father had fallen on hard times, and could no longer support his education.

My sons asked if I could find this young man work. I have several friends always looking for help, so I asked the young man what sort of work he wanted to do. Surprisingly, he picked a hard job delivering produce, working long hours. Honest labour.

In time he finished his education and applied for a private investigator's licence. He apprenticed at an established office. During that time, he paid back my earlier kindness several times over and helped return an heirloom necklace stolen from one of my nieces.

Soon, though, he and a friend of his decide to start their own company. They don't have the need for the kind of "face bank" my father did, but they do need someone to co-sign. It's an honour for me to do that.

I own real estate, so naturally when the young man's partner needs a quiet place to work, I can recommend one that's affordable.

This is the extent of the favours between us, done out of friendship, and a desire to help. Just like this young man I was talking about, Jun Fei, or Jeff, knows many people across many groups. I'm glad to be one. And I'm glad he has a partner so concerned for his integrity.

As for this other matter, I'm saddened by the violence. I hope you find these people, or the police do. There are no obligations between us either way. If I did know someone who was involved, that person might even consider it a favour if you find those responsible. Whatever might happen to them after.

FORTY-TWO
LIGHT IN DARKNESS

Roy Long walked us to the exit. I said goodbye and left to give them privacy. Jeff caught up with me in the Memorial Plaza, near the monument to Chinese servicemen.

"Talk about favours," Jeff said. "I owe him big for that—it's probably more than he's told his kids."

"Just to be clear," I said, "the kid in the story is you."

"Dumbass, of course."

"And that's how it happened?"

"Pretty much. His sons brought me to the Six Companies—that's the name of the group."

"The tong."

"You want to call it that, sure."

"And it's just a club."

"That one is."

We walked east on Pender, turned on Malkin Ave. A light rain fell. Under a black umbrella, a couple stood at slow-dancing proximity, passing a tinfoil and lighter works, taking turns holding the umbrella handle while the other lit up and inhaled.

"There's really a group where all the members have the same last name? Or family name?"

"Common ancestor," Jeff said. "You wouldn't understand."

"What *you* think. You haven't met my friends at the Lodge of the Fabulous Wakelands."

Shaking his head, Jeff said, "Anyway, that's what happened."

"No crucial details he left out?"

"Well, I was fucking the niece," he said, deadpan. "Crucial enough?"

In the lobby of the Strathcona Community Centre there was a row of vending machines, including a coffee maker that boasted it could concoct a nonfat chai latte. Sometimes you have to tempt fate. I plugged three dollars in and watched the paper cup fall into the chamber and fill with the spewings from the guts of the machine.

It was an odd fit for the offices, which had the yellowed, pleasantly out-of-date look of most underfunded bureaus. Over the beige island of the front desk, I could see a fax machine, a few CRT monitors and a Xerox that might have been an original.

Among the services offered at the centre was a distribution point for the *Light in Darkness* calendar. I had no idea if the calendar program lived up to its name; such programs are hard to evaluate, which is why they often end up getting cut. It's only years after a program is gone, when you see the crime rate surge, or the homelessness on your block proliferate, that you get a sense of what's been lost.

On paper it sounded swell. Each year the city would appoint a committee to select the most inspirational photographs taken by entrants living in poverty. The fourteen best would be compiled in a calendar, printed up by the city and sold by street vendors.

The pictures ran from Hallmark cheese—wheelchair-bound grandmas being pushed by broad-grinning orderlies, the mayor standing in front of totem poles—to outright startling. One showed the point of view of a diner patron, sitting at a counter with soup and coffee laid out. Raining outside, the corner of the frame rouged by the out-of-focus edge of a neon sign. You could almost feel the heat from the kitchen warm the last of the rain from your skin.

It was a popular program from what I'd seen. The Calendar Man was by no means the only one hawking these. He seemed to be the most diligent, though, and I was reasonably sure he'd be known wherever he picked up his stock.

Jeff waited at the desk for the receptionist to finish his phone call. I scanned the bulletin board, empty save for a repressive list of what could and couldn't be posted. The thumbtacks had been globbed together at its empty centre.

When the man hung up he looked at Jeff as if he had just walked in. My partner asked about *Light in Darkness*. The receptionist selected a binder from the shelf behind him and placed it on the counter.

"What do you want to know?"

I let Jeff run this one. He said, striking just the right note of yuppie bashful: "We run this business, my partner and I. Lot of opportunities opening up. There's this guy we see 'round the neighbourhood selling calendars, really putting his heart into it. I tell my partner, who better to get in on the ground floor?"

A sympathetic nod from the receptionist.

"Only here's the thing." Jeff's voice went down to hit a desolate note. "We don't know his name—talk to this guy every other day, but… you know how it is."

"Sure," the desk clerk said.

"So we were wondering if you could help us out. We just want the guy to drop us a resumé. Don't need his address or anything, just his name."

"I'm not really supposed to—" the clerk began.

"Oh, totally. Like I said, no private info or anything. How would you describe him, Dave?"

"Short, hair long in the back, losing it up front. Caterpillar eyebrows."

Jeff nodded at me. "The main thing, the guy really puts an effort in."

The receptionist killed the beginnings of a smirk. "Think I know who you're talking about," he said. "May I give you a piece of advice?"

"Never turn it down," Jeff said.

"Mr. Boudreau might be enthusiastic on the street," the clerk said. "When dealing with others, though, he can be belligerent."

Jeff looked at me, a bit worried, like it had been my idea and he'd known from the start it was too good to be true. "Sounds like you got a story," he said.

The clerk gesticulated, taking in the room. "My job is simple. I dole the calendars out and record the signatures. That's all. I don't control when the deliveries are made. To Mr. Boudreau, you'd think I personally drove the truck into mid-morning traffic."

"You can't control that," said Jeff "Mr. Sympathy" Chen.

"Because I have quite a few other responsibilities."

"Of course."

"None of which matter to Mr. Boudreau. Mr. Boudreau has to have his calendars now. Or else I'm 'cutting into his profits.'" The clerk made finger quotes.

"You're just doing the guy a favour," Jeff said. "Tell you what. You probably did us one, warning us off this, what's his first name?"

"Gabriel."

"Right. Anyway, doesn't sound like he'll work out, does he, Dave?"

I started to shake my head, then qualify it with a shrug, well, maybe we should...

Jeff turned back to the desk, rolling his eyes. "My partner's gonna play philanthropist, waste my afternoon talking to this guy. Might as well give me his phone number, if it's not too much trouble. Hey, thanks. He live in the area? We could maybe drop by while we're in the neighbourhood..."

Walking out of the centre I handed Jeff the coffee cup. "Nicely done," I said. "The Chen System in action."

"Thanks. Where's yours?"

"Finished it while you were talking. Drink up and let's go."

He put the cup down on the top of the access ramp as he dialed for a cab. I thought for a second he might leave it there, untasted.

"You really think this guy's in on it?" he said.

I wasn't sure. Gabriel Boudreau had played some part in the scene—weeks later, with the memory beginning to lose definition, his image was still preserved in all its detail. He was picking the calendars out of the street, up Keefer, away from the doors.

He could be a full partner, or the one who put them on to the building. Or uninvolved and a witness. But there must have been some interaction between him and the people in the van, before the shooting commenced.

"Even if not, we'll want to make sure he's okay," I said. "Keep track of all the pieces. Drink up and let's go."

Jeff tucked his phone away, belted his coat. Only then did he take a sip of the frothy swill in his cup.

"The fuck—" The white foam washed down his chin. He coughed. His face seemed to be trying to retreat from his mouth.

"You think that's funny?" he said. "What was that?"

"Chai latte. Machine said 'barista quality—subtle flavour.'"

"Cinnamon, mucous and shit," said Jeff.

He shook his fist like a silent film villain.

"You'll fucking pay, Wakeland," he said. "Last thing I do."

FORTY-THREE
THE BALTIC

Gabriel Boudreau's address was the Baltic Hotel, an SRO that calculated its rents at sixty-five percent of the average assistance cheque. I'd been there a lot over the years. Jeff parked in back and we told the desk clerk we were here for Mr. Boudreau, room 27, he in today? She told us we were welcome to check.

The outside of the building had a weathered, rundown charm to it, set off by the vertical art deco sign. The inside was quaintly apocalyptic. Scars and scabs on the wallpaper, water stains. Closet-sized rooms with fold-out beds and hot plates. Washrooms at the end of the hall.

I remembered Nikki Frazer telling me Ryan had been called out here and nearly got stabbed. It didn't surprise me.

Polite knocks on Boudreau's door led to no response. I knocked louder. Someone in another room told me to shut the fuck up. "He ain't here."

"Where is he?" I called out.

"Fuck you," was the reply.

I tried the handle. Looking through the space in the warped door-frame I could see the light was on inside.

Jeff was trying Boudreau's phone one more time. We could hear its generic tone somewhere within the apartment.

The door had double locks but a slight pressure caused the frame to sink inward. I wouldn't be the first person to break down the door.

"Should we get the manager?" I said. I had little problem risking an infraction or invading Boudreau's privacy. A family man might not share my enthusiasm.

But Jeff said, "Go for it," and stood guard while I pushed. As I thought, the wood gave easily. Someone had busted in and then made cosmetic repairs, fitting the nails back into their holes.

Cockroaches on the floor skittered to the baseboards. The room had a fungal smell. A fold-down bed and cubbyhole shelving, a chair by the window and a TV tray but no television. On the wall, a rayon tapestry of a weeping bloody Jesus.

Surveying the few items of clothing on the shelves, I couldn't tell if the room had been evacuated, abandoned or had never held much to begin with. By the bed, a small pile of newspapers and one chipped coffee mug,

LOVE THY NEIGHBOURS

printed on the side.

The drawers held a flotsam of pencils and paperclips, government correspondence stuffed back into envelopes. No photos. There was a closet with a towel and toiletries kit. A cloth-sided suitcase of mid-seventies vintage.

"He didn't pack up," Jeff said.

On the windowsill, half a yardstick held up the greasy windowpane. A pair of votive candles on the sill. Paperbacks. *The Sackett Brand* by Louis L'Amour, *Runaway* by Evelyn Lau.

"What's missing?" I asked Jeff.

"Beats me. Can we get out of here? My shoes are sticking."

"Guy with a picture of Jesus on his wall, what's he gonna have with him for sure?"

We went back to the front desk and told the manager Boudreau's door was unlocked but he wasn't home. If she didn't believe us, she didn't make the effort to say so.

"You seen him around?" Jeff asked.

"You mean lately?" Her brow furrowed. "I guess not, actually. But then he's an early riser."

"He has a cart," I said. "Know where he keeps that?"

Her nod expressed aggravation—*do I ever*. "The storage is around back. He's not exactly quiet getting that thing out in the morning."

"And you haven't heard him do that recently."

"Not for... least a week or so, I guess."

"Can we take a look?" Jeff asked.

She pushed off her stool and led us outside. Locked the front door and walked around to the parking-lot side. It took some finesse for her to open a utility door with no handle and an odd-looking lock.

"'Sposed to be long-term storage," she said. "Gabe wanted to put his cart there—save him hauling it up to his room. Eventually we just gave him a key."

"He's pretty trustworthy?" I asked.

"I dunno."

"Any reason he can't take the cart up to his room?"

"His back," she said. "He told me he had some sort of disk problem. Scolio-something. Stubborn sonofa—here we go."

Inside were boxes, luggage, skis, half a bicycle. And prominently, next to the door, a wire-framed handcart with a canvas bag.

We unsnapped the top flap and loosened the drawstring. A neat stack of *Light in Darkness* calendars, and on top of them, a worn King James bible.

I handed the good book to Jeff and lifted out the calendars. Nothing else inside. Jeff flipped through the bible but no clues fell out.

Scanning the shelves on our way out, Jeff found a receipt and a storage key. The manager looked at the note and said it was Gabe's handwriting.

"It's for me," she said. "'Dear Sandra, going away for a while here's the key God bless p.s. don't let anyone touch my stuff.'"

She looked guiltily at us and led us out.

"He's not that bad a guy," she admitted. "Just particular about his things."

"You're on call, right?" I said. "Why wouldn't he drop this at your desk?"

"Maybe he didn't have time," she said.

"Or," Jeff said, "didn't want anyone seeing him come home."

FORTY-FOUR
NAMES OF THE DEAD

We had a late lunch at the Ovaltine, grilled cheese, fries and coffee. At some point in the afternoon the sky had chosen to force out every drop of liquid. Rain spilled off the awnings in a continuous sheet, coating the windows, puddling in the streets. People lingered in the diner, postponing their return to the deluge.

We'd taken a booth. I stretched out and yawned. The warmth was getting to me. I thought of the picture in the calendar, the faceless diner patron.

"Two possibilities," I said. "Boudreau's in on it."

"Guess you don't need your shaving kit when you got fifty grand," Jeff said.

"The other possibility being, he lit out after he saw them."

"He's afraid."

"I would be." I finished my tea. "I was."

Jeff accepted a refill, handed our empty plates off to the waitress. "I'd say it's the second."

"Me too. You first with your reasoning."

"The bible," he said. "I don't see him being involved in this. From what people say, Boudreau's the type that gets up every morning, then throws himself into his work." Jeff smiled and sipped his coffee, and I knew what was coming. "Like you," he added.

"Makes sense," I said. "But I get the feeling he wasn't always like this. Maybe it's an act."

"Yeah, maybe. But him putting the bible there, doing the right thing with the key, points to a conscience. A total skel would've tossed it and ran. What's your thinking, Dave?"

"When I saw him, he was up the sidestreet, away from the entrance. Away from the shooting."

I used a few sugar packets and creamers to diagram.

"Boudreau usually set up out front, here, near the corner. Get the foot traffic from the bus stop. But that day he's way out of place."

"On purpose?" Jeff asked.

"They moved him."

"The shooters did."

"Tossed his stuff in the street, away from the entrance." I slid the Boudreau packet ninety degrees around the napkin dispenser.

"Clear him out of the way," Jeff said.

"Which they wouldn't've done if he was in on it. If he was spotting for them, he'd've been closer, and he'd've hightailed when it started to go south."

"So we're both right for different reasons," Jeff said. "Big question, though, where is he now?"

I slid the packet to the edge of the table, left one end hanging over the side.

"These guys knew the area," I said. "If they knew we rented an office in a nearby building, they damn sure knew who set up shop out front."

"Which means what?" Jeff prompted.

"They drive away, lay low. Then if they start thinking about loose ends, they start with the guy they crossed before the shooting."

"So Boudreau's dead," Jeff said. "Or lamming it."

"Right."

"So maybe they're looking for him too."

I hadn't considered that.

"Even if they aren't," I said, "he might think they are. After the shooting he doesn't even go home. Maybe gets a taxi to drive him up to the storage shed, or a friend. He stows his cart, 'cause it's his life, then takes off for parts unknown."

"So we just have to find him," Jeff said. "Simple."

I watched him test a forkful of cherry pie, survive it and tear in.

"One more thing," Jeff said. "Maybe nothing. The victims inside the room—Huang, Zhou, Ma and Chang Chia-Yang."

"What about them?"

"Chia-Yang is Taiwanese style spelling," Jeff said. "The others are current Pinyin."

I looked at him. "I like to think I'm not totally ignorant about Sino-English nomenclature," I said. "But for the sake of argument, let's pretend I don't know what you mean."

"One name can be spelled different ways," Jeff said. "No spelling's really perfect but some are closer. Like Zhu, can be Z-H-U or C-H-U. Or C-H-O-O or C-H-E-W. But Zhu is pretty standard now."

"I'm with you," I said.

"You see older spellings with families that've been here a long time— *Louie* instead of *Lui*." He exaggerated the pronunciations to drive home the difference. "I'm simplifying the shit out of this, Dave, but sometimes how a name's spelled tells you where someone's from."

"So Huang and the others are more standard, but Chang isn't?"

"Could be nothing," Jeff said. "Could be he just liked that spelling. But y'know that song, which of these is not like the other…"

"Chang Chia-Yang is not the same."

"Right."

We pondered that. I watched him finish his pie. We lingered as long as we could, but there's only so long you can put off slipping back into a wet raincoat.

FORTY-FIVE
WITNESSES

I parted ways with Jeff at the office. He said he'd follow up on Chang and the other victims, leaving me to look for Boudreau. First, though, I owed a visit to Diane Cui. She'd been discharged from the hospital a few days ago. I was dreading this visit.

Before I left the office, I rummaged through the storage closet, found boxes of cameras, motion sensors and something called "the newest in coded-entry, deadbolt technology." Samples from a security professionals' conference Jeff had attended. No shortage of free gizmos in our line of work.

Augmenting my home security had never seemed all that important. I had no rare possessions, other than some aged bourbon and hard-to-find vinyl. And it was East Van—people came over the fence, smoked dope on the patio, occasionally rattled the handle of the sliding door. I hadn't seen the need to hermetically seal myself off from the neighbourhood.

Inside the front door of my apartment, I saw a Safeway bag full of Sonia's stuff, bath gel and cosmetics. Moving them back in. Any doubts I had faded, and I set to work. It took an hour, and I blew the fuse twice, but I installed the coded locks and set motion sensors and cameras to cover the patio.

I took the remaining boxes of gizmos next door and did the same job for Marty's place. My neighbour stood with Lea on his hip, wincing once when I gouged the wall.

We had coffee after. He told me they might move to the suburbs, probably Port Moody or the Sunshine Coast, depending on where Sami could get a transfer.

"We live on the ground floor," Marty said, in a tone that acknowledged the realities that went with that. "We lock our doors, take precautions, but I know it's always a possibility, someone decides to break in. I accept it, y'know? But this..."

He shivered. In the living room, Lea took two quick steps, falling onto all fours, giggling. Marty held his arms out, come to me.

"I never thought I'd be shot at," he said. "With my child in my arms. I really don't know what's happening to this city."

I looked at the family photo on the fridge, Marty and his husband and daughter at the PNE Fairgrounds, Lea holding a plastic sack of blue cotton candy.

The lies are catching up to us, I wanted to say. *A city founded on racism and land theft, that lets people die on the street and pretends it never happened. No matter how much yoga wear we sell, how many killer whale statues we put up. We're not separate from the history of the west. Vancouver is just where the west ends.*

But I said none of that to the frightened father, mouthing instead encouraging words about how safe we were. Peace of mind is fragile, and not always based in fact. Marty thanked me and said he hoped I was right. Neither of us would probably ever look at the electronic security display as a source of comfort. If anything, it would be a reminder of how safe we weren't.

Diane Cui lived in a four-storey red brick building that had once been a warehouse. A two-block walk from where she and her daughter caught the bus every morning. To Diane that life must have felt mythical and lost, part of a long-gone once upon a time.

When I buzzed her, a voice told me Diane was sick and resting. I explained my purpose. The voice said she'd be right down.

Standing in the lobby, watching the elevator, I felt unprepared and empty-handed. What do you bring someone who's convalescing and bereaved? What can you really do?

The elevator let out a tall, Black woman who introduced herself as Adele Niang, Ms. Cui's private nurse. She said if I was quick and didn't agitate her, I could have a brief visit. The nurse warned me that her patient had been tranquilized and was still in a lot of pain.

She drew her hand across her belly. "They removed part of her intestine."

Diane Cui's apartment was on the third floor, facing the alley. The thermostat was cranked to a sweltering heat. The living room had an ornamental fireplace, its mantelpiece cluttered with photos. Jingjing Cui smiled out from a dozen frames.

I waited while Nurse Niang prepared Diane. The photos captured the trajectory of a life. Diane holding a baby, a grey-haired man's arm around them both. Childhood through graduation. She'd been what, twenty-two? So fucking young. I hadn't gotten my shit together until I was past her age. That meant I'd spent more time adrift than she'd been granted in total. Judging by the smiles in the photo, at least there had been happy moments.

The nurse called. I entered the bedroom, where the lights were off and thick oatmeal-coloured curtains blocked out the world. Diane lay in bed. She waved slightly and smiled at me, but there was nothing behind either gesture. She'd been weakened by injury and hollowed out, cored, by grief.

I stumbled through a few remarks about how sorry I was. If she remembered me, it was only vaguely and without strong emotion. I asked if we could talk about what she'd seen.

Diane sighed and looked at the ceiling, but the smile didn't leave her face. Nurse Niang touched her brow. The injured woman spoke quietly.

"We see the van, waiting. Hear loud…" Diane made soft gunshot sounds, each fading into the next, *keee, keee, keee*. "Jingjing look, and the man, he…"

What sounded like the start of a belly laugh erupted into a deep-pitched, shuddering sob. Pure anguish, dying out in a fit of feeble coughs.

Diane regained her drugged composure. The awful smile returned.

I asked if she'd seen the shooters before. No. Had she seen a man with calendars standing across the street? She couldn't remember. Ever been inside that building, or seen anything strange happen there? She shook her head, eyes closing. Nurse Niang said that was enough.

On my way out, as I laced up my shoes, I mentioned to the nurse that Ms. Cui must be all right financially. Home health care was expensive.

"She has good friends," the nurse said.

"One of them covering your costs?"

The nurse's shoulders locked in a pose of indignation. "Why do you care?"

"Just if she needs anything else," I said. "She have any other visitors? Maybe an older man named Long?"

"Her business," Nurse Niang said pointedly, "is not your business."

True enough. If Roy Long felt like paying Diane Cui's nursing bills, that proved generosity as much as a sense of guilt. Maybe she'd talked to him in detail about what she'd seen. Or maybe I was her only visitor.

I left Diane Cui to her sickbed, to her nurse, to the mantelpiece shrine to her daughter. I took the stairs down, wondering if finding the shooters would mean anything to her. Jingjing was lost, another victim of the city, and the details were irrelevant.

In the end you lose everyone.

FORTY-SIX
RELIANCE

"Wakeland," said the voice on the phone. "Know who this is?"

"Nuh."

"I'm outside your door. Wake the fuck up."

I held the phone away from me and yawned. The digits said 3:40. I couldn't place the voice, but it was male, angry and urgent.

Sonia muttered next to me, turning away from the soft glow of the screen.

"What's this about?" I said. "It's three—"

"—don't give a shit what time it is. Buzz me the fuck in."

I sat up. A feeling like a cold hand pressing against my collarbone sobered me. The voice belonged to one of Rhodes's men, the redhead with the beard.

I struggled into my jeans and buzzed him in, then stood in the hallway as Redbeard approached.

"Took you fucking long enough," he said, his voice thunderous in the hall.

"Some tea?" I asked. "It's a little late for a caffeine boost, but let's make an exception."

"We don't have time for that shit." Redbeard was dressed in a denim jacket over jeans, steel toe boots. No weapons in sight. I held the door for him. He shoved past me, walking straight into the barrel of Sonia's service weapon.

"Hey now," he said, in a much less dictatorial tone.

She beckoned him inside and I closed the door behind us.

"You won't shoot," he said.

Her posture and expression didn't change. Redbeard's shoulders slumped and he sighed, petulant, a kid warned by his teacher not to misbehave.

"What do you want with Dave?" Sonia said.

"'Sposed to take him somewhere." Reluctantly adding, "This apartment close to False Creek. 'Sposed to meet someone there."

"Who?" Sonia said.

"Not 'sposed to use his name. Says if we use his name to anyone he doesn't tell us to, we get hurt."

"Who," Sonia repeated, a nasty smile on her sleep-deprived face.

"Terry Rhodes," Redbeard said.

I finished dressing and filled the kettle. Put it on the stove and brought the stainless steel teapot out of the cupboard.

"He just wants to talk," Redbeard said. "That's all I know."

Sonia looked over at me. "I should probably see what he wants," I said.

She told Redbeard, "You're in charge of making sure he gets home. You personally, understand? Anything happens, it's on you."

"Hey," Redbeard said, "I just do what I'm told."

The smile returned to Sonia's face.

"Exactly," she said.

Redbeard steered the Avalanche down Kingsway, which slashed diagonally across the city grid. We entered what had been a light industry area, warehouses and storage lockers, but was now dominated by a cluster of bullshit high-rises with bullshit names. As we drove past Chad's Auto Repair, I saw the silent red and blue lights of parked patrol cars. I asked if we were heading to a crime scene.

Instead he made two lefts and dropped me at the side entrance to a tower called The Reliance.

"Buzz 712," he said.

I did and was let in, and took the elevator up to the seventh floor. The elevator was locked down, one way, no stopping anywhere but seven. Guests weren't trusted with the run of the building.

The door to 712 was propped open. I pushed past the two giants, now out of their leather and wearing dress pants and charcoal blazers, off the rack from Mr. Big & Tall. They carried aluminum softball bats.

The apartment had parquet floors and stainless-steel appliances, mirrors on the closet doors, all the trappings used to remind the owners that two million dollars was a fair price for a one bedroom with a view of False Creek. In the kitchenette, a rattled-looking man made single-serve coffees, holding the flaps of a salmon-coloured bathrobe around his midsection.

Terry Rhodes stood on the balcony, smoking a cigar and tapping ash into a bone china teacup. His eyes had thick purple-black slugs clinging below them.

"Big Dave," he said. "What do you know about this?"

I looked down and across the street, wondering if being dangled over the balcony would alert some of the police below.

"Get him a coffee," he called to the man in the kitchen. I gathered the man had little say in what was going on.

Rhodes pointed down at Chad's. "I've been taking my bikes there thirty years. Before the idiot son took over. Never missed a payment, never fucked up a repair."

"Someone bust up the place?" I asked.

"Left a body there. Fucking calling card."

I squinted, seeing only lights and patrol officers, the forensics crew suiting up for evidence collection.

"Calling card from who?" I asked.

"Slopes, I guess. Smashed up her hands just like the other."

"Her," I said.

"Not a whore, either, what I saw." He lobbed the stub of the cigar over, left the teacup and walked inside.

"Chad calls me first. We take a look and see this bitch laid out on the hood of some rice-burner. Shot in the chest. Hands like spaghetti. Can't figure the angle on it. One of my crew, I'd understand, but her?"

The coffee was some caramel-hazelnut abomination, offered by a trembling hand. I took a sip to be polite.

"One of the shooters was a woman named Shelly Axton," I said. No harm giving her up if she was dead.

Rhodes was incredulous. "A fucking *girl* robbed Uncle Roy Long?"

"If it's Axton, this is a message from someone who thinks you hired her."

"Like Roy himself," Rhodes said. "Or his asshole homeboy son." He spat on the carpet, then paced back toward the balcony. "Felix Long's the toughest little rich kid I ever met. He thinks he can fuck with me, though."

To steer him away from his fantasies of revenge I said, "You know who shot at me the other night?"

Rhodes looked puzzled for a moment, then his mood lightened. "I heard about that—.22s. Why not just throw little pink dildoes at you?"

"One .22 to the back of the head is all it takes," I said.

"So consider yourself lucky." Turning back to the scene below. "Got my own problems here."

We watched the techs in their bunny suits enter the garage. Some trace of Rhodes would be there. He didn't seem that worried.

The man making coffee came out with an extra cup and scooped the empties off the railing. He looked down at the cops below for a second, tantalized. Rhodes inclined his head, *back inside*. The man scurried.

"Nice of him to invite you up to share the view," I said.

"He'll do all right out of this. You, though. What've you got on these people?"

"You wanted me on them," I said. "I'm on them."

"But what d'you have now?"

"Nothing."

He was growling, staring at me.

"I'm not going to waste your time with anything I haven't verified," I said. "We both want them found. I'm on it. What can you do to help me?"

That stopped him. Rhodes, flummoxed, let himself move from front line to tactician. He deflated a bit. His anger took an inward turn.

"Nobody's been spending that count room cash," he said. "No one's talking it up either. Means they're pros, and they know how to keep their mouths shut." He lit another cigar, adding, "Wish I *did* hire 'em."

A weird thought struck me. Rhodes, with his ear to the street, might have a different perspective on the official investigation.

"What have you heard about the police response?" I asked. "Typical homicide?"

He gestured down at the lights, see for yourself.

"I mean big picture," I said. "How wide are they casting the net? How enthusiastic has the canvass been?"

"They're knocking on doors. Lot of pressure to solve this." Rhodes looked down, trying to glean something new from the pavement figures. "You don't think cops were involved."

"I don't think anything yet."

"I've known some dirty fucking cops," Rhodes said. "They'll help themselves to a share of what you rob, but doing it themselves? Doesn't fit their style."

"You're probably right."

"So why fucking ask?"

Salmon Bathrobe appeared at the balcony door, holding yet another cup. He offered it to me, smiling like a condemned man at a judge. I wanted to tell him I knew how he felt.

Rhodes took the cup and didn't look at him. Salmon Bathrobe slunk back inside.

"Cops must live for shit like this," Rhodes said. "Must beat shaking down hypes and bangers."

"Or upstanding citizens like us."

Rhodes stabbed his cigar into the cup, the force sending the cup and saucer pitching over into the black. We were too high up to hear a crash.

"Think they can fuck with me."

FORTY-SEVEN
THE FALLS

No ride home was forthcoming. I left the building through the side exit and walked to my office. The sun was coming up, backlighting the Coast Mountains in violet and amber hues. The only other people on the street wore hospital scrubs or high-vis construction vests.

I phoned Sonia and told her I made it out unscathed.

"That's good, love," she said. "Don't forget your appointment."

Her catch was that I meet with her friend the counsellor. I'd agreed to it—I would've agreed to anything to keep her with me.

There hadn't been any paralyzing flashbacks in the last few days, fewer bloody visions. Maybe the case's momentum kept me from dwelling on what I'd seen. Like a cartoon character racing over the cliff's edge but not looking down. It was only when you realize that the fall is inevitable that you begin to plummet.

So keep busy, and don't look down.

Gabriel Boudreau, the Calendar Man, had been featured on the *Light in Darkness* website, interviewed about how the program gave him purpose and helped him turn his life around. He mentioned addiction and alcoholism, the forgiveness of Christ and how it was necessary to take each day as it comes.

A search of provincial court rulings hit pay dirt. A G. Boudreau had been sentenced to fifteen years in prison for manslaughter, had appealed after four and again successfully after six. He was sixty-three now, and had been out for almost a decade. The victim had been Connie Boudreau, thirty-six, his wife.

A paroled murderer at the scene of a multiple homicide. I didn't know what to make of that.

Boudreau lived downtown, and odds were he worshipped in his neighbourhood. I started at Burrard and worked east, interrupting choir practice at St. Andrew's-Wesleyan, catching the tail end of the food service at the Gospel Mission on Carrall.

I knew some of the pastors to say hi to. I'd made the rounds looking for other people over the years. A few trusted me, to the point they'd break confidence to put me in touch with a runaway teen. Others regarded me as yet another interloper, well-intentioned perhaps, but in pursuit of something other than salvation.

I knew when I walked into the Sacred Heart that this was Gabe Boudreau's choice. Ground floor, tucked between a pawn shop and a Portuguese grocery, folding chairs stacked in the corner and a coffee urn atop a scarred side table. On the door, a list of service times and programs.

The minister was a volunteer and a harm reduction advocate named Perry. I was a fan of hers. The kind of person who could shame a politician off a podium for failing to support safe injection sites, then smother the needy in attention and home-baked goods. More than that, be genuine doing both, because both came naturally.

Bran muffins on the table today. She was talking informally with a couple in the far corner. I stuffed a ten in the parmesan cheese tube that served as a donation box and bought myself breakfast.

Perry saw the couple to the door, hugged them. She turned to me with the resignation that suggested today's efforts might be wasted. That didn't make the effort unworthy, just difficult to sustain.

"Dave," she said, shaking my hand. "After another stray?"

I'd barely mentioned Boudreau's name before Perry cut me off. "I've been wondering for days what's happened to him. Gabe rarely misses the early service."

"I think he's running from someone," I said. I described the shooting, leaving Boudreau's involvement ambiguous.

"When I saw it on the news, I remember thinking, that's Gabe's area. Who are you looking for? I mean, on behalf of?"

"A client very invested in finding the shooters. Gabe might have witnessed them. They might know that."

"And he's hiding," Perry said. "How much danger is he in?"

I sketched out my run-in with Kent. Perry shook her head throughout.

"Horrible," she said. "You know Gabe?"

"Just by sight, and a few early morning words."

"If you know the guy, you know violence isn't in him anymore. He's worked so hard."

I filed away the *anymore*. "If you know where he is," I said, "or can get a message to him."

"I don't, but if Gabe shows up, I have your number."

She called me back as I was leaving. "Dave. You know about his wife, right?"

"Just read about the trial this morning."

"Some people come here reluctantly," Perry said, "by discovering the kind of rock bottom most of us couldn't dream of. Gabe is like that. He's a different man now. I'd venture to say, a good man."

Tell that to his wife, I thought, but said, "Hope so."

"People do change."

Sure. And change back, for reasons unfathomable to the rest of us. Either Boudreau was a part of the shooting, a spotter, maybe, or he'd stumbled into this like I had. Either way, he needed to be found, and now.

FORTY-EIGHT
THE NEON CALL

I forget what was demolished to put up the Waterfront Casino. But there it was, a long dull rectangle on the northern shore of False Creek, aproned with long-term parking. Less the glittering jewel the pamphlets had promised than another tacky coin box more fitting for smalltown Washington State.

It's a grand hustle I never caught the urge for. Cage lighting and velvet and a wasteland of gaudy, squawking, reverse cash machines. Not even the enticement of coins and bills shifting hands. Just diminishing slips of barcoded paper.

But up above the floor, in the private salons, you saw real opulence and real despair. I'd once worked a security detail for a woman who'd walked in with seven hundred thousand in cash and a guaranteed line of credit. It had taken three days, but they'd got it all from her, shuffling her among the salons and private rooms, her fortunes up and down, up, down, then out. I'd bought her breakfast the morning of day four.

Chang Chia-Yang's brother worked in one of the salons dealing poker, Big Two, Pai Gow, Heaven Nine. The salons were themed: the Vegas, the Monte Carlo, the Macao. All varieties of hedonism umbrellaed under one roof. Chang Yan-Ting dealt in the Macao and was shortly due for his lunch break.

A junket of seniors arrived, all women, a sixty-forty split between white and Asian. They took in the casino floor like penitents at a cathedral, making loud plans about pacing themselves or checking the room. The book says always look around first before picking your machine.

Most slid down into the penny slots near the entrance. My mother would have fit right in.

I cashed a twenty and threw bets at a blackjack dealer whose luck was about the same as mine. Seventeen beat sixteen. Twenty and bust. I cashed out as soon as Jeff walked away from the cage.

He avoiding looking at the tables and machines, waiting for me in the alcove where the ATMs were, a stranded coffee trolley nearby.

"Any luck?" I said.

"Should ask you that."

I held up the paper slip. "Broke the bank. Thinking of turning pro."

"Yeah, good. Let's walk outside."

We did, passing between the red lion statues that guarded the front gate. Once outside, Jeff said, "Yan-Ting's due to come off shift in half an hour. He'll talk if we buy the drinks. Not here, though. There's a bar in the hotel next door."

We ordered coffee in the hotel lounge, drawing the bartender's ire. We brought our drinks to a corner with a view of the door. A piano player wedged Oscar Peterson runs into Billy Joel and Blondie.

"Roy Long have an interest in the Waterfront Casino?" I asked.

"I don't know what he does or doesn't." Jeff bent the plastic stir stick between his fingers. "Wouldn't surprise me."

There had been gambling dens in Chinatown, not the opulent night-clubs of years ago, but working-class places where you could bet on a horse or a lucky number, grab a cheap dinner, be among your own. In the wake of legalized gambling and online poker, those places had faded. If the Longs had a piece of the Waterfront Casino, that gave them legitim-acy, as well as opportunities to launder money. It also put Long in with the viper's nest of politicians and developers who ran the city.

"You should have kids," Jeff said, breaking my reverie.

"That's rather forward of you. What would my father think?"

"You don't have a father," Jeff said.

"Ouch. Why bring this up now?"

"I see you looking around at this place like it makes you sick. You care too much about things you can't change. Having kids is good for that. Clears up your priorities."

"Wouldn't it make you more concerned, watching the place you live change?"

"There are other places to live," Jeff said.

"So just stay till it gets shitty, then bail?"

"What d'you think your ancestors did? Or is Wakeland an Indigenous name."

"You have a responsibility to the place you live, not to fuck it up."

"Bullshit."

"Bullshit—you think it's okay to watch things go to hell?"

"No, but it's not changing just 'cause you don't like it."

Jeff gestured toward the entrance, where a gaudy bus let off two dozen elderly women in the turnaround. More junketeers, eager to get inside the casino.

"You can't fight it," Jeff said. "Can't really look at it as a fight, actually. Just have to accept that shit mostly won't go your way."

"And have kids," I said.

"Before you're too old."

"Says the voice of maturity and wisdom, who's three years older than me."

"You can pack a lot of wisdom into three years," Jeff said.

I drank my free refill and noted how Jeff watched the junket buses. He'd hurried away from the casino like someone susceptible to the neon call. Maybe the talk of kids was his way of weighing all he had from the straight and narrow against his temptations.

A man walked into the lobby, paunchy and waxen-faced. Jeff flagged him over. He was in the black-suit-black-shirt-red-tie uniform of the salon dealers. Name tag pinned to his breast, ANSON.

Jeff made room for him in the booth. Chang Yan-Ting ordered a double scotch and soda and a basket of fries. Jeff and I ordered beers to be sociable. Chang worked through the peanut dish as he waited for his drink.

"So yeah," he said. "Something about my brother. You looking for the killers—why you interested now?"

"We're good citizens," I said.

Jeff's hand raised from the tabletop, slid left. His signal to let him lead.

He said to me, "Yan-Ting's brother worked for a friend of ours. There's no reason for what happened. We all want to find answers. Dave, I could use a clean glass."

"No problem, buddy."

I took our beers to the bar and waited. Jeff's posture had changed from the non-threatening slouch in which he greeted witnesses, to a more authoritative demeanor. At the same time, he'd staked out an Asian connection with Yan-Ting, with me as the negative third. *Let's us two get down to business, now that I've sent my* gwai lo *employee away.*

It was a good strategy, well-deployed, and Jeff played his role like a young Montgomery Clift. For that reason, it rankled me a bit. I sat and finished the beers and waited for Jeff to wave me over.

He'd also alluded to Roy Long, letting Yan-Ting think he might be our client. *Jeff's* client. The fetch-it insult might have triggered it, but a thought came to me that I was being played. As I watched, Jeff was telling Chang Yan-Ting to feed me some bullshit, let me think I'm close. It was an unworthy thought, and I dismissed it, but it had had its moment.

FORTY-NINE
THE COUNT ROOM

Jeff worked on Chang Yan-Ting for twenty minutes before signalling me to bring fresh drinks. I did, another double scotch, a beer for Jeff, nothing for me.

Once I sat down, Jeff said, "Yan-Ting's brother was in charge of the count room. Before that he was a counter at a casino in Richmond. Yan-Ting got him the job."

"He was scary good," the brother said. "Could count thousand, hundred thousand, million, like that." He snapped his fingers. "Could spot fakes too. That good."

"He lost the casino job after he took responsibility for someone else's mistake." Jeff paused to see I'd caught his meaning. "It was unfair."

"Total bullshit," Yan-Ting agreed.

"But Chia-Yang had good *guanxi*, and ended up with a job at a smaller casino." Again, checking to see I followed. "He also ended up overseeing the count room as a favour to a friend. More specifically, the son of a friend."

"It's good to know people," I said. "How did it work?"

"It was a roving count," Jeff said, "a different location each week. Money from different sources would come in. Different currencies. Lots of small bills. Chia-Yang started out as one guy on a crew. After a year he was put in charge. Vincent Ma—Lee Hun Ma—started at the same time as Chia-Yang. They were friends."

Jeff looked at Yan-Ting for confirmation. The brother nodded.

"Vincent's a smooth guy," he said. "Liked to hit the club. Always talking 'bout his connections, what a tough guy he is. Why Chia-Yang end up in charge."

"What about the other two?" I asked. "Zhou and Huang?"

"New guys," Yan-Ting said. "Never met 'em. 'Bout four months ago, his boss says get rid of your guys, I got new ones coming in. My brother took care of his people. But Fel—his boss, be all like, 'Teach these guys be as good as you.' Like a compliment. Can't say no."

"Were they working out?" I asked.

Yan-Ting shrugged and gazed vacantly at the empty tumblers in front of him. The ice had dwindled to small silver scales. There was a grief threatening to bubble up through his bluster and patter, a disintegrating despair he kept back by biting down on his lower lip, staring at nothing.

He said, "I got another four-hour shift about to start."

"Of course," said Jeff. "We're almost done. You were talking about Zhou and Huang."

"I just know what Chia-Yang told me. He said Huang was okay, just do his job and go home. Zhou he thought might be on drugs. My brother wanted his own guys, but Felix told him he had to."

"Any guess why?" I asked.

"My brother got hired 'cause he's the best," Yan-Ting said, again mauling his lip. "But he thought they maybe don't trust him."

"Anyone ever threaten your brother?" Jeff asked.

"Sure." Yan-Ting tapped his name tag. "Dealer gets used to threats. Goes with the job."

"But no enemies you know of?"

"Not Chia-Yang."

"Thanks for your time," Jeff said.

"You get that sonofabitch, okay?"

We watched him leave, pausing to straighten his uniform by the mirrored pillar near the doors. You had to be impartial as a dealer, bland and unreadable and a mechanic with your cards and tiles. And neutral, of course. As neutral as the Fates.

FIFTY
MEANINGFUL CHANGE

Jeff's theory was that one of Chang Chia-Yang's original crew had passed along details of the count room to the shooters. Disgruntled and out of work, that person had let slip where, when and how the room would be guarded. If it was true, that meant a line of communication existed from that person to Kent and the others. Jeff wanted to run with that lead, and without saying so, made it clear he'd get better results on his own.

Which left me Boudreau. I spent the afternoon talking to *Light in Darkness* vendors on street corners around the city. None of them had seen Boudreau in the last two weeks. All of them were glad of it. He was universally described as a pain in the ass. Subspecies of pain in the ass included: a straight-up asshole, a try-too-hard, a loudmouth, pushy, scruffy, preachy and phony. Gabe Boudreau had carved a strange niche for himself out of capitalism and charity, and didn't mind losing friends to do so.

No one I spoke to had seen Boudreau act physically violent. No close friends. No secret addictions. No neighbourhood spots where he liked to hang out.

Either he was with the shooters or hiding from them. Or dead. Each scenario painted a different portrait of Boudreau.

In the office, I dropped the half-dozen calendars I'd purchased onto the reception desk and took my laptop into the boardroom. I read through the archives of the *Alaska Highway News*, piecing together the story of Boudreau and his wife, starting with the first mention of their names.

The death of Connie Boudreau, 36, has been ruled a homicide. Mrs. Boudreau was found by a neighbour in her home, having been struck multiple times about the face and hands. She was admitted to Fort St. John Hospital, where she died Sunday from complications resulting from her injuries.

A part-time veterinary assistant and fixture at Queen Elizabeth Secondary School stage band fundraisers, Boudreau is remembered as "a real jewel of a person" by her neighbours. She is survived by her husband, Gabriel, and daughter Olivia. A spokesman for the RCMP says the investigation is a priority...

A week later, from the same organ of public record:

Charges have been laid in the death of Connie Boudreau, which occurred on May 8th. Gabriel Boudreau, the deceased's husband, was taken into custody this morning after a brief pursuit by RCMP officers. Boudreau, 44, unemployed, worked for more than twenty years in the forestry sector, most recently as a senior logging technician for Logan-McDevitt Industries. Boudreau has been charged with second-degree murder, as well as one count each of battery and drunk and disorderly. Mr. Boudreau's hearing will be this Friday.

Boudreau served six years of a ten-year sentence in Matsqui after pleading to manslaughter. Connie's family presented an impact statement to the court during sentencing: "This man is remorseless, and because of him we are robbed of our loving daughter, sister and niece."

"Robbed" of someone described as a "real jewel." Odd choice of words to measure a life. But then what could words get across?

No further mention of Olivia Boudreau, no one by that name in the Fort St. John directory. I wondered if Boudreau might be in contact with his daughter. Almost sixteen years had passed. Hard to say what their relationship was like, if in fact they had one.

At half past six I met Sonia's friend, the counsellor, at her office on Mel-ville Street, a few blocks west of Wakeland & Chen. Dr. Miyami Shibata was twenty-eight and beautiful, accredited by SUNY Albany and UBC, and looked as far removed from personal grief and trauma as a cosmet-ics model. That made it hard to trust her. Fighting the impulse to hide behind the imaginary wall of you-can't-possibly-understand-what-I've-been-through, I told her the truth. At the end of my recitation, I sprang the jackpot question on her: can you help me?

"Your symptomology isn't uncommon," Dr. Shibata said. "I've had success with people who've dealt with worse."

"Cured them."

"I'm uncomfortable with that term, but most people learn to func-tion better and gain some measure of control."

"That's why I'm here," I said. "Control."

Dr. Shibata looked at her notepad, back at me. "Some people view counselling as a means of self-understanding. Fulfillment."

"I know who I am," I said.

"And who is that?"

I thought how best to answer.

"An educable brute," I said.

She waited for me to elaborate.

"There's a way to be in the world. When I hold to that, the world makes sense to me. My part of it, anyway."

"And the rest of the world?"

I shrugged. "'Here be dragons.'"

Dr. Shibata nodded. "This isn't an easy process, but if you're willing to work at it, I'd like to help."

The consultation seemed designed to end there. I told her I'd think about it. Before I left I asked if she could advise me on something else. A case.

"That's not really my realm of expertise," Dr. Shibata said.

"Call it a philosophical question. Someone kills their spouse, goes away for it. When they come out, they get a job. They work hard, a decade passes and everyone seems to think they're no longer a threat."

"Are you asking me whether or not it's possible for someone to change?"

"No," I said, amending it to, "sort of. This person showed up at the scene of another violent act, unconnected to what he'd done before. At least it looks that way. My question is, does it make sense to assume he's a part of it? Isn't it farfetched to put it down to coincidence?"

"I wouldn't call it farfetched at all," Dr. Shibata said. "You're no stranger to violence, from what I've heard. Why would we assume that predisposes you to avoid it entirely in the future? In fact, perhaps it's more likely to draw you in."

"That doesn't make me feel better," I said.

"No," Dr. Shibata said, "I imagine not."

FIFTY-ONE
RIP TYDE

Overnight, the Wakeland & Chen boardroom had become crammed with stacks of wall panels, tiles, replacement doors and cans of paint and primer. The table had been shifted to an odd diagonal that cut the room in half. Five people could barely fit side by side, with little in the way of elbowroom. Hard to maintain a Knights of the Round Table vibe when you're forced to array like the Last Supper.

It was Sonia's day off, and she accompanied me, if only to see what my lunacy had wrought. Kay and Blatchford were early, and Jeff was right on time. No donuts this morning, only weak coffee, made with the last scoop and a half of drip fine grind.

Jeff went first. The disgruntled count-room personnel theory was a dead end. Jeff had asked about former count-room cashiers, been given two names. One lived in Toronto now. The other was enrolled at BCIT, working toward his electrician's ticket. When I suggested that forty grand might help finance his education, Jeff shot me down.

"He's not the type," he said.

"How can you be sure?"

"Talking to him, he seemed pretty remorseful."

"Maybe he didn't anticipate there'd be shooting."

"It's not him, Dave."

Jeff's expression told me not to push him on this. I let it go for now.

"How about the vics?" I said. "Huang, Zhou, Ma, Chang."

"Chang Chia-Yang was arrested for fraud. He was implicated in scamming the casino he worked for. The place fired him, but he wasn't charged. No criminal record."

"The others?"

"Vincent Ma has a sealed juvenile record," Jeff said. "As an adult, a couple DUIs. Nothing on Huang. Multiple vehicle infractions and a suspended licence for Zhou. The last two were moved into the count operation a few weeks before the robbery. Chang wasn't happy to have them, but it was on Felix Long's orders."

"Any idea why?" Blatchford said. He grimaced as he tasted his coffee.

Jeff was silent.

My turn. I went over Gabe Boudreau's trial and sentencing transcripts. I still didn't know where Boudreau fit into this. How much had he reformed? How strong was the temptation, after years of scraping out a living selling calendars, to make a play for easy money?

I finished by saying, "By all accounts Boudreau has been clean since he was paroled. A hard worker and a religious convert."

"Which could mean nothing," Sonia said. She'd grown upset after hearing how little time Boudreau had served for beating his wife to death.

"Assuming he's not working with the shooters, or dead, Boudreau is likely hiding out. He doesn't have a lot of money, and with his record he probably won't try to cross the border. There's a daughter he might get in touch with, but if not, I'm betting a friend helped him get out of the city."

"If he did get out," Sonia said. "How can you be sure?"

"Just a feeling. Boudreau is a creature of habit. If he's in town, he'd probably drift back into his familiar routines."

"Your feeling and four bucks will buy a coffee."

"Long as it's better than this shit," Blatchford said.

Kay interrupted us. "Can I go now?"

She had held back, fidgeting, going over her notes. Now she began her rundown of Rudy Czechowski's military history, her voice rushing to get to her grand reveal. Stumbling a bit, backtracking, trying to be thorough. Blatchford looked on with pride.

"Shelly Axton was also in the military," Kay said. "Like Czechowski, she also worked in security. They served in different units and worked in different states, for different companies. Their lives don't really overlap."

"Veterans society?" I asked.

"Way, way better. Her husband Percy is a vet too. Again, no connection with Czechowski. There's only one thing they have in common." Kay paused to soak it in, and said with satisfaction, "Rip Tyde."

The name didn't produce the thunderbolt of recognition she'd hoped for. Kay plowed forward.

"Rip Tyde International does overseas security," she said. "Contract work. Kind of a private army. They were in the news a lot during the Middle East stuff, a bunch of controversy over whether or not the Americans should use them."

"That was a different company," I said, trying to recall the name. "Seven Hills, wasn't it?"

Kay nodded. "Seven Hills had billions in government contracts— 'civilian contractors' was the term. They got a lot of bad press for an incident where an Iraqi man died at one of their checkpoints. That pretty much ruined their good name."

Blatchford made a mock sign of the cross over the corpse of Seven Hills Security.

"But here's the thing," Kay said. "John Laidlaw, the CEO of Seven Hills, changed the company name before he sold it. Then he started another company, sold that one. Now he consults for both. His firm is called Rip Tyde."

"Interesting sleight of hand." I looked at Jeff. "Let's hope we can shuffle Wakeland & Chen that successfully, one of us ever ruins our reputation."

"Guess which of us my money'd be on," Jeff said.

"Laidlaw doesn't take meetings," Kay said, impatient to get back to her report. "I mean, unless you're on the Joint Chiefs of Staff. So I can't totally confirm this. But."

Here she unfolded an elegant, painstakingly diagrammed chart of all the companies that had once been Seven Hills. Three pieces of printer paper scotch-taped end to end.

"Czechowski worked for Mountain Sec Corp, which is their Tennessee branch. Shelly Axton worked for White Knight, which turned into Good Knight Security, based in Dearborn, Michigan. And her husband Percy"—Kay tapped the centre of the page, the bull's eye—"Rip Tyde, their home base in Raleigh, North Carolina. It's possible, Dave, all the shooters worked for this company, or some variation."

"Excellent work," Jeff told her.

She blushed and aw-shucks-ed, and gave Blatchford too much credit. It was excellent work, as good or better than I could do. But it raised a very ugly question.

"All these branches," I said, pointing at the chart, "are all based in the Eastern US. Rip Tyde specializes in international military operations. Overseas and government funded."

"So what the fuck are they doing in Vancouver," Sonia said, on behalf of everybody.

PART THREE:
MY BUSINESS ALONE

FIFTY-TWO
GIFT EXCHANGE

The second I got my debts in order, I bought a Cadillac. It was a black ATS with a rebuilt engine and enough mileage on it that even the salesman had blushed. But I'd wanted it, I'd had the money and I felt I could justify it as a business expense.

The car had given me six years of reasonably faithful service before Kent stole it. When, ten minutes after our staff meeting, Jeff phoned me from the office parkade to ask if I'd bought a new car, I told him I hadn't had time to even consider it.

"Thought not," he said. "You should come down here."

"The parkade?"

"You'll want to see this."

Parked next to my rental Saab was a gleaming new Cadillac Blackwing in metallic gold. Jeff pointed at the note under the wiper blade, my name on it.

From a friend. Enjoy.

Up close I saw nicks and abrasions on the side mirror housing, slight wear on the mismatched tires. The odometer was digital, but I doubted it would read absolute zero.

"What do you think?" I asked Jeff.

"It's a nice car."

"Gold's not really my colour," I said.

"Mine neither."

"Whose colour you think it is?"

Jeff unbuttoned his blazer and crouched near the rear fender. He ran his finger along the seam, which showed two slightly different shades of gold. Someone had swapped out parts, maybe exchanged vehicle identification numbers.

"It's Felix Long," Jeff said.

He stood and smartened his jacket. Knowing Jeff's connection to the Longs, I knew his response—our response—had to be delicate. Jeff circled the car once more as he made his decision.

"We'll take it back to him," he said.

The car had no licence plate, but it would only be a seven-minute drive along side streets and speed-controlled residential lanes. We popped onto Main Street long enough to spin into the parking garage below the Red Lantern.

"Could this be on his father's behalf?" I asked.

"Not likely," Jeff said. "Sometimes Felix works with his dad, but his gang is his gang. It's separate."

"What are they called?"

"Red Snakes."

"For a gang name, that's not bad."

Instead of entering the dining room, we waited by the reservation stand at the entrance. Jeff instructed the hostess to bring Felix Long. Judging from Jeff's tone he wasn't asking politely.

When the hostess disappeared, I asked Jeff what he wanted me to do. Hang back, let him handle things? Instead he placed the Cadillac's keys in my hand.

"Give these to him," he said. "It's a show of disrespect, but it's not a gift he should've given in the first place, and he knows it."

"How will he react?"

"Be pissed, probably."

"So why'm I doing the talking?" I asked.

"He'll be less pissed at you."

Felix emerged from the kitchen, scowling. As he strode through the dining room and spotted us, his plastic smile snapped on, like a motion-sensor light. Felix wore a silk dress shirt, tight across the chest, lapels flared to the edge of good taste. Following in his wake was a squat bearded man in a nondescript suit.

"Hey, Dave," Felix said to me. "Jeff." A taunting approximation of friendly banter. "Howja like the drive over here?"

When we shook hands I pressed the key fob into his palm, closed his fingers around it.

"Appreciate the gesture," I said. "Unfortunately I only have the one parking space."

Confusion crinkled his forehead, though his smile held. "I heard your car got took. Sure you don't want it?"

"Respectfully."

He looked at Jeff. They both shrugged. Felix pocketed the keys.

"Never seen these before. Thanks for the car, Dave. You here for food?"

"Just to give you that," I said.

"Guess you boys walk back, huh." He gestured to the man now standing at his side. "Tell you what. I'll have my friend Mr. Gu drive you to your office. Don't worry about directions, he knows where it is."

"We'd rather walk," Jeff said. "Nice day for it."

"Sure is. Mr. Gu walks with you."

Felix Long fixed Jeff with his empty smile. Jeff met his gaze. For his part, Mr. Gu looked somber but fundamentally indifferent, a professional mourner at a poorly attended funeral.

After a tense few seconds Jeff gave an inconsequential shrug.

"After you," he said to the man in the suit.

FIFTY-THREE
BAMBOO

We walked out of the restaurant and down Main, under a canopy of pearlescent clouds. Gu donned black Oakleys and kept pace behind us. Glancing at his reflection in the storefront windows, I caught him adjusting the shoulder holster beneath his jacket.

I waited for Jeff to intercede, to talk to him. Eventually it wore on me. At the next coffee shop we passed, I turned to face Gu.

"We're going inside," I said. "I don't have enough cash for three coffees, so let's part company here. You can tell your boss, message received."

"Good," Gu said. "He wants you two to have the best."

"Nice of him."

"He's a nice guy."

"No other instructions?"

Gu casually unbuttoned his suit jacket. He had none of the put-on, tough-guy aggression some short men develop. He appeared blasé and spoke without seeming invested in our response.

"Felix says, 'Go get a real case.' He's very worried you might get hurt."

Too focused on the gun, I didn't register Jeff's movement toward Gu until they were grappling. Jeff's left hand held onto the holster through the fabric of the jacket. His right forearm pressed into Gu's throat, forcing the smaller man against the glass window of 49th Parallel Café.

"You don't threaten him," he told Gu.

Gu stared up at him, unflinching. His hands formed fists but didn't move from his side. Jeff held him there, finally releasing him with a hard shove that panged Gu's head against the glass.

Once free, the short man pushed his shades up the bridge of his nose, then pivoted and started back up Main.

"Burl Ives," I said to Jeff once Gu had gone.

"What?"

"Was trying to think of who he looks like. He one of the Red Snakes?"

"Maybe," Jeff said. "He's a bit old."

"Usually, someone tells you to lay off like that, it's self-protection. Felix ran that count room for his dad, right? Any chance they could be at odds?"

Jeff didn't respond immediately. We continued walking.

"It's possible," he finally said. "Maybe I didn't want to admit it, because if Felix was involved, that means real trouble."

"You said there wasn't much connection between his group and his father's."

"There isn't," Jeff said. "Only there is."

"Oh good," I said. "I love obfuscatory language."

"Felix and Roy Long both belong to Six Companies," Jeff said.

"So do you."

"Only Felix is part of the Red Snakes."

"All right."

"But," Jeff said, "only Roy Long is part of the Lucky Bamboo."

How Jeff explained it, Number Eight Bamboo, or Lucky Bamboo, was the syndicate. Not a mafia with a don at the top, but a loose affiliation of big brothers and sisters, connected in myriad ways. There were branches across North America, with ties to Hong Kong and the Mainland. Most members were quasi-respectable, made use of their legitimate businesses for credit card fraud, identity theft, robbery, extortion, human trafficking, drugs.

The Red Snakes were small-time criminals that kicked back to the Bamboo, and had several business ties. The Six Companies drew protection from, and exerted influence over, the other groups.

I saw why Jeff hadn't told me this before. The overlapping members made distinguishing the connections formidable. Jeff, like most of the Six Companies members, wanted nothing to do with crime.

The turmoil of history. You leave your home for a country that uses you for cheap labour, to participate in a colonial enterprise you're not supposed to benefit from. You're taxed, exploited, scapegoated, left to fend for yourself. What is crime when the law counts you as less than? Who else should you turn to, but the bloody and powerful among your own?

And when things change, what happens to groups like the Lucky Bamboo? Each wave of immigration had altered the syndicate, ultimately being incorporated. The Longs had been born into that world, and Roy Long was its Vancouver head.

"Put yourself in his place," Jeff said. "You're Roy Long, what future do you want for your kids?"

"Business degree. Yacht club. Resort vacations where the only locals you meet are serving you drinks."

"Right. And his older kids are right on track. But Felix ..." Jeff paused. "Why don't we actually get a coffee?"

"Long as you're paying," I said.

We backtracked to 49th Parallel and chose a table near the back, away from the MacBook brigade occupying the window seats. I ordered a London fog, Jeff a cappuccino. He took his time formulating his words.

"It's not that I didn't think Felix was capable of violence," he said. "I had hoped he wasn't. You ever have that friend of a friend, maybe a relative, who you know is a shithead, but to keep the peace you overlook their faults? You tell yourself, he's young. Sooner or later he'll have to smarten up. That's Felix. I've seen him at his worst, what I *thought* was his worst, and I let it go because of his dad."

"There's a story there," I said.

Jeff drank coffee and wiped foam off his upper lip.

"When I first started working as a PI at Aries, Felix asked me for a favour. He was a kid then, maybe eighteen. Middle of the night he calls, asks me to come over right away.

"I get to his place, a condo he's sharing with his friends on Bute. There's a girl sitting on a stool in his kitchen with a broken nose. Blood everywhere, all down her blouse. She's holding a packet of frozen peas to her face. No Felix in sight.

"I clean her up, stop the bleeding and offer to take her to emergency. She says she's afraid to leave him alone. Turns out Felix locked himself in his bedroom after hitting her. He called me from there.

"The girl and I hunt around for something I can use to pop the lock open. Think I ended up using part of a DVD case. All the while Felix is talking to me through the door, a mile a minute, saying don't come in. I open up and he's sitting on his bed, naked, with a gun to his head. Crying. Obviously on something. Worried what his father will say when the girl presses charges."

"What happened?" I asked.

"Neither of them would tell me why he'd belted her. I get him calmed down, take the gun from him. He paid off the girl. She was so scared, she wouldn't have said anything anyway. I drive her to the hospital, bring the gun with me. Later I go back and clean the place up. Burn everything with her blood on it.

"And that," Jeff said, "is how I know what Felix is capable of. Why I didn't want to say anything to you until I knew for sure."

I digested this. For all his idiosyncrasies, Jeff was someone I respected. As a business partner, but also as a man. I'd thought his upright business nature was how he'd always done things, rather than a reaction against something he'd done in the past.

"If you were working at Aries when it happened," I said, "that was probably only the eighth most fucked up thing an employee did that week."

"But I should've been better than that. Damn it." Jeff made to smash the table with his fist, then held off, staring at his curled fingers. "I feel like I helped create this guy who thinks there's no consequences. Makes me responsible for him, doesn't it?"

That wasn't a question I had an answer for. Felix wanted to steal from his father, hurt him. He reached out to someone at Rip Tyde. Hired professionals from out of town so the shooting wouldn't be connected to him. I was still missing puzzle pieces, but the half-finished picture that was emerging was ominous. If Felix felt we'd wronged him, what would stop him from reaching out again?

FIFTY-FOUR
CRAWL SPACE

Connie Boudreau's sister Lucille had been granted custody of Olivia. Lucille still lived in Fort St. John, and the voice that answered her telephone was wary but cordial.

She hated Gabe Boudreau with a fury undimmed by sixteen years. He'd been an alcoholic and woman beater from the start, driving Connie away, only to woo her back with limp promises of reform. Lucille had watched Connie fail to break away from her tormentor too many times to count. Lucille's sister had become timid, joyless, a walking corpse created by Boudreau years before he killed her.

"Hell is too good for that piece of shit," is how Lucille ended her refrain.

I was inclined to agree with her. I asked if Lucille thought he might try to contact Olivia.

"He better not," Lucille said. "Livy is in Dublin now, studying at Trinity." Yes, she would probably talk to me, but her aunt implored me not to push too hard. "She's had a rough go of things."

"What's she studying?" I asked.

"Anthropology and criminal psych."

Despite the time difference I got through to Olivia Boudreau-Baker, now legally Baker-Brill, after her stepfather. It was four in the afternoon my time and midnight hers. She was at a pub with friends. As we spoke, a bit of the Temple Bar revelry leaked out of her voice.

"Aunt Lucille said you had questions about my dad. That he's mixed up in something. Maybe in trouble."

"I think so," I said. "Anything you can tell me would help."

"I don't really know the man," Olivia said.

Boudreau hadn't contacted her recently. The last time had been three years ago, she estimated, close to her twenty-first birthday.

"He told me he was sober, had been sober for a while. Said he was sorry. We both cried a bit. Gabe—he wanted me to call him Gabe, not Dad, since he hadn't earned Dad—said he was living in Vancouver selling stationery supplies. He wanted me to know that it was up to me whether we spoke again. Whether we had a relationship. I was pretty fucked up myself at that time, depression, y'know, so I just said I'd think about it."

"And that's it, the last you talked to him?"

"He phoned once more," Olivia said, "like a year later. I think he was drunk. All I heard was crying and mumbles so I hung up. Didn't realize it was him until after."

"Don't answer this if you don't want," I said, "but if he contacted you today—"

"Would I help him?"

A long pause. I heard plates clatter and the clink of glasses, an exuberant whoop and laughter. I imagined her standing in the quietest corner of a loud bar and wondered how often her fun nights out had been tainted by calls like these.

"Don't worry about it," I said.

"No," she said, "it's that, I just don't know. I'd like to hear more about him, our family and stuff. But part of me just wants to forget it all. Not forget. But just—just be me right now. Maybe that doesn't make sense."

Before I could answer, Olivia said she had to go and hung up.

Just to be me right now. As a means to survive, it made all too much sense. I had biological parents I didn't know, an older sister I'd never met. I'd never delved into their lives before, perhaps because, like Olivia, it had been difficult enough handling what was in front of me. Or as my friend Ken Everett had once said when we were teens discussing parental failings: "Fuck 'em if they don't want you."

Ryan Martz's text caught me as I was about to drive home in my rental. *Meet me at our friend's place, he's asking for you.*

"Our friend" meant Ritesh Ghosh, father of Jasmine, who'd disappeared and hadn't been seen in more than a decade. One of the cases I'd brought with me to Wakeland & Chen, that hadn't solved, that wouldn't solve.

I'd long ago stopped accepting money from the Ghoshes, but I kept in contact. I'd drive to their two-storey house in Burnaby, have tea with the father while upstairs I heard the footfalls of his wife. Mrs. Ghosh had confined herself there, most days, while her husband's hope grew more desperate.

Ryan was standing outside their house when I arrived, not looking as pissed as he used to. Time spent with the grieving hardens you. Eventually it teaches you how not to show it.

"'Round the side," he said, gesturing.

I followed him to where three steps led down to the entrance of a crawl space. Mr. Ghosh stood over the small staircase, giving me a cursory smile before grabbing my forearm in a hearty handshake.

"Dave, thanks for coming. Officer Ryan wanted to go but I said you should be here too, for when we find her. If, sorry. You'll look hard for her down there, I know you will."

"Sure," I said. "What's down there?"

"She is. Jasmine."

Brown fragments of leaves covered the bottom third of the landing. Last year's atop those from the year before. They'd been shuffled aside recently, forming a small half moon of cleared space where the doors opened out.

"Have you been down there?" I said.

"No, we waited for you. But I remembered—how could I be so stupid!—we moved things down there when Jasmine was small. A hutch she used to play inside. She loved hiding there. We never checked, all these years. No one did. Dave? *Dave*. She's in there. I know."

Ryan's jaw was clenched, his brow furrowed. I couldn't tell how serious he took Mr. Ghosh's claim.

"Doesn't hurt to check," I said.

I'd carried my Maglite with me from the car. I kicked the leaves away from the door and teased up the bolt. The door stuck. I passed Mr.

Ghosh the light while I pried the door open two-handed. I went first, the father behind me.

Mouse shit, swirls of soil, a Coffee Crisp wrapper faded by age. Drag marks across the floor. Boxes too small for a child to hide in. We checked them anyway.

"The hutch," he said, pointing. "In the corner over there. I can't look."

How the Ghoshes had managed to Tetris the thing in in the first place was a miracle. No way to open it until we brought it out. Lying on my belly, I slid around to the dark side of the heavy rosewood hutch, pushed, hearing it scrape on the floor beams overhead. Hanging pipes caught the ornate knobs of the drawers unless you turned it just so. One knob was already missing from the last time the hutch had been moved.

We got it through the door and Ryan deadlifted it onto the backyard mulch. We exited, Mr. Ghosh first. Crawl spaces make you appreciate fresh air and light, and realize how much we take those for granted.

The hutch locked at the top and bottom. Ryan and Mr. Ghosh worked on the latches. My stomach felt empty in a way that had nothing to do with hunger.

The one in a million, billion chance…

They opened it.

A few beetles and a spiderweb and nothing, nothing.

Ryan smiled and patted the father's dust-caked shoulder.

"But I thought," Mr. Ghosh began to say. I busied myself returning the hutch to where it had been, and didn't hear the rest.

Inside the house we scrubbed up and had a long cup of tea. The house had the same stuffy feel the crawl space had, as if it only existed to enliven other spaces, to hold what couldn't be held elsewhere. I didn't see Mrs. Ghosh, but heard creaking steps and running water.

Ryan let out a three-second "fuck" as we walked to our cars an hour later. "I feel so bad for them, and so good getting the fuck out of there."

"It doesn't get easier," I said.

"The look on your face when we opened that hutch," Ryan said. "For a second you thought she might be in there, right? Admit it. You hoped, at least."

"The first time, maybe."

"What do you mean?"

"The last couple years I've opened that hutch four other times," I said. "Same routine as today."

"Jesus. Why do it?" Before I could answer, Ryan said, "It makes him feel better. Lets him know she's not forgotten and we still take it seriously." He nodded to himself. "One good turn deserves another. Sonia said you're looking for Gabriel Boudreau?"

I told him I was.

"He's tatted up, left arm and shoulder. Get this: a skeleton holding an axe, swinging the fucking thing into the chest of another skeleton wearing a Davy Crockett hat. You know, the coonskin, with the tail. Weird piece of art, done by a guy who served time with Boudreau. Lucas Cormier, from the Carrier Nation up north. Lucas is back inside, in Mountain this time, but his wife Heather still lives near the reserve. She won't speak to Borden or any other cops. Hung up when I phoned."

"Boudreau could be staying with her," I said.

"That's why you're the private eye, Wakeland. Nothing gets by you."

I thanked him for the lead. Ryan drove off, but as he passed my Saab he stopped and rolled his window down. I did the same.

"You hear what Mr. Ghosh said to me while you were closing things up? I can't get it out of my head."

Don't tell me, I wanted to say.

"He said, 'But I thought I heard her kicking in there.'"

FIFTY-FIVE
THE HAPPY DEAD

A line from *The Third Man* rattled through my head as I drove once more out to UBC. The Ferris wheel scene, Orson Welles telling Joseph Cotten the dead were happier dead. Justification for the guilty living. But also, maybe, a necessary lie.

I bought two hours' worth of parking at the Museum of Anthropology, hoping I'd only need ten minutes. I bought another ticket to the cʼəsnaʔəm exhibition and wandered through in the direction of Martha Youngash's voice. Tonight was her last guided tour.

As I walked by the video testimonials, I tried to picture the city before the city. The video loop showed settlement and encroachment over thousands of years. The very geography had changed, the channel mouth opening, islands pulling away from shore. A strategic point becomes vulnerable, distances expand. That put my troubles in perspective.

Lucas Cormier's wife, Heather, was a member of the Carrier First Nation, with traditional territory in the Central Interior of the province. The Carrier had connections to French settlers and voyageurs. I had no contacts in their territory. I was hoping Martha Youngash could help me with that.

I hung back as she wrapped up the tour, ending with a line that caused a ripple of bright laughter through the oddly dressed assortment of tourists and college kids. Applause, the end, a gradual drifting away. Martha stayed to talk with a few hangers-on.

When she was finished, I followed her to the museum cafeteria. We had tea. I asked her how Jaycen was doing.

"Not too late to get my money back, is it?" she said. "I'm joking. Jaycen is Jaycen. We've talked a couple times."

His case and his problems seemed a million miles away, but I asked what Jaycen had decided to do with his inheritance.

"Wants to open a coffee shop, of all things." She gave a wide-eyed shrug. "Not like Vancouver's in dire need of another. But it's his dough, and it's something he cares about."

As we milk-and-sugared our tea, I told her about Gabe Boudreau, and his friendship with the Cormiers. Martha looked into her paper tea cup, drew the bag out by the string and placed it on the upside-down lid.

"It's not that I don't trust you," she said. "I'd rather not get involved, if there might be consequences for her."

"It's possible there are people after Boudreau," I said. "They might make the same connection I did and show up there."

"This is about that shooting, isn't it?"

I nodded. "Honestly I don't know how Boudreau fits—if he fits. I need to talk to him, though, and I'd rather not bring trouble up to the reserve."

Martha consulted her teacup. I watched the line of irritable customers grow, the Korean woman at the till doing her best to ring up muffins and sandwiches and keep the espresso machine burbling out the more expensive drinks. A white woman made passive-aggressive complaints to her partner for the barista's benefit, that the two-percent jug hadn't been replenished. The terrible burdens some of us are forced to bear.

After a minute Martha said, "Here's what I can do. I know someone on the band I can ask, discreetly, to see if this Boudreau is around. If he is, I can tell my pal to pass along the message that you'd like to talk. Give him your number. I can't promise much more."

"I appreciate it," I said.

She nodded. "You do talk to him, you make sure he stays out of danger. I'll have your word on that, before I do anything."

I gave it, thinking of Boudreau's wife, and how the man might embody danger himself. How do you keep someone apart from their own nature?

FIFTY-SIX
DRAWING HEAT

When I parked in front of my building, Sonia was sitting on the wet front steps. Her left foot was extended as she massaged the underside of her knee. Barefoot, her coat still on, her hair an unruly shock of damp tendrils.

"I'm okay," she said, before I could ask. "I'm fine."

Someone had been standing on my patio when Sonia got home. Examining the repaired window and looking inside. She'd bolted when she spotted Sonia come through the door.

"Young woman, dark hair, Asian?" I said. When Sonia nodded: "That's the same person who George Foreman'd my eye the other day."

I helped her inside and checked the surveillance. Sure enough, there she was, in the same rain-soaked green coat, a Canucks toque on her head.

She'd sprinted away, hopping the fence. Sonia pursued her, but made a bad landing onto the sloping concrete on the other side of the fence.

"There is a gate," I said.

"It happened fast, dickwad."

She flexed her bare leg. I ran an appreciative hand over the contours of her calf, thigh. Bruises and stubble and knots of muscle. I kissed the arch of her foot.

"If it hurts in the morning, I'll see someone," she said. "We shouldn't stay here. The patio is too exposed. One kick to that glass. And plus, people know you're here."

"Your place?" Even as I suggested it, I shot it down. "Second most obvious, after here."

"Ryan and Nikki have an extra room," Sonia said. "We could impose on them."

"You impose. If I'm drawing this heat, I should keep it away from them." *And you.*

"And go where?" Sonia said.

Good question. There was my mother's house, but Kay was staying there, and the basement had been rented to another family. Jeff and Marie and their kid lived in a two-bedroom condo in English Bay. Families and kids ruled out both.

"I'll figure it out," I said.

Tim Blatchford rented the top floor of a two-storey house off Renfrew. Every house on the block had been similarly partitioned. His was suite B. The staircase to his apartment was just inside the front door of the unit below, left unlocked, the foyer as dark and narrow as an attic.

He didn't lock his door, or answer to knocking. Inside, a young man was asleep on the couch, his legs contorted around a crocheted blanket. The TV quietly showed *Antiques Roadshow*, an indignant man quibbling over the value of his Frederic Remington cowboy statuette.

I sat down in the easy chair. The apartment was messy in a lived-in way. No food containers or suspicious stains. The walls were decorated with a poster of Roddy Piper in *They Live*, as well as a few push-pinned clippings from local wrestling promotions. One featured a much younger Blatchford in a cage match with Bad News Allen.

On the ottoman was a framed photo, face-up, of a teenage Blatchford with a grey-haired woman. A segment of a drinking straw lay on the frame, next to a few smudges of cocaine.

Blatchford appeared from the bedroom. He was wearing an oversized T-shirt and nothing else, a look I found fetching on Sonia. On Blatchford it was a costume of lost youth. I caught a glimpse of fuzzy testicles as he sat cross-legged on the end of the couch.

"He'll sleep through anything," Blatchford said, gesturing at the kid on the couch. "He's twenty-three, from Thunder Bay. Needed a place to crash." His eyes fell on the picture frame. "Not mine," he said. "Maybe a couple times recreationally. Never on the clock."

"I'm being surveilled," I said, not wanting to get into it. "Mind if I crash here?"

"Knock yourself out. Handle on the side works the recliner."

"Appreciate it."

He looked down at Thunder Bay, half-covered by the mangled blanket.

"How bad's this reflect on me?" he said. "That I'm forty, and he's half that, just about."

"What happened with Stuart?"

Blatchford's on-again, off-again had graced a few company events. I hadn't seen Stuart Royce recently.

"Stuart's in his place downstairs. Not sure what happened between us. We're just different. He wants things nice and quiet."

"And you want what?"

He gestured at the kid, the coke, and smiled.

"I had to give up a lot of things," he said. "Wrestling most importantly. You got no idea how it hurts not being able to perform. The pills and the lifestyle, sometimes I feel it's all I have left of who I was. I give that up and I'm just a fuckin' square."

It was hard not to laugh, his words juxtaposed with his balls draped on the cushion, beneath a stretched-out Danzig logo. Delusions of normalcy.

But I said, "I feel that same pressure sometimes, society setting you up for something you're not sure you want. Respectability."

"Ugh," Blatchford said.

"And I know it's bullshit, that pressure. But I feel it anyway."

"It's that tension," he agreed. "It's worse for me 'cause marriage is a political action. For years I thought it was stupid, before it was legal. Now I don't know." He looked down at Thunder Bay, asleep on his couch. "Might be a good example for others."

After a while we said goodnight and Blatchford went back to his room. I caught a few hours' sleep, bathed in infomercials. In the morning I showered in a filthy tub, made pancakes for Thunder Bay, then headed to the gun range in Abbotsford.

FIFTY-SEVEN
A THOUSAND ROUNDS

Nikki Frazer set up her targets at intervals of five yards. She loaded her CZ Shadow and holstered it. Assumed the stance. Ryan, holding the timer, told her ready, set, wait for it, go.

She drew and fired in one smooth action. Shot the clip empty. Sidestepped and swapped out clips. Fired again and repeated till she'd reached the last target.

We inspected the humanoid outlines of the targets. Centre mass, no strays. The grouping a bit wider as the targets moved farther back. Still, better than I could do with a hole punch.

"Want to try?" Nikki asked me.

I'd brought my .357 Smith & Wesson. Wheel guns were about my speed. I took the belt from her, threaded my holster on, drew the empty gun a few times, letting muscle memory accept the new motions. Then I loaded the gun.

I drew, steadied and put one in the hairline of a fifteen-yard target.

"Not bad," she said. "Were you aiming for the head?"

"I was aiming for the paper," I said.

I tried again and then gave the harness back to her. Ryan took a turn with his service weapon, doing better than I had.

As natural a couple, I thought, watching them, as any other. Sonia told me Ryan had even built a display case for his fiancee's trophies. The gun range was their garden, waterfall, beach path.

"Too bad Sonia had to work," Ryan said. "That'd be a double date."

I agreed half-heartedly, listening to the sound of tires on gravel. I went to the door of the covered range and watched a white-haired man pull three rifle cases from the bed of his Mazda pickup.

"Earl Tanner?"

He nodded. I helped him with one of the cases. We were in the pistol range, at the far right. I could hear the crack of shotguns and rifles from the other ranges.

Nikki ignored us and continued her practice.

"We spoke on the phone," I said to Tanner. "These are your replacements, huh?"

He had a matte-black .308 Ruger outfitted with a tripod, two wood-finished Chinese SKS rifles, and a .30-30 Winchester, its side plate gleaming.

"The pistols are still coming," Tanner said. "Insurance on restricted weapons is a real pain."

"And the shotgun?"

"They sent me the new model, the plastic one, and I told 'em what they could do with it. We're going back and forth on that one."

I introduced him to Ryan. "Earl had his home broken into a month ago. Lost most of his gun collection."

Tanner rattled them off. ".22 target pistol, Colt 1911, Remington 12-gauge, the .308 and both my SKSs."

"They catch who did it?" Ryan asked.

Tanner pointed at me. "Nikki said this fellow might know something."

Ryan shook his head. "I knew it," he said. "Can't have one fucking nice morning out." It clicked into place for him. "These are the weapons from the shooting."

The .22 I'd seen Kent holding in my office. He'd had the Remington that day in the street. And the SKS, one of them, had been the gun the blond man had fired into the crowd.

"What a nightmare," Tanner said. He repeated the phrase as I explained this to Ryan. Someone who cared for his guns as Tanner did would be disgusted, and probably feel responsible, at seeing them put to that use.

"The ammunition at the scene was steel and brass," I told Tanner.

"The SKS is a cheap gun," he said. "North American market's flooded with the things. Each of mine came with a thousand rounds of steel-jacketed ammo. The stuff stinks to high heaven when you fire it. I had some brass, too."

"How'd you find this?" Ryan asked me. I cringed as Nikki fired off another volley. Retreating to the parking lot did little to lessen the noise.

The description that others had given amounted to a group armed with automatic weapons. People who know nothing of firearms often mix up the terminology—automatic and semi-automatic and assault rifle and machine gun all become synonyms. There were no fully automatic weapons in Earl Tanner's collection, but the SKSes were easy to modify.

I'd researched exactly how. The guns were built to fire full-auto—one trigger pull cycles through the rounds—but factories had begun building semi-auto versions to comply with laws, putting pins in the magazines to limit the rounds to five.

It was a simple enough matter to build a sere and insert it into the gun to restore full-auto capability, and remove the pins to give you clips of fifteen or twenty rounds or more. I'd found instructions and a sere schematic online.

"How often do you shoot?" I asked Tanner.

"Twice a week, before the robbery. The scumbags. Wish I'd been home."

You really don't, I thought.

"Last few times at the range, did you see anyone you didn't recognize?"

Tanner thought about it. I saw the range light flash green as Nikki inspected her targets.

"Shoot," Tanner said. "I never put it together, but those two—I shoulda known."

"Who?" I asked.

"Can't remember their names," he said. "We spent one morning shooting the breeze. And shooting. Darn it to heck."

I held my hand up to my own height. "Black guy, quite tall, military hair?" I asked. Lowering my hand to my chin. "Blond guy, a bit shorter?"

"Son of a gun," Tanner said.

There was a locked kiosk next to the club's hundred-yard range. Every club member had a key. Inside was a clipboard hanging from a nail, a lockbox, a pencil on a string.

When you arrived, you signed in. If you were a member who was bringing guests, you'd get them to sign and then pay the guest fee, cash only in the box below.

Ryan took down the clipboard and flipped back. There were two weeks' worth of pages. He phoned the number of the club president, who told him the older sheets were in the office, probably stacked on the fridge.

Earl Tanner recounted to us how, one early Tuesday morning, he'd arrived at the club to find a couple of men waiting by the pistol range.

"Friend said he'd meet us here," the blond man had told him.

He'd given a name that Tanner didn't recognize, but it was a big club, and Tanner preferred to shoot when he could have the range to himself. Nevertheless he invited them onto the range to wait, making sure they signed in.

They watched him sight in his .308s, adjusting between shots. They were aficionados. Hunters, ex-servicemen of some sort.

Tanner had allowed them to try out the .308s. He remembered the blond man had preferred the SKS. He shot from a one-knee stance. The Black man had taken a few standing shots with the lever-action, admiring its smoothness. They'd discussed old and new Winchesters, the merits of each.

The blond man had taken a call from their friend and they'd left to meet him. Tanner had offered to see if he could get their money back, but they'd told him it was fine, getting to fire a few guns and talk with someone who knew his stuff was worth the twenty.

Ryan found the sheets and Tanner flipped through, remembering as he looked. "Guess it had to be the twelfth," he said. "Right, 'cause I had to be back early to get the turkey because Margaret couldn't be bothered checking the downstairs freezer." His finger tapped the list of names. "There."

Clive Kent and *Lester Nunn*, spelled out in blue ink.

"You remember them writing this?" I asked.

"Pretty gosh darn sure. Clive was the dark fellow, Lester, Les, the white one. Can't believe I didn't put it together with the robbery."

"You reported it, though," Ryan said.

"Of course. I've been broken into before. Usually it's punk kids, and that's what the officer told me it probably was. He told me to check the pawn shops, they usually ended up there after a while."

Nikki finished her practice and joined us on the gravel lot. She knew Tanner from the range. They shook.

"After we talked, I remembered hearing about Earl's robbery," she said. "I keep checking the stolen-goods lists, but nothing's turned up. Really glad you put this together, Dave."

"Ryan deserves the credit."

"Bullshit," Ryan said. Tanner winced.

"Well, you get the credit. Borden needs to know. And it won't be hard to explain how you came up with the lead."

Ryan nodded. He returned to the range office to phone it in.

I asked Nikki if she'd seen Sonia that morning before she left.

"She's just wasting away without you," Nikki said, adding seriously, "You should come over tonight. We can find another mattress."

My back ached from the broken spring in Blatchford's recliner. "Might take you up on that."

I told Tanner I'd prefer that he left me out when he talked to the police. Nothing criminal, mention me if you have to, but Constable Martz is who you should commend. "Police don't like me much," I confessed.

Tanner had returned his rifles to the bed of his pickup. He looked at the molded plastic cases mournfully. Hard to see your life's joy transmuted into misery and death.

FIFTY-EIGHT
FINAL ORDERS

Odds were, Lester Nunn and Clive Kent were aliases. Still, I was happy that Ryan was running them. If one of the names clicked, and Borden's people were able to pick them up, so much the better. I wanted answers, not a shootout.

Kay had done stellar work tracing out the skeleton of Rip Tyde International. She'd phoned their PR department, swum upstream against a current of doublespeak and gotten through to a vice president of operations who'd promptly hung up on her. Now she was working her way through the directory of the Raleigh headquarters. As for the CEO, John Laidlaw, she had a plan.

"He's not listed," she said, "but he comes from a pretty posh family. If I go through the Laidlaws in Raleigh, odds are one of them will know of him. Might be another way to get at him."

"Do it," I told her. "But be polite."

"As long as he is," she said. "Want I should use the blocked number?"

"No point. I expect he already knows we want to talk to him."

Before I left the office I checked in with Jeff. He'd dug up addresses on Zhou Li and Huang Shao Wei. As we headed to Zhou's apartment, I asked if he'd heard anything from Felix or Roy Long.

"Roy asked to see me." Jeff didn't betray how he felt about that. "I think it's about Felix."

"Are they at odds?"

"Roy is very old school, and Felix is, I don't know what the word for it would be." He thought it over as I pulled the rental out of the garage and aimed it toward Cambie. "North Americanized, I guess you could say.

He thinks he deserves what he has."

"Is there any chance," I said delicately, "Felix pulled this off? Ordered Chang Chia-Yang to replace his men, then hired Kent and Nunn to knock over his dad's count room?"

"It's not his dad's," Jeff said, "it's the Number Eight Bamboo's."

"Which his dad runs. Any chance Roy orchestrated it himself?"

"He'd never," Jeff said. "He's responsible to others. He's not the fucking godfather, Dave. There's no sense in ripping himself off if he'd be expected to pay it back."

"So he's on the hook for the two hundred thousand?"

I remembered what Long had told me at the Garden: *That person might even consider it a favour if you find those responsible, whatever might happen to them after.*

"It reflects badly on him no matter what," Jeff said. "A lot of that money probably ends up overseas. If certain people don't get it, they'd want to know why."

"You're saying Felix wouldn't do that to his dad?"

"It threatens everything—Felix maybe more than anyone, 'cause he's just stupid enough to think about doing it. But it could be anybody, Dave."

Zhou Li had lived in an unremarkable apartment complex near Oakridge Mall. The building was covered in grey aggregate and featured a single, narrow-framed, glass door, the building number stencilled in faded gold. Jeff told the landlord we were in the market, and asked could we take a look.

Zhou's apartment was on the top level, white painted and radiant from the uncurtained windows. A wide wraparound balcony shared by the neighbours. On the floor of the kitchenette, an empty birdcage, dirty newspaper still carpeting its plastic yellow tray.

"Brand new fridge," the landlord pointed out.

As we scoped the place, the landlord's body language became nervous. He stepped in front of us, corralling us near the kitchenette. I looked to Jeff. He immediately engaged the man in a technical conversation about water damage, slipping into the role of a prospective renter who needed reassurance. The landlord was happy to expound.

I opened the fridge door, blocking their view of me, and slipped around the corner, into Zhou's bedroom.

No furniture on the floor. A mattress with cheap white sheets, a pillow greased from a season's worth of night sweats. A television sitting right on the carpet, turned toward the bed. Accounting textbooks and a backpack with binders, pencil case, Pocky, gym strip rolled up in a T & T shopping bag.

The front pouch of the binder held Zhou's schedule for the spring semester. Accounting, Econ, English, Japanese. No notes; he hadn't made it to his first class. The address on his tuition slip was different, an apartment in New West.

The landlord shooed me out, Jeff following to pull his attention back to the crown molding. I had time to pocket the tuition slip and another scrap of paper covered in Chinese characters, before I rejoined them.

Back in the car I handed Jeff the papers. "Different address," I pointed out. "How'd you hear about this place?"

"Chang Chia-Yang's brother. The two of them stayed here when they were students."

"And I wonder whose name's on the lease," I said.

Jeff ignored me. He'd picked up the Chinese paper and was staring at it, transfixed.

"Where'd you find this?" he demanded.

"Zhou's bag. What's it say?"

"It—" He paused and ran a hand over his mouth. He reread it, shaking his head. "We shouldn't have this."

"What does it say, Jeff?"

He pointed at a row of figures. "That's Chia-Yang's name." Tapping further down the page. "Vincent Ma. Huang is below." Looking at me, he said timorously, "It—it's a list, Dave."

"List of what?"

"Orders." Shaking his head again. "We shouldn't have this."

My breath caught in my chest. "Orders for what—drugs? Payoffs?"

"See here?" He pointed under the ideograms for Chang Chia-Yang. "That says, 'Roast beef and cheddar, Orange Crush.' And here, 'Tuna, no tomatoes, Brisk Iced Tea.'" He looked at me with grandiose dread. "No tomatoes, Dave."

I took the list from him and crumpled it. "You asshole."

Laughing, Jeff said, "Told you, bitch, I'd get you back for that coffee."

FIFTY-NINE
NOBODY HOME

The address on Zhou's tuition slip turned out to be a homestay family's spare bedroom. A young woman from Singapore occupied it now. It was a mail drop for Zhou's school correspondence, to be kept separate from what he did for the Longs.

In the car, on the way to Huang's address in the West End, my phone went off. I answered, heard breathing, asked who was there.

The call died. I hit dial back, listened to the tones. No one picked up. An out-of-town number.

I said to Jeff, "I think Boudreau just tried to call me."

"Tried? Think he'll try again?"

"No idea." I sent a text to the number, *must talk, urgent.*

I was still waiting for a reply when we reached Huang's house. A semi-detached near English Bay, no view of the water but an easy four-block stroll to the beachfront. I asked Jeff what he figured a place like that went for. Three million?

"Three million probably gets you a look through the fridge," Jeff said.

"This guy Huang independently wealthy? A gentleman gangster?"

"Maybe his family's place," Jeff suggested. "Get that money out of the country. Part of our big plan to push out all the white people."

He was being sardonic. Chinese investment in Vancouver real estate was a factor in housing inflation, but most foreign ownership came from the States. White Vancouverites who saw nothing wrong with owning a second home in Mexico or a cottage in the Interior were suddenly up in arms at the thought of sharing their backyard. The Yellow Peril was alive and well in Canada.

We waited a few minutes, taking in the stillness of the house.

"This feels wrong," I said. "I'm going on record saying it."

"'Cause everything else has felt so right," Jeff said.

We squeezed into a space up the block on the other side of the street. Walking back I noticed drawn curtains in the nearby buildings, everyone seemingly asleep at two in the afternoon. No smells coming from any kitchens, no one on the stoops. Like walking onto a set with the film crew out to lunch.

"You have your gun in the car?" Jeff said.

"Locked up, yeah."

He held back as we reached the steps. "Maybe let's go get it."

"You grab it," I said, handing him my keys. "I don't come out, you kick the door in and shoot somebody."

"Not kicking anything in these shoes," Jeff said.

But he hung back by the car. I made the gallows walk to the door of Huang's place and pressed the buzzer. I heard the chimes inside, *cling, clang*.

I knocked. Looking through the smoked glass inset in the door I could see into a dark hallway. A staircase with a white bannister, coat rack on the wall, each peg empty, save one. A baggy green raincoat, its tail brushing the floor.

"Don't move, sir. Hands up."

Those contradictory statements came from behind me in an earnest, guileless voice. I complied.

In the glass, I could see my own reflection. I didn't look petrified.

Behind me a man took the stairs, pointing a pistol at my head. He wore a track suit and had one of my least favourite haircuts, the shaved sides with the unweeded garden on top.

I was muscled to the ground, seeing, as I spun, the pantlegs of three other people. Falling into that forest of legs, my knees hitting concrete, I saw that the shoes were all black, thick-soled lace-ups. I'd owned a pair, once upon a time.

I felt steel bite into my wrists.

As I was raised to my feet, I craned my head to look for Jeff. The rental car was gone. Smart move.

Turning to find the face of the person who'd cuffed me, I saw one opened window in the condo across the street. A face was there, watching me, then pulled back, away from the glass. A familiar young woman's face, the one who'd been following me, who'd struck me in the eye.

Nothing can ever be fucking simple.

SIXTY

BLEACH

Mr. Track Pants and Bad Haircut ignored my questions as he drove me to the station. His car was an unmarked black Charger, and he steered with the intensity of a frazzled parent dealing with a misbehaving child. Whatever his orders were, keeping silent seemed a part of them.

He led me into my favourite interview room and undid my cuffs. I was given a cup of tap water and a takeout container with mushy french fries and an actually-not-half-bad grilled cheese. Then he was gone. Alone with my thoughts, I was keeping poor company.

Private investigation is dependent upon the police—a cop might say it's a parasitic relationship. I've met cops who have fucked up badly. Who fuck up regularly. Cops unsuited for the job. Power-trippers, the self-obsessed, those who can't handle criticism or insults. Humans in a job that demands the superhuman. I'd done no better in my own brief stint in patrol.

But bent cops—sociopaths or the absolutely corrupt—I've only known three. One was given the chance to resign quietly and did. One was promoted to a personnel job where she could do the least harm. The third shot himself through the mouth when his schemes came to light.

There were reasonable possibilities for why the police would have Huang Shao Wei's house under surveillance. Huang could have been an informer, or a weak link chosen as a focal point to break into the Long organization. Maybe he was the finger: maybe he'd helped cook up the heist. His house could be a meeting place for Kent and the others.

It didn't fit, nothing fit, especially when Huang had been dead for days. What fit was corruption—an oil slick that covered everything, soiled everyone, brought us all together in suffocating death. Kent and Borden and Nunn and MacLeish, the Longs and the Changs and the Axtons. Jeff, me, Rhodes, Boudreau...

And the young woman: connected to Huang? To the police? Watching me for what reason?

More than an hour passed. I turned the paper cup into a castle tower, built a ketchup moat around it on the Styrofoam takeout container. I'd begun building parapets and portcullises using leftover fries and plastic cutlery.

Borden entered, alone, carrying a pitcher of water and two glasses.

"Cute," she said, looking at my garbage castle. "My six-year-old can do better than that."

"Abstract art. You wouldn't get it."

"Probably not," she said wearily.

The lost sleep and stress had battered Borden. Her face had become a mask of veins and furrows under unkempt hair. Even her breathing betrayed a bone-deep lassitude.

She sat down and said, "You were picked up by officers assigned to a special detail. A detail headed by the deputy chief constable. You're lucky MacLeish is in a meeting today and I got here first. That means we have a very brief window in which to speak candidly."

"I'm listening," I said.

Borden removed her glasses, dipped fingers in her water and moistened the lenses. Drying them on her shirt, she said, "I've been tracing the weapons used by the shooters, thanks to a tip we received."

"That's all Ryan Martz," I said. "Hell of a police officer."

"Certainly a hell of a friend. We found the van, with Earl Tanner's shotgun and rifle inside. They'd been soaked with bleach. The rifle had been modified to fire fully automatic, which I'm told isn't all that difficult."

"And Nunn and Kent?" I asked.

"Just names," she said. "False passports used to cross the border. Very high-quality."

"The kind you might need connections in high places to get," I said. "From the beginning there's been something off about this."

"Bullshit. We all want this solved. MacLeish more than anyone."

"Does he want it solved," I said, "or does he want it to go away? Czechowski turned up dead. Ditto Shelly Axton. The only other witness has split for hell and gone."

"MacLeish is not," Borden said, and caught herself. "There's a lot more going on, is all I can say."

"No shit."

"Ryan said his informant had a theory on how Nunn and Kent connect to Czechowski and the Axtons."

"Ryan's confidential informant?"

Borden nodded. I looked up at the CCTV camera in the corner of the room. She shook her head.

"You know Czechowski and the Axtons are ex-military," I said. "All three worked for companies associated with Rip Tyde International, a security company. Odds are Nunn and Kent were employed there too."

"Ugly, but it fits," Borden mused. "I wouldn't've put that together."

"Me neither. Ryan's informant must have a sister so good she's starting to outshine him."

Borden smiled. "Thank her for me," she said.

"Let's say it turns out certain people in authority are a part of this. How willing are you to take this where it leads?"

"I can't believe anyone would knowingly sabotage a case of this scale," she said. "But I can't argue that it's been made difficult—and not just by you."

"Nice to know I'm not alone."

"I'll follow up to find where it leads," she said. "You have my promise. Though if worse comes to worst, don't be surprised to see me dropping off a resumé at Wakeland & Chen." Borden stared at her water, adding, "I hope not," as if it might come down to hope alone.

SIXTY-ONE
JUST US

Borden personally dropped me off three blocks from Ryan's house. I made sure I wasn't followed. I went around the side and knocked on the door of their den. Sonia let me in.

It had been too long since I'd held her. Standing on the threshold, I inhaled the smell of her hair and felt her pulse through her thin nightie.

"Missed you," she said.

Inside I saw the den had been painted cyan. A corner had been designated for baby stuff: a stroller, boxes of hand-me-down clothing from friends. Sonia was camped out by the door on an air mattress, her suitcase laid out with work and casual clothes.

It was eleven. Ryan and Nikki were asleep upstairs. I showered and joined Sonia on the mattress. She presented her back to me. I cuddled behind her, my lips brushing the hard jut of her vertebrae.

"There seems to be something poking my butt," she said.

"Seems to be. What are we going to do about that?"

"I could reach over like this."

"That works."

"Are you going to get up early and do the laundry?"

"Do the what?"

"We can't just soil their bedsheets," Sonia said.

"If I do, you think you could use more than your hand?"

"Two hands, maybe?"

"Mouth, maybe?"

"And you'll just lie there, I suppose?"

"Have I ever refused to do the honours?"

"*Quid pro quo*, Clarice."

"Always."

"And you'll do the laundry."

"Fabric softener and everything."

"Now that's a fucking turn on," Sonia said.

The Martzes didn't have fabric softener. In the morning, after the three of them had left, I put the load on, sat down at the table in the dining nook and tried the Fort St. John number again. I hoped Boudreau was an early riser, or I'd catch him unawares.

But there was no answer. I moved the clothing to the dryer, had cereal and made instant coffee—instant, Ryan? really?—and thought of what to do.

Part of me wanted to go back to the Huang house. I'd been taken into custody but not charged, which meant there was some reason I was being kept away. The woman was there. Answers could be there.

I put clean sheets on the mattress, found the spare key Ryan had left me, along with the slip of paper with their alarm code. As I was locking up, my phone rang. A pleasant male tenor said hello.

"Mr. Boudreau?"

"No," the voice said. "Who would that be?"

"Nobody. Friend of my uncle's. What can I help you with?"

"You're David Wakeland?" I assured him I was. "My name is John Laidlaw."

I was midway through pulling on my shoes. I said, "Hunh."

"Is that all you have to say?"

"Sorry, meant to say hello."

"Your secretary has been trying to reach me." Before I could correct him: "I didn't think we had much to talk about. Now I've been informed the police department in your city would like a word. A Miss Borden. Figured before I talked to her, I'd hear you out. What do you have to say for yourself, Mr. Wakeland?"

Here goes, I thought. "There was a shooting a few weeks ago."

"Heard something about it. Not too many in your neck of the woods."

"One is too many," I said.

"I take your point."

"Three of the shooters have ties to Rip Tyde. Rudy Czechowski, Percy Axton and Shelly Axton. There's at least two others. I have the aliases they use, and reliable descriptions."

"And you want access to our personnel records to identify them." His tone made the idea seem ludicrous.

"That would be awesome," I said.

"Why would I let you do that?"

"Justice?"

"Try again," Laidlaw said.

"Because you're going to talk to Borden, and she's going to ask you for the same thing. Only her request will be formal. It'll go through diplomatic channels, and bureaucracy, and all that other jazz. And it'll probably end up in the papers, however it happens."

"I've survived more than bad PR," Laidlaw said.

"If you talk with me, though, it's just us. If I find anything, you can spin it your way, Rip Tyde volunteering to help the police. And if I don't, I'm out quietly. No fuss, no muss."

"Definitely more appealing," he said, "though saying nothing edges out both options."

"Only in the short term. If the shooters are caught and it comes out you knew—or worse, if they kill again. Your company's mandate is anti-terror, right?"

"My personal mandate," he said, "since the events of September Eleventh."

"Imagine how much terror the shooters have caused. Are capable of causing."

"Tell you what," Laidlaw said. "You make the trip out here. I'll clear a couple hours tomorrow afternoon. We'll talk."

"That sounds fine."

"Hell," he said, "maybe we'll even have time for a beer."

At the office I found Kay in the boardroom, explaining to Jeff how she'd be extra careful, she'd text him and bail at the first sign of trouble. I asked what they were talking about.

"Huang's house," Jeff said. "Where you were picked up. I talked to someone in real estate and he said the whole block has been leased recently, at below-market price."

"So Huang got a deal," I said.

"Too good a deal for a count-room guy. This is high up, Dave. Someone with reach or money or both."

"What are you thinking?" I asked.

"Huang gets into the count room, tips off the shooters. Then they take him out to cover their tracks."

"We know Felix installed him in Chang Chia-Yang's crew," I said.

Jeff waited for Kay to leave before answering. On her way out, I told her to keep special watch for the woman in the green jacket. Kay nodded at me like I didn't need to say it.

"Maybe Felix is behind it," Jeff admitted once we were alone. "Maybe someone else. His father's well-respected. It would take a lot to turn Roy's friends."

"Define a lot," I said. "We're talking money?"

"Stability also."

"Not Felix's strong suit. So who's in his corner?"

"Probably one of his father's partners," Jeff said.

"Not a deputy police chief?" I suggested. "Maybe Felix has something on MacLeish. Blackmail."

"Maybe."

"Or"—I massaged my fingers into my jaw—"what if it's Terry Rhodes? He and Felix partner up. That's a power base Roy Long couldn't rival."

"Felix wouldn't take Rhodes's side over his father's."

"For money and power? Respect his dad won't give him?"

"It's possible," Jeff conceded.

The Rhodes-Felix axis could explain why the shooters seemed unconnected to either outfit, yet had inside knowledge of Long's activities. It made a lunatic kind of sense. Even if true, it wasn't the full story.

"That fucking brat," Jeff said abruptly. There was a note of personal betrayal in my partner's words.

SIXTY-TWO
BUSINESS OR PLEASURE

The closest thing to a direct flight from YVR to Raleigh involved a two-hour layover in Chicago. I packed a toothbrush and a change of clothes, a paperback novel and my phone cable. Death before checked luggage. I slung the overnight bag across my shoulder and met Blatchford in the alley behind my apartment. No goodbyes to Sonia. I wouldn't be gone that long.

It was a freezing ride through rain. The canopy of Blatchford's Jeep had ripped along the seams and it fluttered as we crossed the Arthur Laing Bridge. The interior smelled of old soap, and the chipped windshield had the integrity of a tobacco lobbyist.

Behind us a pair of high beams blinked on and off. I couldn't make out the car through the rain-soaked vinyl of the Jeep's rear window. Blatchford switched lanes and drove through the airport's long-term parking until we were sure no one was following.

He dropped me at the departure gate and bumped my fist. "Safe flight, man. We'll hold'er down till you get back." It was a nice stab at reassurance.

I checked in, endured security, sat down in the Starbucks to have a latte and settle my nerves. I cracked the novel, *Keeper'n Me* by Richard Wagamese. I'd read it before, but not recently.

Soon the table to my left was occupied, then the one in front. I put down my book as Felix Long took the seat across from me, smirking.

"Fancy meeting you here," he said.

"That was you behind us?"

"Wouldn't want you to leave, nobody say goodbye."

There was a line of patrons at the counter, a maintenance man in overalls pushing a trundle cart. We were alone in our corner. Felix and his associates had somehow gotten through security.

"Lot of trouble just to see me off," I said.

Felix smiled. He took my drink from me and pushed it aside.

"Wanted to talk without Jun Fei around," he said. "Jeff doesn't need to hear our private talk. You didn't like the car?"

"Nice gesture but it's not for me."

"How do you know?"

"I'm very picky about who I take bribes from."

The stool was the wrong height for him. Felix wobbled, grasped the table to settle himself.

"No more poking around," he said. "I got things under control."

"Good to hear."

"You don't believe me?"

I didn't reply. He looked at the other tables, swore, directing the words at me. *Get a load of this guy.*

"You don't think I'm for real," he said.

"No opinion on you whatsoever."

"My dad makes the same mistake. He doesn't think I'm real."

"But he will when you get his money?"

His smile soured. A nod of his head at the soldier to my right. The tall man shifted his chair, blocking any chance of escape. Gu watched closely from the other table. No visible weapons, but my imagination worked fine.

"When I get his money *back*," Felix said, "Pop'll think different of me then. But you, Dave, you should stay out. Not your business."

"It is," I said. "People were shot in front of me. I've been threatened, attacked, my apartment shot up. Which you wouldn't know anything about, right?"

"Bad neighbourhood you live in," Felix said. He shook his head as if I'd disappointed him. "Dave. You think maybe you're in over your head?"

"Always," I said.

"Glad you know it."

Felix grabbed my coffee cup by the base and began rocking it, just hard enough so the liquid sloshed to the brim, spattering the table.

"Your girlfriend know it? Your sister?"

"I think you know more about the shooting than you let on," I said. "More than you'd tell your dad. Does he know about Huang Shao Wei?"

Felix Long's jaw clenched. He took hold of the table and kicked his stool back. Hunched over me, he seemed determined to unnerve me with his stare. He wasn't failing.

"Sore subject?" I asked.

Felix's expression softened. He looked at his men. The easygoing smile slowly slid back into place.

He tipped the coffee cup into my lap, blanketing my crotch with dark roast and foam. His soldiers laughed.

"You're all wet," Felix said. "Have a good trip, Dave. Don't worry about anything, I'll take good care of things here for you."

SIXTY-THREE
HANDMADE TERROR

Raleigh, half-lit by sunrise, scrolled by the window of my taxi. Temperate compared to Vancouver, the skies clear and rose-coloured, traffic heavy as we drove through the outskirts. Yet another place I could say I'd been to but hadn't seen.

Rip Tyde International occupied two floors of a downtown office tower, its windows looking out on Moore Square. I'd expected something more nefarious, something less banal. Instead there was a reception area that looked like a splash page from an IKEA catalogue, replete with honey-haired receptionist and a vat of passable coffee. Only the reading material hinted at the company's purpose, glossy magazine covers showing political turmoil, firearms and business news.

I was there at eight. The receptionist told me Mr. Laidlaw wouldn't be in till ten, and couldn't see me till twelve. I left, walked to my hotel room and cleaned up. I found a diner near the square that served a working-class clientele. The counter man insisted I try grits with cheddar and fried green tomatoes. He sent me away with a warm, greasy paper sack of hush puppies, which I had with tea on a bench in the square.

Still killing time, I strolled through the nearby history museum, stared at tattered Confederate flags, a display case of primitive firearms, a Ku Klux Klan hood that looked like a jester's hat as drawn by Todd McFarlane. *Handmade Terror* the title of its display placard.

At eleven I returned, and Laidlaw himself met me at the door. He was in his mid-forties, a tall man with an athletic build, wearing a blue dress shirt with the sleeves rolled up, black slacks and loafers, a gold tie with a military pin. Hair jet black and grown out from a buzz cut, slightly moussed. His smile carried a hint of chagrin.

"Long way to come on short notice," he said. "It's appreciated. I wish we had more time, but I've got another meeting shortly. Let's find a quiet corner and have a powwow."

He led me into the elevator and we stepped out on the floor above, into a white tiled hallway. Glass-walled offices, furnished in the pressed-wood and plastic style. Each room the same as the next, and all of them empty.

As if in answer to my unspoken question, Laidlaw said, "Most of my staff is overseas now. I admit it gets a bit lonely, being left back, but that's the boss's curse. Last to leave and all that."

He chose a room with drawn blinds and adjusted the dimmer to full bright. We sat on the same side of the boardroom table, in chairs similar to Jeff's. Laidlaw put his phone on the table, stealing glances at it as we talked.

"We're a company focused on solutions," he said. I groaned internally, hoping this wouldn't be a corporate lecture. "I built Seven Hills to be more effective than the public sector, to do what no one else could. I don't mind being seen as the boogeyman by people who aren't in the game. Armchair critics always need something to talk about, and America isn't anything without free speech. My people, though, are a different story. There I draw the line. International security is incredibly high-stakes, and the fact that the media likes to demonize us, focus on our failings, that does bother me."

He tapped the screen of his phone. The lights dimmed, and the projection screen on the wall slid down. On the ceiling a projector purred, its blue light blinking.

"Privatized security is the future. No, it's the recent past and present. We're already here. Rip Tyde is effective on such a scale because we're not organized along the lines of a government bureaucracy. We're a business. Businesses must be efficient. As you well know."

Jeff Chen might quibble about my efficiency. But I nodded.

"I guess that entails all kinds of resources," I said. "Right tool for the job."

"Precisely," Laidlaw replied.

The screen showed a personnel photo, Shelly Axton in khakis looking into the camera. Raw, livid scars encrusted her cheek and chin.

Laidlaw's gaze was cool. I'd thought that came from his military background. Now I recognized it for what it was—a businessman's need to commodify what should be uncommodifiable. Casualties, illnesses, missing limbs—these had a set price to him. His product was people and there was a certain amount of acceptable loss.

"Shelly was part of an incident, the details of which I won't go into. Afterwards, she went to work at our training facility in Dearborn. Her husband was an instructor there too. Good people, but we just didn't have the budget to keep two schools open. In February their contracts weren't renewed."

A tap of Laidlaw's finger changed the image to a similar photo of Rudolf Czechowski. His uniform was navy blue with a gold insignia sewn to his breast.

"Rudy was also future-endeavored, so to speak. We didn't feel he had the potential to move above entry-level. Nice enough kid, though."

Another click. Percy Axton in a white shirt and black tie. "No sense in repeating myself when we're short for time. You get the idea."

The receptionist knocked and entered with coffee and tea, and told Laidlaw she was taking her lunch.

"Thanks, Trudy." Laidlaw poured out a coffee and sweetened it for himself, then passed me a cup of black tea.

"What do Rip Tyde employees usually do," I said, "when they're let go?"

"'Employees' isn't exactly the proper term. We hire independent contractors. Keeps things simple. Turnover isn't high, but it's steady, and to answer your question, they explore various options. Work for other companies. Teach. There are no guarantees in this business, as you know, only opportunities."

"Percy and at least two others are still at large." I described Kent and Nunn. "I could probably ID them off photos like these, given the chance."

"'Fraid not," Laidlaw said.

"It could save lives." When he didn't respond, I added, "And save your company some grief."

"You seem to be under the impression I'm some cold-blooded businessman," Laidlaw said. "No heart, only cares about the bottom line. I can tell you've never served your country."

"Guilty," I said. "The shooters still need to be found."

"I wish you the very best of luck with that."

Laidlaw walked me to the elevator, used his security fob to call up the car. He escorted me down to the lobby, then surprised me by walking me outside, into the balmy noon sun.

"I know you smoke," he said, moving to a bench on the sidewalk away from the entrance. He lit an American Spirit.

I took one from the offered pack, justifying it as tourism. Raleigh was a tobacco capital, after all. Do as the locals do. Only after I'd lit up did it occur to me that I'd broken my promise to Sonia.

Laidlaw held the flame of his Ronson lighter close to my face. "Occasionally," he said, "in a business like ours, you need to rely on outside talent." He crossed his legs and leaned back on the bench. "I'm doing that now, to an extent. Hoping you'll clear this up for me."

I coughed, days without a cigarette making this one taste both foul and fair.

"A few years ago, let's say three, we hired some outside talent for a project which, again, the details aren't pertinent. The man's name was Mustafa Said. At least his bank account was in that name. He worked with Shelly Axton and a man whose name I honestly don't remember. They were more than adequate at their job, but expensive. Our clientele had misgivings about our use of them."

"Mercenaries," I said.

His hand made a swatting gesture as if to dismiss the term. "Our line of business, everyone is. Who works for free? We're all whores, except for fanatics, and as someone who's dealt with both, I know which I prefer."

He lobbed the half-smoked cigarette at the curb, where it smoldered.

"Apologies, Mr. Wakeland, but I can't help you find your shooters. Your description of Kent just reminded me of Said, and the blond man of the other. Be very careful, and happy hunting."

As Laidlaw strolled back to his office I felt relief, like finding your way out of a hall of mirrors. Since the start of this I'd been surrounded by violent men and women. Yet something told me I'd just dealt with the most dangerous of them all.

I tossed my cigarette next to his and walked back to the hotel to get ready for the flight home.

SIXTY-FOUR
WELCOME HOME

Never buy cheap when it counts. My replacement cell phone cut out while I was in line to board, in the middle of my call to Sonia. I didn't have a chance to tell her I loved her. I texted the words, hoping she'd receive them through the digital ether.

Kay had sent me a half dozen photos she'd taken the day before. She and Blatchford had surveilled Huang Shao Wei's house. They'd observed the young woman in the green jacket. The photos showed her filling a backpack, eating cereal with an older woman, then being escorted from the house by the plainclothes cop with the bad haircut.

The last photo showed her walking through the entrance of Langara College. A student on her way to morning lecture.

Huang's daughter, maybe. She'd watched me on the news, followed me because of that. She wanted answers, like the rest of us, and thought I could provide them.

I couldn't, not yet, but I felt close.

Sleep is impossible for me on planes, and since Kent had my credit card, I couldn't buy drinks. I spent the flight sober as a German pope, with plenty of time to mull things over.

Felix Long was at the centre of this, along with the shooters. If he'd hired them, why tell me he was hunting them? To cover his tracks? Had he killed Axton and Czechowski for that reason? And who was in possession of the money?

The plane landed on time. Bypassing the luggage carousel, I headed out of the terminal. It hadn't occurred to me that Felix might repeat his trick, until I saw the two men converge from either side of my peripheral, someone else swoop in from her post near the exit.

Not Felix. A tall white woman and a tall man who might have been Indigenous, and Mr. Bad Haircut himself. He seized the fabric of my shirt, pushed me through the door.

"Into the fucking van," he said.

It was a Mazda MPV that hadn't been outfitted as a police vehicle. No onboard computer, no police band. That was worrisome. I sat in the back, sandwiched between the unfamiliar man and woman on what was a three-person bench in name only.

Instead of heading into the city, the Mazda followed Marine Drive along the outskirts, crossing into Burnaby. A neighbourhood of older houses and corner stores now abutting highways and outlet malls.

The van stopped in the driveway of a two-storey house that had been broken by renovations and never quite healed. Paint-cracked exterior over malformed humps and annexes, half a porch that had collapsed onto the gravel yard. Dead flower beds like craters, a picket fence and gate that resembled a set of snarled wooden teeth. A shed along the side, dirty windows looking in on furniture stacked to the ceiling.

Around back the property curved to a steep decline down to double basement doors. At one point you could've driven from the alley right into the basement. Maybe the house had been a business at one point, a delivery entrance no longer needed.

We marched down the ramp. The woman unlocked the door and led me through. Water stains on the concrete floor, mold on the painted concrete walls. A faded, earthy smell of piss hung in the dank air. I was reminded of the crawl space beneath the Ghoshes' house.

In an unfinished room near the skeletal stairs sat MacLeish. Out of uniform, in a zipped-up track jacket and grey Dockers, he sat on an ancient stool looking ready to spit hot fire.

I was seated in a rolling chair that looked older than I was. Hands cuffed in front of me. My three escorts stood to the side, leaving me face to face with the deputy chief constable.

"You can smell urine, can't you," he said. "Long before your time, when I was starting out, this is where we'd bring punks like you. Give them a little talking-to, away from the world. It was common for them to mess themselves. Some got the message quicker than others, but they all got it."

"I'm sure they did."

MacLeish looked at me with regret. "It didn't have to be like this, David. Your father was no stranger to this room. I heard he once tuned this kid up so hard he knocked him out of his shoes. Nearly took his head off."

I tried to imagine the man who raised me standing behind MacLeish, arms folded, ready to do the deputy chief's bidding. I found it was only too easy. A legacy of fear and pain.

MacLeish stood and removed his watch and jacket, made a show of rolling up his sleeves. "You know why you're here," he said. "What I need from you."

"I do," I said, nodding seriously. "But redecorating tips won't be enough, not with this place. You'll have to go full home makeover. There's this show on the Garden Network my mother watches—"

MacLeish slapped me. It wasn't as hard as he could, or as hard as he wanted to. He made up for it with the next one.

"Laidlaw told you who did this." MacLeish clamped a hand under my chin and forced eye contact between us. "Now you tell me."

"He gave me the name Mustafa Said. That's it."

MacLeish swatted me on the temple. "That's not it, not all of it. Now tell me what you know. Everything, David, or I swear to Christ you won't leave here."

He'd left his seat to slap me and now stood close, his fury cloaking fear of his authority's irrelevance.

"You're responsible for this, aren't you?" I said. "The scary car ride and slap fight, it's all about you trying to cover for your failure."

His fist struck me in the solar plexus, hard enough to knock me out of the chair. He kicked my shoulder, my ribs. My bound hands moved in anticipation, far too slowly.

When I looked up, the deputy's eyes shimmered with tears.

"What do you know about failure?" he said. His boot nudged my chin, pressed into my throat. I felt the freezing floor against my cheek.

"Huang Shao Wei." I coughed out the name. "Your fault he's dead. Does his daughter know? Does yours?"

The pressure lifted.

MacLeish snagged my collar as he steadied himself to keep from falling into me. His head sank. He staggered back to the chair and fell into it. A fatigued, eerie laughter escaped him.

"You have no fucking clue what it's like," he said. "Having someone put absolute trust in you, risk his life on your order. Your whim."

He snorted and spat. I cautiously sat up.

"Let's level with each other," I said. "Come clean. I can help."

He looked at me doubtfully, unable to believe. There was no reason for him to speak to me. When he did speak, it was compulsive, as if the need to unburden himself had overwhelmed him. I'd seen it in criminals. Never in cops.

"My arrogance killed him," MacLeish said. "A goddamned hero. His family is suffering, and I can't even acknowledge him."

"You're talking about Huang," I said.

He looked up at me, eyes opened wide to push back tears.

"Yang," he corrected. "Staff Sergeant Martin Yang."

SIXTY-FIVE
JUST A JOB TO DO

MacLeish's story suffered from self-pity, a story which made him the tragic instigator of The Fall of Sergeant Yang. It was MacLeish who lured Yang from his post with the Toronto OPP, who fired him up with the idea that they could clean up Vancouver's underworld and break the back of organized crime.

Yang was perfect for the role. His family had emigrated from the same Four Counties area as the Longs, so not only did he have a grasp on the Taishanese dialect, he knew the references. More importantly, his family had criminal ties, distant cousins involved in smuggling and extortion. By tweaking his name and linking him to a credit card fraud, the newly minted Huang Shao Wei was born with the aura of someone outside of the law, but canny enough to avoid being imprisoned.

MacLeish had given Yang some money to gamble with, enough to draw the attention of the Changs. Huang had a mysterious income and a flawed love of Pai Gow and horse betting. Pretty soon the Changs had introduced him to Felix Long.

Most undercover operations are short-term, cops posing as johns or drug personnel. This was the second type, long-term and long-reaching. It required complete immersion in the role. Martin Yang became Huang Shao Wei for weeks at a time. He saw his wife and daughter infrequently, called them on holidays. The time between visits grew longer as his duties in the Red Snakes grew.

Regret seeped into MacLeish's rendition. He'd leapt at the chance to insinuate his agent with Roy Long's son. He'd underestimated Felix. It had been too good to be true.

Huang had assisted Long's people in some minor crimes—unloading boosted shipments from the ports, laying off bets or collecting them. He'd once seen Felix slap around a man who'd worked for him. No drugs beyond recreational, no direct links to Roy Long or the Lucky Bamboo. A slow creep through the capillaries, but tantalizingly close to the main artery.

Yang/Huang had picked up gossip too. Uncle Roy's son was a disappointment to him, while Felix thought Roy was intractable and behind the times. The Vietnamese and Fukienese and Hong Kong crews would support a change in leadership, so long as profits weren't disturbed.

Felix felt locked into the small-time, cut off from the narcotics limb of his father's affairs. That segregation was deliberate. As much as ninety percent of Canada's heroin was imported through Vancouver, which meant the Lucky Bamboo had obligations to powerful people across the globe. Roy Long ran it as a wholesale business, minimizing exposure and risk. That called for patience and tact and discretion, and a host of other skills the father felt the son was lacking.

So Felix stewed and Yang was there to hear it, to document it, to feed info to MacLeish—

—and then the shooting, and then Huang Shao Wei was dead, taking Martin Yang with him.

"I should've seen it for what it was," MacLeish said. "It was a dream operation until then—and I shouldn't've been asleep to the dangers. And Martin suffered for it."

"Tell me about his promotion to the count room," I said. "How'd you arrange that?"

"We didn't have to," MacLeish said. "That was all Felix. He moved his men in, we think as the first step to making a move on his father."

"Did Felix get wind of Huang's undercover status?"

"He couldn't've," MacLeish said. But behind his words there was doubt. It fed into his narrative of failing, betraying his friend.

"So Felix plans this heist to steal from his father," I spitballed. "He learns Huang is undercover and has him shot. Make it look like a casualty of the robbery rather than an execution. Two birds, one stone and two to three hundred thousand dollars."

It fit. It was the first scenario that did.

By this point MacLeish's people had untied me. I rubbed my wrists, thinking of the scene in the count room. Huang's face reduced to bloody nothing. Not just killed but erased.

The others in the room had been dispatched, either to throw attention away from the true purpose, or as a move made out of panic. Kill 'em all and let God sort 'em out. Same as with the bystanders on the street.

MacLeish had known all this from the start and steered Borden's investigation toward the shooters, away from the truth. Each one of us operating with missing puzzle pieces, desperate to take them from the others.

As unseemly as MacLeish's despair was—as melodramatic—he'd fucking earned it.

"What about Huang's/Yang's family?" I asked. "I take it they're under your protection?"

"Of course," MacLeish said. "They know something happened, but—I haven't told them everything. How could I?"

Yang's daughter must have sought me out to learn what happened to her father. Maybe she thought I was involved. And I was—not as a shooter, but part of the evil mechanism that kept the shooters free.

"So what happens now?" I asked MacLeish.

"I need what Laidlaw told you about these shooters."

"Just the name, as I said, and that they're dangerous."

MacLeish's eyes studied mine, decided I was being truthful. He gripped the legs of the stool beneath him, and in a quick motion hurled it against the wall. It clanged off the concrete but didn't break. He kicked it into the corner.

"I have to stop these men," he said. "I have to make this right. It's my fault. Isn't it?"

Maybe it was, but it felt like we were beyond assigning blame. Felix Long had set something in motion, and only finding the shooters and learning who was killing them would stop it. If anything would.

SIXTY-SIX
BOUDREAU

MacLeish's people dropped me downtown, passing me my overnight bag, which I'd forgotten about. I hadn't been home and wouldn't be for some time yet. My office would have to do.

On the ride up in the elevator, I caught a look at my reflection in the brass. Haggard, bestubbled, more grey hairs peppered throughout. One cheek bruised yellow from MacLeish's blow. In the office I ran tap water over my face, an ugly, cold rejuvenation.

A note with my name on it had been thrust through our mail slot, no postage or address. I smoothed it. Written in dull pencil, half an oily palmprint where the author's hand had rested. It read:

Back in town   *Need money*
Will talk   *One thousand*
Not desperate   *Not full of it*
      You maybe wont like what youll hear.

And a number, which I dialed.

"This Mr. Wakefield?" a raspy male voice asked.

"Close enough, Mr. Boudreau."

"You got my note, right?"

"We need to meet," I said. "Tell me where the garage is and I'll bring the money."

"How'd you know about the garage?"

"I know what brake fluid smells like."

Gabe Boudreau chuckled, a tobacco-addled sound that broke apart into snorts and coughs. "Good for you. My buddy's place is above her shop. Mo's Mufflers in Delta. She'll be out for the day. You show up alone and with the money, although, smart guy like you, I prob'ly didn't need to specify. See you soon."

This is a trap, I muttered as I donned my coat. *This is a trap*. I drove to an ATM and withdrew a thousand dollars, the limit on my temporary replacement card. By then I'd made a chorus of it, imagining Chris Cornell belting out the harmonies. *This. Is. A. Trap.*

Mo's Mufflers was in a part of Delta I'd never been to, though the environment was familiar enough. Sharp-cut hedges around the houses, a lot of cul-de-sacs. Like they'd built the neighbourhood off blueprints for the most anodyne community, then realized upon completion the place had an irremovable sense of menace. Chain-link snuggled the property lines, graffiti overlaid traffic signs and, in turn, had been splashed out by more paint, all of it delible, leaving its trace.

Mo's was a ramshackle garage built on what had once been the front lawn of a house. The two bay doors of the shop had been drawn wide open, leaving parabolas in the wet gravel. They gave the place the look of a drunk welcoming you with open arms.

I walked in through the doors toward a desk. The shop was unevenly lit, smoky and cavernous, especially near the back. Every surface was jammed with greasy auto parts or yellowed papers or tools.

Gabe Boudreau came out of the dark, holding a Slurpee cup and a snub-nosed revolver.

"Easy," he said, dropping the cup on the desk. He patted down my coat pockets with no real conviction, the way a background actor might.

His hair contained veins of rust and chrome, his face powdered with cigarette ash. Eyelids plump and half-closed beneath thick eyebrows, as if he didn't want to look too carefully at this life of his. I noticed the tattoo on his arm, the frontier skeletons locked in combat. He put the gun in the front pouch of his overalls.

"You really are by yourself?" he said.

"The army's decamped a block away, waiting for my signal."

He nodded thoughtfully, no-selling the sarcasm. "And you brought the thousand."

Boudreau took the stack of twenties and counted out ten piles of five. He pushed seven of those together and stashed them in a drawer of the desk. The rest he fit into his pouch, adjusting the gun to do so.

"I appreciate the way you got in contact," he said. "Not bringing trouble up to the rez. Those people got enough, and the last thing I want to do is add to it. The money's not for me, just so you know. It's to compensate those that helped me."

"Your note said I wouldn't like what you had to say," I told him.

"You won't, if you're trying to catch them."

Boudreau tucked his ass onto the desktop and sucked on an e-cigarette. I leaned against the edge of the doorjamb, hoping a breeze would carry away the smell of blueberries.

"I didn't see much once it started," Boudreau said. "Most of what I know I read later in the papers."

"But you heard enough."

"Enough to know to get the fuck away."

"Your calendars were lying in the gutter around the corner, up the block. I saw you gathering them."

He nodded. "The Black guy threw them there."

"Why? Did he attack you? Threaten you?"

"He saved my life," Boudreau said.

SIXTY-SEVEN
THE GOSPEL OF GABE BOUDREAU

He woke up that morning at four, as he did every morning. Woke up and knelt on the floor of his SRO and prayed to Jesus for guidance, knowing forgiveness was too much to ask.

Boudreau spoke of his life as a series of eras or epochs. There'd been the young, dumb, violent youth. Then prison. Then the lost years. The bottom. And then where he found himself now, which he was too modest to call a resurrection.

What had ultimately saved him was the structure. Always up early for prayer, then down to the storage shed to unlock his cart of calendars. A coffee at the Korean grocer's, always paid for with nine quarters. He'd flog the merchandise, eat a cheese sandwich, then home at seven, eight in the summer, unless there was a meeting.

That morning he'd followed the same routine. He knew the other early risers. He said hi to Theresa, the receptionist at Gentrification Central, knocking a knuckle on the window nearest her desk. She smiled and waved. At first she'd been wary of him loitering outside, until one morning in November, when she'd seen him set up amidst a light frosting of snow. She had brought him a cup of tea. Shitty tea, but still. He'd reciprocated by kicking snow from the building's walkway.

That morning he'd gone to the corner, sipped his coffee and began to set up. He'd seen the Black man approach from Keefer, up the block. He'd thought nothing of it, because he'd seen him out this early before.

The Black man was staying at the Western Lodge on Cambie, above the Cambridge Pub. Boudreau had seen him twice on other mornings, smoking a cigarette, walking around in the stillness of the pre-dawn. The man looked like he didn't want to be bothered.

Some people had to be up that early; others preferred it. To Boudreau the man seemed to fit neither category. He looked like he'd simply found himself awake, couldn't change that fact and was killing time. In retrospect, Boudreau realized that the man was probably familiarizing himself with the neighbourhood.

There might have been something different in the man's face that morning. He'd been wearing blue coveralls under a black peacoat, some sort of scarf around his neck. He'd walked straight up to Boudreau, grabbed his arm and the handle of the cart, and dragged both up Keefer.

The cart had been upended into the gutter, calendars kicked out into the street. The Black man had spoken something to Boudreau that, in his rage, Boudreau couldn't hear. Then the man had pulled the scarf-thing over his nose, revealing it to be the mask with the dog skeleton design. He brought a gun out of the folds of the coat and turned the corner.

Boudreau had been too angry to be stupefied. He'd bent and recovered his merchandise, finally kneeling on the edge of the gutter to save his back. No purpose to what happened, he thought, just another guy who got off on bullying poor folks. Boudreau had faced worse. He'd been working up the strength to forgive the man. And then came the shots.

Boudreau hadn't paused, unsure what the string of noises signified. He'd heard the gabble of voices across the street, at the bus stop. He hadn't been deterred from rescuing his calendars.

But then the shouts and the gunshots, coming from around the corner. Boudreau froze, thinking the man might retrace his steps. He righted his cart and dragged it up the block, running now, ignoring the sounds.

Of course he'd been afraid. Boudreau used the alleys to put distance between himself and the scene. He walked and doubled back, zigzagging through the streets. Only once he felt safe could his mind start processing what he'd witnessed.

And it had sunk home, what the man had done, and what he'd done for Boudreau.

He still didn't know what the Black man had said, but the gist must have been to get clear, to get to safety. The man had thrown the cart knowing it would place Boudreau away from the violence.

Boudreau wondered why the man had done that. Strategically it made sense to clear the field. Maybe that was all it was. But Boudreau couldn't help reading kindness into it. The man had wanted to spare an innocent. Boudreau wouldn't say he qualified for that, but none of us deserves His pity.

He'd gone to a bar and called Mo, whom he knew from one of his programs. She'd been sober three years, believed she owed him one. He took a cab to her place, stopping at his SRO to lock up the cart. Mo drove him out of the city, up to where his friend's wife had a property near the Carrier reserve.

From there he'd pieced together the story of the robbery and murders. It hammered home the extraordinary blessing he'd received. That was what was hardest to accept: that of eight souls, his had been granted a reprieve. The least deserving. There was truly no accounting for His mercy.

Boudreau had remained up there for weeks. When his friend's wife received a visit from the tribal chief, asking for Boudreau on behalf of a band leader in Musqueam territory, Boudreau had realized something.

"At first I felt I owed it to the guy," he said, loading a fresh cartridge in his e-cigarette. Spittle collected on the stained shop floor. "That man could've shot me and he didn't. Thing is, running away wasn't showing gratitude, it was showing fear."

"I don't understand," I said.

Boudreau hauled a roll of paper towel off the bench and blew his nose. His eyes seemed moist. What I'd first read as fervency I now saw was the anguish of conflict. He spoke convincingly in the hope of convincing himself.

"There's always an easy and a hard choice," he said. "You know. I saw you on the news wanting nothing to do with this."

"I was scared."

"And damn right to be. So was I—but I thought it was gratitude. Not saying anything as a way to pay back the man who saved me. What did I owe the cops? Or the dead folks? I'd almost convinced myself it was the right thing to do."

"But you had second thoughts," I said.

"'Cause of you." Boudreau's look was less of gratitude than grudging acceptance. "I figured I owed it to the dead to speak up. Figured if you'd worked up the faith, then so could I."

"The police could make sure you're protected," I said.

He unbuttoned the pouch of his overalls and handed me the pistol. "If you've been listening, you'd know I got that department covered."

The weapon was light in my hand. Harmless, a replica. I handed it back.

"I told you what I know," Boudreau said, "on faith that you'll show them the mercy they showed me. I don't want to see any more dead."

"I'm not in any position—"

"Catch 'em, see they stand trial, but show mercy all the same." His hand pressed to his heart. "I'll testify to what I heard and saw, just as I'll testify to what that man did for me. I'll put it in His hands."

Boudreau began walking away, farther into the shop, as if I'd already agreed. And maybe I had.

SIXTY-EIGHT
A VIEW OF THE STREET

Ryan Martz agreed to meet me at the Western Lodge at noon. I felt better about my vow to Boudreau knowing I'd be escorted by an armed officer of the law.

When I got there, Ryan was sitting on a bench in the street outside eating a slice of takeout pizza off a paper plate. Sonia sat next to him.

"Figured you'd want someone to cover the back door," Ryan said between bites. "Figured I'd get someone expendable."

Sonia punched his shoulder hard enough to knock half the toppings on his pizza to the ground. I kissed her, held her.

"Missed you," I said.

"You should've called when you got in."

"I got a ride from MacLeish's people, and after that, things popped up."

The Western Lodge front-desk duties were split between an old man and a teenaged girl in braces. I described Mustafa Said and asked about his aliases. A Clive Kent had taken a room four weeks ago and paid upfront for a month's stay. The girl couldn't say exactly when he'd checked out. The credit card he'd given was a prepaid disposable.

Had Mr. Kent left anything in the room? I asked. The old man scooted his chair forward so the girl could dredge up the box holding the lost and found.

"I cleaned his room," she said. "I clean all the rooms. I think—yes." She fished through the box and brought up a pair of beaten paperbacks, Mack Bolan, Donald Goines. Also a comb, a razor and a tourist's map of downtown, bordered with local business ads. Finally, a folded printout of the ferry schedule. Tsawwassen to Victoria, to Port Angeles in

Washington. A long touristy way to get to the States. Someone travel-
ling with stolen money and forged papers would have an easier time
crossing the border by ferry than by car or plane. Less chance of being
searched.

I asked to see Kent's room. I was in luck: it hadn't been rented since.

The girl let me in and scurried back to her front-desk duties. "I'm
pretty thorough," she said, letting me know I wouldn't find anything.

The room was on the second floor, the window dirty, double-paned
and speckled with mold. We began to search. Bed, wastebasket, drawers, closet. Four strikes. Washroom: toilet back, vents, underside of sink.
Nada. Nada for the TV stand. Air ducts—that old cliché—nada.

I worked the mattress up and peered around the seams, finding human
hairs and bloody traces of bedbugs, but no secretly sewn pouches. No
edge to the carpet, no baseboards.

The three of us tore through the place. The girl reappeared; her opinion of my authority perhaps bolstered by the appearance of the two
officers.

"What do you think?" I asked Sonia.

"What do I think what?"

"Good enough for our honeymoon?"

She shook her head but a small tired smile escaped her.

"I didn't know you guys were getting married," Ryan said.

"Neither did I," Sonia said.

"Congrats. When—" Ryan paused to read us and let himself in on
the joke.

I watched as Sonia ran her hands over the rust-coloured blackout
curtains that might as well have been burlap. "What?" she said.

"Want to get married?"

"Of all the places," she said.

"You're right. Sorry."

"Yes."

"Really?"

She smiled. "You thought I wouldn't?"

I stumbled forward. She dropped the curtain long enough to
embrace me.

"This is what I want," she said. "Us. Sharing this—even the dirty shithole apartments. There's no one else I'd want to share it with."

"*Ahem*," said Ryan.

As we left the room, Sonia said, "I still demand a real fucking proposal."

"Of course. Knee and everything."

"And a real honeymoon. Someplace nice."

"Only the best for you," I said. "I'll rent us the country bar on Hastings. Little line dancing, some "Achy Breaky Heart," what do you think?"

As I descended the stairs I felt her boot between my shoulder blades, miming my imminent demise.

I caught the railing, turned.

"What?" Ryan said.

"We missed something," I said, rushing past him, back up the stairs.

The view from the window took in the approach to the front door. Both corners of the street were visible. With the window up, I could crane and see almost to the corner of the street beyond.

Ryan called up, "What d'you got, bloodhound?"

"Explain in a sec," I said as I started down.

The front-desk girl had a beleaguered look as I entreated her again. "Did Mr. Kent choose that room?" I asked. "Did he *choose* 211?"

"Not specifically," she said.

"But he asked for a second-floor room."

"School's back in," she said. "Without students we got a lot of vacancies. He wanted—yeah, I remember, I showed him a couple of rooms and he chose that one. He said he didn't mind the street noise, that it helped him sleep."

"He was by himself," I inferred.

"Didn't see him with anyone else. I don't like to bother people unless they ask."

"But you got the sense," I said, "he was a loner."

"I guess, yeah." She corrected the tension of the scrunchie that pinned back her dark curls. "He was up real early, quite a few times, so maybe the sleep thing didn't work. I left coffee out for him after the second time."

"And no forwarding address," I said, hoping she'd correct me. She didn't.

Outside I backed up to the edge of the curb, stared up. I saw the fat grey lip of the window ledge. Saw Sonia's dark eyes through the scuzzy glass.

Why that room?

To watch the street.

This street?

Or *any* street?

Was this habit? Him expecting something?

Someone with Said's training and experience might pick that room as the safest. High enough to see, an easy drop if necessary. Backed into a corner, he would choose the most favourable corner he could.

Maybe he'd already taken the ferry, but more likely he was still in town, at another place, similar to this. Did he somehow lose control of the money? Was his escape route compromised? Or, with the deaths of Czechowski and Axton, was he looking for revenge?

Maybe, like me, he just wanted to understand.

SIXTY-NINE
HIT AND MISS

Ryan returned to work, while Sonia and I spent hours checking hotels and hostels. No hits on Said, his description or his aliases. We asked at the stores and restaurants near the Western Lodge, but nobody remembered the man.

We ate dinner at The Ramen Butcher off Main, slurping noodles and broth at a communal table with other couples. Normalcy, if only for an hour. Coffee after at the hipster place next door, and a sunset walk back to my office.

"Going to buy me a ring?" Sonia said in the elevator.

"If you want."

"I'll pick it out."

"You don't trust my jewellery-buying skills?"

"When's the last time you bought any?"

"I bought a watch once," I said. "Before cell phones. You hit a button and the face lit up green."

"That sounds classy as hell, Wakeland, but all the same, I'll pick my ring."

In the reception area we found Jeff and Blatchford, both looking on edge.

Before I could ask, Jeff said, "Two things. Kay isn't answering her cell. She was supposed to be back here, this afternoon." He added quietly, "So were you."

She'd been watching the Huang house—the Yang house. "Why didn't you tell me sooner?"

"Your phone's off," Blatchford said.

I took it from my pocket, saw the black screen. He was right. Plugging it into the wall charger by the reception desk, I said to Blatchford, "You were with her, right?"

"All yesterday and earlier today. Didn't see anything weird."

"So what happened?"

He blushed. "I had to take a shit real bad. I was only gone about half an hour. When I got back, she wasn't in the van."

"And since then what have you been doing?" I caught my anger growing, stifled it. "Not your fault. Will you check out the area again? And call if you see anything."

As he left, Jeff said, "It's only been a few hours."

It was like Kay to pursue something to the point of forgetting to stay in contact. But with all that was going on, I couldn't dislodge the pearl of cold dread forming in my stomach.

Once my phone had power, I checked the messages. Nothing from Kay. "What's the second piece of news?" I asked Jeff.

"Felix Long was shot last night."

Jeff's face gave away nothing, but the stiff way he sat told me the news had affected him. There was obligation if not friendship between them. He knew how Roy Long would take the news.

"He's not dead," Jeff said. "The woman he was with, though, she's in critical care. Felix took two bullets in the shoulder and arm."

"Do you know who?" I asked.

"Only one possibility, isn't there?"

If Felix Long had hired the shooters, there was the possibility he'd double-crossed them. That meant Felix was not only behind the robbery but also the murders of Czechowski and Axton.

Jeff told me it had been an ambush outside a night club in Richmond. Felix and a date had been leaving the club around two. Shots had been fired from a car near the entrance to the parking lot. The shooter had hit Felix, Felix had found cover and his bodyguard, Gu, had returned fire. In the resulting firefight Felix's date had been shot in the throat. The shooter then drove off.

"So fucking pointless," Sonia said, taking the seat opposite Jeff.

"He was always like that," Jeff said. "So convinced he was smarter than me and his brothers."

"Does Uncle Roy know?" I asked.

Jeff looked forlornly at the phone. "I imagine so. 'Magine he knew before anyone."

I drummed nervous triplets on the chair's backrest, thinking about Kay. Like Felix I'd set something in motion, and other people were paying for it.

My phone exploded in its preset ringtone, startling us. I picked up, hoping to hear my sister's voice. Instead it was a husky, out-of-breath man's voice asking for me.

"This is Wakeland."

"Good. Stay on the line. Someone wants to speak with you."

I set the phone on speaker, Sonia and Jeff watching it like a ticking explosive. Kay was on a stakeout near a police operation. It was unlikely someone would try violence so close. The word *unlikely* never felt more tenuous.

Finally a dark, familiar voice filled my ear.

"Got something you need to see," Terry Rhodes said.

SEVENTY
TERMINAL AVENUE

The Exiles owned a chain of music shops across the Lower Mainland. The address Rhodes provided sent me to their head branch on Terminal. Instrument showrooms on the ground floor, offices and classrooms above. The yellow-painted chain that barred the parking lot had been flung aside, and the freight entrance was propped open. Unlit signs for Yamaha and Pearl decorated the dark glass.

Inside the door, a woman with jagged-cut purple hair nodded to me, sniffled and led me through the store. There was a narrow, carpeted path that weaved between the stacks of drum kits and amplifiers. The showroom lights were off, illumination leaking from a backroom.

Terry Rhodes and Redbeard took up most of a sound-baffled booth full of speaker monitors and keyboard synths. Rhodes leaned against the controls of an enormous mixing board, staring impatiently at something lying on the floor.

Percy Axton reposed on the carpet. His left leg jutted out as if he were doing a heel step in a line dance. Up close I could see the wounds in his abdomen and right breast. Very little blood on the floor. He'd shit himself, the small room rank with the smell.

Rhodes gently kicked the corpse's head. "This one of 'em?"

"The woman's husband," I said. "I think he was the driver."

Axton's hands bore no signs of torture. His right fist was balled up, at his side, like a petulant child's. I worked the fingers open, but nothing was hidden inside.

I started checking Axton's pockets. Rhodes pounded his fist into the mixing board, leaving a crack in the frame and knocking loose one of the faders.

"I didn't bring you here to play fucking Columbo," he said. "You're here to give me answers. Like who the fuck are these people?"

"Working on it," I said.

"The fuck you are."

I gambled that in this case, anger was better met with more anger than with passive acceptance. "You tell me to find these people," I said, "then piss and moan about how I do it. All because you can't be patient and let me fucking go about my work. You want to search him? Knock yourself out. But one of us has to."

"Mind who you're talking to," Redbeard said.

Rhodes looked at me with amusement. It was the look I'd gambled on, that told me I provided more entertainment to him alive than otherwise.

I gestured at the corpse, and he extended an open hand, you go right ahead.

"The Axtons are ex-military," I said as I patted down the corpse. My olfactory sense rebelled, and I had to look away for a moment. "They and the others worked for an international security company."

"Seven Hills?" It took a lot to impress Terry Rhodes.

"Called Rip Tyde now. One is using the name Lester Nunn. The other"—I thought of whether to mention Said's name, held off, figuring I might need a hole card—"I'm still working on the other."

"Better hurry, then," Rhodes said. "Else Felix'll beat you to them."

"You know it's Felix," I said.

"Of course. The fuck else would do this—hire people to rip off your old man and then shoot 'em over the money? Thought he could make people think it's me that did it instead. Keep Uncle Roy from finding out. Kid makes up in balls what he don't got in brains."

"You shot him, then."

"I will," Rhodes said easily.

"But that wasn't you last night?"

He seemed puzzled. I told him about Felix.

"Piss fucking poor job," Rhodes said. "You want to kill someone that bad, you do it *in* the club. The guys that dink hired must've got their backs up. Desperate, I guess."

He regarded the corpse and then stepped over it. Redbeard followed suit.

"This rate I won't get to kill anyone," Rhodes said.

Percy Axton had no wallet or keys. I peeled up the blood-caked jacket and patted the liner pockets. The store manager watched from the doorway, her thumbnail tucked between her teeth.

"Can I go?" she asked me.

"I won't stop you."

The corpse's jacket yielded nothing. I felt through the breast pocket, worked my way down to the pants.

"That man said he'd let me go when he was done." Curiosity and revulsion kept her eyes on Axton's face. "He's not coming back, is he?"

"There's no predicting him," I said.

I worked a hand under the buttocks, thinking how absurd the three of us must look. Right back pocket: nothing. The smell—in some ways it helped keep my thoughts away from the reality of death. We all go out in an undignified mess.

Holding my breath, I stepped over the body and nudged up Axton's left thigh. In the left seat pocket was a tightly folded rectangle of paper. I stood and unfolded it near the light. It matched the one from Mustafa Said's room at the Western Lodge. This was a map of truck crossings from White Rock to Alberta. He'd circled one near Creston.

The shooters had planned separate routes back to the States. Not quite a free-for-all, since they'd planned together. But it raised the question of who was supposed to take the money, and where it was now.

"I shouldn't leave the store unlocked," the manager said. "But if I lock it and he comes back and I'm not here…"

"It'll be all right," I said.

We walked out together. She tossed the keys through the mail slot once the door was secure.

I put the paper down on the roof of my rental as I fetched my own keys. At the bottom of the page was a series of numbers added in faint pencil. Four digits, then two, then three, then six.

I took a picture of them, sent it to Jeff with a question mark. While my phone was out, I texted Kay.

Fifteen digits, separated by slashes. Bank account. Serial number. Coded message. Part of the plan, or something added later?

Jeff texted back, *Damned if I know*. As I punched in clarification, he added, *First search engine hit on first part is address. Lok-It Storage. Send Blatchford?*

I'll meet him there, I replied. *Any news on Kay?*

Nothing yet.

SEVENTY-ONE
TEMPTATION

Lok-It Storage was on an industrial side street near Fourth and Clark, by the train tracks and beneath the viaduct. It was a short walk from the music store. The teal-coloured building had rows of padlocked overhead doors, each painted a clashing bright red. Floodlights lit up the lanes.

The third set of numbers on Axton's paper was 377. I walked along the lanes until I found the corresponding door. Kneeling down, I twisted the last six numbers into the combination lock, two at a time. The bolt released. I unthreaded the lock and raised the door.

A wall of orange boxes cut the storage shed in half. They were printer-paper boxes, and as I lifted the lid off the nearest one, I felt the left battlement topple. All were empty.

Or most. I tapped a finger against each in turn. One made a deader sound than the others. Something inside. I was shifting boxes to get to it when I heard footsteps.

I turned. No one was around, the only sound the buzz from the lights.

Turning back to the boxes, something pressed into my nape. Two fingers. A breathy voice said, "Freeze."

"Not fucking funny, Tim," I said.

"Maybe not to you," Blatchford replied, taking his hand away.

He stooped and entered the locker with me, began opening the boxes. I asked if he'd found any trace of Kay.

"Nothing," he said. "The van is still parked near that house. I asked around and nobody's seen her. But that's the point of surveillance, right? Stay hidden?"

"Safely hidden."

"She'll be okay, Dave, she's a pro."

Together we pulled out the heavy bottom box. I worked off the lid. Inside were six knotted Safeway bags.

Inside those: money. Most had been sorted into stacks of Canadian or US bills, rubber-banded and bundled with like currency. Three of the bags held loose unsorted cash. At a cursory glance, at least two hundred thousand.

"No coins," said Blatchford. Peering closer. "That's quite a chunk of change."

"Ten lives' worth and counting."

"Meaning what?" His look seemed like an appeal, either for direction or permission.

"You really tempted?" I asked.

"Of course not," he said. "That would be wrong."

For the sake of thoroughness I started checking the other boxes. As empty as they'd felt.

"I mean, so what if it's untraceable?" Blatchford said. "Who cares if there's no rightful owner? Wrong is wrong, after all."

"Dead is dead."

Second from the bottom on the next row, I found the hockey bag they'd used to transport the take. Beneath the bag was a pencil, a set of keys and a flip phone.

"You're no fun anymore," Blatchford said.

"I was never any fun."

"Not true, there was a brief couple weeks…"

The phone was dead. I pocketed it and the keys.

"But you'll take those," Blatchford said.

"The real question," I said, "is do we give this to the police now?"

"Or?"

"Hold off."

"Before giving it to them anyway. If that's all you can think to do with it, what's the point of waiting? Let 'em come take it now."

"I'm worried about Kay," I said.

"Dave, I doubt they would have grabbed her."

Voicing it in the confines of the storage locker gave his words a hollowness that cemented my decision.

"We'll move it," I said. "Rent another locker, couple rows over. Stow the money there."

"Least I know where to find the cash for the rental," Blatchford said.

I shook my head. "Clean money. Hit an ATM if you have to."

He opened his wallet sullenly.

"Look," I said, "when this is over, you still want to take some, that's your business. But if I tell someone I have it, it all has to be there."

"Can't steal from the robbers," Blatchford said. "Got it. Makes perfect sense." But he nodded reluctantly and went off to find the manager.

At our office there was a desk drawer full of miscellaneous chargers. One fit the antiquated phone. It burbled to life, stuttered out its boot-up jingle on blown speakers.

Two missed calls. No messages. I looked up the call history, typing the numbers into my computer. Three calls to the Western Lodge where Said/Kent had been staying.

The other calls were to other hotels, one in Surrey, one in White Rock. The two most recent, the missed calls, were from the Convention Inn in Richmond.

They'd spread to the exurbs, split up, the Axtons taking the money. Each with their own preplanned exit. The shooting had complicated things. Then Czechowski—had he contacted Felix, or had Felix known where to find him?

The robbery had subsumed ten lives so far, damaged countless others. Felix, panicking, decides to remove the shooters while they're vulnerable. Blame the robbery on Rhodes, lay the bodies on his property to sow confusion. Then Felix himself is shot, almost killed in turn, when the shooters work out who's been targeting them.

"Jeff," I called, walking over to his private office. Jeff was inside, going over reports, his way of keeping calm. Kay's disappearance had agitated him too. "Let's go talk to Felix," I said.

"He's still in the hospital," Jeff said. "No way he'll talk to you."

"What about to you?"

He thought it over and shrugged. "He might," he said, "if I go alone."

"Cool. I'll go with you."

"Alone, Dave. It's the only way. If he sees you—"

"Tell you what," I said. "We'll try the hospital together, then I'll check out the hotel nearby. Axton called that number. That way, one call, I'm nearby."

"And vice versa," Jeff said.

Before we left I scribbled out a note on the reception desk, telling Kay, if she saw it, to call me right away. We made the drive to Richmond, taking one of the company vans. That feeling of dread was growing.

SEVENTY-TWO
AMBUSH

Visiting hours were long over by the time we got to Richmond Hospital. Felix Long had come out of surgery six hours ago. He was expected to survive, and to keep his arm. We couldn't possibly see him until ten the next morning.

It was three now. We sat alone in the cafeteria. I rubbed my eyes with my palms and downed a large lukewarm coffee that tasted like a dissolved cigar.

I told Jeff I wanted to hold onto the money until Kay was returned. He said I was leaping to conclusions, that she'd probably turn up tomorrow. I said he was probably right, but just in case.

That was the worst part of paranoia: my mind vaulted ahead to the worst possible scenario, so far ahead that I could tell it was silly, and yet … and yet.

In the last weeks I'd doubted everyone, and I couldn't tell if there had been good reason or not. I wondered if that trust would ever return. For now, it was a high-wire balance of faith and lack of options. How silly and melodramatic that sounded, how unlike me. And yet.

Three men in black suits entered the cafeteria, staking out two tables in the corner. They were soon joined by an older woman, a teenage girl and Roy Long. His arm was around the woman's shoulders, and he helped her into a seat. Long nodded at Jeff and me in turn, looking much older than he had the last time I'd seen him. Not frail, though. The men around him deferred, springing to pull his chair out, fetching cups of tea.

"I'll go check the hotel," I told Jeff.

My partner watched the back of the old man's head with concern. "I'll see if there's a chance for a private word with Roy."

Long's wife let out a loud sob and leaned into her husband's breast. The girl wrapped her arms around the older woman's waist, tucked her head tight against her back. As I walked by them Roy Long looked up briefly. In that half-second, I saw his jaw was clenched, eyes vacant with thoughts of revenge. A deity, provoked into wrath by the hubris of mortals. Then his chin lowered to meet his wife's shoulder, and he was once again an old man, grieving.

The Convention Inn had a long, covered turnaround. No one in the upper rooms could see my approach. The lobby was spacious and plush, a rhombus of leather sofas near the elevators, across from a coffee kiosk, information desk and courtesy phone. Like the other hotel across the street, this one drew its clientele from the convention centre nearby.

The desk manager had a capable air and a professional smile she enhanced with brief nods. *Happy to help but time is an issue, sorry to say.*

I played the disorganized chauffeur, asking her to phone Mr. Kent and tell him his car service is ready. Which room? I'm sorry, I wasn't told. He said he'd meet me in the lobby. When she said Kent wasn't registered, I asked about Mr. Nunn. Then I retreated to the courtesy phone, faked a call to my branch manager and approached again, even more sheepish. Would you believe he mixed up the clients? A Mr. Said. He's not here either? Well, I did my job. I'll work it out with numbnuts back at the office. Sorry to be a bother.

It was possible they were there under another name. I walked to the kiosk and bought a pack of Dunhills, was denied matches and purchased the cheapest lighter.

Outside, under the turnaround, I smoked and looked at the area. Strip mall nearby, parking lot. Fast-moving street traffic, highway access. No locals except the staff.

Intuition struck in the form of a question. Would a professional call from the courtesy phone in their own hotel? Or...

I crossed to the Hotel Richmond, not looking up as I passed under the low-set second-floor windows. This hotel was a bit cheaper, and its facade bore some resemblance to the Western Lodge.

I ran the same scam on the desk clerk, this time hitting on Clive Kent. The clerk dialed room 221.

"Mr. Kent seems to be out," he said after the tenth ring. "May I leave a message?"

"Tell him Percy called," I said. "He has my number."

I walked back outside, drew out another cigarette, fought it and tossed the pack. Back to the car, where I waited. No sign of Mustafa Said or the man calling himself Lester Nunn.

Limos and taxis began arriving around eight. A half-hour later two buses pulled in, letting off a wave of conventioneers. I followed them into the lobby. Registration tables were set up, name tags doled out.

I took the elevator to the second floor, noting that the gym and pool were on basement level one. The hallway on the second floor branched off down half a dozen corridors. I found 221, tried the handle. No luck.

A cleaning trolley was parked outside the elevator. I filched a pair of towels and took the stairs down to the lobby, which was still packed with conventioneers. A different clerk now manned the desk, handling a long line of early check-ins.

In a toilet stall of the public restroom, I stripped to my underwear and wrapped a towel around my waist. Bundling my clothing inside the other towel, I doused my hair and face with tap water. I approached the front desk, begging pardon as I skipped to the front of the line.

I told the clerk I was locked out of my room, making my third sheepish look of the morning. Kent, Clive, staying in 221.

A corner of the clerk's smile was missing, exposing his irritation. He issued me another key card. *Is there anything else I can help you with, have a nice afternoon, next, please.*

I listened outside 221 to make sure it was empty, then unlocked the door and went inside. Slowly. I checked the door jamb for hairs, paperclips. No use taking chances. I turned my phone and Axton's to silent.

The room had been tidied but still had a lived-in feel to it. Suitcase on the folding stand near the closet, pile of clothes on the easy chair. In the washroom: haircare products, razor and comb, collapsible toothbrush and full-sized tube of Colgate.

I opened the bottom drawers of the chest/TV stand, feeling I had a good sense of the man. I pulled on the drawer till it cleared the grooves of its track and came out. I reached underneath.

Passport, stack of money, a dog-eared Chester Himes. The .22 target pistol and a box of ammunition.

As I dressed, Axton's phone shook in my pocket. Missed call from an unlisted number.

I took the gun, trusting it was loaded. Replaced the drawer. Tucked myself behind the half-open washroom door. The phone burbled once more and went silent.

The *chuh-chuck* of the electronic lock. The door swung inward. I remembered I'd left my towels on the bed. A shadow moved into the room, paused. He was carrying something. He stepped farther in.

I pointed the pistol at the base of his neck.

"Not much fun when it's your head, is it," I said.

SEVENTY-THREE
HOSTAGES

He turned, saw the gun. I told him to back up, hands on your head, on your knees. His movements were languid. I made him lie face down.

Any weak tilt of my hand, any vocal flutter, any sign I wasn't committed to killing him and I knew he would break for it. Whether he'd run or try for the gun, it didn't matter. He'd read my hesitancy and know the odds were better if he tried me than if he gave in.

So I focused completely on the gun. Said was already dead in front of me. Only complying with my commands would resurrect him, and even that wasn't a certainty.

His automatic was in his pocket. I drew it out carefully, keeping the .22 close but not touching his skull.

"Where's Nunn and the others?" I said.

A delayed response. Mustafa Said finally said, "I don't know."

I eased down onto a corner of the bed, kept the barrel aimed at him. His head was tilted, ear to the ground, as if listening for a cattle stampede. Or a train. I made him turn his head so he was looking at the wall.

With my free hand I dialed Jeff, put the phone on loudspeaker and sat it on my knee. "Got one," I said. "Hotel Richmond, 221."

"How'd you pull that off?" Jeff said.

"Expert detective work. It'd take too long to explain to a rank amateur. How quickly can you get here?"

"There are cabs out front. Want I should phone the cops?"

"No." Said's voice, muffled by the floor.

"It's not up for a vote," I said. To Jeff: "The van is at the far end of the parking lot. Park it closer. And bring the restraints from the kit."

I ended the call. We waited two minutes in silence.

Said moistened his mouth. He said, "I could've killed you."

"You regretting it?"

"Maybe." He swallowed. "I didn't hurt you."

"Caused me great aggravation, though. Tell me why I shouldn't turn you over."

"Lester Nunn," said Said.

"What about him?"

"I'll help you."

"Tell me where he is."

"Don't know but I can get in touch—set something up. Otherwise you won't find him."

"I found you."

He waited almost another minute before answering.

"He's going to hurt more people."

Two gunshots went off. I jolted, nearly fired. It was Jeff knocking on the door.

I stood, backpedalled to the door, opened it with my free hand. The gun barrel never strayed from the direction of the prone man's spine.

Jeff stepped past me, avoiding my line of fire. Crossed over to Said and told him to put his arms behind his back. Jeff carried a bundle of zip ties.

"Was it Nunn that shot Felix?" I asked.

"Probably," Said said. "He wanted to send a message."

"Stupid message," Jeff said. "He's on morphine now, doped up. His first gunshot, so of course now he's acting like a gangster."

"Who else is Nunn after?" I asked Said.

"You. Me."

"Does he have my sister?"

Said shrugged as best he could with bound arms. "He went to pick someone up. A woman and a man, I think."

"What do you mean 'pick up'?"

"Hostages."

I looked to Jeff, hoping he'd know what to say. But he was busy tying Said's arms.

"He'll shoot them both, same as the others." Said's voice was matter of fact. "I can help you get them back alive."

"How's that?"

"Bait him," Said said. "You have something he wants."

"The money."

"Even more than that," he said. "You have me."

SEVENTY-FOUR
PANIC MODE

"Why would Nunn want to kill you?" Jeff asked our hostage.

Mustafa Said was bent forward, his shoulders slouched, bound arms propping up his torso. Despite the circumstances, he looked relaxed. He asked for water. Jeff filled a glass from the bathroom tap and held it to Said's mouth. When he was done drinking, he moistened his lips and said, "Lester put the job together. He told us we would take at least a hundred grand apiece, with minimum exposure and low chance of casualties. If done right. He repeated that type of phrase a lot. "No one gets hurt if we do this right."

"We planned it out like any other operation. At first it went as planned. We neutralized the girl at the front desk, disarmed the sentry in the hall. We had control of that room. As we were loading the money, Les shot the one man. Claimed he was reaching for something. Then he turned the gun on the others.

"In the moment, there was nothing to do other than back his play. We've all seen good men make mistakes under pressure. We proceeded with the plan. Les hung behind."

"To finish the man in the hall," I said, "and the receptionist."

Said nodded. "He seemed to be in panic mode. We didn't know at the time, but it was an act. Les knew what he was doing. Why else would he reload before exiting the building? Why engage with the civilians at the bus stop? He could have walked to the van like the rest of us. He planned for it to happen the way it did."

I saw Lester Nunn walk out of the building, opening fire. I pushed away the memory.

"We split up soon after debriefing," Said said. "Shelly and Percy took the money. At the last minute, Les told Rudy to switch outs with him."

"Outs?" Jeff held the glass for Said.

"Escape plans. We were going to split up. Different hotels and vehicles. Stagger our border crossings. Rendezvous in Seattle in a week's time. Les demanded Rudy swap hotels and vehicles. Rudy was the youngest and didn't argue."

"Czechowski was the first to be caught and killed," I said.

"He was a good soldier who deserved better," Said said. "That was when I knew Les had lied to us. He knew someone might come for him, so he put Rudy in his place."

"What about the Axtons?"

"Percy contacted me. He said Shelly had been picked up by someone. He'd escaped with the money, and he was worried for her. He said the man who took her was short, Asian, had a goatee."

"Gu," I said to Jeff.

Said watched us exchange a look. "I don't know his name," he said. "I agreed to meet with Percy, even though it wrecked our plan. By that point everything had gone tits up, and I wanted to know where we stood. Percy told me he'd already talked to Les. Les wanted Percy to stay in his hotel room, that he'd be there soon. I didn't know what angle Les was working, but I told Percy to get out of there. He didn't listen."

"Gu works for Felix Long," I said. "Felix was shot last night. So was Axton."

Said coughed and Jeff gave him the rest of the water. "Les and Percy go back a long way together, back to the early days at Seven Hills. I think Les used Percy to try to remove this man Gu. When they failed, Les shot him."

A weight seemed to fall on Said's shoulders. He slumped and closed his eyes, exhaled. Weeks of running, hiding, terror and confusion. I knew the feeling.

"There's just the two of us left now," he said. "I'm the only one who saw Les shoot those people. He'll deal with you, release your friends, to get me."

Jeff said to him, "Given what you just told us, why wouldn't Nunn shoot all of us, you included?"

"He'll try to," Said said. His tone made Nunn's decision to kill four people sound like strategy rather than slaughter. "If you can control the terms of the engagement, you could make it so Les has no chance."

"Worth thinking about," I said.

"No." Jeff had moved closer to the phone stand next to the bed. His hand touched the receiver. "I'm sorry," he said, "but this is police business all the way. We are not prepared or capable, Dave. Too much can go wrong. Kay's better off if the police handle this."

"If it was Marie," I said, "or Shuzhen, would you make the same case?"

"Yes, I would." He shrugged. "I don't know, okay? I *do* know we can't go along with this."

He was right. If Said was telling the truth, of which there was no guarantee, then Lester Nunn was better dealt with at a remove, by the authorities. The stakes were too high to consider the alternative.

Sensing our change of heart, Mustafa Said spoke quickly, an urgent edge to his tone. Even with him lying in repose, it had been hard to view him as anything other than a killer biding his time. I saw him differently now. He was afraid of what would happen to him in custody, or at the mercy of Lester Nunn, and he stated his case emphatically.

"Les is a thirteen-year professional," he said. "He knows how cops think, how they're trained to respond. If he senses anything, he will neutralize his hostages and disengage. You have the right bait and just enough time to draw him out, and I know there is no reason to trust me, but I've done this almost as long as he has, eleven years, and I swear, on my mother, I will help you so long as I can leave when it's done."

"You'd guarantee you'll get his sister back?" Jeff said.

"No, I can't," he said. "I can do my best, though."

"And you'd take Dave's word—he'd let you go at the end of this."

"I would."

Said looked nervous, yet confident in his skills, and Jeff looked on the verge of being convinced. Going with the police would be the safer, smarter option. It would also put our lives in the hands of MacLeish, or someone less involved.

Before I could decide, my phone buzzed. Sonia's number. As I answered I thought of what to say. *Hey, darling, how are you? I'm thinking about doing something really fucking stupid. Endangering myself, my partner and friend, my sister. You too. Which means, depending on how things go, this might be our last—*

"Dave," Sonia said. "Kay and I are at Ryan's house. What happened?"

"Kay's with you?" I nearly shouted, causing Jeff to flinch. "Put her on."

"Don't be mad with her, all right?"

"Not mad, been worried out of my fucking mind, put her on now, please."

Kay's voice was groggy, slurred. "Hey half-brother. I got my first concussion. Pretty tits, huh?"

"How? What happened? Why haven't you called?"

"One at a time, fella. I was in the van and that kid saw me, the girl with the jacket. She came up to the van, all crying and shit. I thought I could talk to her. Next thing I know I'm on the ground with a bad fucking headache."

"Christ," I said, "and you didn't phone?"

"The girl hit me, and I fell bad. Badly, sorry. I fell badly and she felt bad. She drove me to the hospital. That's where I phoned Sonia."

"Why her and not me?" I asked.

"Didn't want you to make a big fuss. Never hear the end of it. Y'know on TV, when you get knocked on the head, you just wake up later with a teeny headache. This feels worse, like my head is a broken, you know, pain, and—"

"Rest up," I said, "and put Sonia back on."

"Dave." Sonia's voice was agitated. "She called me because she didn't want you to worry. To think less of her."

"So instead she tries to hide a concussion. Real fucking smart."

"Like in her position you'd do differently," Sonia said. "I'm taking her right back to the hospital. Is Ryan with you?"

"Just Jeff," I said, looking at Said and thinking of what to say. The truth was easiest. "I've also got one of the shooters with me. Long story, but he says his partner took hostages. Up till now I thought that meant Kay—"

"Oh Jesus, Dave," Sonia said. "That's why I phoned you. We're standing in their house and the door's wide open. He's got Ryan and Nikki."

SEVENTY-FIVE
FAREWELL RIDE

We stood Said up, draped a blazer over his restraints, and escorted him out through the lobby to the parking lot. The convention was still in full swing, and no one looked twice at us. Jeff had moved the van close to the entrance. A few spaces over, I spied a familiar Cadillac. Said had exchanged the licence plates, but I recognized the scrapes on the door and fender.

We seated Said on the middle bench, strapped the seat belt across him. Jeff sat behind him holding the target pistol.

I dialed the number Said gave me, held the phone below his chin. The speaker was on. Said was perspiring lightly.

"It's Kent," he said. "I'm here with Wakeland and his partner."

"Chen," the disembodied voice said. Jeff bristled.

"They say they have the money. They want a straight trade for the items."

A long pause. What could have been a sigh.

"Put Wakeland on."

I turned the phone. "He's been listening," I said. "Are they okay?"

"No harm to them yet. That changes if the police are involved. Or anyone else but you two."

"All right."

"One hour, the Garden in Chinatown, the public entrance. The money in a soft nylon shoulder bag, the kind you'd carry onto a plane. You two dressed in T-shirts, no concealed weapons. We trade there. Any deviation whatsoever, I won't even show up. Does that register?"

"So long as no one's harmed," I said. "If that changes, I burn the money, and you'll never see your buddy here again."

"Acceptable." The voice oddly inflected, as if both were inconsequential, irksome at best. "At eleven, then. Be on time."

It was past ten now, and we were at least a half-hour from Chinatown. Add ten minutes to retrieve the money and we'd just make it. As I started the van, I asked Said where the keys to my Cadillac were.

"Behind the front wheel," he said. "I tossed the wallet and phone."

"How exactly did Nunn know about the Sun Yat-Sen Garden?" Jeff said.

"I told him." In the rearview, Said's face was reflective, almost nostalgic. "My family used to be from here."

"Used to be."

"Hogan's Alley," he said. "Vancouver's Black neighbourhood. It was displaced in the seventies to make way for the viaduct. My parents relocated to Seattle, but I still have cousins here. They'd tell me about eating at Jimi Hendrix's grandmother's place. They had friends in Chinatown. Now, though"—Said shrugged—"it's a different city."

I turned out of the lot, but before I could reach the on ramp I was nearly broadsided by a black Dodge. Another cut diagonally across the road in front of us, stopping with one tire on the curb. I barely shifted into reverse before the first car swerved to block us in.

Dead, if that's what they want, I thought, and then saw Sergeant Dudgeon at the wheel of the car in front. Superintendent Borden was already approaching us from the passenger's side.

"Out of the car," she called to me. A cheerful grin on her face.

I complied, thankful no guns had been drawn. From behind, another officer took hold of my arm.

Borden opened the sliding side door of the van. Said lunged out. In a quick move, she clipped his head, knocking him to the curb. He writhed, and she directed Dudgeon to cuff him.

"One out of five, at least," she muttered.

Jeff came out with his palms in front of his head.

"We need him," I told Borden. "His partner has hostages, Ryan Martz and Nikki Frazer. We've got less than an hour to make the trade."

"It's true," Jeff said.

She nodded at me, neither believing or discounting what we said. "He can tell us where his friend is."

"There's no time—"

"We'll sort it out," she said. "Back at the station, when we're not hold-ing up traffic in Richmond RCMP jurisdiction."

Dudgeon walked a resisting Said toward the caged back seat of his car. Jeff and the other officer stood on the curb. The cop behind me tugged on my arm.

"Please," I said to Borden.

"Weeks spent looking for this man," she said, "and you think you're going to talk me out of this? When everyone else has ended up dead? Is that truly the result you want?"

She pointed at the officer leading me away. "Separate them. No cuffs if they come politely. We'll talk before deciding on charges. If they don't want to now, the ride might change their mind."

Dudgeon turned on the flashers but not the siren. Borden slammed Said's door and resumed her place beside Dudgeon. The car reversed and disappeared.

Soon they were another streak on the highway, another loud metallic *shush*.

"Are you carrying any weapons, sir?" the cop said as he led me away from the van. He was redheaded and lanky, taller than me. His partner, a South Asian woman, finished patting down Jeff and directed him toward the back door of the Dodge.

"Nothing on me," I told the cop. I let him finish his frisk before say-ing, "There is a handgun on the floor between the seats."

His head turned slightly to look through the glass, and I headbutted him.

Stars popped and the world pinwheeled. Headbutts hurt the giver almost as much as the recipient. My skull connected with the redhead's temple, and he staggered. I hit him in the jaw with an overhand right and he went down.

I bolted.

Through traffic, back into the lot. I hurried down the aisle of parked cars, turning, seeing Jeff and the other officer locked together on the pavement. I jogged to where I'd spotted the Cadillac, ducked and groped for the keys.

Front wheel well, he'd said. No sign of them.

Crouching, I checked the front right wheel. There.

I took a different exit out of the lot, rushing down the highway at a speed that made the car shudder. Thirty-eight minutes till the meeting with Nunn.

SEVENTY-SIX
WHEN YOUR NUMBER'S UP

No weapons. No partner. No hostage. What exactly was I left with? The money, and not enough time.

As I drove I texted Blatchford, told him to have the hockey bag filled and ready when I arrived at the storage unit. I wanted to phone Sonia, but even thinking of her turned my thoughts maudlin. Panic clawed its way up into my throat. Absurd rationale: all the good I'd done. What I deserved. Everything I'd left unfinished, unsaid.

Martin Yang must have had similar thoughts in the moment before Nunn shot him. No bargains or equivocations, no making peace. You die seeking closure, which is ironic considering that's all death is. Like an answer so obvious you overlook it.

On the curb in front of Lok-It Storage, I took the bag from Blatchford. It was heavy. I set it on the passenger's seat.

"Don't worry, it's all in there," he said. "Want I should come with you?"

I shook my head. "He said alone. In about twenty minutes, though, call the police. Tell them to check the Sun Yat-Sen Garden."

"All right, boss. Luck with this."

I pulled up to the entrance of the Garden two minutes late, abandoned my car and sprinted through the gate. A few couples and loners wandered along stretches of the winding path. The bright afternoon sun gave the plants a golden tinge, though a spattering of rain rustled the leaves and left concentric circles across the face of the pond.

Unsure where to go, or if Nunn was still here, I followed one arm of the path, over a bridge and by the terrace where I'd sat with Jeff and Roy

Long. I looked at the museum, across the pond, and saw a security guard make his way between displays.

Following the path, I disrupted a couple necking, tallboys of Pabst concealed by the feet of the bench they occupied. The last time I'd seen Lester Nunn in public he'd shot and killed Jingjing Cui in front of her mother. This time—

The path turned, opened onto a miniature promontory. Barely more than an outcropping of mossy rock, it was the turnaround point for the path. From there I could see both entrances.

I dialed the number Said had given me but after six rings it cut to a programmed voice saying the user has not set up their voice mail, please hang up and try again.

A cloud the colour of unspun silk passed above, and the rain increased, then waned. I watched beads of water roll down the nylon skin of the bag. Too late by two minutes. Ryan and Nikki had been dragged into this because of me, and their fates sealed by a hundred-and-twenty miserable seconds. Nunn could be anywhere. Hell, maybe he'd never planned on honouring our meeting at all.

What exactly had I expected—a heroic rescue? Our plan hadn't been much, but now two thirds of its participants were in police custody. I'd be terrifically lucky to join them, if that was the worst to follow.

What next, though?

And then I saw Nunn pass through the side entrance.

He'd dyed his blond hair an unnatural Elvis black. Dirty blond stubble covered his face. The clash, together with pale blue eyes, gave him the look of a black and white image that had been hastily colourized. He wore black gloves, hiking boots, jeans and a padded suede jacket. Alone.

He held up his hand, the gesture meaning, stay there. I did. He disappeared along the path.

I thought of surprising him, hiding, but there was little I could do other than wait. Soon I saw him at the end of the trail.

Up close I could see the wear on his face. Nunn was past forty and looked sleep-deprived, spurred on by pills. Something else beyond that, though. A calm that had nothing to do with training or drugs, something in the basement of his personality. I study faces as part of my job, look for physical signs of the guilt mechanism. Sometimes they're obvious. Other times, the lack of these signs tells you something is broken inside.

But occasionally people surprise you. The tearful widow who twisted a knife into her husband's guts only hours before. The teenager playing street hockey who forced a teacher over her desk after class. Pathological cases, troubled, antisocial, some I'd even categorize as evil. They throw off your readings, compel you to admit this is a business of guesswork rather than science.

In Nunn's case, for a second as he approached I saw the aura of death that surrounded him. He was monstrous, a natural void, and it was all I could do not to run from him. How could others resist? How could every face in the Garden not be turned in horror at what they saw?

But then he nodded at a woman heading the opposite direction, side-stepped to give her right of way, and Lester Nunn was then just a person. It wasn't a mask he wore to hide his evil. If anything it was the opposite. Nunn traded on fear.

The moment we were alone, his face assumed a tight scowl.

"Where's my friend?" he said. "And where's your partner?" He tut-tutted, clucking his tongue. "Not what we agreed."

"I don't see Ryan and Nikki either. Jeff figured he'd wait to see if you were going to hold up your end."

"They're here," Nunn said. "Why don't you hand me the money and bring out my friend, and then we'll hand them over."

"Is he really your friend?" I said.

Nunn's smile was tight, eyes heavy-lidded. "Mustafa's all right."

"He saw you kill Martin Yang," I said. "Did you know you were shooting a cop? Or did Felix Long hire you without telling you who you were after."

Being confronted with his deeds didn't change Nunn's expression. "Not my business to ask, 'less it's pertinent to my objective."

"You shot Percy Axton too, and injured Felix Long. How's that pertinent?"

Nunn held out his hand for the bag. I unslung the strap from my shoulder.

"That whole night was a clusterfuck," he said. "I was planning on handing Percy over to them, but he wouldn't stay put. Before I could say boo, he broke off and started shooting, and then they were returning fire at us. I had to do what I had to do. Bad form to let someone kill your bankroll."

"Then—"

Nunn waved a hand over his head at someone behind me. I turned.

Ryan Martz lurched out from the museum entrance, hands folded in front of him. Nikki Frazer was next. Felix's associate, Gu, herded them forward, a rifle pointed at their backs.

SEVENTY-SEVEN
A COLLISION OF SHADOWS

Every bad ending spun through my head, a doomsday merry-go-round.

Gu and his captives skirted the edge of the pond. I pulled in a breath and called to Ryan and Nikki, "You two okay?"

"Been fuckin' better," Ryan answered.

His hands were tied with what looked like wire. When I stared at him, I saw fear writ on his face, unalloyed, like a cringing child awaiting punishment.

I couldn't see the security guard. Turning, I held out the hockey bag for Nunn.

"I'll give you the money first," I told him. "Let them go, then I'll call my partner and send in Said."

Nunn's left hand was buried in his jacket. He shook his head. "Not the deal we discussed."

"But it'll work. No one gets hurt, we all walk out of here."

He took the strap and let the bag fall to the path. "That's all right," he said. "We can find Mustafa ourselves, later, need be. Chen too. For now, come with me."

His hand slid out of the jacket, showing half of a large automatic. Earl Tanner had listed a Colt 1911 among his missing firearms.

I looked back at the others. Nikki had her hands up to her forehead, a gesture which looked like prayer. Gu stood behind them, the barrel of the rifle aimed over Ryan's shoulder at my chest.

"Never mind them," Nunn said to me, dropping the strap of the bag. "You carry that."

I ignored the strap and held out my cell phone, as if it contained the answer. "One phone call and we all get what we need."

Nunn took the phone from me. "Many thanks. Now pick that up."

I stole one last glance across the pond and guessed what Nikki was planning. Bringing a knee up and her bound hands down could snap her restraints. I crouched and picked the bag up by both ends, stood, and thought, *now*, and palmed the bag up into Nunn's face.

I saw Nunn lurch backward, the phone spin from his hand, and I heard a gunshot like the ones from that morning, and every instant between then and now collapsed. There was no time.

Nunn was off-balance. Before he could recover, I lunged at him, spinning the both of us to the ground. We hit the grass and rolled, struggling.

His arms were free, one hand creeping across my face, his thumb searching for the fleshy recess of my eye. I punched at his throat and missed, felt my knuckles drag through dirt and small stones. I reared back as his thumb dug into the socket, a pain like nothing I'd ever felt, and I knew, worst of all, it was only a distraction to earn him time to free his gun.

Blind, I grabbed hold of something—hair, an ear—and rolled back, taking it with me, plunging us both into the pond.

It was cold and slightly oily. Not deep but we were on our backs. Retching, thrashing, my hands brushed lilies, held on to the side of Nunn's head. As we spun, my head cleared the water. Breath filled my nostrils, all too briefly, followed by another rush of dark liquid.

Nunn squirmed and freed himself. I leapt to get hold of something, keep him from taking in air. His boot caught my kneecap, his shoulder beneath mine, lifting me up. I became dead weight and sunk an elbow into some fleshy part.

I saw the gun in his hand.

I was behind him, both of us sputtering as our heads bobbed in the water. His arm was extended away from me, searching. I grabbed for his arm, my underwater movements unfolding at nightmare tempo.

He turned. I was on his back. I saw his mangled ear hanging from where the lobe had been. I locked my arms around his throat and fell backward, back into the nightmare.

Our struggle had stirred up clouds of silt. Even my good eye couldn't make out more than shadows colliding, breaking away. My hand brushed Nunn's ear, I felt it tear away, and I jabbed two knuckles into the sputtering mess.

Nunn howled, and threw me away, and pointed the gun at me

at the people near the bus stop

and shot me.

I felt my blood thrill and carbonate. No pain but a terrible numbness in my side. I couldn't raise my arms to fend off another shot. Nunn aimed. He seemed to be deliberating. Then he canted his head, spun his body to the side, noticing something curious. Another shot echoed above us.

Nunn reeled and slunk down into the water, till all I could see above the murk were a few black strands of hair along a pale white stretch of forehead.

I leaned back, looked up. The world was upside down. Nikki Frazer stood on the bank, holding the rifle. Something recognizable lay at her feet. I'd figure out what that was in just a second.

Instead, I sank.

SEVENTY-EIGHT

FOURTEEN CONVERSATIONS FROM A HOSPITAL BED

Jaz Sanghera, Registered Nurse:

...some damage to the spinal cord, severe hematoma. Dr. Wei won't know until she's through the second surgery and the swelling goes down. Vertebrae fractured...alive, though. Not the best of news, Mr. Wakeland, but you said he's your friend, and I thought you'd want to know.

Sonia, day one:

My god, Dave, do you have any idea how fortunate you are? They told me you were this close to it. If Nikki hadn't...your eye. Can you see out of it? Good. Rest, love. Sleep. You're all right now.

Kay:

I won't keep you, but holy shit, Dave, holy shit. I can't believe I missed it. The guy's fucking ear...

Me? Yeah, it was a concussion, but the doctor said I'm fine now. How Blatchford put it, just "got my bell rung." He said it happens, he's had at least six or seven...Seriously, though, I'm glad you're okay.

Natalie Holinshed:

Of course, it's a friendly visit, and I'm not here as a journalist, officially...when you do want to tell the story, though...

A thought I had on the way over: Diane Cui is at home, and maybe... nice picture to go with her visit...To be honest, with all the layoffs and buyouts going on, a feel-good piece like this could help.

Superintendent Ellen Borden:

Well.

Honestly I don't know quite how to feel about what you did. Constable Frazer says you saved their lives. If we'd been there, maybe the injuries to her fiancé might have been avoided. But then again, maybe not.

All of them dead except one. And we're no closer to pinning anything on the Longs. There are already rumours that Felix wants to partner with the Hayes brothers and the League of Nationz. But that's a problem for tomorrow...

Mustafa Said will have his day in court. He'll be in protective isolation, I imagine. The worst of them usually are.

Jeff:

Most important is you're okay, and they're not charging us, at least I don't think. The security guard Gu knocked out has a few stitches, but he's fine. Yeah, I heard about Ryan. Sad.

What Felix did is unforgivable. Roy knows it. For us, I think it's best we keep out of things for now.

Wakeland & Chen could use some good PR out of this. I'm just saying, if Holinshed does bring Ms. Cui to see you? Be nice, Dave. For a change, be nice.

Sonia, day two:

Fucking idiot, Dave. Alone? Really, you couldn't ask Tim or me to back you up? After everything, you had to go alone. Yes, I *know* they said no one else, but since you broke every other goddamn rule—let's not have this conversation now, all right?

No, I don't blame you. Nikki doesn't, either.

I haven't asked Ryan.

Constable Lawrence Jagyr:

Some hard fucking head you got there, brother. Ryan's a buddy of mine. What you did for him, or tried to do, obviously I can't fault you for that. I'm just saying, I was distracted, okay? The superintendent said you wouldn't be a problem. It was kind of a dirty shot. In a fair fight, it wouldn't happen like that. We both know it, don't we?

Sergeant Benoit Dudgeon:

I know what Borden thinks. I wish I felt the same.

Me, I don't call it rescue, you go in half-ass. If anything, Frazer, she rescued you. She's the one that got Gu and Nunn. Way she told it, Nunn was about to shoot you.

Your friend might not walk again. Remember that first time we talk, when I ask what you saw? A different answer then, maybe things don't happen this way. For next time, you consider it.

Rongrong Yang:

Um. Yeah. Hi.

I guess I'm sorry for hitting you, first off. Your poor eye. And your cousin, I really didn't mean to hurt her.

They wouldn't tell us anything. I was so angry. My mom was crying. That white-haired old cop said we couldn't talk about it, even though dad's face was on the news. I just thought I'd talk to you, but I guess I got nervous. Sorry again.

Now they're saying my dad's a hero. I wish that made me feel better. You ever lose anyone? It sucks, doesn't it? Just sucks.

Adele Niang, on behalf of Diane Cui:

She says, thank you.

John Laidlaw, via phone:

Obviously capture would have been preferable, but nevertheless, it's an outcome you can be proud of, Mr. Wakeland. I'm impressed, with both you and Ms. Frazer.

Normally, it's true, we recruit from the armed forces. We find that discipline isn't always there with civilians. Aside from that, you're everything we look for in a Rip Tyde associate.

You should be making a lot more money than you are, and your leadership skills are a valuable asset. Vancouver is a growing market, and it might be the right time for Rip Tyde to expand. "Gateway to the Orient," right? A partnership is what I have in mind, or maybe more of a franchise opportunity. Private security is a booming field. Just think about it.

Nikki Frazer

Shit, Dave, I don't know what to say. I wish it had been me.

He looks so different lying there. Like a kid.

I got loose and fought with Gu over the rifle. It went off and hit Ryan. If only I'd had my pistol. But I got hold of the weapon and shot him, yeah, a clear case of him or us.

I didn't have a shot at Nunn until he had the Colt pointed at you. It was training more than skill.

You're welcome.

I'll tell Ryan you're thinking of him.

Sonia, day three:

Come on. Let's go home.

SEVENTY-NINE
SPIRITS

The swelling went down. I began to feel better, to be able to move without pain. The day after I was released I was back at St. Paul's to visit Ryan. Nikki went to the cafeteria and I took her place in the warm, sterile room.

Ryan slept. His body looked frail beneath the hospital blanket, amongst the machinery. Nikki was right, he did look childlike.

So much of my own childhood had been comprised of events I didn't understand. Birth parents leaving me to follow their strange religion, my adoptive mother and father not knowing how to fill those roles. I'd walked around feeling that everyone around me deliberately withheld answers, not able to understand concepts like fate, tomorrow, the unknown. And I still didn't, really. Those first few years I'd gone to bed expecting it all to end, anticipating being sent away.

Ryan's face reflected that same feeling. Asleep, at the mercy of what comes next.

A few days later we had a company dinner. Jeff reserved a large table at the Red Lantern. His family, Kay and Blatchford and their dates, and Sonia, her hand displaying the ring. True to her word, she'd picked one out for herself.

Dishes were dropped off and circulated around the table. After days of hospital food, it tasted like manna. Gai lan, spareribs, vegetables in black bean sauce, fried tofu with green onion. The works.

At one point I left to use the washroom. When I returned I saw Roy Long at a table near the kitchen. A teapot in front of him, along with a bottle of *baijiu*. His back was to our table. I wasn't sure if that was on purpose.

I motioned to the seat across from him. He nodded and poured me a cup of the clear, strong liquor. "I was very sorry to hear about your friend," Long said. "My son and the man that worked for him are a very great…" His voice faltered. "I apologize for them."

"If you could answer a question for me," I said.

"If I can."

"When you hired Lester Nunn to kill Martin Yang, did you know the others would be killed, including the people in the streets?"

"I'm sorry?" Long said.

"Somehow you learned Huang Shao Wei was an undercover officer named Martin Yang. You needed him gone, unable to testify, and for the blame to fall on someone else. Nunn did his job pretty well in that regard. At first the shooting looked like the Exiles, the beginning of a gang war. Then later, when it seemed like an inside job, and Felix the likely culprit, that was okay too. Until he was shot at."

The *baijiu* warmed my throat, a spicy note to the white liquor.

"Of all the people to be involved, Felix was lucky enough to survive."

"You too," Long said quietly.

"So far."

I refilled our glasses, sloshing the tablecloth.

"Nunn kills Yang and the others inside, shoots the bystanders. He helps Gu and Felix to eliminate his accomplices, except Percy Axton gets trigger-happy and injures Felix. So much death. And there'll be more, won't there? Now that Felix has survived a gunshot, his gangster credentials are way up. If people think he was behind it, what does he care? He's invincible, after all. And who knows who'll pay for that? Probably not him, not at first."

"I'm sorry," Long said, "but I don't know what you're saying."

"Gu worked for you. He's too old and too professional to be one of Felix's Red Snakes. Maybe you delegated the whole thing to him. But I think it was your plan from the start. It was audacious, and almost foolproof."

Roy Long peered into his cup before draining it. The man who looked up was essentially the same, though the eyes now sought sympathy, understanding, rather than pretend they held those for others.

"He's my son," he said. "A father can't let anything happen to his child."

"No matter who he hurts."

Long didn't need to verbalize his answer to that.

"You have people waiting," he said. "People you love."

He poured out the last of the bottle, a taste for each of us.

"There's a very old saying: 'A loss, no bad thing.' It comes from the story of an old man whose horse escaped, only to return in the company of another."

"Meaning, fortunes change," I said.

Roy Long nodded. He raised his cup. I tilted mine so the rim touched the bottom of his.

"No one else hurt," he said.

I drank to that, put the cup down and went back to my table, thinking that was a lot to ask.

We were near the end of the meal, Jeff telling a story that had everyone laughing, their troubles forgotten for the moment. I steepled my hands and looked down at the orange stains on the bright white tablecloth. It was too late to give thanks, not the right time, and I wasn't the person to say it. But I bowed my head anyway and said what I could, a very late and very suspect grace. Then we finished our tea, and waited for the cheque to come.

— THE END —

ACKNOWLEDGMENTS

This novel began life as a short story, "Head Down," which appeared in the back pages of the first issue of Image Comics' *The Violent*, at the behest of series writer Ed Brisson. Thanks to Ed and Adam Gorham for the opportunity.

In my research into armed robbery, I relied on conversations with Joe Loya and Les Edgerton, who both graciously shared their expertise, and set me straight on a few things.

On the law enforcement side, Vancouver Police Department spokesperson Constable Brian Montague and retired D.C. detective and author David Swinson answered my questions about police response and procedure.

In the novel, if characters with authority are depicted breaking laws or flaunting procedure, it's done for dramatic purposes, and is not offered as commentary on the real-life people who hold those jobs. Likewise, in depicting criminal organizations, I've done my best to balance research with the needs of the story, while trying my best to avoid perpetuating stereotypes. All errors are mine.

The geography of Vancouver is always changing. The idea for "Gentrification Central" came from several controversial construction projects. I've played with the geography where it served the story. Vancouver itself is a colonial project located on the traditional territories of the Coast Salish, šxʷməθkʷəy'əma?ł təməxʷ (Musqueam), and səl'ilwəta?ł təməxʷ (Tsleil-Waututh) Nations.

I also consulted the following books: *The Last Gang in Town* by Aaron Chapman; *Chinese Canadian Criminal Entrepreneurs, Volumes 1 and 2* by Alex Chung; *Tongs, Gangs and Triads: Chinese Crime Groups in North*

America by Peter Huston; *The Secret Life of Bikers* by Jerry Langton; *400 Things Cops Know* by Adam Plantinga; *Saltwater City: Stories of Vancouver's Chinese Community* by Paul Yee; the *"cʼəsnaʔəm, the city before the city"* exhibit at the UBC Museum of Anthropology curated by Susan Rowley and Jordan Wilson; Kim Bolan's reporting on Lower Mainland organized crime, which is the best in the country; and Carlo Liconti's documentary *Dragons of Crime: Climbing the Golden Mountain.*

Thanks also to Janie Chang, for double-checking my name clue; as well as Naben Ruthnum, Kelly Senecal, Mel Yap, Benoit Lelievre, Charlie Demers, Paul Lazenby, Linda Richards, Dietrich Kalteis, Eric Brown, Gorrman Lee, Brian Thornton, Sheena Kamal, Chris Brayshaw, Chuck Hogan, Natalie Rocheleau, AJ Devlin, Dennis Heaton, Kris Bertin, Andrew F. Sullivan, Amy Stuart, Sook Kong, and Bruce Lord; everyone at the VPL; my brothers Josh and Dan; my mother Linda; and the memory of my father, Al Wiebe.

Thanks to my agent, Chris Casuccio at WCA; to Derek Fairbridge for diligent editing; to Charlotte Gray and Audrey Castillo for their marketing and publicity work; to cover artist Annie Boyar; and to the teams at Harbour and Blackstone.

And to Carly, with all my love. No one means more to me, and without you I would be much less.

Sam Wiebe
Vancouver

ABOUT THE AUTHOR

Sam Wiebe is the award-winning author of the Wakeland novels, one of the most authentic and acclaimed detective series in Canada, including *Invisible Dead* ("the definitive Vancouver crime novel") and *Cut You Down* ("successfully brings Raymond Chandler into the 21st century"). Wiebe's other books include *Never Going Back, Last of the Independents* and the *Vancouver Noir* anthology, which he edited. His work has won a Crime Writers of Canada award and a Kobo Emerging Writer Prize and has been shortlisted for the Edgar, Hammett, Shamus and City of Vancouver awards. He is a former Vancouver Public Library Writer in Residence.

Sign up for the Sam Wiebe newsletter at samwiebe.com and receive "Hollywood North," a free Wakeland story.